Forgo

Luci

MW00875618

Dedication

TO MY PARENTS ANTHONY and Catherine Cifelli, who without their guidance, even from heaven, this book wouldn't have seen the light of day.

Acknowledgments

I CONCEIVED WHILE ATTENDING a Pug Rescue fundraiser in Connecticut. It was over a decade in the making. It just came to me that these women who attended, many including myself, had driven far from their home state. My brain went to the what if? And the story came to me. Although it had a different title and I changed the main character's name, the story remained the same.

This story would have never been published without the following people, Maria Picozzi, Pat Devereaux, Janice Petolicchio, Lori DeVries, JoAnne Sokolski, Jean Joachim, Nancy Brito, Gina Heil, Kay Springsteen, Susan Hunt, Tina Marie, Deanna Manzo, Terry Hammoutene, Robin Cifelli, Renee Waring, Wanda Foss Ospowicz, Carissa Marks, and Patricia Elliott. Special thanks to Dawné Dominique for bringing my vision to life with her awesome talent in designing the cover.

Lastly, I'd like to thank my husband and sons for supporting and indulging me in pursuing this dream.

One

RICHARD ROCKED IN HIS chair, praying, the memories slamming him. Remorse and pain coursed through him. He was lonely and wanted more than anything to be with his bride and only daughter.

He remembered everything about that day, the first stage of failure as a single father. Losing everything he had known. He searched his memory bank to see where he went wrong. What he could have said to make his daughter turn on him.

His thoughts returned to that dreadful morning. Richard and his daughter, Susan, sat bedside. Her eyes focused on the machines keeping her mother alive. Susan glanced at the former vibrant and youthful woman, now frail and sallow skinned. She quickly diverted her tear-filled eyes to the monitors again. Susan remembered her energetic mother, her golden glow from playing tennis, her naturally blonde hair and bright blue eyes. Now her eyes were glazed, and her hair sparse from chemo. They moved Donna from the hospital to a private hospice room upstairs. Donna didn't want to go home to die, didn't want her only child to witness the transition or have memories of it at their home. They filled their home with joy and laughter before her diagnosis. Donna signed a DNR order weeks before because she was aware of the outcome, and she knew she couldn't beat it despite the desire to remain for her only child and her husband.

Richard stared at his wife and knew the transition would be over soon. Her breathing had changed. He leaned forward and grasped her hand as the tears poured down his cheeks. Glancing to his daughter, Susan, who sat with her head bowed, her lips moved, mouthing the word "mommy" over and over.

Donna's eyes opened briefly. With wet eyes, she gazed at her husband and daughter, whispering, "I'll love you both forever."

"Mommy, I love you too. Please stay. You're my best friend." Turning toward her father, she asked, "Daddy, why couldn't you save her?"

He paused and gazed into his daughter's eyes. "Sweetheart, Mommy was too far gone when the doctors diagnosed cancer. The pain she perceived as normal because of exertion was uterine cancer. It's sneaky, honey. Trust me. She had the best doctors." He lowered his head into his hands and quietly sobbed.

"Don't blame daddy, honey. I'll always be with you, sweetheart, both you and daddy. Always." Donna closed her eyes briefly. At Susan's sob, she opened them again. "You are the best daughter, sweetheart. The absolute best," she whispered, taking her last breath.

Susan's scream reverberated in Richard's mind. That moment when she knew her mother was gone, that guttural scream that tore his heart in two.

It was a devastating blow to them when Donna succumbed to the illness that wreaked havoc on her body. She died the week after Susan's high school graduation. Donna was the glue that held their family together. The funeral had been overwhelming for these two lost souls. After hours of receiving guests at the visitation, they found themselves alone, with no clue how to survive without their matriarch.

Richard remembered the day she complained of pelvic pain the morning after they made love. He assumed she'd worked out aggressively or pulled something during her tennis game earlier. He patted her shoulder and said, "Rest today, sweetheart. If you need me, just call." He remembered her smile the most. With her perfect teeth and the genuineness of her beam, she was quick to laugh with her family and was open to any adventure. After she mentioned the irregular bleeding, he insisted she call the doctor, and they learned the devastating news.

He tried to keep his daughter focused. He begged her to apply to colleges, any school she wanted. Although she ignored him regularly, he still begged. Susan had no interest in school or being an active participant in her own life. Her mother supported everything she'd done, but now she died. By August, Susan disappeared, just six weeks after Donna's death. Devastated and lost, Richard hired private investigators and spared no expense to find his daughter. They told him she left with a known drug dealer and a rumored human trafficker. The private investigator told Dr. Kline that the police had found the man dead in a hotel room in San Francisco. This news was just an additional heartbreak added to his overwhelming sorrow.

Losing his wife and his daughter's disappearance changed him. His tan faded, and his lackluster skin alluded to his grief, and he ambled with an air of sadness surrounding him. He moved from the desk chair slowly, as though in physical pain. His loose shirt snagged on the handle of the drawer. When he spoke, his voice was low, as though it was painful to communicate. He lounged in his sleep clothes on weekends, lonely and stricken by grief, missing both his wife and child. His attorney and longtime friend, Thomas Collins, and his wife and son, were now his only family. They had been childhood friends, brothers by heart. Thomas's son, TJ, was close to his Uncle Richard, and his uncle was proud of him. A famous actor and a confirmed bachelor had just landed a role in an action film expected to gross millions. Richard loved TJ like his own. They were his family now and would do anything for Richard and grieve along with him.

Immersing himself in his work, often working around the clock, the only thing he could do to redirect his grief. Occasionally, he took a much-needed vacation to visit one of his resort properties but never stayed long enough to relax. The Beverly Hills home called to him. His need to be there was overwhelming, as this had been the place where Susan would return. Even though Susan had left twenty years ago, he remained desperately hopeful.

Richard leaned back in his desk chair and thought of his daughter Susan as he pressed the bridge of his nose. His thoughts returned to the last time he saw her, as they always did. Their conversation replayed in his mind daily, wondering what he could have done or said differently to stop her from running away. Susan rebelled against any suggestion from him, and he tried desperately to help with the grief. He made appointments with a psychologist who specializes in grief counseling for teenagers. But Susan never went to see the doctor. The day she disappeared played like a bad movie clip in his mind. He's sees her in his mind's eye stamping her foot, just as she had when things didn't go her way throughout her childhood. A brief smile played on his lips. He'd always loved her feistiness, her mother, not so much. Neither of them had a temper, and both were calm and rational. He doesn't remember Donna ever raising her voice to him or their only child. Yet Susan knew when her mother was serious.

Susan stamped her foot as she ran her fingers through her messy blonde hair. "No, Dad, I don't want to go to college. I barely survived high school," she yelled vehemently, tears stinging her eyes.

"But, sweetheart, you are so smart. You shouldn't waste your intelligence. I would love nothing more than to work with you at the practice. Like I did with your mother, God rest her soul." He wiped his teary eyes with the back of his hand.

"Back off, Dad. I can't do this." Susan's desperate tears streamed down her cheeks as she ran past him. The last thing he saw was her back as she stomped through the kitchen door leading to the garage.

The memory of her blond hair swaying, dressed in her ragged cutoff jean shorts, her thin honey-tanned legs as she rushed to the garage. He hated those shorts, but her mother advised him to choose his battles. The door slamming reverberated in his mind. Not knowing that would be the last time he saw his daughter.

Richard planned to visit Myrtle Beach with Thomas to view properties in the area. Thomas and his wife Nicole planned to buy a vacation home. Nicole had other ideas and hoped Thomas would slow down and stay a few months a year. She remained at home until he narrowed his choices down to three of the properties she had chosen from the realtor's website. A Southern girl, Nicole was delicate, respectful, and sophisticated. Growing up in South Carolina, she missed her home and hoped eventually to retire there, longing to return to her roots.

Richard and Thomas landed at the Myrtle Beach International Airport Friday afternoon. They had appointments lined up with a local realtor—Diane Iacone, the top salesperson in the area—to walk through vacation properties on Saturday afternoon. They planned to play golf at their resort on Sunday before heading back to California on Monday morning.

The warm breeze should have been welcoming, yet Richard's heart wasn't in the trip. Nor was he into much these days, not his life and not his practice. He hadn't socialized since Donna's death and Susan's disappearance. Richard couldn't recover from his earth-shattering losses. His heart still raced each time he spotted a blonde woman who appeared to be in her late thirties, hoping to find his daughter. He looked at every blonde in each city, and he sought for Susan in the faces of strangers. Every year that went by without her affected him even more. His hope and his health took a harsh hit.

After his urologist diagnosed him with prostate cancer, he had to decide on whether he wanted treatment. Richard was aware of the outcome and the survival rate based on his PSA numbers. It didn't look promising, and he didn't care. He hadn't told Thomas yet, nor had he told anyone else about his diagnosis. The news just made him numb. He'd lost everything that mattered to him. Why not his life too? A lost soul without his girls. They had informed him that doctors could cure it. But what was the point? He was alone and lonely, so why bother?

Richard took a deep breath as he and Thomas checked in to their hotel. After receiving their keycards, they went up to their rooms to clean up. Thomas called Richard's room and asked him to meet him downstairs in the lobby so they could find a restaurant.

"Rich let's try this amazing seafood place by the ocean. I read the reviews, and the food is excellent." Thomas looked up from his phone, his eyebrows raised.

Richard nodded, and they walked the few blocks to the seafood restaurant on the beach to enjoy an early dinner and drinks. As they approached the table, Richard stared at the ocean's angry waves slam against the shore. The deep blue water rumbled, leaving white foam against the shoreline. Richard glanced toward the bar and noticed a blonde woman waiting. Her elbows leaned on the gleaming bar top. He squinted and peered closer. It was Susan, and his heart pumped rapidly in his chest.

"Tom, look. At the bar, it's Susan. That is my girl."

Thomas followed Richard's finger and admitted the resemblance was uncanny. It could be Susan, an older and more mature version of the teenager long gone. It could very well be her. She looked so much like her mother at that age.

Thomas realized the woman overheard them. Her mouth curled in a smile, and her hands trembled as she reached for the beverages. Thomas tried to calm Richard down. He leaned in across the table and spoke softly, reasoning with him as the woman left and headed to the beach with her order. Richard wasn't going to risk losing his daughter again and jumped from the table to chase her.

Thomas grabbed his arm. "You can't do that. What if it isn't Susan? Look, I see where she's sitting. She's with a friend over there." He pointed. "I'll speak to her, so she doesn't call the police. Calm down, Richard, and I'll take care of this." Thomas stood, his lips in a grim line, his brows lowered over his eyes, shaking his head as he walked away from his friend.

Unable to sit down and eager for Thomas to return, Richard, tapped his fingers on the table. His eyes followed Thomas as he walked from the beach after his brief conversation with the woman. "Well, Tom, what happened? What did she say?" Richard asked as his brows shot up.

"The woman isn't Susan. She looks like what I imagine Susan would look like as an adult, but she is not Susan. She's from up north, and she gave no hint of familiarity. I was a stranger to her."

Richard paced, his face reddening. "What if she messed up her brain with all the drug abuse, and she forgot who she is? What if that terrible man did unspeakable things to her, and she blocked everything out when she escaped him? How can you be sure, Tom?" He flailed his arms. "I'm her father. It would help if you had let me speak to her. I'll speak to her now, and I'll know if she is my daughter."

Richard rushed by Thomas to head the beach, bumping him as he flew by. Gazing onto the beach where she sat, he realized she'd left. Glancing in both directions, he didn't see her or her companion. Richard plopped down onto the hot sand, lowering his head into his hands, so anguished he couldn't move. *I lost her again. Tom shouldn't have intervened. She is my daughter.* Several minutes passed, and Richard stood, dusted himself off, and headed back to the restaurant. Neither man spoke.

They walked back to the hotel in silence, Thomas heartbroken for his oldest friend, and Richard lost, visualizing what might have been if he had reunited with Susan.

Later that evening, while in the hotel room, he plopped on the bed, checking emails on his tablet. His cell phone sent a loud tone into space, the tone he chose for emergencies. He pressed accept and listened as his service described the issue. A high-profile client, an actor, had sustained a minor facial injury on the set and insisted that Dr. Kline examine the wound. "Okay, I'll call and speak with him. Thank you for reaching out. I'll take care of it." He rose and tossed his tablet in his carry-on bag. Richard disconnected the call and then called the physician who worked in his practice, Dr. Maria Ross, who sometimes worried Richard when she deviated from the protocol. It often worked out for her, but Richard was more conservative in his approaches. "Maria?"

"Hey Rich, what's up. Are you still in South Carolina?" she asked.

Richard paced around the hotel suite. "Yes, I am. I'm sorry to bother you, but a patient, Cliff Marrow, received a facial injury on the set earlier today, and he's asking for me. Can you set him up with my first appointment tomorrow? I'll text you the information. I'm calling the pilot to get the plane to leave immediately. I hope to be back in Los Angeles tonight. Please ask Lisa to move appointments so that I can tend to this first thing in the morning."

"Sure will, Dr. Kline. I'll go in extra early tomorrow, just in case."

"Thanks, Maria. I'll check in with you in the morning." Richard then called the pilot to file a flight plan for that same evening.

As he approached the bar, he realized the only time he felt alive was when one of his patients needed him. *Now to drop this bit of information on Tom, he'll probably blow a gasket.* He found Thomas at the bar nursing a Jack and Coke, his go-to drink.

"Tom, unwelcome news. I must fly back tonight, a patient. Do you want to gather your stuff?" Richard asked Thomas, his eyebrows raised and the familiar gleam in his eyes because he felt needed and was eager to get home. He wasn't interested in looking at houses or being away from home any longer.

"Crap, I've had a few drinks, and if I fly like this, I'll be sick. Take the rental car to the airport, Rich. I'll fly out commercially in a few days. Who knows, perhaps I can convince Nicole to come out and decide on one of these houses. Have a safe flight, and don't forget our dinner plans next Friday."

"All right, I'll grab my things and wait on the pilot's call. Catch up with you back home." Richard made his way upstairs and gathered his things.

As he was getting ready, the call came in from the pilot with the flight plan. "Dr. Kline, can you be here by midnight for takeoff?" the pilot asked.

"Yes, I'm leaving the hotel now. Same place as arrival?"

"Yes, sir, same location. The plane will be ready."

Richard tidied up, grabbed his bag and the car keys. He said a quick goodbye to Thomas on his way past the bar. He found the rental car and tossed his bag inside and plopped into the driver's seat and sighed. He popped in the coordinates for the airport into the vehicle's GPS.

Several minutes later, bright orange detour signs led him to a deserted dark back road with windy curves, lit only by the moon, and visibility was poor. Squinting, he followed tread marks on the street in the brightness of his high beams and saw a faint glimmer of vehicle lights in the woods. Finally, he pulled over near the smoking vehicle that had smashed into a tree. He rushed to help, and as he approached the car, a dog barked. He peered into the car and saw the driver, a female, slumped over the steering wheel. Her airbag had deployed. He looked in the back and squinted at the small dog seat-belted in a padded elevated seat, covered in white powder, his bulging eyes glowing in the darkness.

"It's okay, puppy. I'll help your mom. Okay?"

The dog sneezed in response. Richard checked the woman's pulse and then hurried back to the car for his bag. When he returned, he ran his fingers along on the woman's neck and spine, easing her off the wheel with great care. His hand flew to his chest, and his legs liquified. *Susan.* His brain screamed.

Richard carried his daughter and placed her into his car, his breathing rapid from the exertion. She moaned in pain as he fastened the seatbelt and reclined the seat. Then, turning, he ran back for the little dog, sweat dripping into his eyes. He grabbed her pocketbook and sprinted back for the dog's carrier, not wanting the dog running loose on the plane. Finally, he returned to the rental, gasping from his brisk movements, and headed for the airport, driving faster than usual onto the tarmac where the pilot waited.

"Fred, send the flight attendant out to the tarmac with the wheelchair." Richard had his plane amply stocked with medical equipment for the kids he transported to the Children's Hospital of Los Angeles. He volunteered his time for the last decade to recon-struct facial deformities. "My daughter's injured, a car accident. She's hurt, and I need help with her and her little dog."

Janice, the flight attendant, arrived without delay, pushing the empty wheelchair onto the tarmac toward Richard, who insisted on taking care of his daughter. She reached for the leash and the car seat and walked on board with the dog. She read his tag, engraved with the name "Buddy," as she secured him, returning with a damp wash-cloth to wipe the powder from the small pet.

Richard ushered his daughter into the back bedroom, and after he and the pilot laid her on the bed, he gave her a cursory exam. *She needs to be home.* Panic built, and he worried if it were safe to trans-port her. Lines creased his brow. Adrenaline coursed through his body. He nodded to the pilot that it was okay to prepare for flight.

"Doctor Kline, is it safe to transport her to Los Angeles? Do you think we should take her to the local emergency room before we take off? I'd be happy to wait. Then, I'll call for an ambulance."

"Fred, not only am I her father, but I am a doctor. Are you questioning my capabilities as a physician?" Richard caressed Susan's forehead, and his gentle ministrations brought memories of her as a child with a fever. He would sit by her bed until it broke, replacing the cool rags. Richard's heart raced. He prayed to God and his wife for her to be okay. Finally, after twenty years, he found his daughter, and he's delighted despite his panic. *She looks just like her mother.*

"No, doctor, I didn't mean to imply that, heaven's sake no. I want to be sure it is safe for your daughter for the trip." He watched as Dr. Kline checked her heart and her oxygen levels. He left the back room and headed to the cockpit. He announced the takeoff instructions and for everyone to secure their seatbelts. Richard stayed by the bed, holding on to his chair, reciting a silent prayer for a turbulence-free flight. Once given the okay to move about, he further examined his daughter and noticed a scar on her abdomen. Typical of a cesarean section. His brows shot up. *There might be a grandchild, perhaps grandchildren.* Since his diagnosis, hope filled his heart and the willingness to fight for his life for the first time.

Checking Susan throughout the flight, he noted that her breathing wasn't labored. Her pulse, blood pressure, and heart rate were regular. Her eyes fluttered open, but then she closed them again. He caught glimpses of his wife in her eyes. He tended to the nasty gash below her scalp, at the hairline on the right side of her forehead. Cleaning the wound, he pulled a tiny shard of glass from it and tenderly placed a butterfly bandage over it. Susan whimpered in her sleep, and his heart raced. A few times, he overheard a mumbled, "Buddy."

Assuring his daughter that the little dog was fine and with her, Richard remained, his warm hand resting on her arm. Satisfied that

Susan was in stable condition, he planned for his medical transport vehicle to wait at the airport.

Once they landed in Los Angeles, the team boarded the plane and placed her on a stretcher, taking her to the transport vehicle. Richard asked the EMTs to take them to his medical center. He called Dr. Ross and asked if she would meet him. Surprised at such a late hour, she agreed. Richard called his housekeeper Cora to come for the dog and explained the situation.

Cora and Jack McMillan took care of Richard and his house. Richard hired Cora nineteen years ago. He'd met her when she brought in a child in her care for a follow-up surgical appointment. They chatted warmly, and she mentioned that this was her last week as a nanny. Richard asked what she would do, and she said she was looking for a housekeeping position, and he had hired her on the spot. Not long after, Richard hired her husband Jack, a handyman by trade, after seeing how hard he worked. They developed a wonderful friendship, and Cora took great care of him and his home. Cora and Jack arrived at the medical center in record time. Even though they'd been asleep when Richard called, he met them in the lobby.

"Thanks for coming. I'm sorry to drag you here. This little guy is my daughter's little dog. Please take him home and make him comfortable. His tag says his name is Buddy." He looked at Cora as he passed her the leash. "Can you freshen up Susan's room, please?" Richard asked as he hopped into the medical transport.

Once Dr. Kline arrived at his surgical unit, he rushed Susan into the CT suite. With Maria's help, they scanned her for injuries, focusing on her head. She had a slight brain bleed that they hoped would resolve on its own. To be sure, Dr. Kline emailed the views to his friend, a neurologist, Dr. Henry Paulson. As a good friend, he rushed to the practice to read the results and examine Susan himself.

Maria had also examined Susan, concerned that she wasn't awake yet. Dr. Kline stated that he had given her medication for pain, which made her sleepy. Puzzled, Dr. Ross peered at him, her eyes squinting. Her mouth opened to speak, but closed it quickly, changing her mind.

Once Maria completed the exam, Dr. Kline mentioned he planned to take her home to sleep in her bed. He asked for Dr. Ross's discretion until he could find out where his daughter had been and to allow her to recover in peace. Dr. Paulson confirmed that the blood should resolve itself. With specific instructions for Richard, since he insisted on caring for his daughter at home, both doctors agreed she could recover in his care.

Dr. Ross nodded in agreement. "Richard, you took an awful risk, moving her after the accident. Why didn't you call 9-1-1?" She watched his expression. His mouth formed a small 'o', and he shrugged his shoulders. Dr. Ross knew the reason. He was thinking like a panicked father and not a doctor. "If you need anything, just call." Dr. Ross's background was in trauma, with a residency in emergency medicine. But she loved plastic surgery, and after her residency, she moved to New York City to work with a surgical group. When she learned of the Kline facility opening, she applied, and Richard, impressed with her background, hired her.

The medical transport loaded Susan back into the vehicle with Dr. Kline and took them home to Beverly Hills. Richard and the EMT helped Susan into the bed and made her comfortable. Richard walked with the EMT to the hallway outside of Susan's room, and gave him a massive tip for his inconvenience and the help he provided, even though he was on the payroll.

When he went back inside, he brought Buddy into the room to sleep with his owner and gave his daughter another shot for pain. Richard stayed with her for a few hours as she slept before heading to his room, doubtful he would sleep. He had so much to be thankful for and delighted that he found his daughter.

Two

A FEW DAYS EARLIER...

Natalia hustled around the house, getting things for her trip. She rushed through the kitchen, where her husband, Jonathan, sat at the kitchen table, reading on his tablet. She peered at him and raised her eyebrows. "Hey, babe, do you think you can watch the kids for a day while the girls and I head to Myrtle Beach for the fundraiser?" Natalia asked as she flicked her blonde hair off her shoulder and pulled it up into a pony.

"I'm sure I can make that happen, honey. I'll check my schedule and let you know what works best," Jonathan said as he stared at his tablet screen, not looking up.

Natalia leaned in for a kiss. "You're the best."

Jonathan lifted his head, smiled, and said, "No teasing with a brief peck. Plant a proper kiss on me."

Natalia sat in his lap. She pressed her lips against his, kissing him again, this time with more passion. After eighteen years and three kids, their sexual chemistry hadn't diminished.

"Whoa there, keep kissing me like that, and we'll end up naked," Jonathan joked.

Natalia smiled, took his hand, pulled him up from his chair, and led him into his home office. She locked the door, turning to Jonathan.

"Where are the boys?" he asked.

"Not home from school yet. We have time for a quickie." Natalia glanced at him. Passion clouding her eyes as she unbuttoned her denim shorts.

Jonathan pulled her to him and kissed her hard on the mouth. He pushed her denim shorts down her legs, leaving her tiny bikini underwear in place. He moved to her chest, snapping her bra open, exposing her full breasts, taking one in his mouth, while Natalia's fingers frantically worked the button on his shorts. She slowly slid the zipper down, enticing him.

"Nat ..." he moaned.

Jonathan moved her panties down her legs, leaving them in a puddle at her feet. He flicked his tongue across her breast and reached into her moist folds, nudging her to the leather sofa. His erection pressed against her, sliding himself into her wet folds. Natalia made the same sweet noise she always did when he entered her, a half sigh as though he was putting out her fire as he penetrated her. She reached an explosive orgasm after just a few minutes, gripping his shoulder blades. Jonathan followed, nibbling on her lower lip as he pulsed inside.

Later as they dressed, Natalia said, "Honey, perhaps you should coordinate with Matt and Charlotte for the time you can watch the crazies." They referred to all seven kids collectively as the 'crazies' because it was chaotic when they were all together.

Natalia met Jonathan Miller after college. He worked at a well-known financial firm that had hired her for her first full-time job as a Mitigation Loss Specialist. Her career was to assist lenders in finding solutions to avoid foreclosure. She hadn't felt for any man what she felt for him. Every time she said his name, her heart thumped faster, and she felt butterflies dancing in her stomach. Natalia worked for several years until she became pregnant with their first child. While on maternity leave, they decided she would be a stay-at-home mom. Eventually, she had three children, all boys. Their sons were rambunctious, healthy, and fun-loving children. Marc was the first, then Alexander and Anthony.

Natalia volunteered for her children's school and with an animal rescue. She enjoyed a happy life and socializing with her friends, as well as a happy marriage. Natalia's two closest friends from college, Christina and Alicia, were a constant support and love source. The girls enjoyed nights out, vacations, shopping trips, and date nights with their significant others. Their kids referred to them as "the moms on a mission," which meant the ladies would save an animal, help the less fortunate, find the best cup of coffee, or the best cocktail. Natalia didn't like to drink, and the other girls made it their mission to find the perfect cocktail for her.

They would attend a fundraiser in Myrtle Beach on their next trip, just the girls, scheduled for the third week in June. They were meeting up with rescue friends they'd networked with on social media for years. Their kids were on summer break, and the spouses would care for them.

As the trip to Myrtle Beach approached, Natalia kept busy cooking meals and doing household chores. Jonathan repeatedly told her, "Slow down, you'll be back, and the house will be here. The house isn't dirty, and I can cook. Besides that, we plan to eat out a lot as we're taking the crazies on adventures."

Annoyance washed over Natalia. She peered over at him. "You know how I am, Jon. I need to do my thing. Go for a run while I finish up here." Natalia wiped the sweat from her brow and let go of her annoyance.

The blaring of the home phone jolted Natalia. She peered at the caller ID that displayed Christina's name and number. Natalia looked at the screen, chewed the inside of her lip—her sixth sense tingling—and answered.

"We have a problemo, kiddo," Christina muttered.

"Uh oh, what kind of problem?" Natalia asked. She wrapped her palms across her stomach, the sudden drop painful.

"Alicia is in the hospital." Christina inhaled. "Her female issues have reared their ugly head. Matt took her to the ER. She's having emergency surgery to remove a ruptured cyst on one of her ovaries."

"I'm coming to pick you up," said Natalia as the sweat beaded on her forehead.

Christina and Natalia rushed to their friend's bedside. They found Matt in the waiting room, running his hands through his thick dark hair as he paced. The cold and sterile family room reminded Natalia of her parent's illnesses and subsequent deaths. She looked at the clean environment, the hushed tones coming from an office across the hall and the bright white paint. The memories were so vivid. She had waited alone for news of her mother. Her father passed first, and she had her mother to lean on. Here, she was glad to have Matt and Christina with her while Alicia was in the operating room.

"What happened, Matt?" Natalia asked.

Matt replied as tears glistened in his eyes, "Alicia suffered from a ruptured ovarian cyst, causing significant bleeding."

Female issues plagued Alicia throughout her reproductive years—polycystic ovaries and endometriosis. It had been quite a challenge to conceive and maintain her two pregnancies. Eventually blessed with Brianna and Julian, and the hysterectomy was inevitable.

As they waited, an operating room nurse came by occasionally to let them know the surgery was going well. Natalia and Christina waited until Alicia was in the recovery area before they left. Then, Natalia stopped by Alicia's house to give Alicia's kids dinner. That evening, Alicia called Natalia to thank her for taking care of Brianna and Julian, and while on the phone, she cried, upset because she couldn't travel for six weeks.

"Gosh, Alicia, why not give me a heart attack with all the tears. But, no worries, we can do it another time," Natalia promised as she wiped a stray tear from her cheek. "You need to concentrate on yourself."

"Natalia." Alicia sighed. "We looked forward to meeting up with our friends at the fundraiser. It is a fabulous event. Everyone is coming from all over the country. And please don't get upset, but with Matt going out on the sea trials for four months, Christina offered to stay behind and help me."

"Alicia, why would that upset me? I planned to stay behind to help until you're on your feet, too," Natalia replied.

"Natalia, we discussed it. Both Christina and I think you should go. You organized all of this. It would be best if you had this break. We'll all go next year. Please promise me you will not call Christina and decide amongst yourselves who will stay home with me. Christina and I discussed this ad nauseam. She's relentless. I'm grateful for you both, but we agreed, you need to go to this fundraiser. You worked hard on it. Take Buddy with you. There will be other pugs there for him to play with."

"I'll think about it, but I can't bear to leave you behind while you recover." Tears poured down Natalia's face. She wiped them with the back of her hand. "If I go, I'll stop by to see you before I leave." Natalia wasn't even sure if Jon would have an issue with her traveling alone.

"You better go. Don't make me come over there." Alicia teased. "I love you, Natalia, so does Christina, but we need you to do this. Do it for us and text lots of pictures."

"We'll see, and yes, I know you guys love me, and I love you both just as much. Listen to the doctors, Alicia, and don't move about until they tell you to" Natalia warned. "You overdo things."

"Okay, I promise," Alicia said convincingly.

After a discussion with Jonathan and Christina, Natalia decided to go to Myrtle Beach with Buddy. The trip from New Jersey wouldn't be that bad. She planned to stop overnight in Virginia to rest and then make her way to Myrtle Beach the following day to check into the hotel by late afternoon. She'd meet up with all their rescue friends, friendships she had developed with Christina and Alicia over the years.

The following day, after visiting with Alicia, Natalia went home, gathered her things and her pug, Buddy. The little dog jumped with excitement as he enjoyed going out with his favorite person. Buddy loved his entire family, and they loved him, but Natalia was his world, and Buddy was the furry light of her life.

"Mom, where's your stuff?" her eldest boy Marc inquired. "I'll load the minivan."

"Everything is in the bedroom, Marc. Thanks so much." Natalia walked around the kitchen to ensure everything was in order and the family had all the food they needed. After Marc loaded the van, Natalia went into Jonathan's home office, although she didn't usually intrude into his space while he worked. "Hey honey, I'm heading out now."

"Do you have enough money? The credit cards, just in case? Buddy's food, his seat belt harness?" Jonathan inquired as he stood to take Natalia into his arms.

"Yes, my love, I'm all set, and I bought Buddy a car seat just for the trip. He's hooked up like royalty. Did you fill the gas tank for me?"

"Shit, I forgot."

"Ugh, Jon. I've asked a few times, each time you were using the van." Natalia replied, her lips in a grim line, her arms crossed.

"I'm sorry, babe, I got distracted—check in with me when you stop for the night. If there are any concerns about the GPS, as it can be a little outdated, use the app on your phone instead. Don't pull over to walk Buddy on the roadside. Use well-lit rest stops. Also, stay on the interstates, no back roads alone, please. Even if it takes longer," Jonathan said as he reached for another hug.

"Okay, honey, I promise. I'll call you later. Love you," Natalia exclaimed as she kissed him.

"Love you more. Talk to you later."

She left her husband's office and made her way to the driveway, where Marc had Buddy securely fastened in his car seat with his favorite stuffed toy and his bully stick. They had placed the cooler in the front seat with snacks and plenty of bottled water for two. Marc teased his mother about Buddy's new car seat. She hugged Marc, squeezing him tight.

"Gosh, Mom, you'll be back home in a few days," Marc complained, frowning. "You act as though you're moving to Mars or something."

"Sorry little man, that's the mom in me. I love my guys." she said with a shrug. "Speaking of which, where are your brothers?" She glanced toward the house, the breeze blowing through her hair.

"Alex and Anthony are in the man cave playing video games," he said, pointing to the house.

"Okay, can you get them while I program the GPS?" she asked. Natalia walked to the driver's side and tapped on the keypad, the address, glancing up when her two younger boys came running through the door.

"Hey, mom, are you heading out now?" Anthony asked.

"Yup," she replied.

"Are you going to be okay by yourself?" Alex inquired.

"I'll be fine."

"Kiss me, and I'll call you guys later. Behave. And don't eat all the snacks in one day and do nothing dangerous either. Got it?" she warned, waving her finger at them.

Three voices at once replied, "Okay, Mom," whining the word, mom.

Smiling, Natalia pulled out of her driveway. She looked back through the rear-view mirror at her three amazing sons. Her heart filled with pride. How *I love those boys*. She turned and headed toward the Turnpike.

Natalia passed through New Jersey, Delaware, Maryland, and DC and ended her first day at Virginia's southernmost point. Buddy, a cooperative traveler, had enjoyed the trip, especially the rest stops where he could stretch his legs, go potty, and enjoy a snack. Natalia didn't want to leave him alone in the minivan, so she carried him into the rest stops in a baby carrier under her hoodie, trying not to draw attention to him. She bought pre-made sandwiches and snacks they would share and return to the van before staff could reprimand her.

"Hey bud, I'm glad you're quiet and love hanging with me, or in this case from me, otherwise they might toss us from these rest stops. Thanks, little guy," Natalia said as she kissed the top of his furry head. "The first trip for us alone, we need to be creative, dude." She nuzzled her nose into the fur on top of his head.

She stopped for the night in Emporia, Virginia, at a pet-friendly hotel, right off the interstate. After she checked into the small hotel, she took Buddy for his last walk for the evening and called home. The hotel looked like many others, small and geared toward families. In serious need of a remodel. Yet clean.

"Hi honey, I'm here in Virginia. How was your day?" she asked as she yawned. "I didn't realize how lonely and exhausted I was driving this far."

"It was okay, I miss you already and wish I could have gone with you, but I'm still working on this deadline." Jonathan responded.

"Everything will be okay, honey. I've got this. Give the boys my love and tell them I miss them. I'm goanna go to sleep," she mentioned, yawning again. "Super-tired."

"I'll call you tomorrow with your wake-up call. Love you, honey, sleep well, babe," Jonathan told her as he disconnected the call.

Natalia changed into her pajamas and climbed into bed. Buddy's warm body behind her knees as his gentle snores lulled her into a deep sleep.

PERSISTENT RINGING woke Natalia. Still groggy, she thrust one hand from beneath the covers and fumbled around on the nightstand and snagged her phone on the fourth ring.

"Hello," she answered, her voice hoarse from sleep.

"Good morning, my love," came Jonathan's voice in her ear. "This is your official wake-up call."

Natalia cleared her throat and replied, "Good morning, babe. Thanks for calling," she said, stretching and wiping her gritty eyes. "I'm gonna jump in the shower while Buddy eats breakfast. And maybe order room service. I'm eager to hit the road. I'm so excited to catch up with friends, but I didn't realize how challenging it is to eat and take bathroom breaks with Buddy along."

"How is the baby carrier working out?" Jonathan asked.

"Outstanding, but I'm always nervous that someone will see him and not let us in. So far, we've been lucky. It's challenging, but I could use the lady's room and grab a pre-made sandwich on the way out. By the time anyone realized I had held him, we were leaving. I plan to replenish bottles of water and snacks from the hotel gift shop to avoid another stop."

"Okay, babe, I'm leaving for a quick meeting, and I still have to drop the boys off to Charlotte. So be careful and check in. Love you," said Jonathan.

"Love you too, enjoy your day," Natalia responded, her heart giving a little tug. She missed waking up beside him. It wasn't often they slept apart.

She ordered breakfast, fed Buddy, hopped in the shower, and packed their things just as room service arrived with the food. Buddy danced in small circles, wagging his tail when he got a whiff of the bacon and begged for a taste. Natalia finished breakfast, got Buddy and their bags, and headed down to the gift shop to buy snacks and bottled water. Buddy went on an expected walk before they headed out to the interstate. After several minutes of driving, they entered North Carolina.

"Won't be too much longer, Buddy, are you okay?" she asked, glancing in the rearview mirror. Buddy looked up and went right back to gnawing on his bully stick. Natalia smiled at her furry companion and said, "Those things stink, Bud."

Natalia traveled for another few hours, stopped at a rest stop, walked Buddy, grabbed a sandwich, and hopped back on the interstate. Buddy seemed to enjoy the trip and being with his mom, adjusting to the new routine and his adventure quickly.

Arriving in Myrtle Beach in the late afternoon on Thursday after several potty breaks that exhausted Natalia. Having dozed for most of the trip, Buddy was eager to explore. Natalia checked in and unloaded the minivan, plopping on the bed for a few minutes. The air conditioning hissed as the cool air kept the room comfortable. Covered in a fluffy white comforter, the king-sized bed tempted Natalia to snuggle underneath and take a nap. Natalia glanced at the schedule sitting on the dark wood desk. She checked it and learned about the meet and greet in the lobby, followed by a pizza party on the terrace. After she changed into shorts and her favorite Pug Rescue T-shirt, she took Buddy for a quick walk and headed back to the lobby for the meet and greet.

Natalia approached the registration table. She overheard bits of conversation behind it as they greeted old friends and their furry companions. The fundraiser would kick off the next day, with the rescue volunteers selling crafts and pet items to raise money. Tonight, they planned an informal gathering to reacquaint, relax, and enjoy each other's company.

Natalia signed in and received her name tag. As she entered the area where the other pug families gathered, she recognized Kathy and ran over to her, squealing, "We meet in the flesh at last."

Kathy smiled. They embraced, squeezing each other.

"You're prettier in person," Natalia squealed. "We see pictures of each other on social media, but you're even more gorgeous than your pictures."

"Stop, sweetie, you're making me blush," Kathy said, laughing. "Where are Christina and Alicia?"

"Long story short? Alicia had emergency surgery. Christina stayed behind to help with recovery because Matt had to board the ship for sea trials. He'll be gone for at least a month, maybe more if there're issues. They conspired against me and decided I should come to the fundraiser, and they can live vicariously through me." She giggled.

"Wow, sorry to hear that. I remember you mentioning that you've all been friends since college, all of you are like one big happy family, then you bonded over pugs too. How cool is that?" Kathy exclaimed. "Tell me the story."

"Are you sure you want to hear this?" Natalia raised her right eyebrow.

"Every bit." Kathy laughed, her eyes twinkling.

"Well," Natalia began as she inhaled, "we were in our senior year of college. I didn't want to stay in the dorms any longer, and I found the most amazing rental, but it was out of my price range. Alicia had been in a few of my classes and overheard me talking about it to other friends. She came right over and said, 'I can help, I would love to move out of the dorms, and I can swing part of the rent.'"

Natalia continued, "I thanked her and asked if she wanted to think about it and if she needed to see the place first. I also mentioned that we need one more person. I proposed the idea to my friend Christina. She was a business major in her last year. Christina called me after work and said sure. And Alicia just said, 'That's fabulous. Let me know in class tomorrow when we can see the place and how much we will need upfront. I'm excited to meet Christina.'"

Natalia smiled as she shared the memory. "I then told Christina about Alicia, and she said she looked forward to meeting her. In class the next day, I told Alicia they had an appointment that afternoon. Interested, Alicia had asked Natalia to describe the house. I explained the home and mentioned it was mere minutes from the college. I also had to let Alicia know that Christina was gay. Thankfully, she didn't have an issue with it. Otherwise, she wouldn't be a good fit." Natalia smiled at Kathy.

"How did the three of you come to love pugs?" Kathy asked.

"We had been in the house for about three months, and one evening, as I got ready to leave work, I went to take out the trash, and there stood this adorable pug eating garbage that had spilled from the dumpster in the middle of a blizzard. She was so tiny and so cold that I picked her up, brought her into the employee bathroom, and checked for a collar or ID. Nothing. I left her there, ran into the kitchen, and got food for her. Then, I walked home with her snuggled into my coat.

"Alicia and Christina were in the kitchen with their homework. They'd squealed when they saw my bundle. I mentioned we needed to find the little dog's owners, and we made flyers and posted them after the storm. We placed an ad in the local paper with no response and dropped off leaflets at local vets' offices. Finally, we called the police and learned that no one had lost a pug to their knowledge.

"We called shelters and more of the same. At that point, the pup had been living with us for a few weeks, and we had become attached. I called the landlord and explained the situation. He thanked me for giving him a heads up but reminded me that there was a 'no pet clause' in the lease and allowed her to stay until we could find her owners. We took her to the vet, and she didn't have a chip, and other than being too thin, she seemed healthy and about two years old."

Kathy listened. She loved hearing rescue stories.

The rest of the story came with a rush of warm feelings. "The holidays had arrived and gone, and no one claimed the little pug girl. Instead, we provided weekly updates to Joe, our landlord, because we weren't trying to be shady. About three weeks after the holidays, he came by to replace a leaky faucet. Impressed with the house's condition, knowing that all three of us attended classes full time and worked, he remarked the place had never looked so good, cozy, inviting, and clean.

"He asked about the dog, and I told him she was in the bedroom because not everyone likes dogs. He said he did and wanted to meet her. When I opened her bedroom door, the pug flew out like the Tasmanian devil, right into Joe's legs, jumping like crazy. Joe had laughed and roughhoused with her like a little boy. Then he'd said since we kept the house clean, if we couldn't find her owners, she could stay."

Natalia met Kathy's interested gaze. "I jumped in his arms and gave him the biggest hug. Every day, when we returned from work, it overjoyed us when 'Dolly' excitedly greeted us at the door. We worried each day that her owners would come forth. It would have broken our hearts. Anyway, I mentioned Joe's visit and his approval. We called the shelter and the police one last time before claiming her as ours. It had been about seven weeks, and no one called to claim her. We took it as a sign that it meant Dolly to be ours. Dolly became the fourth member of our family, and that's how we all became 'Pug Lovers.' After attending local Pug gatherings, we hooked up with the rescue and became volunteers." Natalia shrugged. "That's our love story."

Kathy flashed Natalia a broad smile. "Oh, my word, a love story for sure. When you all graduated, who took Dolly?"

"We stayed behind in that rental house until we got full-time jobs. I took her with me, as Alicia and Christina were traveling a lot for work. After meeting our spouses, we moved to the same town, my hometown. Dolly died several years ago. She left a lot of broken hearts behind. Dolly was even my flower girl at my wedding to Jonathan."

"No. How sweet is that? Well, I've monopolized you long enough. Let's go meet the others." Kathy took Natalia by the arm and led her over to the rescue group that had organized the fundraiser. The evening was full of hugging her friends, loving on pugs she had only seen in pictures, crying over lost pugs, and enjoying the evening.

Once back in the room for the night, she called home and checked in on her guys, then called Christina to check in on Alicia. Christina stayed at Alicia's, close enough to run home periodically to her own family—her wife Charlotte, their twin girls Carly and Casey, and their rescue Pug Poe. Natalia texted them pictures of the meet and greet and their friends.

Three

AFTER BRUNCH ON FRIDAY, sightseeing excursions were next on the itinerary. Those who wanted to sightsee received free 'pug care' from the members who planned to stay behind. Natalia went to the beach for a few hours with Kathy. Kathy's sister, Deb, stayed behind with their pugs and took care of Buddy.

The beach was beautiful, with the scorching sun glaring on their bodies and warming the sand. Overheated, Natalia turned to Kathy and said, "I'm going to grab a soda." She pointed to the bar. "Can I get you anything?" The heat of the sun flushed Natalia's face, beads of sweat glistened on her nose and forehead.

"Gosh, girl, you read my mind," Kathy exclaimed, wiping beads of sweat from her nose. "Diet for me, please."

Natalia made her way to the bar, placed her order, and waited for the server to come back with the beverages. She tapped her fingers on the bar in tune with the music. In the pit of her stomach, she experienced a familiar dance, butterflies. Her skin pricked, and she sensed that someone watched her. She turned and detected two distinguished gentlemen peering in her direction. Smiling, she turned back to the bar. Her mother always said she had the 'eye.' An Italian saying that meant psychic abilities. For most of her life, she felt as though someone watched.

Natalia overheard the gray-haired gentleman say to his friend, "It is her. The smile, the eyes, it must be. It is *her*. I am telling you I would recognize my daughter anywhere."

The second man responded, "People are listening. Please lower your voice. "

Natalia wasn't sure who they were talking about, but it could be anyone. The place was busy. She paid for the sodas and hustled out of there to return to Kathy. Her body tingled with uncertainty.

"Natalia, your face is all red," noted Kathy. "What's wrong?"

"I'm okay, just overheated from the run back to you. I didn't want the drinks to get warm."

After gulping her drink, Kathy got up to go for a swim, leaving Natalia lost in her thoughts as she gazed at the waves break against the shore. Then, a shadow fell over her, and she looked up and recognized the one man from the restaurant. She almost jumped out of her sand chair, her heart racing.

With a charming smile, he said, "Hello, my name is Thomas Collins, forgive my intrusion, but my friend lost his daughter as a teenager years ago, she was a runaway, and you bear an uncanny resemblance to her. By any chance, is your name Susan or does the name Susan mean anything to you?"

"No, I'm sorry, but I'm not Susan," Natalia responded.

He followed up with another question. "Do you live here?"

"No, I don't," she replied. "I'm from up North, born and raised there."

"Sorry for the inconvenience, and thanks for answering. I'm sorry to disturb you. I'll tell my friend that you are not his daughter," Thomas assured her. "It is truly unbelievable, but the resemblance is uncanny."

Natalia watched as the stranger made his way back to the restaurant. Kathy returned from her swim and mentioned to Natalia to take a dip.

Natalia smiled and said, "I've been quite content sitting here, enjoying the warm breeze and my soda. The beach is very peaceful. But to be honest, I'm about ready to head back to the hotel. I bet my little guy is missing me, and I'm missing him. Are you ready?"

"Yes, I am. That swim will help me sleep tonight." Kathy chuckled as she rolled her eyes toward the sky. "That is if my furry terrors let me."

They strolled to the hotel, chatting, and enjoying the landscape. Natalia inhaled the salt air deep into her lungs. The fresh air was refreshing. Natalia picked up Buddy and took him for a long walk around the resort. The earlier roughhousing exhausted her little pug, and back in their room, he fell asleep, snoring softly. Finally, Natalia called home to check in.

"Hi mom, are you having fun?" asked Alex upon answering the phone.

"Yes, honey, I am. It would be more fun if you were all here too. Is Dad home yet?"

"Yes, he's just pulling in the garage now. Dad, Mom's on the phone." Alex yelled. The shuffling and rustling sounds came over the phone, and Natalia imagined Jonathan rushing into the house to take Alex's phone.

"Hey, baby, how are you? Having fun?" Jonathan's harsh breaths huffed into the phone.

"Yep. But something freaked me out and made me a little sad. I hung out at the beach with a friend for a few hours this afternoon. I walked to the bar for a soda, where these two older guys sat nearby. The gray-haired man made a fuss, looking my way, and he kept insisting I was his daughter. At first, I didn't realize they had been talking about me, but it still freaked me out, and I hustled back to our spot on the beach. Several minutes later, the other guy came to me on the beach and asked me if my name was Sue or Suzy. I told him it wasn't, and he asked if I lived there, and I told him no, up north. He apologized and left. His friend's daughter ran away as a teenager, and he hasn't seen her since. It freaked me out, yet it made me sad for the guy. I couldn't imagine that happening to one of our boys."

"Perhaps you should come home. It sounds a little creepy," Jonathan remarked.

"No, I'll be fine. The beach isn't near our hotel or any of the festivities. I'm not planning on venturing away from the hotel at this point. All scheduled events are here." Natalia sighed. "I miss you guys."

"We miss you too. How is Buddy enjoying all the other pugs? It is too quiet here without him," Jonathan said.

"Buddy's having a blast, running, and playing. He even tried out the agility course and seemed to catch on fast. Tonight, there is a buffet dinner outside, a barbeque. The weather is a little hot for Buddy, so I'm leaving him inside. I'll be right outside the sliding glass doors. He should be fine for an hour or so. Later, an auction is on the agenda inside the air-conditioned ballroom. He'll enjoy it and get to play with other dogs."

"Okay, baby, I'll talk to you later tonight. Call me before you go to bed and give the furry man a high five from Dad."

"Will do. Love you." Natalia hung up and stepped into the bathroom for a shower.

The remaining days flew by in a whirlwind—filled with auctions, contests, agility training, lots of activities for adults, kids, and dogs. Most attendees made their journey home after breakfast on the last day. Natalia planned to leave on Monday after checkout. She relaxed and read by the pool, took an afternoon nap, and had dinner plans with Kathy and Debbie, who planned to fly out later that evening.

After dinner, Kathy and Debbie took the shuttle to the airport. Natalia walked back to her room to gather her things to be ready to leave in the morning. Not tired and unable to read, she viewed pictures from the event on social media, saw a movie, and still found herself unable to sleep. Finally, Natalia decided to check out and head home earlier than planned. She missed Jon and the boys.

"Buddy, what do you say we head out now? I want to go home. I miss my guys. What do you think, little guy? Wait here." Natalia said as Buddy did his happy dance, wagging his curly tail. "I'm going to the gift shop for water and snacks. I'll load up the car and then come back for you." Natalia grabbed her duffle bag, Buddy's stuff, and the cooler, and headed to the gift shop. She bought water, granola bars, and pretzels, and loaded up the minivan. She hurried back to the room for Buddy, who waited by the table where his leash rested. She harnessed him up and strolled to the lobby to check out.

"Until next time Myrtle Beach, it's been fun." Natalia mumbled as she programmed the GPS and headed away from the hotel toward the interstate. After a few miles, she ran into a roadblock with a detour. The road beyond the barricade appeared, flooded from a pipe rupture.

The GPS announced, "Off route, make a safe U-Turn."

"Damn it. Now I'm on a dark-ass back road. Shit. And just my luck, there is no one in front of me to follow. Okay, Buddy, taking this slow. I hope we find the interstate easily."

Natalia spotted another detour sign up ahead with an arrow showing where the darkened road curved to the left. She sped up. *Okay, I've got this. At least there are signs. Ugh, I should have waited until the morning to leave.*

Natalia followed the bright orange signs, hoping she would get to the entrance of the interstate soon. The GPS continued to repeat the instructions to make a safe U-turn. She glanced from the GPS as an animal ran in front of her van. She slammed on the brakes.

Without realizing it, Natalia hit a patch of thick, damp sand, losing control of the vehicle. She lurched forward as the airbag deployed upon impact with a wide tree. The sound of metal crunching, glass shattering, and the powdery acrid smell from the airbag, along with the strong chemical smells from the engine, accosted Natalia. In mere seconds, the only sound was the hissing of the smoking engine as she plunged into darkness, leaving Buddy unhurt and still harnessed in his car seat, whimpering.

Four

PRESENT DAY...

She felt a warm caress fall over her body as the sun's light revealed the fresh new day. She popped her eyes open and heard a dog whimpering. The bright sunlight forced her to close her eyes quickly. She blinked a few times to adjust her eyes to the light, but her vision was blurry, and she had difficulty focusing. The pain in her head was intense, and her hands flew up, cupping each side of her face as if she could quell the throbbing. The little dog popped his head up and rested on the side of her bed, peering at her. She tapped the mattress, inviting him up. The tiny, tan, flat-faced dog jumped up and cuddled with her, laying his head on her thigh.

"Where are we, puppy?" She stared into his soulful brown eyes. Her thoughts were a cacophony buzzing in her head, and she couldn't focus on a complete thought. She moved and moaned, trying to lift herself. The intense pounding in her head forced her to lay back against the pillow. Pain emanated out of every part of her body. As she tried to move again, she froze in place as she listened to the door creak open.

"Oh, you're awake. Good morning. I'm Cora, the house manager. I came to walk the little dog." She held a bright red leash in her hand. "I will bring him back to you along with your breakfast."

"Umm, okay," she replied. "What happened to me?" her voice cracking as she licked her dry lips.

Cora wore a sad smile, her eyes wide with concern. "You were in a car accident, dear," she answered, "I wanted to know if it was okay to feed Buddy the food that we found food in the plastic bag, and I'll send Jack out to the pet store for more food. Is there a brand you prefer?"

"Umm, I'm not sure. I don't remember."

"No matter. Jack will find something." Cora snapped the leash to the dog's harness. "Dr. Kline has you on a light diet. I will bring your breakfast up to you shortly."

"Wait. Can you tell me where I am? Who is Doctor Kline?"

"Yes, you are at home, dear. Doctor Kline is your father," stated Cora reassuringly, smiling at her.

Bewildered, she gazed at the room, and nothing appeared remotely familiar. It was large and luxurious, but foreign. The dog was cute, and she assumed by his devotion that he belonged to her. Her heart thumped in her chest as she placed her palm across it, as if she could calm it down. Her eyes burned from unshed tears when she asked, "Who am I? Where is home?"

"Susan Kline, honey." Cora gave her a sympathetic smile. "Don't worry. Your father will have you well in no time. And your home is in Beverly Hills."

Cora said Beverly Hills as though that meant something. How is it I cannot remember anything? Have I just woken up from a coma?

Cora returned twenty minutes later with breakfast and fresh pajamas. The aroma from the food made her nauseous. She placed her hand over her salivating mouth. Cora assisted her to the bathroom but advised her not to shower alone because she appeared to be too unsteady on her feet. She noticed the crusted blood embedded in her hair.

Cora's care was gentle and attentive. She assisted Susan back to a chair and gave her the breakfast tray. She tried to eat, but she experienced nausea when she moved her head because of the pain. She sipped the juice and ate a few bites of the toast. Cora gave her pain meds and assisted Susan back into bed.

"Shall I take the little guy downstairs with me?" Cora asked.

"He's fine here, thank you," Susan replied. She tried hard to remember something, anything, but her mind was a blank slate. *Who am I, and why can't I remember?*

Susan rested her head on the fluffed pillow. She peered around the room, spacious and clean, yet unfamiliar. She caressed the small dog's head as she dozed off, sleeping most of the morning.

The pain pills brought her little relief as her head continued to throb. She felt confused and sleepy. The little dog—she kept forgetting his name—comforted her. *Someone must take care of him,* she thought. *Maybe the gracious lady,* because he was missing from her bed now and again when she periodically woke up.

This time, the dog was there. She tried to sit up, and he tilted his head and got up too, gazing at her. Susan smiled at him. "You sure are a cute little guy. Am I your friend? I like that. I guess we'll figure this out together. Deal?" The little dog licked her face in agreement.

A few hours later, Cora slipped into the room. "Hello, Miss Susan, can I do anything for you?"

"Yes. Can you help me to the bathroom, please?"

Cora assisted Susan out of bed and helped her into the bathroom. Still unsteady on her feet, she leaned on Cora for support. The gray-haired, blue-eyed woman held onto her as though she were precious cargo. Her smiling face guided Susan.

"Do you think I can take a shower?" she asked.

"Not yet. Your father is bringing a shower chair home. I'll ask him about it as soon as you're tucked back into bed."

"Can I sit in that chair for a little?" she asked, pointing to a plush chair by the window.

"As long as you don't move about by yourself," Cora said with a smile. "Call for me when you want to go to bed."

Susan nodded her head in agreement and reached up, grasping her pounding head.

Cora nodded in sympathy. She passed Susan the TV remote and the magazines she had bought at the grocery store. "If you need anything else, Miss Susan, you can speak into this intercom. It will reach me no matter where I am in the house. Just push this button right here." She tapped the device she'd placed on the table.

"Thank you," Susan replied.

"I'm going to prepare lunch. I'll return in a jiff." Cora glanced at Susan and wondered if she should leave her alone in the chair. She hurried the dog during his walk and prepared a light lunch tray. After Cora had Susan situated with lunch, she called Dr. Kline to give him an update.

"Good afternoon, Dr. Kline. I wanted to give you an update on Miss Susan's progress. She's still in a considerable amount of pain. I just gave her lunch, and she's picking at it. She enjoyed the soup, ate about half of it, and now wants a shower."

"Thank you, Cora, no to the shower right now. I don't think she's stable enough," Richard replied.

"Were you able to order the shower chair?" Cora asked.

"Yes, a chair is being delivered, along with a walker. Maybe she will use it for exercise, walking herself to the bathroom. I expect the delivery later today. Once she can stand unassisted, I'll send over a personal shopper to get measurements for her wardrobe. Please keep me posted on her progress throughout the day," Richard said.

"Will do, Doctor. I sent Jack to the pet store for the dog. He needs toys and treats. He's such a sweet little guy and adores Miss Susan. He brought life into the house."

"I agree. Buddy is a sweet dog. I've never had a dog before, but he is cute and well-mannered. I read tips on the internet at lunch about the breed. I'll share them with you later this evening over dinner. Please ask Jack if he can join us. If Susan isn't too weak, perhaps we can bring her downstairs for the meal. I'll see you at around three o'clock. Bye for now."

Five

JONATHAN MILLER PACED in the kitchen, his brow wrinkling. He rubbed his hands on his jeans as he inhaled deep, calming breaths, his stomach-churning. Finally, he turned to his son, who was eating a sandwich. "That's the fourth time I called your mother, Alex, and the call goes to voicemail. Right to voicemail. Your mom never turns off her phone."

"Relax, Dad, maybe she's out of range," Alex replied, without looking up from his sandwich, his mouth full.

"No, Alex, this isn't our normal. When either of us is away, we call first thing in the morning and check in throughout the day. Either with texts, calls, or silly pictures. I'm seriously concerned. I spoke to her last night. She mentioned she almost had everything packed up for checkout in the morning and planned to go to bed early." Jonathan ran his fingers through his messy hair, his face deeply lined, his eyes moist.

"Why not call the hotel, Dad? Maybe she's sick and stayed until she felt better?" He took another bite.

"That's a great idea," Jonathan said, nodding.

He left the room and strode into his home office, where he had placed Natalia's itinerary. The hotel information was at the top of the page in his wife's cursive. She wrote like a girl, feminine and legible. She always teased the guys about their chicken scratch and said they all had the handwriting style of a doctor.

Reaching for the landline, he tried again and left yet another voice message. Jonathan called the hotel, and the hotel clerk explained she had checked out late Sunday night to head home. The news stunned Jonathan. His heart raced, and he closed his eyes as he sagged in his chair. His gut told him something was wrong. Natalia would have called by now. She would have called first thing to inform him of any change in plans. He didn't want to disturb Alicia and Christina this early. Instead, he called Charlotte because she woke early. Charlotte answered on the second ring, "Good morning, Jon, how are you this sunny morning?" she chirped.

"Char, I am flipping out. Natalia's phone went to voicemail right away, as though she turned the phone off. Has she called you?"

"She sent me a text Saturday afternoon with pictures of harnesses she had made for all the pugs, embroidered with their names. I'm checking my phone now. Yes, Saturday afternoon, at one-thirty. She was excited because she personalized them. She mentioned they would be ready at three. That's the last text I received from her. I'll ask Christina when she gets out of the shower."

"No, tend to the girls. I hear them in the background, and it sounds like they're about to kill each other. I'll call Alicia." Jonathan paced as he called Alicia's number.

"Hey, Jon, what's up?"

"Natalia's missing." he exclaimed, his voice quivering as he rubbed his forehead.

"Come on, Jon, how long has it been since you chatted, twenty minutes? Stop being a clown." Jon was a practical joker, and Alicia assumed it was another prank.

"No, I'm serious. She checked out of the hotel late last night and hasn't checked in with me yet. I've been calling her cell, and it continues to go right to voicemail. I'm worried that something has happened," Jonathan said.

"Come on over. I'm assuming that Natalia took the directions we mapped out on the map program. We'll call the police in each state," Alicia suggested.

"Okay. I'll be over soon. Gotta go, someone is calling in on the other line," Jonathan said. He disconnected and took the incoming call. "Hello?" Jonathan could hear the panic in his voice.

"Is this the Miller residence?"

"Yes, it is."

"This is the Myrtle Beach Police Department. We found an abandoned vehicle on Route 22 East. A Mazda minivan registered to you."

"Yes, that's my wife's car. She's in Myrtle Beach for a rescue fundraiser. Wait, abandoned? What do you mean? Did it break down?"

"No, it appears she skidded off the road. The van hit a tree right by the lake. If the vehicle hadn't hit the tree, she would have landed in the lake. We found blood on the airbag. Was there anyone else in the car with her?"

"Our dog. Where is my wife? Is she in the hospital? Was the dog in the car?" Jonathan spewed the questions without taking a breath.

"Sir, please, calm down. No, the vehicle was empty. No woman and no dog. Can you give me a description of your wife and the dog? Maybe she's dazed and walked with him into the woods."

"You wouldn't ever catch my wife in the woods. She's not a country girl. Not to mention she's terrified of bugs."

"Can you give us a description?

"Yeah, sure, she's five, five and weighs about a hundred and twenty pounds. She has shoulder-length blond hair and blue eyes."

"Mr. Miller, what kind of dog?"

"Our dog is small. A tan pug, his name is Buddy. My wife's name is Natalia. I'll grab the first flight I can. What is the address of your police station?" Jonathan's voice cracked his heart racing. He swayed slightly, grasping the wall for support, and quickly jotting down the address to the police station. He then called Alicia back and told her who had been on the other line and what little he learned.

Christina entered Alicia's room while they were on the call and asked if there were any updates, but Alicia couldn't talk through her sobs. Jonathon tried to relay the information over the sounds of her crying.

"What?" Christina bellowed. "Will someone tell me what's going on."

Alicia took a deep breath, stifled a sob, and began, "The police from Myrtle Beach called Jonathan. They located the minivan in the woods. She hit a tree by a lake. No one was inside, and blood was on the airbag. The police are heading into the woods to search now. They think the accident disoriented Natalia, and she walked with Buddy into the woods."

Christina, the most organized and calm one of all the women, took over. "Okay, Jon, grab your things, and I'll get a flight for you. Have the boys each pack a bag and send them here. I'll get you to the airport. I need to call my office first to tell them I'm not coming in today." Christina had a flight, a hotel, and a rental car secured for Jonathan within the hour.

Jonathan took the boys over to Christina and Charlotte's and begged the boys not to torture their girls and help Charlotte. "Please, guys, don't make me worry about you. I need to focus on your mom." Although they tried hard not to show their emotions, the boys were upset, and his eyes burned with unshed tears. "Keep your cell phones charged. I'll text you every bit of information as I receive it. I love you guys."

"We love you too, Dad. Bring Mom and Buddy home," Marc said.

"That's the plan." Jonathan replied.

Jonathan tossed his suitcase into the back of Christina's car and slid into the front seat for the trip to the Philadelphia International Airport. Sick to his stomach, anxious, and scared, he looked at Christina and cried, "Chris, what am I going to do? How am I supposed to find her? How will we survive without her?" His eyes glistened with tears.

"Okay, Jon, let's not be melodramatic. Our girl is a tough cookie. And the police know what they're doing, and if you doubt their capabilities, insist on calling in the state police."

Christina sped to the airport, anxiety driving her need for speed. They arrived at the terminal, and she said, "Okay, Jon, this is your terminal. Call me when you land. I paid for the ticket and take this cash." She held out an envelope. "I always have some on hand for emergencies." She shoved it toward him.

"I can go to the ATM for cash. No worries," Jonathan responded, refusing the cash.

"I know you can, but there are other things on your mind. Take it," Christina pleaded, and she shoved the cash toward him again.

"Thank you, Chris. Can you do me one more favor? I'm off today, but can you call my boss and tell him I won't be in for a few days? You can tell him what's going on. I texted you his contact information." Jonathan jumped from the car and ran into the terminal. He realized his boarding pass had *TSA pre-check* noted on it. A perk that came with the position and allowed him to avoid lines during check-in. Jonathan breezed through without delay. He'd packed light and didn't have to check his bag, confident he would come home with his wife and dog in a day or two.

The two-hour flight was uneventful, but Jonathan was full of anxiety. His legs bounced the entire flight. Upon arrival at the terminal, he exited the plane and hustled to the rental car area. Fortunately, when he arrived, the clerk was just finishing the transaction for the person ahead of him. Christina was thorough and had arranged for a car to be waiting for him outside, and he was grateful that he didn't have to search for it. Jonathan plugged the police station's address into the GPS on his phone and headed toward the interstate.

When he arrived, he parked in one of the guest spots behind the station and walked around the building's front to the main entrance. At the front desk, Jonathan asked to speak to Officer Trent. The officer at the front desk checked the computer and said, "I believe he just went off duty. I'll page him. What is your name, sir?"

"Jonathan Miller." He stayed where he was as the front desk tried to contact Officer Trent.

"Officer Trent here."

"Officer Trent, a gentleman is here for you, a Mr. Miller."

"Oh, okay, that was quick. I'll be right out there."

"He's on his way," the officer informed Jonathan.

"Thank you." Jonathan paced as he waited, glancing toward the 'wanted' signs. He noticed a photo of a man who the FBI wanted for abducting a woman. He silently prayed that Natalia hadn't crossed paths with him.

Officer Trent appeared in the lobby and went over to Jonathan. "Mr. Miller, I presume?"

Jonathan nodded. His mouth was dry, and his lips stuck together.

"My office is down this hallway." He pointed, "right this way."

Jonathan struggled to breathe as he followed the officer. He shoved his trembling hands deep into his pockets as if he could calm them. Once inside, the man closed the door and asked for identification, opening a folder. The officer showed Jonathan photos of the van, both inside and out. The color drained from Jonathan's face when he saw the damage and the blood on the airbag. Officer Trent mentioned the police had walked through the woods with no sign of Mrs. Miller or a dog. Jonathan shook his head and grasped the edge of the gray metal desk, his knuckles white, tears stinging his eyes.

"These are the pictures of the car," Officer Trent said, placing them on the table in front of Jonathan.

The color drained from Jonathan's face. The accident caused the van's hood to split in two down the center, and the windshield shattered. "Oh, God." *That can't be our van. It just can't.*

His eyes burned with unshed tears, he moved to the following picture, and his chest tightened. "Blood," he said, slamming his finger on the image. "There's blood on the airbag."

"I'm sorry. I can imagine how upsetting this must be."

"Upsetting? Upsetting?" he bellowed, his voice raising an octave. "Is this your wife's car? If not, then I don't think you know anything about how I feel."

"You're right, I'm sorry," the officer said apologetically. We're going to do everything we can to find your wife, Mr. Miller. We had the team scope the woods out, but sadly we saw no sign of Mrs. Miller or her dog."

Jonathan shook his head and grasped the edge of the gray metal desk, his knuckles white, tears stinging his eyes. "She has to be okay. She has to be okay."

"Do you have any recent pictures of your wife?"

Yesterday, Natalia had texted him a great shot from the fundraiser, one of Natalia smiling with Buddy on her lap. Jonathan passed his phone over, opened it to the photo Natalia sent.

Officer Trent took Jonathan's phone and walked it to a nearby copier with a USB cable ready. After he got the pictures, he returned to the office and returned the phone. "I'll distribute these pictures. I've checked the local hospitals and veterinarian offices with no luck. We pulled the van in, and forensics has it now. Mr. Miller, we're treating this as an active crime scene."

"I'm overwhelmed, scared for my wife, scared for our family. Where could she be? The location of the accident, is it safe? Is it residential? What kind of area?"

"Mr. Miller, Route 22 is a rural route. No houses. It is a deserted stretch of road. Detour signs sent your wife in that direction because of a water main break on the road leading to the interstate. Only a short distance ahead, and she would've arrived at another entrance ramp for the interstate. The tire tracks look as though she skidded in sand and gravel on the road."

"My God, I told her not to take back roads."

"It appears she walked away from the accident. Maybe to search for the dog, the accident may have tossed the canine from the vehicle. The rain that night muddied any footprints."

"No, my wife always secured Buddy. He had a doggie car seat and a canine seat belt. I don't see those in any of the pictures. She usually put him in the middle row, on the passenger side." He pointed to the picture. "There, that's how he rides to the vet or the park. Can I see the car and the area they found the car?"

"Mr. Miller, it's pointless, the van isn't there any longer, and the police scoured the area." He glanced at the troubled man and debated asking his next question but knew he must, "is your marriage in trouble? Is there any chance Mrs. Miller had planned her disappearance? Was she having emotional issues? Or taking any medications for depression?"

"Oh, my God. No. Our relationship is amazing. We rarely disagree. I'm married to my best friend, and we are parents to three amazing boys. We love our life. She wouldn't disappear willingly. My wife is happy, well-adjusted, and one of the strongest women I know. Had she wanted to disappear, she could have avoided injury and just left her hotel, abandoning the van there. Trust me. My wife didn't just disappear on her own. Someone has her, or she's wandering around lost and confused. Can't we call the media and issue a missing person report?"

"Did she speak with you during her vacation? Mention what she was doing? Does anything stand out?"

Jonathan thought for a moment and suddenly remembered something. "Yes. She mentioned a man approaching her and her friend on the beach. He thought she looked like his daughter. She told him she wasn't, and he left. It was creepy, but she assured me she was going back to the hotel and not leaving until checkout."

"Did she describe the man?" Officer Trent asked.

"Not that I recall," Jonathan replied. "Just that he appeared to be a professional. Now, can I please visit the accident location?"

"Okay, Mr. Miller. There is an APB out on her. Search and rescue are on it. As for seeing the location, there is nothing there. Your van is in the tow lot. Go rest. I'll be in touch."

Defeated and drained by the emotional stress of the day, Jonathan struggled with the news, his heart raced, and he could settle the knot in his stomach. Lowering his head as he strode to the rental car, reeling from the news. Once inside the rental, he yelled and banged the steering wheel, sobbing as he wrapped his arms around it. Running his hands through his hair, he took a deep breath and composed himself to call his sons, Christina, and Alicia and updated them. Jonathan begged for prayers and guidance. His eyes were dry and gritty from crying. *How could someone just disappear? How do you even find them?* Jonathan tried Natalia's phone one more time. Voice mail. *I can't just sit here. I need to find my wife.*

Six

THE MORNING AFTER SUSAN'S return, Richard checked his email from his tablet as he readied himself for the day. Dr. Paulson had reiterated that Susan's bleed was slight, and he would monitor it and planned to check on her later that morning. In the meantime, Dr. Paulson discussed warning signs should Susan's health change. Richard checked on Susan, who had been sleeping with her little dog next to her. After another shot for pain, she didn't wince at the sting. The little dog glanced up and closed his eyes again, snoring softly beside her. He couldn't remember the last time he experienced joy like this. *Maybe at her birth?*

Richard left for his appointment with the actor earlier than usual. His patients respected Dr. Kline for his discretion and for protecting his client's privacy. In instances like this, he took care of his patients with minimal staff. He paid his employees well and insisted on signing a non-disclosure statement, but one never knew when a tabloid would catch wind of gossip and offer a massive payout for photos or the actual story. Money changed people.

His patient arrived on time with a massive bandage on his face. They escorted him to the exam room, and Richard removed the tape holding the gauze. The wound was just an abrasion. After he assured the actor that there wouldn't be any scarring, Richard cleaned it and applied an anti-bacterial cream.

"Here are samples of the cream," said Richard, passing him small tubes. "It should clear up in a week. If you're filming, your make-up artist can cover it easily."

"Thanks, I appreciate you fitting me in first thing this morning, Doc. I worried it was much worse. This face of mine is my money-maker," he said, laughing.

"You're welcome. Try not to do anything too dangerous to ruin your money maker," responded Richard with a smile. "No need for a follow-up unless you have an issue."

Richard escorted the actor to the back door as he listened to the chattering staff. His receptionist had arrived. Smiling, he returned to his office, where his daily schedule waited on his desk. He perused it and was grateful it would be a simple day—a few Botox injections, facial ablating. Nothing too time-consuming that Dr. Ross couldn't handle on her own. It would allow him to go to his appointment later with his urologist.

He proceeded with seeing patients and handling paperwork. He was happy and had a pep in his step. He had an appetite, something he hadn't had in years. The deli delivered the staff the food he'd ordered at noon into the staff break room. The practice shut down between noon and two. Many of the elite of Beverly Hills "lunched" with friends. Richard ate while he worked on paperwork or returning phone calls during the lunch period. The staff took an hour for lunch and used the remaining downtime for filing, ordering medications, and general catch-up work. Richard's practice was a busy one and profitable. They estimated his portfolio to be worth about twenty million dollars between his medical practice, investments, and properties.

A generous man, Richard paid his staff well and involved himself in many charitable organizations. His wife, Donna, had been the actual volunteer. However, after her death, Richard wanted to honor her memory by contributing his money and time. He hoped Susan, when well enough, would resume her mother's philanthropic activities. Glancing, he realized he should hustle to get to his appointment.

He hurried to his appointment with Richard was unfamiliar with Dr. Taugher. The man had recently moved from New York to Hills Urology. His friend, Carmine Talotta, had started the practice twenty-five years ago and had a high success rate in the regression of male reproductive cancers. Since they played golf together for years, Carmine mentioned that his new associate would better care for Richard. He would be there for consultations and advice.

A nurse escorted Richard into an examination room and asked him to disrobe from the waist down. The cheerful nurse gave him a cotton hospital gown and informed him that Dr. Taugher would be in to examine him in a few minutes.

Dr. Taugher, born and raised in Brooklyn, New York, was dynamic, fun, and knowledgeable. He embraced the California lifestyle and dressed casually in a short-sleeved, printed button-down shirt, khakis, and canvas loafers. His brown hair grew over his collar. Dr. Taugher bounded into the room with a welcoming smile. "Hello, Dr. Kline. We spoke on the phone—however, nothing like meeting in person. I'm Justin Taugher. It's a pleasure to meet you." He reached out to shake Richard's hand.

"Likewise, Dr. Taugher."

"Nothing formal about me, just call me Justin."

"Great, call me Rich." Richard smiled. He felt good about this young doctor.

"Okay, Rich, since you're half-naked," Justin said in jest, "I'll do the exam now, and then we'll discuss the results in my office once you've dressed." Relaxed and with a smile, he proceeded with the exam. A nurse wasn't present as Justin wanted to offer Richard total privacy and anonymity. When the exam was complete, he said, "Put your pants on, dude, and let's gather a treatment plan. My nurse will come in and escort you to my office."

A few minutes later, Richard found himself in a warm and inviting office. It was clean but cluttered. So many exciting photos adorned the walls, mostly of vacations and fishing expeditions.

Justin stepped inside, holding a folder and two bottles of ice-cold water. He offered one to Richard. "Well, Rich, I'm sure they told you it affects both sides of the prostate. There are lymph node involvements as well. We should order a PET scan to rule out any other involvements. I'd like to refer you to a radiation oncologist for treatment. I read in your chart that you opposed it in the past, but I think you should reconsider. You're in great shape for your age, and it would be a shame if you didn't try," Justin explained.

"Okay, give me his information, and I'll make an appointment. I've had time to think, and there is a lot to live for now." Richard rose and shook his new doctor's hand. "Thank you, Justin."

"The radiation oncologist is in this building. I'll see you back after you've met him. Take care of yourself, Richard."

Although the news wasn't the best, it wasn't the worst either. Richard was confident it hadn't spread to other parts of the body. He prepared himself to fight so he could enjoy the reunion with his daughter. It overjoyed him, and he was the happiest he had been in a long time, even with the diagnosis. Richard walked to his car briskly, eager to go home for the first time in twenty years.

When he walked through the door, the little dog ran to him and jumped up to greet him. "Well, hello there, little guy. How are you? It looks like Christmas with all these toys strewn around the room. Did you get lots of new toys today?" Richard plopped down on the floor to play with his new friend.

Cora ran into the living room and gathered the toys.

"Stop, Cora, leave them. The house looks lived in and joyful. Look at this little clown. He just loves them." he said, looking up. "How's my girl?"

"Better. Miss Susan ate lunch, brought her a snack, and ate a little of it. After that, she didn't want the pain pills and refused the last dose. She said they make her 'foggy in the brain,' and she feels she can tolerate the pain. What do you think?"

"She needs to take them for a few more days. The pain will be difficult to manage if it becomes out of control. I'll speak to her. Do you think she can make it to the dinner table tonight?" Richard asked.

"Perhaps we could bring her down in the elevator, and then she wouldn't have to risk coming down that stairs." Cora nodded toward the beautiful marble staircase that sat in the center of the grand foyer. It was beautiful but imposing. For someone in a weakened state, the stairs could terrify her.

"Any idea where Donna's wheelchair is? Have you ever seen it? When I brought Susan home, we used the elevator, but she was on a stretcher. I can wheel her down in the elevator."

"Jack thought of that earlier, and he's in the workshop with it right now. He's cleaning and checking it, making sure it's still stable after all these years in storage."

"I should have thought to order one with the other items. I assume they arrived with nightclothes and underwear?"

"Yes, Doctor. Everything arrived, and I helped Miss Susan clean up. She's dressed in the new pajamas and undergarments. I offered to wash them before she wore them, but she assured me they were fine as they were."

"I'll check on her. Is Susan awake?" Richard asked.

"I don't believe so. She wanted to lie down. Washing up and changing exhausted her, but she claimed she enjoyed it. The hot water helped with her pain," Cora informed him.

Richard climbed the stairs with Buddy at his feet. He knocked on the door but didn't receive a response. Then, slowly opening it, and saw that Susan slept on top of the covers with magazines strewn about her. Smiling, he remembered her teenage years and the times he tried to wake her for school. Buddy jumped on the bed and snuggled in with her.

Deciding not to wake her, he padded into the master suite instead and changed into shorts and a T-shirt, gathering the things he had brought back from Myrtle Beach. Reaching for the jacket, he checked the pockets. He found a dead cell phone along with two rings, a wedding ring set. He had removed them and tossed them in his pocket when he noticed her hand swelling.

Richard sat with the phone at the small table in his sitting area. He stared at them. *Do I invade her privacy and see what's inside? Where has she's been living? Do I charge and scan her phone for photos? There may be pictures of grandchildren.* He remembered the cesarean section scar. *I think I'll just put these away, and when Susan can, she'll tell me herself. I want to start this new beginning with trust.* He dropped the rings into an envelope and placed them into her purse, along with her cell phone. He planned to put the bag inside the safe in his study.

Richard checked on his daughter before heading downstairs, and he found her still asleep. He hurried down to his study, dropped the purse into his safe, and returned a few phone calls. Forty-five minutes later, he headed into the kitchen to speak with Cora. He found Cora and Jack in the kitchen, fussing over the wheelchair. Buddy had made his way down from Susan's room and pawed at the wheels on the chair as though they were monsters, a low growl as he danced around the chair. The adults erupted in laughter at Buddy's antics.

"Cora, the clothing Susan arrived in. Did you throw them away?" Richard asked.

"Yes, Doctor, they are in the trash in the laundry room."

"Would you be so kind as to retrieve her sizes from them? I want to order clothing, things she can wear around the house. The personal shopper will want to take measurements, order other things, and shop all around town, which will take time. Susan also needs personal items. I don't know how to order that stuff. Do you mind ordering everyday things from Nordstrom for now? Bill it to my account. Get her sandals, slippers, and maybe tennis shoes. A bathing suit, too. Once she becomes more mobile, she can relax by the pool. Maybe use the spa for pain relief, whatever she needs to be comfortable." He waved his arms wide.

"Doctor, it would be my pleasure. I'll order them online. Jack won't mind going to the store to pick it up. It will be quicker."

"Thank you." Richard nodded.

"Dinner will be ready in five minutes. You two want to head upstairs with the chair and see if Miss Susan wants to join us down here? But be careful of the pup in that elevator," Cora reminded them, wagging her finger.

"Why don't you entertain him down here? It would be easier without him saving us from the mean ol' wheelchair." Jack said with a hearty laugh. The two men walked to the back of the house and pressed the button for the elevator. Cora often used it to transport the laundry upstairs.

Jack waited outside Susan's bedroom until needed. Susan flipped through a magazine as her father knocked. "Hello, my precious girl, how is your pain?"

"Tolerable," she answered quietly.

"Would you like to eat dinner in the dining room? Buddy is down there nipping at Cora's heels for a sample of the roast she made. Jack is in the hall, with the wheelchair. We can take you down the elevator. Want to try it?" Richard asked, hopefully.

"Sure."

Susan's response thrilled Richard, and he called Jack into the room, and they helped her into the chair. Jack offered to push the wheelchair, but Richard insisted on driving it himself.

When they entered the dining room, the kitchen's aroma caused Susan to salivate, and she thought she could eat an entire meal. When Buddy realized Susan was in the chair, he jumped right into her lap, kissed her, looked down at the wheels, and barked. Jack took Buddy from her lap and assisted her into a dining room chair.

Cora entered with the remaining food. She had made a small feast, prime rib—cooked to perfection—roasted potatoes, fresh carrots, and a salad. She also baked a cake for dessert.

Richard helped serve Susan. Cora cut up a small piece for Buddy with carrots and placed it in his bowl in the dining room. Susan listened to the conversations but didn't take part. While Susan picked at her food, she listened to the unique family banter and the comfortable conversation. Yet, she felt isolated and uncomfortable, almost like an outsider peeking in the window.

She gazed around the dining room. The walls were a warm beige color, and the curved window was covered with blue draperies. The twelve-person mahogany table that they were seated around matched the server and China cabinet and it sat on a thick beige carpet. The room was warm and inviting. She gazed at the strangers, and her heart filled with despair and loneliness as tears burned her eyes. Susan's gaze stopped at Cora, the one person she felt the most comfortable with.

After Cora put the kitchen and dining room back to order, she went into the laundry room and opened the bag containing Susan's things. She made a note of all her sizes, put the bag back into the trash, strolled into her sitting room with a glass of wine, and turned on her laptop. Peering at Jack snoring in his recliner, she smiled. *That didn't take long.*

Cora entered the web address for the Nordstrom website and shopped. By the end of the shopping spree, she had spent several thousand dollars. And ordered everything on Doctor Kline's list, jeans, shirts, T-shirts, bras, Capri pants, Bermuda shorts, tank tops, sundresses, underwear, additional nightclothes, sandals, tennis shoes, bedroom slippers, a robe, and bathing suits with matching cover-ups. Also, personal items including a facial wash, moisturizer, shower gel, shampoo and conditioner, and cosmetics. It would be ready the next day. *An excellent start until she can choose her things. When the personal shopper arrives, she can see what is here and add to it.* She snapped the laptop closed.

Cora enjoyed shopping for a young woman. Jack and Cora had married later in life and never had children of their own. Her family consisted of Jack and a distant cousin who never had time for her. Dr. Kline was such a kind man, and she considered him family, too, as he did them. Cora enjoyed making meals and sharing them with Dr. Kline in the kitchen. Their bright suite hosted a vast bedroom, living room, beautiful bathroom with a jetted tub and a stall shower. Cora especially appreciated the tub after long days on her feet.

Cora stood from the computer desk and strode over to wake Jack. They strolled into the bedroom, holding hands. Jack proved himself invaluable, and the two men genuinely liked each other and often attended sports events together.

As Jack undressed for bed, he said, "Sure is nice to have that little fellow here. I can't tell you how often he made me laugh today on our walks, but I haven't let him off the leash yet. Tomorrow, I'll go over the yard with a fine-tooth comb to make sure the yard is safe for him to run and play."

Cora fell asleep with a smile because of their new life in the house now. She enjoyed that little dog and helping Miss Susan.

Seven

AFTER BEING AWAKE MOST of the night, Jonathan struggled to sleep in the hotel. He had no sooner walked out of the bathroom to turn on the news when he heard a knock on the door. He viewed Officer Trent and another man through the peephole and opened the door.

"Good morning, Mr. Miller. I'm Detective Andrew Peters, from MBPD."

The two men shook hands, and then the detective filled him in. "While reviewing the van and the contents, we found your wife's belongings in the back in a duffle bag. Search and rescue dogs are in the woods with one of your wife's T-shirts. They'll reach out to me once the search is complete."

"Okay, thank you." *Search and rescue?* He couldn't help but worry. "I cannot believe this is happening." Jonathan exclaimed as he threaded his fingers through his hair.

"Mr. Miller, we learned your wife arrived at the hotel where the fundraiser took place on Thursday early evening, after leaving New Jersey on Wednesday. Can you tell me where you were Wednesday through Sunday evening?" Peters asked.

"Yes, in the office Wednesday through Friday. I left Saturday morning with the boys and our friend Charlotte for a trip to the Jersey Shore. We arrived home Sunday around seven o'clock in the evening. We had dinner at a rest stop."

"Were you having an affair with your friend, and could Mrs. Miller have caught on and ran away?"

"No affair. Never, not with anyone. Charlotte is family and the wife of Natalia's best friend, Christina. They're the parents of twin girls. We live within a few miles of each other and have always been there for one other. Christina and Charlotte own a summer house at the Jersey Shore. We always go there for vacations and long weekends. There is nothing improper. Just a group of friends that love each other like family."

"Okay. Can you write the contact information of all the adults you were with and your supervisor as well?"

Jonathan's mouth opened, and he caught on to what the police suspected. It shocked him that someone would even think he could bring harm to his wife. He stepped to the desk in the hotel room, jotted down the information, and passed it to the detective. Jonathan thought it a waste of resources when they could be out looking for Natalia.

"Is there anything I can do to help? I can't sit here going crazy with worry," Jonathan asked as he ran his fingers through his hair.

"Just be available in case we need more questions answered. We've also received a list of the fundraiser attendees, and we're reaching out to everyone."

Jonathan nodded wearily and muttered, "My wife disappeared over a week ago, and you have found nothing? No clues, witnesses? I don't understand how someone could disappear without a trace. Detective Peters, what is your next plan?"

"The Myrtle Beach police now involved the State Police, who don't believe she ran away. They think someone ran her off the road, perhaps an abduction." He rubbed his hands across his stubble. "I think you should head back to New Jersey and your children. Let the State Police take the case over."

"How can I leave? She might need me. I can't leave without her," Jonathan cried out in anguish.

"Mr. Miller, you have a family and a job. Until we find Mrs. Miller, your kids need you. Go home. Your numbers are in the file. Should we receive any leads, we will reach out to you."

Jonathan overheard Detective Peters, and Officer Trent's conversation as Peters turned to Trent and said, "I'm not getting a bad vibe from Miller. He is a mess over this, not the typical crocodile tears or anger. Distraught. I'll follow up with his alibi."

"Agreed," Trent replied.

Jonathan rushed into the hotel's computer room and booked a flight home for the morning. He called Charlotte and Christina's home number.

Charlotte answered, "Hey Jon, please tell me you have good news."

"No, not a thing, no sightings, zero clues. Nothing. I'm flying home tomorrow morning. My flight lands at eleven. Is anyone available to pick me up, or should I grab a cab home?"

"I'll pick you up, don't worry. Text your flight info, and I'll wait in the short-term parking lot tomorrow. When you deplane, text me. Are you eating at all? We can stop for lunch. Christina is working from home tomorrow and offered to stay with the kids. Alicia is up and about and able to be by herself, but we still go over to cook and clean. Matt contacted us from the ship and was so upset by the news that he wanted to fly home. We told him to finish up the sea trials since there's nothing he can do here."

"No need for him to abort his mission. They're sending me home because there is nothing I can do. Oh, Char, I'm hopeless. How can someone just disappear like this? No sign of either of them?"

"Jon, I understand. Try to rest. I'll be waiting at the airport for you. Good night, friend."

JONATHAN ARRIVED AT the Philadelphia airport without issue and texted Charlotte once he deplaned. She pulled up to the terminal door just as he exited. Tossing his bag into the back seat, he climbed in next to her. "Thanks for picking me up. You're a lifesaver."

"Of course. The ride over was peaceful, with light traffic, and I jammed to my choice of music, which is rare. The girls like to put on what they want to listen to, and if Christina is in the passenger seat, she always changes the station."

"Oh, I hear you. Natalia had a rule. No matter whose car it was, the driver chose the station. It worked for us. Oh, Char," Jonathan cried, "what am I going to do without her? I overheard Detective Peters mention they were sending divers to the nearby lake. And now, it is being considered a search and recovery mission. Doesn't that mean they must think she's dead? She can't be dead. I would know it. Damn it. She's alive somewhere. I can only pray they find her."

Charlene cried with him. "I agree, as close as you were—*are*—I agree. Somehow you know these things, the same with Christina and me. We understand many things about each other. I can tell by how she climbs out of the car whether she's had a tough day or a wonderful day. No matter if she greets me with a smile and a kiss. Her body language changes with her mood.

"How were the boys for you?" Jonathan asked, needing to change the subject.

"They were okay. No behavioral issues, but they're not themselves, quiet and withdrawn. They're missing their mom and you. They're scared she isn't coming back. I think after you establish a new routine, get them counseling. It isn't easy for anyone."

"Yes, I'll do that. Thanks for taking care of them for me."

"This is what families do," Charlotte said.

Charlotte and Christina lived in a two-story colonial in Whispering Woods, a neighborhood a mere mile from Jonathan's family. They arrived in forty minutes.

As soon as the car pulled into the driveway, the boys ran out, with Christina behind them. They were anxious to go home and sleep in their rooms and beds. Christina walked into Jonathan's arms. "I love you, Jon. You're the best dad and husband. Our girl is going to come home. You are good people, and this shouldn't be happening to you."

"Thanks, Christina. I love you and your family, too. All I can do is pray my love comes back soon, unharmed. I never, ever imagined this happening to us. It is the stuff you hear on the news. It happens to other people, and you never expect it to happen to your family. I can't tell you what's going on in my head and my stomach. I can't eat. I'm in a panic, worried if she's locked up by some deviant or if human traffickers took her. Are they hurting her? I'm driving myself nuts. Why did she fucking go alone? I should have put my foot down and told her she couldn't go. Why didn't I go with her? This my fault, all my fault." Jonathan lowered his head in his hands and sobbed.

"Oh, Jon, this is not your fault. Don't you think Alicia and I are experiencing the same guilt? We encouraged her. She looked forward to this trip. It was all she talked about, the month leading up to it. The blame belongs to whoever has her and is keeping her from us." Christina rubbed Jon's back to comfort him.

Jonathan went home with the boys, and the house had a stale, closed smell because he'd turned off the air conditioner before leaving for Myrtle Beach. Natalia had always known just what to do, and the house never smelled stale on her watch. She took care of things like that. Jonathan issued orders. "Anthony, open the windows and doors down here. Alex, you take the upstairs, and Marc, could you mow the front lawn? I'll do the back after I go through the mail and pay the bills."

As the boys did their chores, Jonathan turned on the AC to circulate chilly air. Walking into the home office, he sorted through and read the mail, hoping he would find something regarding Natalia. There was no activity on her credit cards. No ransom note, a hint, or anything else from or about his wife. Just bills and junk mail. He couldn't seem to pay the bills as tears poured down his face. Anthony stepped over and asked, "Dad, can we close windows now? The air conditioner kicked in."

"Of course, sorry, I ... the mail distracted me." He mopped the tears from his face.

"Dad, Mom is coming back. She would never leave us. We're a team. She's coming back," Anthony said with conviction. "And Buddy too."

"You're right, little dude. She is. No more tears. I'm sorry, I'm scared out of my mind for her, for them." Jonathan silently prayed his youngest was correct. Leaving the office, he went out front to grab the lawnmower from Marc and noticed him walking it around to the back.

"I've got it, Dad. I'll take care of the back. Finish up inside."

"Thanks, son. I appreciate it."

"No worries, Dad. We're a team. We all pitch in. That's what Mom always said — says." Marc corrected himself. His face flushed.

"I have to call your grandparents. Maybe they could come for the summer while I work," he mentioned to Alexander as he walked back inside.

"No, Dad, don't. Jersey is such a far drive, and then they'll bring the cat. Anthony is allergic to that furball," Alex exclaimed. "Aunt Char said we could go over to her house every day. Can we please do it that way? Do we even need someone? Marc is almost fifteen. He could stay with us. We won't give him a tough time, right, Ant?"

"I'll think about it. Let me ask your mom." He apologized right away. "I'm sorry," he said when he saw his son's eyes fill with tears. "I always confer with your mom, as she does with me. I said it out of habit."

Oh, my God. Oh, my God. Natalia, where the hell are you? Send me a sign or something.

"Okay, Alex, let me think about it and talk it over with your aunts." Jonathan pulled his son into his embrace, whispering, "I love you."

"Love you too, Dad." Alex stepped back and headed down to the man cave. As he passed Buddy's toy box, he mumbled, "I hope you're with Mom and you're both okay. Protect her, little dude." Alex ran downstairs as tears poured down his face.

Anthony was already downstairs, sitting on the sofa with tears streaming down his face. "Alex, how do we do this without Mom? I'm scared."

"Me too, Ant, me too. I guess we pray with all our hearts that Mom's safe and finds her way back to us. Bud too."

Eight

RICHARD ENJOYED SPENDING the evening with his daughter and insisted on helping her get upstairs and climb into bed, making sure Buddy was in the room with her. He asked if she needed anything before he went to bed.

"No, thank you. I'm fine," she said as he handed her a glass of ice water and a pill. "What's this?" she asked, noticing the different colored capsule.

"A pill for pain and inflammation. You need to stay ahead of this, so it doesn't impede your recovery. You want to get back to your old life, right?"

"Yes, the trouble is, I don't know what that is," Susan said miserably. "I feel like I don't belong here, yet I don't know where I belong."

"My pleasure. What kind of movie?"

She shrugged her shoulders. "What happened to me? Why don't I remember you or my mother?"

"Sweetheart, you were in an accident, a car. You hit a tree. Buddy was with you but was uninjured."

"An accident? Will my memories be gone, forever?"

"We don't know that yet. Dr. Paulson diagnosed you with a dissociative fugue."

"What is that? What does it mean?" she asked as she wiped an escaped tear. The pain she could deal with. Where were the memories she wanted? This man claimed to be her father was kind and tender, yet not one iota of recognition. Yet they seemed to know a lot about her.

"It's a psychological state in which people lose awareness of their identity or other vital information. It can affect memories and personality as well. Sweetheart, I'll try to put it in layperson's terms. It's uncommon but reversible. It is a disorder characterized by reversible amnesia for personal identity. The condition affects obviously, your memory and other parts of you, like your characteristics, likes and dislikes."

"Did I have anything with me?" he shook his head and she responded, "Okay. Thank you." Susan was openly crying, and Richard reached into his pocket and dabbed her pink cheeks with his crisp white hanky.

He murmured, "your mother used to call this my magic hanky. It took away all of your boo-boos."

Not thoroughly understanding what was wrong with her, she asked, "You don't mind if I watch a movie, do you?" She lifted the remote, confused by all the buttons. "I'm having trouble navigating the TV. Can you help me find a movie station, please?"

"Well, what if I scroll and you stop me when you see something you want to watch?" Richard suggested. A few minutes later, she found one that piqued her interest. "Your memories will return in time. I'm sure of it. You're safe here, baby girl. Good night, my sweet girl."

Richard left the room and strode down the hall to the place he had shared with her mother, the same room where they conceived Susan. Although he missed Donna dreadfully, he was happy his daughter was back— a quieter, mature version of his girl.

Susan watched TV until her eyes were droopy, yawning. She slid down, burrowed underneath the blanket, and tried to remember something from her past. But remained befuddled and didn't quite feel like "Susan" but wasn't sure who she was. She had to trust this kind man who said he was her father. The pictures around the house looked like a younger version of her. Yet, nothing about this house or her room brought a sense of familiarity. Then again, the little dog was hers, and she didn't remember him either, yet she loved him and felt bonded to him. She fell asleep with more questions in her mind.

THE FOLLOWING MORNING dawned hot and bright, a perfect southern California day. Susan listened to the birds outside her window. Someone had removed Buddy from her bed for a brief time, but he was now back with another noisy toy. She asked him if he liked the toy, and he squeaked it more as if to say, "Yes, I love it."

Susan hobbled to the bathroom, her walker banging on the floor, and struggled into fresh pajamas and underwear. Plopping in a chair by the window, she pulled the draperies aside and gazed outside. *Wow,* she thought. *What a view.* The crystal blue water glistened in the sunlight from the large pool. *Maybe I could sit out today.*

Deep in thought, she jumped when the intercom buzzed, and Cora asked, "Miss Susan, would you like breakfast up there, or would you prefer to eat in the kitchen, dear?"

"Oh, the kitchen, please."

"Great, I'll be right up. Stay put." Cora hurried up the stairs and found the door to Susan's room open. Susan sat by the window, looking outside. "Good morning, love. I hope you're hungry."

Her lips curved into a small smile. "A little."

"Okay, let's get you into the chair."

With help, Susan lowered herself into the wheelchair, gripping the walker for support. Cora pushed Susan, with Buddy in her lap, toward the elevator. When they arrived downstairs, Cora brought her into the kitchen and wheeled the chair over to the kitchen table. Cinnamon and coffee permeated the room.

"My mouth is watering. What are you baking?" Susan asked, salivating.

"Cinnamon buns and a fresh pot of coffee. Do you like coffee? If not, I'll make you tea."

"I'm not sure what I like. My brain is a blank slate. But the aroma is pleasant, so let's start there," Susan said with a smile.

Cora poured a hot brew. "Do you think you want sugar and cream?"

Susan shrugged.

"Here you go. One mug is black, and one mug is with cream and sugar. You decide." Cora placed both mugs in front of her, along with a cinnamon bun.

Susan tried both coffees and liked the black coffee best. And she inhaled the entire bun. "Cora, do you think I could spend time by the pool? It looks like a beautiful, peaceful area."

"Sure, if you'd like, I can wheel you onto the lanai and help you into a lounge chair."

"That would be wonderful. Thank you."

They chatted over breakfast. Jack left to run errands while Buddy lay under the table, munching on a chew stick. Richard left for the practice since he had an early morning procedure scheduled.

After breakfast, Cora snapped Buddy's leash onto his harness and wheeled Susan onto the lanai as promised. She handed the leash to Susan. "I'll clean up the kitchen, and then I'll be out to join you."

Susan enjoyed being outside and basked in the sun. Buddy became overheated, and Cora took him back into the air-conditioned house to cool off. Susan remained out in the sunshine, her face lifted toward the sky, appreciating the occasional breeze that wafted over her.

Cora brought Susan back into the house after noticing her eyelids closing and her head drooping to the side repeatedly. Cora thought it was because of the medication that the doctor had prescribed. "Susan, would you like to sit in the family room or go upstairs to your room for a brief nap before lunch?"

"Oh, the family room would be nice. Is there a television inside?" she asked.

"Yes, there is," Cora replied as she led Susan into the family room. "What would you like to watch? Talk shows? Soap Operas?"

"The movie channel."

"Sure, your father has several movie channels. Here you go, how is this one?"

"That's fine, thank you." Susan was comfortable on the sofa, and when Buddy jumped up next to her, resting his warm body against hers, she fell fast asleep while the movie played. She woke to Cora standing over her.

"Would you like lunch, dear?" Cora asked.

"Maybe something light."

Cora brought her into the kitchen, where she had prepared an Asian-inspired rice bowl with chicken, followed by a fresh fruit salad.

"Cora, this is amazing. The flavors in this are delicious. I can't seem to find the words, but it is heavenly. You're amazing in the kitchen."

"Thank you, dear. I intend to feed you well, so you'll gain your health back quickly. Maybe even put a little weight on you. Your face is too thin from not eating."

"If I continue to eat all this delicious food, I'll be huge in no time."

"You flatter me, sweet girl. What would you like to do this afternoon? Spend time by the pool? Another movie?"

"Can I read by the pool?" Susan asked. "Are there any books around?"

"Yes, Jack is a voracious reader, and he has a lot of books in our suite. Would you like me to bring them out, or would you rather choose yourself?"

"If you don't mind, can I choose? I don't know what I like to read or even if I like to read. I just need to pass the time and stimulate my brain."

Cora wheeled Susan from the family room, down a short hallway, past the powder room, and into a small foyer of sorts. Beyond the threshold. Cora pushed Susan through and wheeled her over to the bookshelf. Books lined each shelf, both hardback and paperback. Susan pulled a few that she could reach and read the brief descriptions. She chose one and turned to Cora. "This is a pretty space, homey. I can sense the love you two share in here. Thank you for inviting me in."

"Thanks, honey. We love the area. Your dad renovated this space for us. Here is our living room. Back there is an enormous bedroom and an enormous bathroom that way." Cora said, pointing further back toward the bathroom. "And that door leads to a lanai." She flipped her thumb in the opposite direction, toward the lanai. We're happy here caring for your father, and now you and Buddy." She beamed at Susan, her face a mask of kindness.

"hank you, Cora. I appreciate everything you do for Buddy and me." Susan pushed herself outside, the book on her lap. After reading for a while, overheated, she headed inside and Cora invited her into the living area of her suite to watch a movie.

AFTER A LONG DAY AT the medical center, Richard was eager to go home. On his way, he stopped at the Coach store and bought his daughter a purse and a matching wallet. He stopped by the bank to get bank cards and cash from his accounts in her name. He placed everything in her new wallet.

When Richard arrived home, laughter filtered through the rooms, coming from Cora's suite, and he didn't want to disturb the "girl talk." He smiled and headed upstairs to change, first leaving the purse and wallet in Susan's bedroom. After he changed, Richard headed downstairs to find both ladies now in the kitchen, chatting like old friends. He listened with a smile for a few minutes before making his presence known.

"Well, hello ladies, aren't we silly today? I could hear the giggles in the front foyer. How are you today, my love?" he asked Susan as he leaned over and kissed the top of her head.

"Okay." She sighed. "A little painful and foggy in the head. But I had a better appetite today. And I soaked up the sunshine by the pool for a little while."

"Continue with the anti-inflammatories, and you'll be on the road to wellness in no time. Richard sat at the kitchen table across from Susan. "Cora, what's for dinner tonight?"

"Tacos. Not my idea. A certain someone," Cora nodded toward Susan, "saw a commercial for tacos and thought she might like to try them. So, it is Taco Night in the Kline household."

"Well, I guess the boss has spoken. Bring on the tacos and antacids." Richard said jokingly.

Cora finished sauteing the beef and chicken while Susan sat at the table, shredding lettuce. Buddy wasn't sure who to beg from and was running back and forth between them.

"Buddy, you're not saying hello tonight?" asked Richard.

The pug ran over for a quick pet and then ran right back to the stove, knowing Cora would slip him a piece of chicken. Richard laughed at the little dog. "He's a character, that little guy. I never realized how much joy a pet could bring into a home."

Cora did an excellent job with the tacos, and everyone enjoyed their first taco night. Each of them ate a couple, adding ingredients from the small bowls Cora provided. She finely chopped lettuce, onions, tomatoes, and a bowl of salsa, along with guacamole.

"I enjoyed taco night, and we should do it again, Cora," Richard said.

Susan nodded her head in agreement as she wiped taco sauce from her face.

"There's a good movie on TV tonight, Miss Susan. Would you like to watch it with me in the family room?" Cora asked. "Doctor, how about you?"

Susan nodded, but Richard said, "I plan to go upstairs early to relax and watch the game. I have an early appointment tomorrow. But you two enjoy your movie." He turned to his daughter. "Susan, you're looking healthier today. Your skin is glowing, and your face is filling out."

"Yes, I am feeling better, thank you."

"Cora, I'll skip dessert tonight. No need to bring anything up. Good night." He bent down to kiss Susan on the cheek. "Good night, sweetheart."

"Night."

Susan hadn't referred to him as Father or dad. He was sweet, kind, and considerate, and he took great care of her, but she didn't have the emotions a daughter should. She felt nothing. It was as though she had just been born the day she awoke in this house. Not any one thing made her feel like Susan, not even Buddy. She had fallen in love with the little dog but remembered nothing of having him in her life before the day she woke up in this house with him beside her.

During the last few weeks, Susan learned a few things about herself. She enjoyed tacos and a good mystery, Cora's company, and Jack's books. Jack was quiet, but kind. He repeatedly asked what he could do for her. After the movie, Jack stepped from their living room to escort her to the elevator.

She could tell he'd been asleep. "Jack, I think I can do this myself. I know the way to the elevator, and I can reach the buttons."

"Well, I'm here now. Let me help you. Cora went upstairs to turn down your bed and give you your bedtime pill. Tomorrow you can try, but tonight, let me help you. Deal?"

"Deal." she said, smiling up at him. He was a tall, lean man, and his face radiated kindness. Cora joked that the more Jack ate, the chubbier she became. He had the metabolism for them both.

Jack pushed her down the hallway to the elevator and again down the upstairs hall to her bedroom. She had a fantastic view of the pool, lanai, and garden from the room. And as Jack said, Cora had everything ready for her. She'd laid out fresh pajamas.

"I see the taco sauce on your pajama top. I thought you would like a fresh set. I wouldn't want you smelling that and craving tacos all night," Cora said with a giggle.

"That's funny, thanks to both of you. I can do the rest. That old lady walker keeps me steady."

Jack nodded and said, "I'm taking Buddy out for a quick walk. I'll bring him right back."

Susan slipped into fresh pajamas, and as she waited for Buddy, she discovered the purse on her table. She opened it and inside found a wallet with cash and credit cards. The cards were in her name, including a black card that read "American Express" and a white card that read "Stratus Visa." Another card, "Visa Debit for City National Bank." But like everything else, nothing in the purse looked familiar.

After spying the closet door slightly ajar, Susan padded toward it, peered inside, and found it dark. Running her hand along the wall, she felt the light switch and flipped it, blinking from the bright illumination. The massiveness of the closet overwhelmed her. A few pairs of sandals sat on the floor, neatly atop the boxes they had come in, along with a few pairs of tennis shoes, several pairs of slippers, both mules and the bootie type. Hanging on the bar were several pairs of capris, along with matching tops. A few dresses hung alongside the pants, shorts, and tank tops placed neatly on shelves. "Maybe

I'll dress tomorrow. No more PJs during the day for me." Just as she left the closet, she heard a light tap on the door and a snort from Buddy. "Come in, all decent," she called.

Jack opened the door, and Buddy rushed into the room. The pug leaped onto the bed, all ready to snuggle for the night. "G'night, Jack. Buddy and I both thank you."

"My pleasure, sweet dreams."

Susan snuggled in with Buddy, and he soon fell asleep. Her pills hadn't made her tired yet. She picked up the book on her nightstand and read until she fell asleep with the book on her chest. Susan woke up to the bright sunlight streaming into her room as the pool water glistened on her ceiling. Buddy wasn't in bed, so she assumed Cora took him for his walk and breakfast.

Still in considerable pain, Susan made her way into the bathroom with the aid of her walker. She looked longingly at the whirlpool tub, but didn't want to take the chance of not being able to climb out of the tub without help. Instead, she opted for a hot shower and found new shampoo and conditioner and a flowery scented shower gel. Susan enjoyed the heated water streaming down her painful spots, the pain that seemed to settle in her hips and lower back during the night.

After the shower, she found cosmetics on her vanity along with brushes and a blow dryer. "Well, first, let's see what we can do with this mop." She had been washing it with whatever shampoo was in the shower, allowing it to dry, then put it up in a ponytail with a hair tie she found in one of the dresser drawers. Today she blew dry it straight, and thanks to the conditioner she'd used, her hair cooperated.

Susan used the walker to make her way to the closet, hoping that the clothing fit. After choosing a pair of blue jean Bermuda shorts and a white top with beads at the neckline, she made her way over to her chair, plopped down, and wiggled into the shorts, happy that they fit. Next, she pulled the shirt on. She'd worked up a sweat dealing with the pain while trying to dress. After resting for a few minutes, she realized she forgot shoes. She opted for a white pair of canvas-type loafers with no socks. Holding onto the walker for balance as she stepped into the shoes. Her goal today was to walk to the elevator using the walker and getting downstairs alone.

She grabbed her book and tied it to the walker using a plastic bag she found in the closet. As she made her way down the hallway, she realized that securing the bag with the book hadn't been such a great idea as it banged into her painful knees. But Susan persevered, and she reached the elevator at last and felt like a naughty child, not listening to her parents. Jack had mentioned she was to call for him, and he would escort her down. Getting to the elevator was only half the battle, but it excited her anyway. She pushed the button, and in seconds the elevator arrived, and the door opened. She entered, the book banging her on the knees all the while.

She made it into the kitchen, out of breath and in pain. Cora looked up from the sink with a start. "Oh dear, what are you doing down here all by yourself? You're flushed. Are you okay?" Cora dragged a chair from the table over to her. "Here, sit down, catch your breath."

"Yes, a workout for sure. I'm weak, but I must do things to improve my health. Need to get the blood flowing to my legs."

"You look nice today, dear. I see the clothes fit you well."

"They fit great. I like everything. You chose the clothes?"

"I did."

"Thank you."

"Where's Buddy?"

"Jack took him for a walk in the neighborhood. I told him to make sure not to let him become overheated. They should be back soon enough."

"What are we doing today?" Susan asked.

"Well, I ordered groceries for delivery, and I'm expecting them soon. And the service is coming to clean the house, so I should stay here. What would you like to do?"

"I'm starving. Can I make coffee for myself?"

"Stay where you are. I'll bring you coffee, and I made an omelet for breakfast. I waited to eat so we could have breakfast together. Your father took his breakfast to work, and Jack inhaled his already. I used the leftover tomatoes from yesterday, taco spices, and cheese. They are warming in the oven." Cora pulled the plates using a pink gingham potholder. She placed a warm plate with the omelet in front of Susan and sat down with the other. "That plate is warm. Watch you don't burn yourself."

"Thank you, Cora, this is amazing. I can see why Jack inhaled it."

Cora smiled. They chatted and enjoyed each other's company. Just as Cora rose to put their dishes in the sink, the doorbell rang. "I'll be right back, love. Stay seated."

The grocery delivery had arrived, and a young man brought the bags into the kitchen and placed them on the counter. Cora tipped him graciously and thanked him. No sooner were the groceries stored than the doorbell rang again. The cleaning service had arrived. They loaded the foyer with their supplies and moved about the house cleaning the rooms.

After being gone a while, Cora and Susan had grown worried. Cora inconspicuously tried to call him on his cell, but she heard it ringing back in their suite. He had forgotten it again, left it on the charger. Jack eventually returned with a happy Buddy, his tongue lolling and tail wagging.

"Jack, where the hell have you been with that puppy? Much too warm out there for him. And you forgot your phone. Again." Cora said, frowning.

"Sorry, we took a short walk. I realized it was hot. We hung out in the workshop with the AC blasting. We played fetch, and when he became tired, I let him sleep on my sweat jacket as I fixed the weed trimmer. I like to keep ahead of the weeds between the landscapers. The next time I buy his food at the pet store, can I buy him a bed for the shop? He seems to enjoy it out there with me. Maybe a water bowl too."

"I think my furry friend has you wrapped around his paw. Why not take the dog bed in my room? He sleeps with me anyway. And I'm sure there's a bowl around here you can take for him," Susan said.

Cora nodded in agreement. "That's a great idea. Take the bed from Miss Susan's room. I'll grab you a bowl to use."

Buddy sat in Susan's lap throughout the conversation, his tongue curling, looking from one person to the other as though he understood they were talking about him.

"I think I'll go to the lanai to read before it gets super-hot. Can Buddy stay here with you, or will he be in the way of the cleaning crew?"

"Miss Susan, if you'd like, I can bring the awning down. The remote is in the shop. It creates a lot of shade and will cool that entire area for both of you, and there is always the grotto. It stays pretty cool."

"Oh, Jack, that's great, thank you."

"I'll be right back." Jack rushed out to the shop, and a minute later, was out back with the remote, lowering the awning. It squeaked, sending Jack running back to retrieve the spray lubricant, "Well, there you go, good as new. It should keep you cool and the little guy too."

"Thanks, you and Cora are both so kind."

In the peaceful pool area for a few hours, Susan read her book, lulled into serenity by Buddy's gentle snoring. He slept on the lounge chair between her legs. He seemed to find comfort with her legs on either side of him.

Cora joined them and sat for a while, making lists. They didn't work on the weekends, and Cora hoped to try the new restaurant in town. Jack wanted to visit the bookstore. She would have loved to take Susan on the outing, but she was still too weak to be out that long. Cora also worried about leaving her behind. Dr. Kline planned to be home, but he seemed off somehow. His face had a grayish tinge, and he wasn't eating well, skipping meals. Dark circles colored the skin beneath his eyes. His movements seemed slower, almost painful.

"Miss Susan, tomorrow is our day off," Cora said. "We're going shopping, and we'll most likely be out all day. Is there anything I can pick up for you? Your father will be here. We're off on Sundays too, but we usually rest and relax here at home. Jack and your father watch the game, and I lounge by the pool. We order food for takeout. That's been our routine for years. I can leave menus to choose a restaurant. We take turns choosing what to order." Cora smiled. "Your father hasn't been eating well, Saturday nights, he has dinner with Thomas, or they grab something out."

"That would be great. Thanks. Cora, do you and Jack have to call me Miss Susan? To be honest, I don't like it. Can you use my name? You're friends. Would that be, okay?"

"Yes, we *are* friends."

RICHARD WOKE EARLY to head to his appointment with this radiologist-oncologist, Dr. Rajesh Patel. Dr. Patel was one of California's top doctors in his field. After reviewing his charts, Dr. Patel was concerned, considering Richards's age and lymph node involvement. "Richard, I'd like to do a PET scan to see the level of involvement. The biopsy results are in, and I'd like to begin hormone therapy as soon as we get the PET scan results. Do you have the time for this right now?"

"Yes, I do. Let's go. I need to win this battle, Dr. Patel."

"All right, a nurse will be in and escort you to the lab. Once you're through, come back here. I'll see you soon."

The PET scan finished, and the technician escorted Richard back to the doctor's office thirty minutes later. When he arrived, Dr. Patel sat and shuffled through a few papers, then looked up. "Richard, we need to schedule surgery. It must come out. You've had symptoms for some time. Why did you wait? You're a physician. You must have recognized the symptoms."

"Life differed from what it is now. I was alone. A widower whose only child was missing. What did I have to lose? Now my beautiful daughter returned to me, and with her, a reason to try."

"Alright, Dr. Taugher will perform the surgery. I've spoken with his office, and the surgical nurse will call you to plan for the procedure. Once you've recovered, I'll proceed with hormone therapy. Any other treatment depends on the results of the post-surgical PET scan."

"Thank you, Dr. Patel." Hopeful, Richard left Dr. Patel's office, willing to do anything to win this battle. But either way, he would see his daughter protected.

Nine

JONATHAN'S FIRST WEEK back to work was rough. His co-workers learned of Natalia's disappearance and brought in frozen dishes to make dinners easier for him and his family. They prayed for the family and checked in on him often. While he appreciated the food and the prayers, the attention became overwhelming. He tried to focus through his sorrow, but the added attention and interruptions just stole focus further away from his work.

On Friday, after the first week of work, his boss called him into the office. "Jon, I can see that your co-workers mean well, but they're driving you crazy. I think I've found a solution. Since you work from home once a week, I requested you to work full time at home. Upper management knows how strong your work ethic is, and we're not worried that anyone on your client list will suffer. But I think you need to be home with the boys, sticking together. I hope you will accept the offer and not be obligated to come in."

"Mr. Fern, I appreciate it. We're having challenges with childcare. I wanted to call my parents to come and stay with the boys, but they own a cat, and my youngest is highly allergic." He sighed and shook his head. "My wife's parents are deceased, and I'm kinda thankful, as I don't know how they would survive their only child's disappearance. Our friends offered to take the boys, but they're parents of two younger daughters, and it is like mixing oil and water with the kids sometimes. They insist they can stay alone, but I'm too far away should anything happen. I appreciate this offer."

"I know that I'm new here, and you're respectful, but please stop calling me Mr. Fern. Just Bob." He grimaced. "Jon, don't worry about it. Go home and try to do something fun with the boys this weekend. If you need anything, research, making flyers, social media to spread the word, please tell me. I'm good with those sorts of things."

"Thanks a lot...Bob. Again, this is much appreciated."

"You're most welcome. We're a family here, and when you need us, we're here. Make a flyer and send it over to me as soon as you can, and I'll jump on social media." A small smile curved his lips. "Also, don't let it surprise you if any of your coworkers insist on cooking for your family. I'm sure they will show up regularly with a meal."

"They're sweet, and I'm thankful for them as those boys eat everything in sight." Jonathan smiled wanly.

Jonathan packed the folders he needed, gathered his laptop, and made his way to the parking lot, relieved, knowing he could keep the boys at home with him. No need to call his parents, and no need to disrupt Charlotte's routine. He'd let them stay home today by themselves as Charlotte had left for the shore house with the girls, and his boys didn't want to go. They loved the shore and the beach, but they were just too worried about their mom to enjoy the time away.

"Hey, guys, I'm home," Jon yelled when he stepped into the kitchen from the garage.

"Hey, dad, we're down here in the man cave. We're starving too. Can we order a pizza?"

"No, I brought dinner. The crew from work cooked up a few meals. Would you boys like lasagna tonight?"

"Is it like Mom's?" they asked all at once.

"Not sure. Let's try it. I'll throw it in the oven to warm while you set the table and clean this room up. Or better yet, two of you clean up down here, and one of you set the dinner table while I change my work clothes. Maybe a swim after dinner? What do you guys think?" Jonathan raised his eyebrows, keeping his voice light. *I've got to try to create a new normal for these kids.* From his bedroom phone, he called Christina.

"Hey Jon, how was your first week back?"

"Challenging, but I made it through. My boss told me I could work from home. Thank you to you and Charlotte for offering to take the boys. Are you going down to the shore tonight? I think Charlotte left with the girls this morning. At least that's what she planned. "

"I may, if not, first thing in the morning. I went into the office today. I completely forgot today was Friday and that I'd be sitting in the normal Friday night traffic heading to the shore. I'm at a stand-still on the freeway. Any news from Myrtle Beach?"

"Yes, the State Police are convinced someone has her, even though there are no signs of foul play. They had divers search the nearest lake. Nothing. The water is murky and lots of dark under-growth. They distributed APBs," Jonathan said. "They're checking hospitals, homeless shelters, animal shelters, churches that assist the homeless. The story will appear on the local news there tonight. They're hoping this helps with any leads."

"I hope so, too," Christina said. "People are praying, and our rescue group is holding a candlelight vigil Monday evening at eight o'clock at the dog park. So far, the response is overwhelming, and most of the town will be there. These prayers need to reach the right ears so we can get our girl back."

"That's amazing. Do I need to do anything?"

"Nothing, Jon. Just show up. Every attendee is bringing their candles, and we have them for you and the boys."

"Thanks, Christina, I appreciate it. Enjoy the weekend at the shore."

Jonathan rushed downstairs into the kitchen. Plates were on the table, and the smell of the lasagna permeated the room. Jonathan tested it and found it still cold in the center. He set the timer on for another fifteen minutes and strode into his office. After flipping through the mail, Jonathan unpacked his laptop, shoved his briefcase in the closet, and then straightened up his office. He wanted it more of a "work" office than a "home" office.

The timer went off just as he finished. He tested the lasagna again and called the boys to dinner. The boys ate quietly and brought their plates to the sink without being told. *These boys are good kids,* Jon thought. *Why is this happening to them? They need their mother.* He felt the now-familiar sting of tears in his eyes.

After Jon cleaned up the kitchen, he and the boys floated in the pool for thirty minutes, but none of the usual shenanigans. They were all quiet, lost in their thoughts. *Thank goodness they're off for the summer. If I had to do the school thing by myself, I wouldn't know where to begin.*

They tried to watch TV, but all four fell asleep in the man cave. Jon woke first and realized it was two in the morning. He gently tapped the boys awake and sent them upstairs. Jonathan followed behind, climbed into bed, and grabbed Natalia's pillow. Her scent was still present, that familiar lavender scent. He broke down, sobbing as soon as he inhaled, pressing his face into her pillow.

The local news station in Myrtle Beach had reported Natalia as a missing person over a week ago, and still no leads. It was as though she vanished, just evaporated into the air. Poof. Gone. An investigative reporter reached out to Jonathan and asked if offering a reward was a possibility. The police were against the idea, but he wanted to. Not that he had a lot of money, but he would give up everything to have his wife back. He telephoned Officer Trent and mentioned what the reporter said. "I strongly advise against it," the detective said adamantly. "We'll receive a lot of bogus calls taking valuable time away from the investigation, and you'd be putting your family at risk for lunatics."

Jonathan wanted the girls' opinions. They were undecided, and Charlotte said, "I agree with the police. If there were a witness, they would have notified the police. It's as though she disappeared into thin air. If you throw money out there, every crazy person is going to respond with false information."

Jonathan decided against offering the reward. He would network and plaster her face all over social media. He often worried about abduction and human trafficking, and he worried about how his boys would cope with the trauma.

Without their mother to plan summer activities, the boys kept to themselves. This emotional nightmare had uprooted their lives. They had a great relationship with their mom and missed her dearly. Stress changed Jonathan, and he no longer pranked the boys and was a mere shell of his former self.

Their neighborhood community helped neighbors, and this time it was his family that needed help. They brought food over and refreshed the flyers around town. One neighbor had business in South Carolina and went to Myrtle Beach, placing flyers all over the resort and the neighboring areas. Jonathan had been in contact with a few of Natalia's rescue friends, and they networked on social media.

"Where is my wife?" he asked himself over and over. Day after day, he asked the same question. Jonathan swore he would know if she had died. Deep in his gut, he would. He couldn't even accept the thought of her being dead, nor would he mention the possibility to their sons. Natalia had done everything with him, and now he's lonely. They enjoyed craft fairs, shopping trips to quaint little towns, and date nights. How he missed those weekly date nights with his best friend.

The aching grief and worry depleted Jonathan. He felt weighed down by the burden, mainly by keeping his tears and his feelings in check for the boys' sake. He peered into the refrigerator and didn't have the energy or the desire to reheat another casserole Ruth had prepared for them. Ruth, a friend from work, was a single woman nearing retirement whose hobby was gourmet meals. She watched the food network and loved recreating the recipes.

Ruth lived alone, and Jonathan and the boys enjoyed her creations. Her house was ten miles away in another town, but she would stop by every Sunday delivering her masterpieces and often stayed for dinner and a swim. The kids liked her, and she took Jonathan's mind off his wife. Ruth and Natalia had known each other from work. And she was kind to his sons, and they enjoyed the grandmotherly attention and the pranks she pulled, trying to make them laugh. When she prepared to leave each week, she gave the boys a grandmotherly hug and asked them to call her if they had any special food requests. The boys always looked forward to her next visit.

Ten

RICHARD ARRIVED HOME on Friday night later than expected. Dinner was just about ready. Susan helped Cora as much as she
could. The housekeeper had such a calming influence. Susan enjoyed
being around Cora. Buddy ate his dinner, walked with Jack, and
snored in their suite, resting on Jack's feet.

"Hello, ladies, did you have a good day?" Richard asked. "What's
for dinner? The aromas are amazing."

"Yes, we did. Thank you, Doctor. I hope you enjoy dinner. We're
eating in the dining room tonight, and it should be ready soon. Why
not change into more comfortable clothes? We thought maybe we
would play games tonight." Cora explained.

"Susan dear, did you have a good day? How is your pain? Are you
eating?" He leaned over and kissed her cheek.

"Yes, okay, and yes." She giggled. "You tossed those questions out
without breathing. she said, smiling. "I ate, hung out by the pool,
read, and napped."

"Good to see you dressed. You look lovely, sweetheart."

"Thanks. Yes, not as much of an invalid in pajamas all the time."

"Where is Buddy? He didn't greet me."

"Oh, he's with Jack. He had a busy day and is a little tired. Those
two are as thick as thieves," Cora replied as she plated dinner.

"Okay, I'm sure I'll see him at dinner. I bought him a new toy. Susan, I bought you a few things too. I'll put them on your bed." He was soft-spoken, and his deep voice, soothing.

"Oh, that's sweet, thank you."

Susan was reflective during dinner. She felt safe, but still no connection to the man who was her father. She had no clue who she was, let alone where she belonged. Her lost memories frightened and worried her. And she couldn't quiet the nagging voice in her head. She tried to pull the memories from the recesses of her brain, resulting in migraines. She hoped her memories would come back soon because she felt empty and alone inside.

They ate later than usual, and Richard mentioned he was too tired to play their weekly card game. Susan headed upstairs to get comfortable. Before bed, Jack took Buddy for his last walk and escorted him upstairs to Susan's room. There, Susan opened her gift from the doctor. Inside the colorful gift bag was an e-reader, set up with an account in her name. Jack showed her how to use it. She was excited because now she could download any book without leaving the house. Susan still dealt with pain and was anxious in the car. She enjoyed reading and had breezed through all of Jack's books. She tried to keep her brain active, hopeful that her memory would return.

She familiarized herself with the e-reader, found word games in the bookstore to help stimulate her brain. *This gadget is fantastic,* she thought. Also in the gift bag were hair ties and barrettes. *For a man, he did an excellent job picking things out.* She fell asleep happier than she could remember since waking in the unfamiliar surroundings. Despite Cora, Jack, and Buddy's company, she had this nagging thought she was missing a part of her life. A vital role.

The following morning, Susan woke, excited to start her day. She kissed the top of Buddy's little head and painfully made her way to the bathroom. Buddy was still asleep, snuggled in her bed. His little head rested on her pillow with the tiniest bit of tongue peeking out of his mouth. Susan dressed inside her closet, donning a pair of khaki Bermuda shorts and a peach tank top. She found a brown clip among the hair things the doctor had bought and gathered her hair into the clip. The weather forecast flashed on the television and read that it would be in the nineties and hoped she could use the pool. She planned on asking the doctor.

Susan woke Buddy, and they made their way to the kitchen. The room was empty. She'd forgotten this was Cora and Jack's Day off, and they'd mentioned they were leaving early. She found Buddy's food in the pantry and fed him. While he ate, she looked for his leash and harness. She found it hanging on the brass hook in the laundry room by the door. Buddy had finished eating and ran into the laundry room. It was a routine. *Maybe this was their home?*

She stared at the alarm keypad by the door. It intimidated her. "Ah, green light, Bud. It looks like we're ready." It was a challenge, but she harnessed Buddy and got him outside. She leaned on the walker for support as Buddy ran into the penned area.

Jack had placed a bright red plastic fire hydrant in the yard and installed fencing so Buddy could enjoy his play and potty area. Buddy ran to the red plastic fire hydrant and lifted his leg. He walked around to find the perfect spot to do his other business. Susan found a scoop and a trash can and cleaned up after him. *Jack was very thorough and considerate when planning this area for Buddy.*

She smiled, brought Buddy back in, and removed his harness. He barked and stared at the box of treats, sitting patiently. Susan laughed and said, "You're a smart boy." She gave him the treat. Buddy took it gently and gobbled it up. Susan ambled to the kitchen, where she found the doctor sitting at the table in his bathrobe.

"Good morning, sweetheart. I woke up early to tend to Buddy, but I see you've taken care of it. How are you?"

"Good morning. Still in pain but getting more mobile each day. I'm using the walker because I'm still a little dizzy. Thank you for the e-reader and the hair ties. I played with the reader last night and downloaded a game to stimulate my brain. I have my eye on a few books that sound interesting. I'll download one or two later."

"My pleasure, sweetheart. As for the hair ties, the sales assistant chose everything because I'm clueless." He raised his palms. "I hope she chose well." Richard smiled sheepishly. "Your mother did those things for you."

"Well, her choices are great, thank you. I can try to make breakfast if you'd like."

"No need." He held up a hand and shook his head, swallowing a gulp of coffee. "Cora most likely left prepared food in the refrigerator, and I see muffins on the cake plate. Cora loves to bake and cook. She always worries I won't eat on her day off. I can make a few things for myself when I'm here alone, although it's much easier to order in."

Susan pushed her walker toward the refrigerator and found a serving plate with a breakfast note resting atop an omelet. "Found it," she said as she took off the wrap. "Looks like a veggie omelet. Are you ready to eat? I can make coffee, too. I learned how to use this machine. I'm amazed at how fast and how delicious the coffee is." She trembled slightly, unnerved in his presence without Jack and Cora. Not fear precisely. She didn't know what to say or how to converse with him.

He peered from his e-reader. "Sure, but let me heat things. Sit down and relax."

"Why don't you heat the omelets, and I'll make the coffee?" Susan suggested.

"Deal. Just be careful with carrying the hot brew using your walker. Better yet, make them and leave them on the counter. I'll bring them to the table."

"Okay, how do you take your coffee? I figured out that I like my coffee black."

The doctor smiled, "black for me as well." Richard stuck the platter into the microwave. While the omelets heated, he set the table for three. Natalia looked over and asked if they had guests for breakfast. "Nope, that's Buddy's plate. The omelet is safe. I thought he would like a little. If that's alright with you?" he raised his eyebrows.

"Oh, sure, that's sweet." She blushed.

Breakfast was a quiet affair. Buddy snorted with joy as if he were eating filet mignon rather than a vegetable omelet.

"I see you use an e-reader too. What are you reading?" Susan asked as she slowly chewed her food.

"Well, right now, I'm reading the newspaper. I read medical journals and occasionally a book. The newspapers are auto-delivered to the device."

"Technology is amazing these days. Read your papers with breakfast, don't change your routine for me," Susan told him. She found conversation challenging.

"Thanks. I appreciate that. I've almost finished this article. Then we'll discuss plans for today." After he finished eating, Richard stood from the table and retrieved a muffin for each of them.

"This is amazing. How are you three not overweight with all these delicious foods?"

"I haven't had the best appetite, but I eat better now that we're a family again." He smiled, peering into her bright blue eyes, Donna's eyes. "Cora also cooks very healthy, uses fresh ingredients and free-range meat and eggs, low sugar and no bleached white flour."

Susan wasn't sure what "free-range" meant. She didn't want to embarrass herself, so she made a mental note to look it up in the dictionary using the e-reader.

Richard finished his muffin and said, "Would you like to hear today's plans?"

"Sure." She secretly hoped the plans were outside of the house. Maybe sightseeing.

"Well, the weather app stated today will be a glorious day. I ordered fresh steaks from the butcher. I invited Uncle Thomas, Aunt Nicole, and TJ over for a cookout and a swim. Doesn't that sound like fun?"

"Yes, it does." She nodded. *It sounds overwhelming too.* "Do you think I'm strong enough to use the pool?"

"Yes, but not alone. TJ can assist."

Frightened and worried because she had no memories of these people, she stuffed her hands into her pockets. Her *family* were all strangers to her. When his face had erupted into an enormous smile, she agreed, but felt the now familiar pang of anxiety churning in her stomach.

Happy that Susan agreed to the gathering, Richard wandered outside to check on the outdoor bar near the grotto's entrance and the kitchen just inside. *Donna had loved the pool and the cave-like space.* His memories flooded back from when they built this area. Inside, they had a big screen TV and comfortable furniture. Donna relaxed on the hotter days inside with the TV on as she cooked in the outdoor kitchen. The pool extended into the area. When Susan was small, Donna taught her to swim inside, shaded from the sun.

Everything was in order. Jack or Cora had refreshed the soft drinks, Perrier, Voss, iced teas, sodas, and wine coolers. Richard made Donna's recipe for Sangria. He was whistling as he worked. He laughed as he thought, *imagine that I'm whistling. I haven't done that in years. I'm happy.* Shoving the Sangria into the refrigerator, he turned to preheat the grill. The hors d'oeuvres arrived earlier, and Richard stuck them into the grotto refrigerator. He found that Cora had made a tossed salad, potato salad, and pasta salad. *Cora is a blessing.*

Susan joined him outside and sat on the lanai with Buddy. She had brought the awning down and was reading her e-reader. She had asked many times if she could help, but he insisted that she relax. Promptly at one o'clock, the doorbell rang. Richard rushed toward the house and turned to Susan. "Be right back, my dear. That would be our guests now."

The knots in Susan's stomach intensified. She licked her dry lips, wishing she had a glass of icy water. She shoved her right hand into the pocket of her cover-up, not knowing why she kept doing it. The panic flamed in her gut like a wildfire, everything surreal. When a deep male voice inside greeted the doctor, tears stung Susan's eyes. She wiped the one lone tear that escaped. Her hands shook, and she held them together to still them.

The doctor returned with a tall, handsome man with bright blue eyes. He combed his hand through his thick unruly, and wavy hair back with the one rebel strand falling on his forehead. Susan couldn't help it, but her eyes glanced to his rock-hard abs, accentuated by the clingy T-shirt he wore. Buddy saw him and jumped off her lap, barking and greeting the newcomer.

"Hi there, critter." The man squatted down to pet the excited dog, then he looked up, squinting from the sun. "Who is this, Uncle Rich?"

"That little guy is Buddy, our furry friend," Dr. Kline said, laughing. "He's a silly little clown. He brings laughter and joy into this house."

"I wouldn't peg you as a dog person, Uncle Rich."

"I am now. Let me introduce you to someone you haven't seen in years. Richard walked him over to Susan's chair. She tried to pull herself up, but the walker wouldn't cooperate. Richard started toward her chair to assist, but TJ got there first and pulled her to her feet. When he touched her hand, little shock waves coursed through her body.

"TJ, this is Susan."

"Susan?" TJ exclaimed, dragging out the syllables. The name came out exaggeratingly slow. "The little shit who put pepper sauce in my tomato juice because she thought a kid that liked tomato juice was weird?" TJ stared at her, recognition dawning on his face. "That Susan?"

"Yes, TJ. That Susan. But I doubt she will do that again."

Relief washed over Susan's body. *This guy was a gentleman, handsome and funny.* "Well, let's just say I'll *try* to behave," she said with a tentative smile. It wasn't as though she remembered doing it, but it sounded like a fun prank.

TJ's brows furrowed together, but he refrained from questioning his uncle or his long-lost childhood friend and lover. In her earlier years, the people she associated with had changed her, and it broke his heart when she became involved in the local drug scene. She had become a different person, not the Susan he loved. But he had to admit that since then, she'd aged beautifully. Her hair was still blond, and she'd kept it long, although she was thinner than he remembered, and it was apparent she was recovering from an injury. The walker was never far from her reach.

He was eager to get his uncle alone, to ask him how he'd found her. Several minutes later, the bell rang again. This time Buddy barked to alert them. Richard strode into the house, and he listened to the greetings of the new arrivals. TJ sat across from her and bluntly asked, "Where have you been?"

She looked at him with sadness and said, "I do not know."

"You were gone for almost twenty years, and you do not know? That's bullshit."

Susan's mouth opened to retort when an unfamiliar voice came from a few feet away.

"Thomas Junior, language." There were remnants of a southern accent clear in the woman's voice.

TJ replied, "Sorry, Ma." He stood and sauntered over to his parents.

Thomas laughed as he hugged his son. "See, son, you might be a big-shot movie star in Hollywood, but she's still the boss."

"Yes, I am, and I will not tolerate such crass 'boy talk' from either of you," Nicole exclaimed, waving her finger between them. Raised in a very political, well-respected family in the south, Nicole demanded good manners.

"Richard, are you going to introduce us to your guest?" Nicole inquired.

"Nicole, Thomas... this is Susan. My Susan is home."

Nicole ran and enveloped Susan into her warm embrace. "Oh honey, I'm happy you're back. You look fabulous. Doesn't she, Thomas? Look at her. She's beautiful, just beautiful," Nicole gushed as she dabbed the happy tears that sprang to her eyes, being careful not to mar her exquisitely applied makeup. "Susan, you look just like your mother."

Shocked to his core, Thomas stared, his mouth wide open. *That's the woman from Myrtle Beach. What the hell is going on? Had Richard lost his mind? Had he kidnapped this stranger?* The thoughts flooded his mind. Not wanting to make a scene, he peered into her eyes, looking for the girl from so long ago. Showing no sign of having ever met him in Myrtle Beach, she greeted him warmly, if a little warily. Worried, Thomas tried to act as normal as possible. Thomas gave her a brief hug as he said, "Welcome home."

Susan replied, "Thank you."

Susan hadn't yet removed her bathing suit cover-up. She refused to ask for TJ's help to get into the pool, as her father suggested. She sensed him staring at her through his dark sunglasses, and she fought the urge to run up to her bedroom, where she always felt safest. TJ stood with his arms crossed, and Nicole seemed overjoyed. TJ removed his shirt and dove into the pool, hoping the refreshing water would cool his temper down. His body had earlier betrayed him when he grasped Susan's hands. Those long forgotten yet familiar longings returned.

Dinner was delicious, but all the participants were on edge except for Richard and Nicole. Susan's thoughts were in a jumble. The accident had taken every bit of her memory. She tried so hard to remember that she gave herself a migraine, and she felt it intensify. She wished this day would end.

Richard knew Thomas wanted to discuss Susan's return when he was alone with him in the kitchen, but he spoke incessantly, not allowing his friend to get a word in edge-wise.

Annoyed, confused, and angry, TJ stood to leave, claiming he had an early call on set, thanking Richard for such an enjoyable day and a sumptuous meal. He hugged his father, kissed, and hugged his mother, and curtly nodded to Susan. He shook Richard's hand and then showed himself out.

Nicole chattered on and on about what a lovely woman Susan had turned out to be and how she couldn't wait to bring her to the club for lunch. They made plans for Wednesday before they left, and Nicole offered to pick her up if she would like an outing.

Cora and Jack returned after they had finished cleaning up. Susan thanked her for the salads. "Did you enjoy your day, honey?" Cora asked.

Susan shrugged. "Just an okay day."

Cora studied Susan, a frown on her brow. "Just okay? I thought the change of routine would be good for you."

"Well, I picked up weird vibes from the doctor's friend Thomas, and his son, TJ, was rude and cold. Nicole was sweet, though. She wants to take me to a salon and to her club for lunch on Wednesday. What do you think? Should I go?"

"Honey, you're an adult. You can decide for yourself. I'm sure your father won't mind."

"He didn't seem to mind when Nicole brought it up at dinner. But I'm uncomfortable since I don't remember these people at all."

"I'm sure your father told them that, and they'll respect your position and not pressure you," Cora said with conviction.

"I want to go. Hopefully, I'll be better on my feet. I don't want to take the walker out in public. It makes me look like a senior citizen."

"We'll work it out, don't you worry." Cora said.

"Did you enjoy your day off? Buddy pined for Jack, and he ran into your suite several times today."

"Oh, that puppy. He's so sweet. We went to the farmer's market, and Buddy has extra surprises. Jack is enjoying him." Cora unpacked her bags and placed them into the kitchen pantry. "We stopped at every single pet stand, and he bought an item from each," Cora explained. "Miss Susan, if you ever need to talk, I'm here for you. No judgments and in total confidence."

"Thank you, Cora. You might regret telling me that. Today was exhausting. I think I'm going upstairs to change for bed." Susan glanced outside. "Buddy is outside, playing with Jack. Should I wait for him down here?"

"No, you go on up. I'll bring Buddy up to you. Sleep well, honey."

"You're so kind, Cora. Thank you, and good night." Susan kissed Cora's cheek, turned, padded down the hallway, and pressed the button to call the elevator. It arrived in seconds. Once on the second floor, she exited the elevator, and the doctor's snores wafted through the hallway. Susan noticed that during clean-up that the doctor's pallor had changed. She wondered if he felt okay. He worked long hours, but rarely looked as exhausted as he had today. Susan felt compassion for him because of his kindness toward her. But regrettably, the emotion wasn't because he was her father. The people that visited today, Thomas and his son, intimidated her. She had caught them staring at her several times, ice in their eyes. Nicole welcomed her and seemed grateful that she was home, and the conversation flowed smoothly. She would enjoy an outing with Nicole and hoped the doctor would agree.

Smiling, she made her way to her bedroom and closed the door. She took several deep breaths to calm herself. She grabbed a quick shower and dressed in her nightclothes. By the time she made it back into her bedroom, she had found Buddy on the bed waiting.

The small family barbecue had taken every ounce of Richard's energy. He slept but didn't wake refreshed and was surprised at how tired he was, since he usually had an abundance of life. *Thank goodness it's Sunday,* he thought. Cora, Jack, and Richard usually stayed home and relaxed by the pool. Jack traditionally cooked in the sheltered area or on the grill. They spent Sunday evenings watching movies or sports while Cora read or surfed the web, searching for new recipes. Cora had some computer skills. She could email, use search engines, and find recipes. She also learned to order groceries from several stores and loved this convenience.

Cora glanced from the stove when the steady gait tapped on the marble floor. "Good morning, Doctor," she said with a smile. For years he had asked her to call him Richard. Cora, old-fashioned, still called him Doctor. "Are you alright? You're pale."

"No, I'm not myself at all. I think yesterday took a lot out of me," he said with a heavy sigh. "Probably the heat."

"That surprises me, as you're always overflowing with energy. Why not just stay comfortable today? Jack is outside, prepping the smoker for lunch, and he has dinner planned. He's in his swim trunks."

"I think I'll change into my trunks as well and float around the pool. It's always so relaxing. Maybe with Jack in the pool, Susan can join us. She looked forward to it yesterday, but she hadn't bothered to use it."

"Jack would be happy to help. Perhaps I'll get in myself. I hope I can trust Jack not to push me under the water. That man is still a child." Cora laughed as she made the statement.

Richard laughed too. "He's an admirable man-child, though. I don't know how I survived before you both moved in. If anything should ever happen to me, you'll be protected financially."

"Oh, Doctor, don't talk like that." she said as she wiped a tear. "You're fine. You're just exhausted."

Jack strode through the French doors from outside. Buddy ran over to him like he hadn't seen him in years. "Good morning Doc. Are you alright?"

"Just tired. Gee, I must look bad if you both commented. What's for breakfast there, Cora? Smells great."

"Blueberry and apple pancakes. Blueberries and apples fresh from the farmer's market. Organic."

"Cora, you're a wonderful chef. I wonder if Susan is all right. She doesn't sleep this late."

Jack jumped up. "I'll go check on her." Just then, the elevator door opened, followed by the banging of the walker.

"Susan's coming now, moving faster with that thing," Richard said. "Perhaps soon she won't need it at all. But I prefer she uses it because she is still dizzy. She should see Dr. Ross again. I'll reach out after breakfast."

"Are you guys talking about me? Oh my gosh, what is cooking?" She grinned at the doctor's smile.

"Yes, we said how much better you were getting around with a walker, and your father mentioned making you a follow-up appointment with Dr. Ross." Cora smiled warmly.

"Who is Dr. Ross?" Susan asked.

"A physician in my practice that cared for you after your accident. You need a follow-up to check on your healing progress."

Cora placed the hot pancakes on the table, her cheerful face flushed from the stove. There was a gentle tapping of Buddy's nails on the tile as he jumped from person to person, begging for a sample and which each adult provided.

Richard ate half a pancake and was full. "I'm heading into my office for a few minutes. I'll meet you out back in a little while." He trekked to his office, his head lowering as he shuffled.

Richard's office had become his haven. Donna decorated it in warm tones, masculine and comfortable. The service didn't clean this room, only Cora. It only needed a quick vacuuming and dusting, as the doctor was very meticulous about his space. He reached for the phone and called Dr. Ross.

"Hello and good morning, Dr. Kline."

"Good morning, Maria. How is your weekend so far?"

"Very relaxing. Is everything okay? You seldom call me on weekends unless it's an emergency."

"Yes, everything is fine. I wondered if you could re-examine Susan. Either first thing tomorrow or your last appointment? She's still dealing with pain, and although she's stronger, her legs are weak, and she's still experiencing headaches. Sometimes dizzy spells."

"My first appointment is at ten. Bring Susan first thing tomorrow morning. It will give me plenty of time for an exam and conversation. How is her memory?"

"It has not returned." He sighed. "We're having a lazy day today and using the pool, cooking on the grill. Why don't you join us? I'd like you to assess her behavior and personality in a relaxed setting. I fear she will be apprehensive tomorrow, and shut down. She is quiet and doesn't express feelings, not to me at least. Most times, she seems withdrawn. If you have plans, don't worry about it. We can do it another time."

"I'd planned to go to the complex's pool for sun and relaxation. I can't pass up on an opportunity to swim in your gorgeous pool and enjoy a delightful meal with friends. What time would you like me to arrive? I'll bring dessert."

"Is one good for you? And bring nothing. Cora is testing a new Quinoa salad recipe. I imagine she's testing a lot of different recipes. She loves being in the kitchen."

"One is perfect. See you then."

Dr. Ross arrived, wearing a giant sun hat along with her big smile. "Hello, Cora, you're looking great as usual."

"Hello, Dr. Ross. Thank you for coming. Doctor Kline is on the lanai with Susan and Buddy, but first, follow me. I want you to try my latest creation."

"Plying me with your delicious treats?"

"Well, not exactly a treat, a new salad."

Cora took a huge cold bowl from the refrigerator and scooped out a spoonful into a small bowl. "What do you think? I found this recipe for confetti salad, and I added Quinoa and citrus dressing. Be honest. I'm not sure if it needs more flavor."

Dr. Ross took a forkful. "I love it, and there are healthy eats in there," Maria said, pointing to the bowl. "I try to eat better, but I'm constantly on the run. I don't have time to prepare anything elaborate, but I can make this salad on my days off. Can you share the recipe?"

"Of course, I'll write it down, or I can email it to you at work."

"Email is great, thanks, Cora."

Cora wiped her hands on her apron and asked, "Shall we go outside?" Maria followed Cora to the back door.

Susan glanced over at the slight squeak of the French door as Dr. Ross and Cora stepped onto the lanai. Susan sat in one lounge chair, an open book on her lap. Dr. Kline in another. His face lifted to the sun, and Jack stood by the grill, pre-heating it. Jack rushed over and greeted Dr. Ross. Richard had fallen fast asleep.

"What would you like to drink, Maria?" Jack asked.

"A wine cooler would be great."

Jack opened the refrigerator and chose a tropical-flavored cooler. "How's this, Maria?"

"Oh, perfect, delicious. Thanks." Maria peered over at her colleague and then at Cora. Cora shook her head. Susan watched with interest as the guest stepped over to her. "How are you? Do you remember me?"

Susan replied apologetically, "No, I'm sorry, I don't. But Doc told me a lot of wonderful things about you. Why not grab that chair and let's become acquainted?" She pointed to her left, and her hand quivered. The two women talked while Dr. Ross assessed Susan and enjoyed the conversation. They're the same age, and Susan seemed comfortable with her. Dr. Ross asked if she enjoyed being home.

Susan responded candidly, "I guess they're kind, but I sense as though I don't belong."

"I heard you met TJ in person?" Dr. Ross asked. "I'll admit I have a crush on him."

"I found him to be rude and obnoxious. He left me feeling very uncertain. He was aggressive about sins of the past of which I don't remember."

"Maybe that's the famous movie star coming out in him," Maria suggested.

"He's a famous movie star? Doc told me he was acting in a movie but didn't realize he's famous. No matter, he's an ass."

"According to your father, that ass has been in love with you since you were both kids. You're a lucky girl."

"Who's lucky, and who is an ass?" asked Richard.

The women giggled as Susan exclaimed, "No one."

"Oh, I see. Girl talk. I'll mind my business." Richard saw Jack leaning over the grill and strode over. "Hey, Jack, what's cooking?"

Susan laughed. "Do I look lucky? Gimpy legs, walking with an old lady walker, a family I don't remember, a lifetime I don't remember. I had to be somewhere these last twenty years. I have a scar on my stomach with no clue what caused it."

"Okay, tomorrow during your appointment with me, I'll examine you and give you my opinion on what that scar is." Dr. Ross offered.

They talked the entire day. Susan enjoyed what she hoped would be her new friend's company. She also wondered how that would work, with her being her doctor. She speculated if Maria even wanted to be friends. The rest of the day went perfectly. For the first time, she laughed, enjoyed her food, and used the pool. Maria showed her exercises to do in the water to strengthen her legs. Maria mentioned to Richard that Susan should use the spa for pain relief if she could climb in and out safely.

Richard enjoyed watching the two women interact. He didn't use the pool, but he moved between the lanai and the grotto to escape the sun.

"Jack, who taught you how to grill? Dinner was fabulous." Susan exclaimed.

Everyone concurred. Maria peeked at her phone and said, "Wow, seven-thirty already. I should get going. Thank you, Richard, for inviting me. I had a lovely time."

"Thanks, Maria, for your advice, and we will see you first thing in the morning," Susan said.

Richard walked her to the door and thanked her for coming. He mentioned he would be in contact with her after the exam tomorrow. "Be safe," he said.

"See you tomorrow, Richard."

Maria went home, deep in thought. Susan seemed confused, with absolutely no memories of her past. Nothing before when she woke up in Dr. Kline's house. *Perhaps I should refer her back to the neurologist tomorrow.* Maria was apprehensive about the exam tomorrow. It wouldn't reveal Susan's past, and the scarring concerned her. *What if it was a cesarean section scar? That would mean there might be a child or children. How would this affect her? Maybe she had the child adopted, or had been a surrogate?* Maria didn't like being in this position. Her obligations were to her patient, but Richard was her colleague and her patient's father. "We'll see how tomorrow goes," she said out loud as she turned into her condo complex. Maria observed how ill Richard looked during her visit.

Richard felt unwell, but he relaxed and tried to enjoy the cook-out, he dozed most of the day, yet he felt worse. Could he be coming down with a bug? He listened to the conversations but didn't take part. He had never experienced exhaustion like this. He returned to the kitchen after seeing Dr. Ross out and found Cora and Susan. "Ladies, I'm heading upstairs." He leaned over and kissed Susan's cheek. "Night, honey."

"Good night. I hope you feel better tomorrow."

Richard made his way up the marble staircase and thought, *I should use the elevator. These steps were never so long and tiring.* He padded into his bedroom and called Thomas. "Hey Tom, can you set aside time for me? I want to update my accounts and will."

"Sure, what about one night this week over dinner at the Club?" suggested Thomas.

"That's fine. Call me tomorrow after you've checked your schedule. Sleep well, my friend."

"You too, Rich."

Richard ended the call and went to bed without reading or turning on the TV. He wanted to arrive early to speak with Dr. Ross before she examined Susan. He fell into a deep and restful sleep and arrived at the office by seven-thirty, well ahead of Susan's appointment at nine. Dr. Ross waited in the break room, reviewing the chart she made the night Susan had come in almost a month ago.

She had a gash on her head, which had healed, and the scar was virtually indistinguishable. She had also suffered a minor brain bleed and a concussion, and she'd had bruises all over her body. The pain medications and the trauma to her legs left her weak and lightheaded, leaving her father, Dr. Kline, in a panic. He was overprotective, insisting she uses the walker and a shower chair.

Richard joined Dr. Ross in the break room. "Good morning, Maria."

"Good morning, Richard. I'm glad we've got time for this before Susan comes in. There are several things we should discuss."

"Shoot," Dr. Kline said with a smile.

"First, Susan needs to walk on her own. No more walkers or any aids. She needs PT and to move about again. Second, I think she should see the neurologist again. I want to find out if the memory loss results from head trauma or something else. I'm aware the neurologist diagnosed a concussion and dissociative fugue, but I want to be proactive. Last, we need to bring in a gynecologist. She has visible scarring on her abdomen, indicative of a cesarean."

"Okay." Richard said as he rose from the chair. "All of those specialties are right here in the center. Aren't you friends with a gynecologist? I play golf with the neurologist on the ninth floor who read her results and saw her the night of the accident. My utmost concern is her health and her privacy."

Dr. Ross replied, "I agree. As for my assessment of her on Sunday, she was open and forthcoming. Susan has no sense of familial ties to you, the house, Thomas, TJ, or Nicole. Nothing has jarred her memory, and she complained that the medications made her foggy. While I agree she needs care, perhaps we should re-test and try alternatives. But I feel weird now. We've bonded and formed a friendship."

"Why not see how things go today? We can have the staff make the appointments with the specialists once you decide on a doctor. You can choose anyone, not just my suggestions. I want to respect her privacy," Richard said as he opened the door to the break room.

"Understood, Susan should be here for her appointment soon. I'll check in with you later."

"All right," Richard said as he left the room.

Eleven

JACK ENJOYED THE AFTER-dinner walk with Buddy. They usually went a few blocks each evening. Buddy begged for a treat upon their return to the house, and he quickly learned where they stored his treats. Stepping into the family room with Buddy after the walk and treat, he asked, "Do you need me to bring him upstairs, Miss Susan?"

"No, thank you, Jack. We're watching a movie. Cora found a movie to watch, one of snarky TJ's. I am curious about his skills," Susan replied, giggling. "Would you like to join us?"

Jack glanced at the TV. "No, thank you. I've seen it several times. A good movie, though, enjoy."

Cora carried in bowls of fruit salad and sat next to Susan to watch the movie. The scowling, pompous ass from yesterday was talented. She turned to Cora. "Wow, how about that movie? Could he be the same smart ass that visited here yesterday? He made me extremely uncomfortable."

Cora smiled. "Well, supposedly, you were the love of his life."

"Seriously? Doc hadn't mentioned that little tidbit. It's a shame I don't remember, or is it?" Susan laughed. "Thank you, Cora, for watching with me."

Susan moved toward the kitchen with Cora. They said their goodnights, and Susan and Buddy strolled down the hallway to the elevator. Once in their room, Susan gave Buddy belly rubs as he snorted gleefully. By the time she climbed into bed, the little dog was fast asleep.

The following morning, she woke early and changed into a floral sundress and sandals and banged her way to the elevator. She peeked into Richard's room, noticing his bed made and the room empty. *He must be downstairs at breakfast,* she thought.

She found Cora by the stove, and Jack let Buddy into the backyard. She saw a contractor outside fencing off a more extensive area by the laundry room door for Buddy.

"Good morning, Cora," she said. "What is for breakfast?"

Cora smiled. "Good morning. Apple muffins. I also scrambled eggs. Can I make you a plate?"

"Sure," Susan responded as she hobbled over to the brewer to pour a cup of coffee.

"How are you, my dear?" Cora continued stirring the eggs until they set.

"I'm much better. I think whirlpool helped. I'm a little apprehensive about the doctor's visit today, though. Where's Doc?"

"He left for the practice early. Jack is taking you to your appointment. That dress suits you, and your makeup looks lovely, just enough," Cora said, smiling, her bright eyes shining.

"Thank you, Cora. I wasn't sure I could do it properly, but I tried. My arms are still a little shaky."

Cora brought a plate to the table, along with a fresh fruit cup. She placed the plate in front of Susan and returned to the stove briefly to make sure she turned it off.

Susan picked at it. "This is delicious, Cora. You could open a restaurant. Sorry, I couldn't finish. I'm nervous about today's appointment."

"I hope, as time goes on, your appetite will improve, and you'll be more yourself."

"Hmm, myself? I wonder who that is." she exclaimed.

Jack stepped in from outside. "Are you ready to leave, Miss Susan?"

Susan nodded. "Yes, just give me a few minutes."

Susan limped into the powder room, near tears, frightened of what the exam would reveal—terrified of what it might not show. With her stomach in knots, she banged the walker as she made her way back into the kitchen to Jack.

Cora handed her a purse. "You forgot this, honey." She gave her the bag the doctor had left in her room.

"Oh, thank you. Yes, I did."

"The garage is this way, Miss Susan. Since you're using the walker, we can take the Town Car. The air conditioning is on, so it should be nice and cool for you."

They walked down the hallway and made a right turn, opening a door leading to the garage. The garage was brightly lit, clean, with six cars housed inside. Susan had no clue what the vehicles were. Jack guided her toward a black car with darkly tinted windows. He opened the back door for her.

"Can't I sit in the front seat with you?" she asked. "I promise I won't be annoying or distracting."

"Miss Susan, it isn't how we do things here," Jack replied.

"Well, it is now." She hobbled closer to the front passenger seat, opened the door as much as she could with the walker in her way, and climbed in the front seat. "This is how I want to do it. Does that work for you?" she asked, with laughter in her voice.

"Whatever her highness wants," Jack said, laughing as he folded her walker and placed it in the trunk. He backed out of the garage and used the remote to close the door behind them. He drove down the long, curved driveway and made a right onto the road.

At the sight of the large estates lining the street, Susan's eyes almost popped out of her head. "Holy moly. Look at these mansions. Who lives in these?" she asked in awe.

Jack pointed to the right. "Well, that house belongs to a former actress and her husband. They own several high-end restaurants in town now." He gestured left. "That one there belongs to a comedian who is also a talk show host." He went further, and he pointed left. "That one, he owns several Casinos in Las Vegas and somewhere else in Europe. Doc told me where, but I forgot."

"Wow, I'm blown away by the size of these homes, the opulence," Susan said.

After several blocks of residential traffic, Jack steered the car to a business district. Here gorgeous palm trees towered overhead. Mesmerized, Susan felt almost as though she were in a new world. Nothing was familiar, but not frightening at all, but remarkable.

"What is this town called, Jack?" she asked.

"Beverly Hills," he answered.

"Oh." She wasn't sure what that meant yet, but she sensed from his tone what a well-known, famous place it must be. They traveled another fifteen minutes, and Jack pulled up to an impressive building. A young valet rushed to them and opened the back passenger door. Susan laughed, seeing his face as he realized there wasn't a passenger in the back seat.

Jack smiled and said, "her highness is in the front seat." Jack and Susan laughed when the valet's orbs opened wider.

Apologizing, the young man opened the front passenger door. "Welcome, your highness."

Jack and Susan laughed again, and the valet's face turned red.

Susan gently placed her hand on his arm. "No, no, I'm not royalty. My friend Jack thinks he's a comedian. He was joking. That's just his nickname for me when I'm obstinate."

"Oh, I see. Well, nice to see the smiles this morning. Have a great visit." The young man smiled, his eyes shining.

Jack walked around and handed the valet the car keys. "We may be a few hours. That's Dr. Kline's car. You best be careful with it," Jack said with a teasing wink.

"Yes, sir. I will," the young man replied.

Jack and Susan walked toward the glass doors. She hadn't been as lightheaded lately, so she left the walker in the car and took Jack's arm to steady herself. They walked through the doors and into the lobby. The gleaming cream marble floors, the gold elevator doors, and the cool crisp air and soft music flowed through the vast space. The gold-tone mirrored windows blocked the intense southern California sun. The building mesmerized Susan, amazed that this was a business and not a ballroom. They walked to the elevator and ascended to the top floor. The button imprinted with the name "Kline."

"Wow, Jack, this is unbelievable."

"Yup." Jack replied. "Your father is pretty famous for what he does, and he works hard."

"I struggle to believe he is my father. Not that I think he's lying," Susan said with sadness as she shrugged her shoulders.

"I understand, or at least I'm trying to, having never experienced what you're going through."

Susan and Jack exited the elevator on the twelfth floor into a vast waiting room. A receptionist greeted them, looking as though she just stepped out of a fashion magazine. Her dark hair flowed to her shoulders, not one out of place, and a simple silver chain dangled at her throat, a crisp white blouse tucked neatly into the navy-blue pencil skirt, which accentuated the slim waistline. She wore navy blue stilettos. Susan wondered how she wore those all day.

"Good morning and welcome. I presume you're Miss Kline. My name is Lisa, and I'll check you in. Your nurse today is Nancy. Can I get you vitamin water, juice, or green tea?"

"No, thank you. I'm fine." Susan sat in one of the plush chairs in the waiting room. "Jack, these chairs are crazy comfortable. Toss one in the trunk, will you?" she said in jest.

"Yes, they are, but I don't think they would go with your father's décor."

"No, I guess not."

A nurse stepped into the waiting area. "Good morning, Miss Kline. A pleasure to meet you. My name is Nancy, and I'll be your nurse for today's appointment. Would you be so kind as to follow me? Do you need help?"

"No, I'm fine. I walk a little slow."

Nancy replied with a smile, "Take your time. The exam room isn't far."

They walked together at Susan's pace and turned into an exam room. Nancy passed her a hospital gown and a robe. She motioned to the dressing area and stated that she could change into the wrap inside. "I'll leave you in privacy. I'll return in a few minutes to take your vitals."

Susan stepped into the large changing room with a bench seat covered in a plush tan fabric. A white terrycloth robe hung on a hanger, with matching slippers on the floor underneath. She undressed, then slipped into the soft cotton wrap, robe, and slippers before walking back into the exam room.

Nancy knocked on the door. "Are you ready for me? May I come in?"

"Yes, ready as I'll ever be." Susan shivered from the chill in the room, her skin breaking out in tiny bumps.

Nancy checked Susan's blood pressure, temperature, and pulse and asked her if she was okay today. "Any pains or anything you need to discuss with the doctor?" she inquired.

"Painful all over, a tightness in my hips. My hands and arms are weak, and I'm experiencing frequent headaches. Sometimes I'm lightheaded," Susan shared.

Nancy made notes in her chart and stated that Dr. Ross would see her in a few minutes. Susan sat on the exam table and waited for the doctor.

"Hey, Susan. Long time, no see," she joked.

"Hey. I hope you had a wonderful time yesterday."

"I did. Based on our conversation yesterday, I'd like two other opinions—one, the neurologist that saw you the night of the accident, and a gynecologist. Second opinions are helpful to explain what's possibly causing the continued memory issues and to explain the scar on your abdomen," Dr. Ross said.

"That's fine. The scar, could it be from childbirth?" Susan asked. "That could mean there may be a child missing me. Or perhaps even children?"

"That's possible, and one reason I think those specialists should examine you. I'll ask Nancy to set up the appointments. Any preference for days or times?"

"No preference. Today is the first time I've even ventured into public. Gosh, the things I saw today. The mansions, the biggest palm trees, swanky buildings like this one. Fancy cars. All I can say is, wow. What an excursion, and all just for a checkup."

Maria laughed out loud. "You'll get used to it. All right, can you lie down on the exam table? I promise not to hurt you," she said with a laugh.

"Don't scare me. I'm nervous."

"Don't be. I was teasing you." Maria proceeded with the exam and then assisted her in a sitting position. "Well, you seem to have a lot more mobility in your legs and hips. You didn't cry too loudly when I manipulated them," the doctor teased.

"Funny, ha-ha," Susan responded with a smile, recognizing the teasing again.

Maria smiled, her dark eyes shining. "Your scar is fading and will diminish even more with time. And the headaches, did you ever experience them before?"

"Before when? There isn't a before, just an after. After I woke up in a bedroom at Dr. Kline's."

"Sorry, I haven't had a patient without history before. Be sure to tell the neurologist about the headaches. I'm changing your medications. Let's see if we can eliminate the dizziness. However, if it continues, let the neurologist know or me, and we'll order a repeat CT scan or an MRI. However, I'm sure the neurologist will order those tests."

"Okay. Thanks, Maria."

"Change, and I'll see you in a minute," Maria said, as she scribbled notes on her chart.

Susan entered the dressing room, changed, and sat in the chair to wait. Maria returned with her prescriptions and a cream for the scar. She also warned her to use a moisturizer and sunscreen when going out, even in the car, as the sun was intense in California. The two women walked out together. Maria mentioned her father was with a patient. Otherwise, she would take her back to his office.

"How does he look this morning?" Susan asked. "He looked unwell yesterday. Both Cora and I remarked about it."

"Yes, he's fine today. His normal Energizer Bunny self," Maria said with relief.

"Oh, good."

"What are you doing with the rest of your day?" Maria asked.

"Going back to the house to hang with Buddy and Cora."

"My last appointment is early today, around two. What do you say I pick you up around four? Early dinner and catch a movie?"

"I would love that. Thanks for asking. How do I dress? I see everyone looks like they stepped out of a magazine here."

"Oh, casual. Jeans, capris, anything." Maria walked her out to Jack. "Hey Jack, how are you?"

"Hello Doc, how is her highness? Doing well?"

"Her highness?" Dr. Ross inquired.

Susan laughed. "He's sarcastic because I refused to sit in the back seat. I sat in the front next to him. Now I am known as 'her highness.'"

Jack chuckled and shrugged his shoulders at Dr. Ross.

"All right. See you later, Susan," Maria said, laughing.

Jack escorted Susan to the elevator. As they descended, Jack turned to Susan and said, "I'm happy that you're smiling." She peered at him, and he grinned.

"I'm happier," she said. "The exam was okay, and I've gained a new friend. She's picking me up tonight, and we're going to dinner and a movie. I enjoy the movies."

"I'm aware," he snickered. "You and my wife and those movies. Your return brought joy to Cora too. Your friendship fills a void for her. Thank you for being kind to her."

"Jack. I'm grateful. You both are kind and welcoming. You two are amazing friends."

"I appreciate those kind words, your highness, but they won't get me to build you a throne." Jack laughed.

"Funny guy." she snarled playfully. "Let's go home. I'm hungry. I wonder what deliciousness Cora has planned for lunch."

"I'm not sure, but she could've mentioned it, and I didn't hear her. She claims I have 'man ears.' I hear what I want to."

Susan laughed and asked, "Well, do you have man ears?"

"I can't answer that. You women stick together," he replied, casting a glance at Susan.

"Can you take me home a different way so that I could see more of the area?" She enjoyed the ride like a child on Christmas morning. As they approached the house, she remarked at the size. "These houses are huge. I've only seen my room and those few rooms downstairs. Is there more?"

"Much more. I'll ask Cora to give you a tour. It is amazing. Your Dad had this built for your mom before you were born." He pulled into the long driveway and backed into the garage and into the space he had vacated earlier that morning. He came around to open her door, but she had stepped out. "Your highness, I'm supposed to open your door," he quipped.

"Where is that law written?" she asked with sass.

Jack shook his head and opened the garage door to the house. Cora sat in the family room with Buddy, where he enjoyed chewing on a bully stick as Cora listened to the daily news during a quick break. The food smelled wonderful in the kitchen. Buddy ran to Susan when he realized she was home. Susan ambled from the garage into the kitchen.

"Hey, little man, did you miss me? I sure missed you." Susan turned to Cora. "Hi, Cora, what magic is going on in the kitchen? The aromas emanating from the kitchen were divine."

"French onion grillers," Cora replied, walking into the kitchen to check on lunch. Susan followed, anxious to see what they were.

"Wait until you try them." Jack exclaimed. "They're my favorite."

Cora slid the broiling tray from the oven and placed them on plates. She brought the food to the table and served iced tea along with a small green salad. Susan's mouth watered. The garlic toast and slices of meat covered in au jus were visually appealing and delicious.

For the first time since she had been living in this house, she ate her entire meal. "Cora, it was excellent. Thank you very much."

"Cora, her highness, would like a tour of the house," Jack said to his wife.

"Her highness?" Cora raised her eyebrow in question. "Where did that come from?" Jack explained how he had come up with her new nickname.

"Jack, you're terrible." She turned to Susan. "My husband sometimes forgets his manners. My apologies for Mr. Sarcastic."

"Not to worry, Cora. I gave it right back to him. I enjoyed the tour of the area."

Cora reached for the plates. "As soon as I tidy up the kitchen, I'll give you that tour of the house."

Cora started at the lowest level, the basement. Susan wasn't aware there was another level below the living area. Downstairs, Cora showed her a huge game room with colorful pictures reminiscent of a billiards room. Susan followed Cora into the next space, "This is the media room." Susan glanced at the carpeted media room with slightly elevated theater seating. They mounted a large TV in the room's front, high on the wall. Another area with light wood flooring contained two bowling lanes, a small kitchen, a gym, and a full bathroom. Cora pointed inside a meticulously organized storage room where the toys from her youth sat on shelves. She inside but had no interest in looking at any of the items.

They finished upstairs, with Cora showing her the guest rooms. Tastefully decorated, the house was welcoming. Susan loved her room, just as large as the master suite. This room brought her comfort. Not because it was huge, but now it was a familiar and comforting space.

THAT MORNING, RICHARD began his day in good spirits. His weekend was terrific, and he was grateful that his daughter was coming out of her shell. He whistled in the halls of the office now, something he hasn't done for twenty years. Finishing with his patient, he searched for Maria, who was inside an exam room. He hoped she was still with Susan. Maria stepped out, closing the door where she found Richard.

He smiled and asked, "Hey, are you heading in to examine another patient?"

"No, I have a thirty-minute break between patients."

He nodded toward the door. "Is Susan inside?"

"No, she left. Jack waited for her in the front room."

"Oh, I see. Well, my next patient is my last—Botox, quick and easy—and then the discussion of a facelift. I plan to leave early. Do you have a few minutes?"

"Let's go to the break room. I need coffee." Maria gave him an overview of what their plans were. She mentioned his daughter was on board with seeing the neurologist again and a gynecologist. Nancy was setting up the appointments. "We're having dinner tonight and seeing a movie. Girls' night out. I'm looking forward to it."

Before he left, Richard made a few calls after his discussion with Maria. When he got home, he found Cora and Susan in the kitchen and overheard part of a conversation between the women.

She mentioned to Cora that she was having dinner with Maria and going to a movie. "I'm not sure how late this movie is. If you go to bed, how do I get inside?"

"Oh honey, isn't there a set of keys in your purse?" Cora asked.

"Oh gee, I didn't think to look." She grabbed her purse and rummaged inside it, but didn't see a key. "Not one I can see."

"No matter. I'll wait up for you," Cora said.

Twelve

SUMMER FLEW BY, AND Jonathan was still shell-shocked and missed Natalia terribly. It had been almost three months since she disappeared. The schools would be open in less than a week, and Jonathan needed to prepare the boys. He panicked at the thought of it, and he didn't know how to get them ready.

Marc was beginning his freshman year of high school. At eleven, Alexander was attending middle school, and Anthony was still in elementary school at eight. Jonathan planned to go back into the office after the first week of school. But what did he need to do for the boys? Natalia had always handled it, and she'd made it seem effortless.

He couldn't rely on Alicia and Christina and had to do this by himself. He and the boys agreed that today, Sunday, would be the day they would go to the mall and buy new clothes, backpacks, and sneakers.

"Okay, guys, let's get busy. I'm ready to go."

The three boys came from different directions.

"I'm sitting in the front," called Alex.

Anthony complained, "But it is my turn."

Jonathan expelled a deep breath. "Here we go again. Guys, I'm not in the mood for this crap today. Can you just get in the damn car, and let's go?"

When they arrived at the mall, Jonathan glanced around, over-whelmed. "Okay, who shops where?" He groaned as all three answered at the same time. "Please, one at a time."

"Mom always takes us one at a time on different days, like a date," Anthony explained, distraught.

"Yeah, Dad, we'd each eat lunch with Mom and go to our favorite store and buy a few things to start school," Alex agreed.

Saddened and overwhelmed, Jonathan wracked his brain. How *did he not remember this*? If he could ask Natalia, she would say he never listened when she talked. It was an ongoing joke. *Damn it, Natalia, come home, and I will listen to every word that comes out of your mouth.* Tears stung his eyes. *Man up.*

"Okay, guys, well, a little late for that now. School starts in a few days. Whose favorite store is closest to where we're standing?"

Marc pointed to a store thirty feet away. "That's where Mom buys my stuff."

"Okay, Marc, you're the oldest. Pick out what you need. Be smart with your choices, son. Get nothing that wouldn't meet your mother's approval. I'll meet you at the front of the food court in an hour." He handed Marc cash to buy what he needed.

"Dad, you look tired. Are you okay?" Marc gazed at his dad, worried. The lines on his face seemed more profound, and his eyes no longer bright and reflected his pain. The hair at his temple showed some gray.

"Yeah, son, I'm okay," he forced a smile to reassure his son. "Who's next?" Jonathan asked.

Anthony was the next one to point out a place. "That's the skateboard store. Mom usually buys me stuff in there."

"Alex, what about you?" Jonathan asked.

Alex pointed to a store across from the skateboard store. "There. They sell the jeans that fit me best." Alex was tall and lean, built like Jonathan's father.

"Okay, do your thing. Here's the cash. Same rules as your brother."

Jonathan took Anthony into the skateboard store. Anthony ran over to the skateboards. "Son, we need to buy school clothing, shoes, and a backpack. Not another skateboard."

By the end of the shopping trip, each boy had new school clothes and most of what they needed for the first few months. Despite being overcome with sadness, Jonathan tried to make it a fun day. They had dinner at the food court, but he couldn't eat. He pushed his food around on his plate. The last time they were at the mall, they were with Natalia. Each chose a meal from a different restaurant and sampled each other's food. It was what they did with their mother. He visualized Natalia's smiling face, and his heart ached.

When they arrived home, Marc said, "Dad, the message light is blinking on the landline."

Jonathan hurried into the office to retrieve it. They rarely used the home phone. He and Natalia used their mobile phones for most communications. Most people reached him on his cell, which he found lying on his desk. He had forgotten to take it with him.

He dialed the voicemail. There was a message from Detective Peters. "Mr. Miller, please call me as soon as you receive this message. It's important."

Jonathan stared at the Detective's business card on his desk. After he took a deep breath to fortify himself, he dialed the number and closed the office door, his hands shaking.

"Peters," the detective answered.

"Jonathan Miller, returning your call."

"Mr. Miller, I regret to tell you we've found a body. We retrieved it from a marshy area in the lake. We only know that the corpse is female with blond hair, around the age of Natalia. Your wife's suitcase is here in our evidence lab. We're going to use her hairbrush for the DNA match."

Jonathan gripped the edge of his desk so hard his fingertips turned white. Tremors wracked his body as cold sweat trickled down his back. His mouth worked, but no sound came out. *Natalia...dead?* He thought as his brain screamed, *No.* His stomach churned, and tears slid down his cheeks. *Please, God, no. Don't let it be her.*

"Mr. Miller, are you there?"

"Um... Yes, I'm here," he replied, his voice cracking. "I'll fly out at once."

"No, don't do that. We don't even know if it is your wife. Stay put. We'll tell you when and if you need to come. Mr. Miller? Are you okay? Please try not to panic."

"No, I'm not okay. I will never be okay. At least not until my wife comes home. Please call me as soon as you know anything." Jonathan disconnected the call and stayed in the office for a while longer. He didn't want to upset the kids, so he waited until he had his emotions under control. Jonathan locked the door and felt extreme grief wash through him. If any of the boys knocked, he'd say he was paying bills.

By the time he left the office, it was dark. The boys were in bed, fast asleep. He peeked into their rooms to check in on them, then went to his and Natalia's bedroom. He could almost smell traces of her perfume still lingering.

"Natalia, where the fuck are you? I can't do any of this without you."

Never in a million years did he see his life being this way. He thought he and Natalia would grow old together and enjoy grand-children, as their parents did with their boys. He knew, deep in his heart, that she was alive. And he also knew that wherever Natalia was, she was fighting to get back to them.

THE WAITING WAS UNBEARABLE, and Jonathan was beside himself. After the longest two weeks of his life, Jonathan caved. He plopped down in his office chair and called Detective Peters.

"Mr. Miller, I didn't receive the results yet, which is why I didn't call you. I can't even imagine how difficult this is for you and your boys. We requested Mrs. Miller's dental records. The DNA test was inconclusive, and they've just arrived, and forensics is comparing them to the deceased. The minute I hear anything, I'll call you."

"Okay. To say things are difficult is putting it mildly. We have three kids who miss their mom. I miss my wife." Jonathan sighed.

"Understood. I have three, two girls and a boy. If anything happened to their mom, I couldn't function. These girls of mine are a handful. Like you, I have a wonderful relationship with my bride, even with the challenges of being a cop and being an ass. I assure you, the second I hear anything, I'll call you."

"Thank you," Jonathan said. He glanced at his favorite photo of his wife, it was a candid shot, and she wore a massive smile on her face. He remembered vividly the day he took it. She was sitting at a picnic table at his parent's, watching the boys play. He called her name. She turned and smiled, and he shot the photo. He still hadn't told the boys about the body they'd found. He glanced around the room. They had the house built right after they'd married. Every aspect, each item they bought, they'd carefully planned together. Their home reflected his wife and her love for her family. She wouldn't just up and leave it all. Of that, he was confident.

The following week, Jonathan sat in his office in Philadelphia, digesting the news he received from Detective Peters. The decomposed body wasn't a match for Natalia. The long wait had been agonizing, and the many setbacks left him mentally battered. That the remains weren't Natalia's left him relieved. However, it was short-lived. The pain remained, and the unknown remained. Where was she, and would the next body be hers?

Thirteen

"WHO IS WAITING UP FOR whom?" Richard asked. No one realized he had come in. He was dangling a set of keys in his hand. "Hi, sweetheart. You look lovely in that dress. Here are your keys to the house. A little birdie told me that tonight is "girls" night out. I also want to show you the alarm system."

"Oh, thank you," Susan followed, their footsteps echoed in the foyer. They tested the new key, and Richard explained the alarm. He then realized she didn't have a phone should she need to call home.

"Honey, take a quick ride with me?" he suggested. "I want to pick up a mobile phone for you."

"That's unnecessary. I wouldn't understand how to use it."

"I insist, and the Apple store will teach you how it works. The store isn't far."

Richard directed her to his favorite sports car. He tried to get the door for her, but she opened it herself and climbed in. He laughed at her independence as Jack had filled him in on the fun they had that morning and his new name for her.

Richard took her to the Apple store and told her to choose the phone she wanted. She picked the smaller smartphone. The associate had it up and running in mere seconds. He gave her a tutorial on how to use it. She told him she only needed to make calls and doubted she would remember everything he'd shown her. The Apple associate had plugged her father's info into her contacts app. That was it. One entry, and she realized how alone she was. She placed the phone into her purse and peered out the window. There was an overwhelming sadness deep inside her. Her heart was missing vital parts of her life that her brain couldn't retrieve. Her knees bounced as her lower lip trembled.

They arrived home in enough time for Susan to freshen up, play with Buddy, and get changed. Her closet appeared even fuller than when she'd left earlier and guessed the things had arrived from the personal shopper. She decided on a pair of white jeans with a turquoise top. Everything fit her perfectly. She slipped into a pair of white sandals.

As she walked down the hallway from the elevator, Richard stepped out of his study. "Wow, don't you look nice? That outfit is perfect for you. If you need anything else and you're up to shopping, either Jack or I will take you, and I'm sure Cora would like to go with you. There are credit cards in your wallet that will work in any of the stores. I want you to buy whatever you need or want."

"Thank you. I'll assess the closet tomorrow, but by the looks of things, I believe I'm more than adequately stocked." She smiled at him. "I'm very grateful."

"My pleasure, sweetheart." Joyful just to be in her presence, it warmed what he had thought of as his cold and broken heart. Even if she didn't remember him, he was confident she eventually would. The doorbell interrupted his thoughts.

"That would be Maria. Bye, everyone. Buddy, Momma loves you. See you later."

"Enjoy yourself, sweetheart," her father called out.

"Bye, your highness. Try not to dictate orders to the valet tonight," Jack said with a grin.

"Be quiet, silly man. I can do whatever I want, right?" Susan was laughing as she left the house.

"I enjoy the banter between you two. It's very refreshing," said Richard. "This once-quiet house is now full of laughter."

Cora nodded in agreement. "As much as my sarcastic husband worries me, he has a great relationship with Miss Susan."

"Hush, woman. She'll tell you off if she hears you call her 'Miss Susan.' She's as real as it gets. No putting on airs with that one," Jack warned. Although in his sixties, Jack kept fit and enjoyed his new-found friendship with Susan. He never had kids, but if he had, he could imagine them being just like her.

"A refreshing change," Richard commented, prideful.

Cora looked pensive as she bustled about the kitchen. Both men looked at each other and then back at her.

"What?" she asked.

"Well, you look concerned or worried. What about?" Richard asked.

"I'm just concerned whether she feels up to this. I'm a worry-wart."

"Hey, did any of us give her a curfew?" Jack asked, snickering as they joined in with laughter.

MARIA TOOK SUSAN TO Sur where they talked and connected better. Immediately after they ordered, she heard someone call her name. She glanced around and spotted TJ sitting at the bar, his stool turned, facing their table. As their eyes met, he slid off the seat and strode to their table. Anxiety coursed through her, and she licked her lips, reaching into her pocket for God knows what. She glared at him. "Well, it didn't take you long to be out and about town, did it?" he said snidely.

"Are you always this snarky or just with me?" Susan asked.

"You deserve it." He turned and went back to the bar and picked at the label on the beer bottle.

Humiliation heated Susan's cheeks, and she turned to Maria. "I have no clue what his problem is with me. That was embarrassing and uncalled for." A flush crept up her neck to her cheeks. She pushed in closer to the table as if it were armor.

Maria sighed and shook her head. "Let's ignore him, finish our dessert, and catch that movie."

"Please don't tell me the movie is one of *his*."

"Nope, you're safe." Maria laughed.

The movie was fun. Both women laughed throughout the entire film. As they walked back to the car, Susan said, "I don't want to sound corny or anything, but I needed this, and I enjoyed your company. Thanks for asking me."

"I did too. I haven't found many friendly women here. They're stuck on themselves or wrapped around being seen or married to famous guys. Or all they can discuss, once they find out I'm a plastic surgeon, is the benefits of Botox or other procedures to keep them young. I like to enjoy normal downtime with a female friend—just a casual girl's night. Let's do this again. I'll call you later this week to set a date. What kind of stuff do you like to do?"

Susan laughed out loud and shrugged her shoulders. "Remember, I'm a newborn?" Both women laughed.

"Until we figure that out, I'll choose things for us to do," Maria said.

"Agreed."

Maria brought Susan home, and they giggled like schoolgirls. After such a busy day, Susan fell asleep with a smile on her face. She enjoyed girl's night out and hoped there'd be more.

The ringing phone woke Susan. The bright sunlight streamed through her room as she reached for the phone, almost dropping it, pressing the button, and before she mumbled 'hello' she heard Maria's voice, "Well, your first foray into public has landed you publicity."

"What does that mean?" Susan inquired, yawning and stretching.

"Well, I can't help it. My guilty pleasure, I buy the local entertainment newspaper, and there is a shot of TJ at our table during your little 'discussion.'" Maria laughed.

"What does it say?" She laughed.

"I'll save it for you. If I don't see you today, I'll send it home with your dad, but it alludes to, 'is there trouble in paradise with confirmed bachelor TJ and his mystery woman? Stay tuned.' was the bold headline. It is hilarious, Susan." Maria exclaimed.

"Well, let's see where this story goes and if they identify the mystery woman," Susan commented. "Crazy."

Fourteen

JONATHAN TRIED TO MANAGE day-to-day tasks. He pulled back from his extended family in Christina and Alicia and hadn't attended a family function in months. Now thanksgiving approached. *Should he pack the kids up and take them to Florida to visit his parents? Should he invite them here? Did he even want to celebrate without his wife?* These questions kept going through his head. His thoughts were all over the place as he struggled daily to function. The unknown was the worst. Had the remains been hers, they could have grieved and tried to move on. But he and his boys looked for her in every crowd, every store. She was never far from their minds and hearts.

It was the second month of school and back to school night for the two older boys. Jonathan had to follow their classroom schedules. He thought, *How the hell can I do this with my boys in different schools?* Anthony's was the following evening.

The boys' grades were failing. All their teachers were giving them leeway because they were aware of the situation at home. The staff tried to reach them, but the boys were sad and fearful and missed their mom. They didn't take part in school activities as they had in the prior school years, sports, clubs, no extra-curricular activities. They missed Natalia, her family, close friends, and the school because she was an active member of the PTA.

Jonathan didn't have it in him to deal with it, but he knew he had to and told his kids to go back to working hard and being active, even if he couldn't bring himself to do the same. He was a frustrated, emotional mess. This situation riddled him with anxiety. He couldn't cope, yet he must. He tried his best to map out a route with Marc's help. Johnathan met the first teacher, introduced himself, and told the teacher that he had another school to get to for his other son.

Most teachers were sympathetic to his plight. Others were just speaking about their class, eager to finish and go home. About halfway through, Jonathan left. He couldn't do it anymore. He'd email the teachers he missed the following morning. Jonathan was beside himself with grief when he arrived home. The kids were in their respective bedrooms, watching TV.

He went into the bedroom he shared with his Natalia—his missing wife—the woman he hadn't talked to, seen, or kissed in months. Jonathan stepped into their closet and stared at her clothing hanging in a neat row. He buried his face in her bathrobe. Natalia's scent enveloped him. He inhaled it as though the deeper he breathed, the closer he was to her. Dropping to the floor, defeated, he sobbed and prayed that they'd find her. He didn't know which avenue to pursue that would lead him to his wife. His boys worried him, too. They've changed, they're quieter, sadder. They should have fun.

Anthony's room was next to his parent's room. He ran into Alex's room, upset when he overheard the meltdown. "I can hear Dad. He's losing it. What do we do?"

"Leave him to get it out of his system. It would embarrass him for us to see him," Alex said.

"Can I stay in your room tonight? I hear dad, and it makes me sad. Where is Mommy? Why can't we find her?" Tears were sliding down Anthony's cheeks.

"Yes, you can stay, but I have to finish this book for class tomorrow. Can you just chill without the TV?" Alex asked.

"Yes, g'night, Alex."

"Night Ant."

They felt Natalia's absence more as time passed. The boy's routine had changed. They missed all the extraordinary things their mother did with them and for them. Jonathan tried, but being out of the house for ten hours a day while Natalia raised them left him at a disadvantage. He wasn't privy to all that she did for their family, but he knew she doted on all of them.

Natalia loved all holidays, more so after she became a mother. She decorated the entire house and the outside for each holiday. Not once did she miss a special occasion. Valentine's day, too, hearts all over the place with their names and sweet messages. On the boy's birthdays, they woke to balloons in the family room and a small gift to open before school. She prepared birthday pancakes, and it was the only day she added candy sprinkles to the batter. She delivered cupcakes to the classroom, beaming with pride at her sons.

Natalia did the same for Jonathan, his favorite breakfast, a love note, and a small gift to begin his special day. They'd celebrate as a family with dinner and presents, typically on the weekend when their parents could attend. Jonathan and Natalia's parents got along wonderfully and took pride in their grandchildren. Catarina never referred to Jonathan as her son-in-law but as her son.

Jonathan's parents invited him and their grandsons to fly down to Florida for a few days in November. They knew the boys had a week off from school in early November for teachers' conferences. They lived in a three-bedroom ranch-style home in a fifty-five and older community, with plenty of things to keep their grandsons entertained. Besides spending time with them, they had another reason for being so determined that they visit. They wanted them to move down so Jonathan's parents could help with the boys.

Jonathan mentioned it to the boys, and they wanted to go. He refilled Anthony's allergy medicine at the pharmacy. He planned the vacation time at work, and the family of four flew to Central Florida in November. The boys swam in the pool every day, rode the golf cart, and played volleyball in one of the larger community pools. For the first time since June, they enjoyed themselves. The night before they planned to leave, Jonathan's father called a family meeting out on the lanai.

With his hands in his pockets, his father paced. "Jon, your mother and I want to help. We think you all should move down here. There is a school right in the area, a great school, and you can get a job down here. It might not pay as much, but you won't need as much down here. The cost of living is more affordable."

Anthony had silent tears falling down his face. Marc's mouth opened, his face and ears red, as he tapped his finger loudly on the tabletop, and Alex's eyebrows shot up. Jonathan and the boys never expected this. Throughout the entire conversation, Jonathan shook his head no.

"Dad, Mom, while I appreciate the generous offer, we're doing a lot better. We've got a rhythm now and plenty of help back home whenever we need it. The thing is, I don't need it as much. We." He pointed at his sons. "The four of us are learning as we go. We have this, Dad." Jonathan turned to Anthony, "Wipe the tears, son. We are not moving."

"Good, because Mom wouldn't look for us here. We need to be home so she could find us." Anthony replied, running his arm across his face, clearing the tears.

On the flight home from Florida, Jonathan had time to process his thoughts. While grateful for his parents' offer, he wouldn't leave the house he built with Natalia. He wasn't ready to make a move. He couldn't think beyond the current day. Natalia's disappearance took a toll on his sons. He understood she wouldn't do this purposely, and was keenly aware of the love his wife had for her sons. He never doubted it, but the unknown taunted him mercilessly.

The boys nagged for a dog. Jonathan didn't have it in him to add another living being to his responsibilities. He tried putting them off, and it worked for now, but he knew that the issue would eventually resurface. In the meantime, they returned to their routine. The boys went back to school, with Marc being the caregiver for a few hours until Jonathon arrived home from work.

On one day when Jon worked from home, the doorbell rang. He opened it and found a police officer waiting on the porch. Jonathan panicked, thinking he would tell him that Natalia was gone forever. "Mr. Miller, sorry to intrude on your time. We need to talk."

"Of course. Come in."

The officer's movements were jerky, and he was blinking rapidly. "I'm here about your wife's disappearance. Although the state police verified your whereabouts, higher-ups want a lie detector test. Would you be willing?"

"Absolutely. I love my wife and am lost without her. I couldn't, wouldn't ever see harm come to her at my hands." Jon agreed to go to the station the next afternoon and submit to the test. "Why do I need to do this when they verified everything? Do I need an attorney?"

"Someone high up is looking into unsolved cases. Your wife's disappearance is still on their radar. It's probably someone stretching their wings. As for an attorney, that's your decision." Before the police officer left, he took a business card from his wallet and handed it to Jonathan. "Mr. Miller, a good friend of mine, is a Private Investigator. He's a retired Detective. He's excellent and has a way about him that gets people to talk. Here's his card, do yourself a favor and contact him."

After the officer left, a sense of peace and happiness came over Jonathan. The investigation was still active. He was going to contact the P.I. immediately. If only a lead or clue would surface to guide them. He prayed to God, to his in-laws in heaven. Natalia always said that she would speak to her parents in heaven when she needed anything. She swore they still led her in the right direction. Jonathan tried, feeling a little foolish as he cruised into the dining room. Their cremains in the China cabinet, combined in a wooden box. "Mom, Dad, please watch over our girl and help her and help us find each other again. The boys are distraught. I'm a mess. We need your help."

Sighing, Jonathan shook his head and thought, *my wife and her notions,* but somehow, that slight gesture brought him hope. He smiled, thinking of the small rock she carried in her pocket. Her mother painted it with the word, "Blessed." She had it since childhood and whenever worried, she'd slip her hand into her pocket and hold on to it. He flipped the business card in his hand and decided he'd pay for the services with the insurance money to replace the van. He called, and after being advised of the fee schedule, he set up a meeting—just another waiting game.

As if life wasn't challenging enough for the Millers, the washer broke. Despite it all, Jonathan kept trying to work, ensuring the boy's grades improved and running the household, but his familiar, well-organized persona no longer existed. Stressed, scattered, and scared out of his mind, he reached out to Charlotte. Since Natalia and Charlotte were stay-at-home moms and spent much of their time together, he figured they'd use the same repair companies.

"Hey, Jon, you sound terrible. What is wrong? Besides the obvious?"

"Washer broke, and I'm behind in the laundry. Who fixes these? If it were a normal washer, I would attempt it. But it has a motherboard."

"Ace," she answered. "I'll text his contact to you. Bring the laundry here. I'll do it."

"No, but thanks. I'm going to the 'Suds and More' place over by the liquor store. Maybe I should buy a bottle or two and drink until I can't think any longer."

"Jon, don't do that. I wouldn't want you to have an issue. You're my favorite man," she said with conviction.

"Thanks, Char. You're a dear friend, and I love how you love our family and are always there for us. Text me the company's info. I'm heading out now to the laundromat."

Jonathan raided Natalia's coin jar and loaded up his car with the laundry. While waiting for the laundry, he called the contact Charlotte gave him and made an appointment to have the washer diagnosed in two days. Laundry took him all afternoon, and that was with tying up three washers and dryers the entire time. With every piece of laundry, he thought of Natalia. *Am I doing this, right? Is that how she would do it?*

His heart kept telling him she was alive as he vacillated between hope and despair.

Fifteen

AFTER HAVING THE BIOPSY, ultrasound, PET scan, and receiving the results, the doctors established a treatment plan to treat Richard's advanced prostate cancer. Richard had ignored the symptoms for an entire year, as there was no reason to treat it. He had been alone but not any longer. Now he had his Susan back. The surgeon scheduled Richard for surgery to remove his prostate. They planned hormone therapy to reduce his testosterone level along with an aggressive chemotherapy protocol. They set his surgery date. Now he had to tell his daughter.

With Richard's health issue and his upcoming surgery, he set up a meeting with his attorney to prepare a new will, leaving his entire estate to Susan. He would also generously appropriate funds for Cora and Jack, leaving them fiscally stable for the rest of their lives. Besides the house where they all lived in Beverly Hills, Richard had properties in Maui and Telluride and a beach house in Malibu. All his holdings would go to Susan, including stocks, bonds, mutual funds, cash, Donna's jewelry, and the properties.

Richard planned to teach her how to manage money, beginning at once. He thought everything should be in place legally and ironclad, just in case. *I can frankly say Susan spends judiciously,* he thought. *She buys only what she needs, not what she wants, because she can afford it.* He often transferred money into her checking account, but she never came close to spending it, nor did she go overboard with her credit cards. The most significant expense to date, the monthly car service, was at his request because he worried about her driving in the area. When Jack wasn't busy, he would take her. However, when unavailable, the car service was. Once he had everything in place with the attorney and financial advisors, Richard would discuss his health and Susan's plans.

They scheduled Richard's surgery for the following week. He spoke with Susan privately about his serious health issues once he learned of the date. Tears spilled down her cheeks, and for the first time, she hugged him. She assured him she would be there for every treatment and surgery. He lovingly gazed at his daughter. She was ashen, her chin quivered, and she wrapped her arms around herself as though cold. It broke his heart, as he never wanted to cause her any pain. He wanted to be her lifeline, and not a source of anxiety. Susan's behavior was quiet and reflective around her father since he shared the news.

Three days before the surgery, he asked, "Darling, why are you quiet these days, particularly around me? You aren't joking or taunting Jack like before," Richard pointed out.

She offered a small smile and looked at him. "I don't want to be annoying since you aren't well." Her gaze darted around the room.

He laughed. "Baby girl, hearing those taunts and banter back and forth brings joy to my heart. You bring joy to my heart. Please be yourself and continue to make this house lively again. Deal?"

"Deal." She smiled at the man she grew to love and respect.

SUSAN WAS GOING ABOUT her usual morning routine after speaking with Maria about her few seconds of fame the night before. Susan took her vitamins and waited for the coffee to brew while her father read the paper. As she reached for a cup, her phone rang.

"Unknown number," she whispered. Oddly, this frightened her. The few numbers listed in the contacts were her father's cell, their home landline, Cora and Jack's mobile, Maria's, her Aunt Nicole's, and Buddy's vet. She answered with trepidation, her finger hovering over the green button.

"Hello?"

"Susan, TJ here," he said, his voice abrupt and brisk.

"How did you get this number?"

"Your father. I'd like to take you to dinner tonight. I think we need to clear the air." She peered at her father and held out her hand, palm up, wanting to ask why he would give TJ her number.

"I don't need to 'clear the air.' The issues seem to be yours," she said.

"Are you still playing the memory game? Seriously?" he asked rudely.

"Mr. Smart Ass, this isn't a game. It's my *life*. Do you think I want to wake up every damn morning not knowing who the hell I am, where I've been?" she demanded heatedly. She didn't recall ever being so angry. Her father snickered, trying to hide behind his e-reader, and Susan stuck her tongue out at him.

"Okay, calm down. I'm sorry. Can I pick you up Friday night at seven? I must make a quick stop at a cocktail party. Then we can head to dinner. Cocktail attire in case you *forgot*." His tone was sarcastic when he said he stressed the word, 'forgot.'

"Friday? I don't think so. Why would I subject myself to your rude behavior?" She glanced at her father, who was nodding and mouthing the word "go."

"If I promise to behave, can we please discuss things?" he asked.

"I guess, but be honest, is your mother behind this?" Susan inquired. Nicole and Susan bonded after they spent an afternoon together. She had planned a lovely lunch, haircuts, and massages. Nicole was sweet and easy to like.

"Yes, while my mother may be a meddler, we should talk," he responded.

"I'll go with you, but only because your mother wants it."

"I'll pick you up at the house."

Curious, she thought when she hung up. TJ referred to it as "the house" and not "your house." Susan disconnected the call and sensed that someone was staring at her. She turned and saw that Cora was smiling. Jack wore a foolish grin. One she recognized as whenever he would say something sarcastic or funny. The doctor was about to combust from holding in his laughter.

She looked around the room at them. "What? Why are you all looking at me?"

Jack responded first. He couldn't contain himself and teased, "Her Highness has a date. Her first date—with a movie star."

"Jack, step away from the coffee mugs. They may become flying missiles soon," Susan exclaimed as she laughed at her friend.

Her remark brought her father into a full-blown laughing fit. Susan shot him the death stare, and he laughed even harder.

"Cora, you're smiling. Why? I agreed to meet him because of his mother. Why is this such exciting news? He's a rude, pompous ass, and I just agreed to subject myself to an evening with him."

"I was just going over items in your closet mentally. Would you like help in deciding what to wear?" Cora asked, ignoring Susan's complaint.

"Sure. I'm heading to work the first day," Susan said as she reached into her skirt pocket and mumbled, "I don't know why I keep doing this." Sighing, she addressed Cora, "If you can spare a minute or two, do you mind pulling out a few things? Please call me later if I need to grab anything from Nordstrom. I haven't attended a cocktail party before, not that I'm aware of, anyway." She shrugged her shoulders and walked away, shaking her head.

Richard struggled not to laugh out loud. His girl was sassy, quick-witted, and didn't take well to rudeness. He enjoyed watching her personality shine through. He could not believe his blessings at being reunited with her. Susan's physical health improved rapidly since her follow-up examination in his office when she had discarded the walker. And her mental health had followed suit. She followed Maria's orders to the letter and exercised in the pool, and she used the spa for pain relief. She tried to use the gym on her own but had found herself overwhelmed. Richard ordered physical therapy three times a week in their small home gym.

Once the therapist found she had mended, he hired a personal trainer to help her with her strength. After a month of training, Susan looked physically fit, and her pain had significantly reduced. She asked if Doc had a job she could do at the practice. Thrilled, he nodded his head vigorously. Richard would see his beloved daughter at work and home. He assigned to Susan the tasks he shared with Maria and Nancy. They had talked about the company each night over dinner, and now that the doctor released her from medical care, she could start her new position.

Susan arrived, not long later, for her first day of work with trepidation. Nancy was a complete professional and helpful in getting her familiar with the office. After a brief break for lunch, they reconvened in the supply room to gather their inventory sheets. Then, it was off to a computer to place orders. Nancy took her to the last room in the corridor and opened the door.

"Wow, pleasant office, Nancy."

"Glad you like it. It's yours. My office is across the hall and is just as nice."

"This is my office. You're serious?" Susan walked around the desk and discovered that someone had placed a framed picture of Buddy on her desk, and she smiled, knowing it was Doc. Nancy motioned for Susan to sit behind the desk and pulled up a chair alongside her.

She explained how to boot up the computer, asked her to set up a password, and logged her into the ordering sites. She passed Susan a card with all the web addresses in case her computer crashed.

Susan found the instructions straightforward and placed several orders herself. The delivery service would bring the supplies by ten o'clock the following day, at which time Nancy would assist her in storing and securing the inventory. Susan completed the computer work and investigated her office.

The large office boasted two doors, one a closet, where she found colorful lab coats hanging with her name, position, and the name of the practice embroidered on them. The other door led to a full bathroom with a shower. Susan assumed a doctor used it previously, in case it was necessary after a messy procedure. She was going to enjoy having a bathroom to herself. She took her purse from the storage room and placed it in the closet.

ON THE MORNING OF THE cocktail party, Susan kissed Buddy and stated she was leaving for the office. She waved to her family and went into the garage, where Jack was waiting for her. She hopped into the front seat next to him.

"You all set, your highness?"

"Yep. Let's go, a busy day ahead." She giggled. She wanted to be there when the shipment of medications arrived. Her father or Maria usually ordered the medicines. Now she had taken it over, and it freed them up to spend more time with their patients. Traffic was horrendous, as expected, because of rush hour. Susan made it to the office just before the shipment arrived and unpacked, counted, and secured everything. She realized the most common breast implants were missing from the order, but they were on the invoice as being received. She'd have to call the supplier and have the issue corrected. Susan and Maria referred to the implants as the "boobies."

Maria walked by the storage room, carrying two cups of coffee. She placed the black coffee on the table. "Good morning, Susan. Were you mumbling from the break room? Are you alright?"

"Good morning. What a morning. Do you have a minute, or are you headed to see a patient?"

"Nope, the first patient is in an hour," Maria said, glancing at the clock.

"I was mumbling because I'm missing boobies, but I'll resolve it." Susan then told her about the phone call from TJ. "Maria, I don't want to go. I agreed because Nicole asked him to do it. To clear the air." She made finger gestures when she said, 'clear the air.' Her face was crimson.

"Calm down. It's a cocktail party, not a firing squad. You can't talk there, but you can at dinner. Don't panic. If TJ raises his voice, it will call attention to him, and I doubt he wants negative attention. Paparazzi feed off that. We'll go to lunch and talk. Would that help?"

"I don't need an excuse to go to lunch with you. I'd love to," Susan agreed happily.

"What do you say we buy you a cocktail dress? A knock-your-socks-off cocktail dress? I'm happy when I look fabulous," Maria gesticulated, waving her hands.

"Well, there are several in my closet. We should check first. I'll call Cora, or we can pick up food for lunch on the way. If we find nothing suitable, we'll go shopping after work? What do you think?"

"That sounds wonderful. I'll stop by your office at noon. My next appointment isn't until three o'clock, just a follow-up. It won't take long if you want to leave early and get a jump on the shopping spree in case you don't luck out at home."

Susan finished in the storage room and called the company about the missing items. They assured her they would send the missing items at once. Because it was just the implants, she didn't need to be there when they arrived. Medication deliveries were a different story. Since most were narcotics, she required an accurate inventory. Susan telephoned Cora from her new office and asked if she wanted anything for lunch as they planned on takeout and to scope out her closet.

Cora said, "Don't you buy food. I'll make your favorite Asian bowls for lunch."

"I love those bowls, but I don't want you to go to any trouble," Susan said.

"No trouble at all. Jack requested them. It seems your partner in crime has the same tastes in food. Do you need Jack to come to pick you up?"

"No, thank you. Maria is driving. Thanks, Cora, for making lunch. I'll tell Maria. See you in about forty-five minutes."

Susan hurried down the hallway toward Maria's office. Just as she walked out with her purse and keys, Maria exclaimed, "Hey, you. Right on time."

"Yep, that would be me. Hey, how do I find TJs number on this thing?" Susan handed Maria her phone.

"Right here in recent calls. Why?"

"I don't think I can do this. It feels wrong," Susan said as she clutched her purse.

"It's just cocktails and dinner, not a weekend in Malibu. How's this for a plan? You go, and if things get weird and you want to come home, text, and I'll come to pick you up. I think the cocktail party is about networking, and your conversation won't take place there. He may talk in the car, though. Be yourself and not ashamed. You are not that person anymore and don't owe him anything. Good?"

"Yes, good. Thank you." The traffic was horrible as usual, but Susan and Maria made it in time because Maria learned the shortcuts.

Cora had lunch ready. The two women greeted Buddy and enjoyed their lunch outside by the pool. After lunch, they went upstairs and into Susan's room.

"Wow." Maria said. "This room is exceptional. Huge."

Susan said, "I love it. And I love that I have views of both the pool and the neighborhood." She pointed in both directions. "This is the closet." Susan walked to one of the two sets of double doors in her room and opened them, turning on the light. It was massive, and one side was full of clothing. The back and the other side were empty. There were purses, both casual and formal, same with the dress and shoes—a free-standing cabinet in the center with pull-out trays for jewelry.

Maria followed her inside and spotted a gorgeous royal blue dress through the plastic protective cover. Rushing over to it, she pulled the plastic back. The dress was sleeveless with a nude illusion top and back, making it appear strapless. The beads at the neck and sleeves matched the belt. Form-fitting and the fabric was incredible. "Try this one on while I look through the others," Maria said.

"Okay." Susan went into the bedroom to disrobe and tried on the dress. She peered at Maria. "What do you think?"

Maria held a pair of strappy high-heeled sandals in the exact color of the dress in her hands. "Wow. Here, step into these shoes. I'm glad that we treated ourselves to that pedicure the other day."

Susan slipped on the matching shoes. "Well, do you think this is appropriate for a cocktail party and dinner? I'm clueless."

"Perfect. Others are in the closet too, a black dress and a cream. Do you want to try those, too?" Maria asked, stepping back into the closet. "This closet is impressive."

"No, I think this is good for a first venture out into the party scene."

Maria returned with a matching evening bag, sighing. "I wish I had the space to update my closet. Maybe someday."

"You don't think this is too monochromatic? All the same color, from dress to shoes to bag?"

"I think it looks great. But if you want to add a bit of diversity, I found a pair of silver shoes with crystals like those on the dress. Would you like to try them on?" Maria asked.

"Sure," Susan replied. Maria carried the shoes and bag from the closet and placed them on the floor. Susan replaced one blue shoe with the silver and held a bag in each hand. "What do you think?"

Maria studied her pensively. "I do like both looks, but since this is an evening cocktail party, perhaps go with the silver." She had difficulty choosing, peering at each foot and then in the mirror. "Well, here's a thought. Why not call Nicole? She's always attending these things." Maria suggested.

"Great idea. I'll call now on speaker."

Nicole answered the phone on the first ring. "Hello, darling girl."

"Hi, Aunt Nicole. Can you help me with a decision? I have a cocktail party this evening. And dinner following. I have a question about the accessories that go with a blue cocktail dress. There are matching blue shoes and a bag. Also, silver shoes with similar crystals as on the dress and a matching bag. I'm out of my element here."

"I would say since this is an evening affair, to go with the silver. I should mention, however, if it were an afternoon affair, the matching blue would be fine," Nicole informed Susan.

Neither woman mentioned TJ and the fact she was going with him. "Thank you," Susan said. "I wish I had the sense to do the right thing in this town."

"Listen, honey, how about this? Next week, let's go shopping. I can give you pointers on how to dress for functions here. How is Wednesday?"

Susan glanced at Maria, who nodded her head. "That sounds great. Can I bring a friend? Perhaps she might learn a thing or two, providing her schedule is clear. What time do you think would work?"

"Well, I sleep late. What do you think about one o'clock? I'll pick you up at the practice," Nicole said. "Does that work?"

Susan glanced at Maria, who nodded. "Yes, Aunt Nicole. That's great. See you then."

"I hope you don't think I didn't value your opinions. I thought it would be a fun girls' day out."

"Susan, not at all. I'm excited to step out of my New York City box and embrace Beverly Hills," Maria said with enthusiasm.

At the loud ding of the bell, Cora pulled the door open and TJ stepped in. Susan was ready and was walking down the marble staircase. TJ greeted Cora and raised his head to the stairs as Susan descended.

Before he could catch himself, he exclaimed, "WOW. You look gorgeous." Realizing how excited he sounded, he turned off the charm and asked if she was ready, his tone abrupt. Buddy ran to greet TJ and bounced around him, tapping at his leg for attention. Worried at first about the dog hair getting on his suit, but he stooped down, gave Buddy a few pats on his head, and said, "Dude, chill. I'm taking your mom to a party, and I can't go all hairy. You understand, right?"

Buddy ran to his mom for love. She bent down and kissed his head. "You behave for Cora, you hear?"

Dr. Kline hurried from his study and into the foyer. "Hello there, TJ. You look good, son."

TJ preferred a casual, rugged look. He didn't wear suits often. "Thanks, Unk. I'm meeting with a potential producer for my next flick. My agent advised me to dress for success."

"Susan, you look breathtaking, honey. That dress is lovely. Enjoy your evening, you two," Susan's dad said.

"Thanks, Doc. I have my key should I be late," Susan said.

TJ escorted her to his vehicle and opened the door for her. After he strapped in himself, he looked at Susan and asked, "Doc?"

"Well, what would you prefer I call him?"

"Dad? Father? You used to call him Daddy,"

Susan whispered, "I don't remember." She stared at him like he was an opponent. Her heart raced, and her face heated. *What would make him think she was lying?* They rode in silence. Susan was angry but decided not to let her fury ruin her trip to Malibu. She hadn't been this far from home since arriving.

They arrived at the producer's house, it sat high on a hill, and the ocean crashed loudly against sand in the distance. TJ walked around to the passenger side, opened the door for Susan, and helped her climb out of the small sports car. He guided her to the front door, his hand on the small of her back. Despite her annoyance, the heat from his hand felt as though it branded her, leaving his mark on her skin.

The staff escorted them outside where the pool, full of artificial lotus flowers with lit candles, glistened. "there's my agent." TJ grabbed Susan's hand and walked toward him. "He is with the producer who is interested in signing me for his movie." He murmured out of the side of his mouth, almost in a whisper.

His agent introduced TJ to the producer and then asked, "Who is this beauty?"

"My apologies. Susan Kline, an old friend."

Susan received kisses on both sides of her face from the men. She smiled and said, "Hello, my pleasure to meet you both."

The producer asked, "Kline, Kline, why is that name familiar?"

TJ volunteered the info. "Her father is Richard Kline. He's a plastic surgeon who created the pathway to redirect damaged nerves to treat facial paralysis."

"Yes. Yes. He performed a procedure on my oldest son, who was born in India with a cleft palate. It was severe, but you can't tell now. Tell your father I said hello."

"I will. Thank you."

TJ introduced her to a plethora of people. She would never remember who they were and their relationship to the producer, even if she tried. She was also apprehensive about the conversation that was about to come during dinner. As TJ talked about business, she wandered around outside, smiling at people, but mainly enjoying the phenomenal view. TJ found her looking out over the wall to the ocean. "You will not jump, will you?" he snorted in a half-laugh.

Susan glared, her chin lifted, her eyebrows pulled together in a V. She was fearful that she might have used colorful words if she responded verbally. She counted to ten before she replied, "No, I'm not. But I must ask you, are you always this snarky or only to me?"

He didn't answer her question but said, "We have reservations. Are you ready to leave?"

"I am."

He took her hand and walked her through the pool area. The sun had set, and the photo flashes were more noticeable. *Someone was taking a lot of pictures.* Her grip tightened with each flicker of light.

"It's okay, Suzy Q, you'll get used to it," TJ said.

"Suzy Q? Where the hell did that come from?" Susan's eyes shot daggers at him.

"That's what I called you back when we dated." he shrugged his shoulder, confused as to why it offended her.

"Not to be rude, but I don't like that name. I'm an adult, and it sounds childish."

"Alright then, Susan, it is." He laughed, raising his hands. "I surrender."

TJ maneuvered the car onto the road leading down the mountain. It had significant curves, and she gripped the armrest and tried to take deep breaths to calm herself. Her head pounded and her heart raced. When they reached the main road, he took her to a lovely, upscale restaurant with beach views. The valet met them and guided Susan from the vehicle as TJ hustled to join her. He reached for her hand again as they approached the restaurant. Flashes went off, almost blinding her. Once inside, the maître d' approached. It seemed everyone knew TJ. "Right this way, Mr. Collins. Your table is ready."

TJ escorted Susan to the table, and the maître d' pulled out her chair. The table was by the window, with a superb view of the ocean. The sommelier arrived and presented the wine list to TJ. "Good evening, Mr. Collins. How are you and the lovely lady this evening?

Susan smiled and said, "Hello."

"Why don't we start with champagne. My favorite?" he asked the sommelier.

"Yes, Mr. Collins." the sommelier nodded and left them.

The server appeared with menus. "Good evening, Mr. Collins. Good evening, Miss." He handed them each a menu and announced the evening's specials. TJ ordered a steak and Susan a Cobb Salad.

TJ shook his head and remarked, "Don't tell me you're one of those that order a salad on a date."

Her temperature was rising again. Susan's face turned crimson. She glared and wanted to crack him on his head with the newly arrived bottle of champagne. She counted and inhaled audibly. "Number one, this isn't a date. Number two, I don't recall trying a Cobb salad, and it sounds delicious. Number three, I'm an adult and do as I see fit for *me*. Got it?"

TJ was appreciative that she kept her voice down, and her assertiveness surprised him. "So, noted." He said, exasperated. "I'm having a lot of trouble comprehending your loss of memory. For years we thought Susan was dead. And then suddenly, out of nowhere, you pop up. I will admit, you look exactly like what I presume Susan would look like as an adult, but your personality is the opposite of the Susan we all remember," he said.

"And when were you in my company last? What were we, seventeen, or eighteen, perhaps? Wouldn't you, looking back now, say we were kids? You have those memories. I don't. Are you the same person today you were at that age? Did you mature and become a better person?" she asked.

"Yes. I would say I'm a better, more mature version of myself," TJ agreed.

"Well, I'd like to think the same of myself. I have no memories of my past before waking up in my room. Not one. Not even the dog they found with me. I have scars I don't remember and that a vital part of my life is missing. Trust me. My life isn't easy. I can tell your father doesn't believe me. He thinks I'm after Doc's money. I don't ask him for anything, nor do I expect anything from him. I'm just trying to be the daughter he needs."

"Okay. I can't say I understand what it's like to lose your memories. I'll back off. Truce?"

"Truce," she said.

Being with TJ drained her, and she was eager to get home. When the food arrived, she ate most of the salad before laying the fork down. She gazed at TJ, who ate his entire meal, surprised by how fit and trim he was, and thought that his body wouldn't look this good for long if he eats this way all the time. It was apparent how solid he was. She saw his muscles through his suit jacket. Susan was out of her element and uncomfortable. She tried to make conversation, asking him questions about interests outside of filming.

"I love to surf on my time off, and I still love being on the water. Do you still surf?"

Susan laughed and shrugged. "Did I used to surf?"

"Sorry, I forgot. Yes, you were crazy good at it."

By the time dessert came, they were getting along much better and enjoying each other's company. Susan relaxed, and they shared the dessert special, laughing as the melted chocolate slid down his chin. She leaned over to wipe it with her napkin.

Her gentle touch sent a rush of heat to TJ's loins. The server arrived with a small, elegant folder with the check inside. TJ signed it and passed it back, leaving a hefty wad of cash next to his empty plate. He had slipped a substantial tip into the sommelier's folder earlier. TJ escorted her from the restaurant, hoping she wouldn't notice the customers taking pictures with their cell phones, aware that it made her uncomfortable. His car waited. TJ passed cash to the valet and assisted Susan into the vehicle.

She smiled and said, "Did you see how many customers took your picture?"

"I try to ignore it. I don't want to be *that* guy and make a scene. Let's face it. My 'fans' are how I make my money. I wouldn't be rude to them. Just concerned that you were unnerved by it."

"No, mostly, they tried to be discreet. I became a little nervous with all the popping sounds and the lights flashing from the street photographers. Are they always in your face like that?"

"A few of them hide and take a quick photo. Others are more aggressive and get right in my face. It comes with the territory." They were almost back to Beverly Hills when he asked if he could take her to Malibu Saturday into Sunday to practice their surfing skills. "We could stay at your dad's house. He gave me a set of keys."

"That sounds like fun. Can I let you know tomorrow?"

"Sure. Give me your phone." She handed him her phone. He added all his numbers to it, along with his address.

She looked at it and laughed. "Not sure I needed your fax number, but thanks."

"Just in case you ever want to fax over a little love note," he teased.

Sixteen

RICHARD FELT MUCH BETTER. Just knowing things were in place and that his daughter was aware of his issues made his stress level decrease. He took his medication orally, and mostly, he was tolerating it. While he felt well, he planned to take Susan to Telluride to show her the property. Now that it was cold enough, perhaps they'd ski. He planned to invite the Collins'.

He wanted to go for Thanksgiving. He had all these ideas as he prepared for the day. When he appeared in the kitchen for breakfast, he asked Cora, "Do you and Jack have plans for Thanksgiving? Invitations from family?"

Cora replied, "No, Doctor. My only family is my cousin Clara and her brood, and they're going to Disney in Florida. It beats me why they would go all the way there when the actual Disneyland is right here."

"I think for Disney fans, it's all about seeing different venues," Richard replied. "I wanted to speak to you about something. I'd like to take Susan to Telluride to show her the snow. Perhaps over the Thanksgiving holiday? I hoped you and Jack would come too, but not in a working capacity. I'm also planning to invite the Collins'. We'll fly over in the jet. What do you think?"

"That sounds lovely. I don't mind taking care of things."

"No. I'll order dinner from a caterer. I'll make the caretakers aware when we arrive. They'll go over and freshen the place and stock

152

the pantry. I just need a headcount so they can buy ample supplies. Do you want to check with Jack?"

"I'm sure he'd be delighted. That 'man-child' of mine loves and misses the snow. He was born in the cold," Cora said.

"I'll call Nicole once I arrive at the office. I hope they can make it."

"Doctor, once you get the headcount, please give me the number. I would prefer to reach out to the Telluride staff and mention a few things to stock. Would that be alright with you?"

"Of course. I'm sending the contact to your phone now. Thank you, Cora." He glanced into the family room. "Has Susan left for work already?"

"Yes, she wanted to get an early start on ordering supplies."

Susan had been coming into the office daily and was now the official Office Manager. She was a fast learner and excelled in her position. He was confident that everything would run seamlessly under her management. She'd proven herself fully capable of running the office and managing the non-medical staff. In the waiting room, Richard often found her chatting with patients, calming their fears, or reassuring advice. She made him enormously proud. He beamed with pride whenever she was in his presence. Every week, Richard's accountant directly deposited a salary commensurate with similar practices paid for the same position.

Richard took his car to the office, since Jack wasn't back from taking Susan yet. Once he arrived at the office, he looked at the highlighted printout on his desk. The printout displayed that day's appointments with colored highlights to identify procedures. There were alerts for anyone with health issues in their chart. He liked to review anyone with health concerns or reactions before the next operation. He studied the charts and walked to Susan's office to say good morning as her laughter and TJ's voice filtered from the speaker through the office. "TJ, you are a terrible man. Yes. I'll go to dinner with you, and if I order a salad, you will keep your pie hole shut."

"Pie hole?" TJ roared with laughter. "Where did you hear that phrase?"

She replied, "Jack."

"You're getting quite the education from Jack. Okay, silly girl, I'll pick you up tonight at seven."

Richard waited a few more seconds before entering Susan's office. She looked up from her computer and said, "Hey, Doc, what's up?"

"Good morning, sweetheart. Did I overhear you planned another date with TJ? What is that? About ten now? Would you say you are an 'item'?"

"Yes. We're going to dinner. And I don't know about an 'item' as you say. What does that even mean?" Susan asked, laughter in her voice.

Richard laughed with her. "Just a phrase I overheard." Shrugging his shoulders, he continued, "I wanted to go to Telluride for Thanksgiving. I've invited Cora and Jack, and I talked to Nicole. They're coming. Do you want to ask TJ, or shall I?"

"I'll ask him tonight. Would you mind if I asked Dr. Ross and her boyfriend to join us? Since the practice will be closed, you don't need Maria here, do you?"

"That would be wonderful. Tell Cora? She's reaching out to the caretakers with a grocery list and a headcount, so they prepare the correct number of rooms."

"Sounds like fun." Susan said. "I want to go shopping for winter things. I so dislike shopping," she whined, rolling her eyes.

"Here." Richard reached into his wallet. "This is the card of the personal shopper I used for most of your clothing. She has a record of your sizes. Call her, just tell her where you're going and for how long. She'll get you what you need. Relax, honey. We're all hoping to sit by the fire and relax unless you want to ski," Richard said.

"Sounds amazing. I'm looking forward to it."

TJ HAD ASKED SUSAN to go to Malibu for a weekend weeks ago. It never happened. The plan was to go this morning and stay at her father's house. TJ told her he was very punctual and would be there at ten. She had packed her bags the previous night and had her clothes ready for their excursion. She didn't own a wetsuit, but TJ told her that if she needed one, they'd buy one at the surf shop.

TJ texted Susan to wake her and told her he was leaving in five minutes to pick her up. Having overslept, she tossed the bed sheets back to get ready. She dressed in denim shorts, a pink tank top, and Sperry's. Susan hurried downstairs as she pulled her hair up into a messy bun. Finding the kitchen empty and the house seemed oddly quiet.

She walked toward the laundry room and discovered the door open and the gate to Buddy's yard wide open. She heard Cora and Jack yelling Buddy's name in the distance. Susan realized what had happened. Buddy had gotten out. Her heart pounded in her chest so vigorously she felt it would open her chest wall. Susan screamed, a pure guttural sound coming from deep within her, "Buddy." stressing the syllables. Fear paralyzed her, and she slid to her knees. TJ had come into the house as an earth-shattering scream bounced through the empty foyer. He followed the sound to the laundry room and found Susan hysterically on the floor.

"Susan, honey, what's the matter? Talk to me." he asked, stooping down to her. He leaned forward and his brows furrowed.

Between Susan's gut-wrenching sobs, TJ deciphered Buddy had somehow gotten out. He saw Cora walk toward the house as Jack wandered farther away. Cora saw Susan on the floor. "Miss Susan, the landscapers left the gate open. We told those men to leave that area alone. And that Jack takes care of it." She was wringing a tissue in her hands. "We should have put a lock on the damn gate. Honey, Jack will find him. I promise you."

TJ ran outside to help Jack. They came back several hours later, empty-handed and sweating. Susan was distraught and sobbing uncontrollably as she rocked in the kitchen chair, a pile of tear-filled tissues in a heap on the table.

TJ asked Cora, "Should I call her father?"

"He has back-to-back surgeries today. I'll call Dr. Ross." Cora left the room. Susan vacillated between the front door and the laundry room door, hoping Buddy remembered his way home.

After his procedures, Dr. Kline rushed home. Buddy loved his golf cart rides. Richard and Jack perused the neighborhood in the golf cart to search. They hoped he'd hear the motor's hum and would come running. Richard worried about the heat and the effects on the little guy. When they arrived home empty-handed, Susan made flyers. She found a template on the internet and included the most recent picture Jack took of Buddy.

She asked Jack to take her out to hang them up. In this affluent area, residents didn't post flyers and such in the neighborhood. Jack looked to Dr. Kline for guidance. He nodded. Jack, Susan, and TJ hopped into TJ's car and coasted the neighborhood, looking for places to put the flyers. Susan walked up to mansions and stuck them on the front gates.

A week later, Susan remained distraught and grief-stricken. She hadn't been to the office and went out each day to distribute more flyers and walk the area looking for her little pug. Her eyes were red, her face blotchy, and her clothes hung on her from missing meals.

Richard was sick. Not from the treatments, but from seeing his daughter so distraught. He had no clue how to make her happy. Susan was despondent. He had placed ads for Buddy, offered rewards, very pricey rewards. Nothing. He assumed the coyotes captured him, and that sickened him. *That joyful little dog,* he thought. He didn't mention coyotes, but the fear was ever present in Richard's mind.

Since Susan was so inconsolable and hysterical, Richard stayed out of her way. When at home, he rode the golf cart looking for Buddy, hour after hour, day after day. His heart broke for his little girl and the dog. He loved that little guy, his little cookie thief. Whenever Richard took his nighttime snack into his study, Buddy would follow, jump into Richard's lap, and sneak an entire cookie. Richard enjoyed watching Buddy be naughty. Buddy's favorite toy was still under his desk. He picked it up and placed it near his wife's picture. He picked up a photo of his wife and said aloud, "Donna, you flew our daughter home on your angel wings. Now I need you to bring her puppy back to her. She's breaking my heart. Can you please do that from heaven? Please send Buddy back home?" Richard kissed his wife good night, as he did every night before heading upstairs.

TJ came by every day after he finished on set. "Honey, why is this affecting you this much? You loved him, and I imagine how difficult it is for you, but you're not eating, not functioning, and crying all the time."

"Because he was mine, a connection to my past. They found him with me. I'm so alone and worried that I failed my precious little pug boy. I can't imagine how he's surviving alone. He was always with one of us." She fidgeted, her palms clammy, then hunched over, grasping her stomach as though she would be ill at any moment.

"I understand. Why don't you change into your pajamas? I'll go get us food." He leaned forward and gripped her hand. Kissing the top of her head, he up righted himself.

"Okay." She walked upstairs, her head down, taking one step at a time. She shuffled into her bedroom, took clean things from her bureau, and jumped in the shower. Sitting on the shower floor, she cried, with her head resting on her bent knees. After, Susan pulled her wet hair up into a ponytail and went into the kitchen where TJ waited, unpacking the food bag.

"Look, I bought comfort food. Burgers, fries, and ice cream." He tried to smile, eager to help.

Susan was pale, red-eyed, and hoarse from crying. She tried to eat, but her throat was dry, making her pick at the food.

TJ asked, "Are you sleeping?"

She shook her head.

He said, "Okay, let's go to your room, and I'll tuck you in and stay with you until you fall asleep."

She nodded again. TJ held her hand, and they walked up the vast staircase together, each lost in thought. Susan worried if her Buddy was alive, and TJ wondered what he could do to bring her smile back. She cried herself to sleep. He removed her from his chest, and she'd soaked his shirt with her tears. He tucked her in, kissed her forehead, and slipped out. On a break from filming for the next two days because the film was in the editing process, he called his gym friend whose girlfriend volunteered for an animal rescue. He called Chad and explained what happened. "Hang on a sec, dude, let me put Lexi on the phone."

TJ heard him yell, "Hey Lexi, my buddy TJ is on the phone. He needs to find a breed-specific rescue. Can you come to the phone?"

"Be right there." She was tending to several foster dogs. She rushed over to the phone and grabbed it. "Hey TJ, this is Lexi. How can I help?"

"My girlfriend's pug is missing, and she's heartbroken. Do you know of any rescues that shelter pugs? The question is twofold. Should he come in as a stray, and if not, I'd like to adopt one for her. Not that it could replace her little guy, but it would give her someone to love. If you knew her story, you would know why this is especially important."

"Yes, someone in Los Angeles that I network with. Her name is Sophia, and she's known as 'The Pug Angel' in the rescue world. Can I share your phone number with her? I'll call her now."

"Yes, please do," TJ informed her.

"One of us will call you soon," Lexi said. She passed the phone back to Chad and strode into the spare bedroom she used as an office. She picked up her cell phone from the charger and called Sophia.

Sophia answered, "Oh, no, Lexi. Don't tell me you found a homeless pug. I'm overwhelmed with the puppies."

"Puppies?"

"I didn't tell you. I rescued a pregnant mother a few months ago. She has the most adorable pug puppies destroying my house."

"No. I'm not calling with a rescue. However, my man's gym bud lost his pug. Well, not his, but his girlfriend's pug got out. Landscapers left the yard gate open. He's been missing for about a week. Did you get any male strays in from the shelter recently?"

"That's sad. Nope. No new strays. Did they call the shelters?"

"Yes, they did. I'm know how busy you are, but can you reach out to him? His girl is a mess over this and not functioning. He wants to rescue a pug to help heal her."

"I'll call him, but gifting animals is never a good thing in my book," Sophia said.

"I agree, but Chad says this would be okay. They wouldn't surrender. The entire household is troubled."

"Okay, text his number, and I'll speak to him."

"Thanks, Sophia, you're the best." Sophia tended to the puppies before making the call to TJ.

When he answered, she said, "Hi, this is Sophia from Pug rescue." He was grateful she called. He explained Susan's story and asked him if he could come to her house in Los Angeles. She agreed, and he was there within the hour. He rang the doorbell, and with it, the chaos ensued. High pitched barking and screaming coming from inside the home. He flinched and thought, *perhaps I should've tapped on the door*. Sophia appeared at the door with a tiny pug puppy in her arms.

"Hi Sophia, I'm TJ." If she recognized him, she didn't acknowledge it. She invited him inside. They talked in the puppy playroom. He sat on the floor with the puppies, and the other pugs in her care were all over him. He asked about the adoption process. She mentioned she had an application process and adoption donations. He asked if she could expedite the application process if he gave her his girlfriend's name and references. Sophia handed him a paper version of the application. He completed it, still on the floor, with Susan's information, and asked the adoption fee as an older pug fell asleep, her head on his thigh.

She reviewed the application, called the vet. Her reference was Dr. Kline. She looked up at TJ, "Dr. Kline? The famous plastic surgeon?"

"Yes."

"Okay, you've played with all the pugs. Those three are mine and not up for adoption. The puppies and the chubby girl sleeping on your leg is."

"How old is the chubby girl, and how long has she been with you?"

"She's six years old and has no known health issues. She needs to lose a little weight. She's good with kids, pets. She has been here for at least five months."

"Why is she in rescue?"

"Owner had a baby and no time for the dog," Sophia said.

"How sad for her," he said. "I think a puppy for Susan. If Buddy comes home, I fear he will be too feisty for Candi."

Sophia's heart dropped, and she wanted to cry for Candi. She thought she had a home for her at last.

"Is it okay if I adopt Candi for myself? I'm on the set a lot, but my housekeeper lives with me, and she is an animal lover. Candi could also hang out in my trailer when I'm working."

Sophia erupted into tears. "That would be wonderful."

"Please, don't cry. I've had about enough tears for a while. Is it okay for me to take this lovely lady and to pick out one of these little terrors for Susan?"

"Of course. Let me grab Miss Candi's harness and leash. And I'll get you a carrier for the little one."

TJ sat on the floor again, playing with the tiny terrors. The little black one was very demanding and playful, and he couldn't resist it. Sophia came back into the playroom with everything he needed.

"Sophia, I think I like this little black one. Is it a male or a female?"

"That little monster is a female. She's a terror awake and a cuddle pug when tired."

"She's the one. She's feisty, like Susan."

Sophia offered him iced tea. He accepted, and they talked for what seemed like hours. He received quite an education. After listening to her story and what she does for animals, it amazed him. She did it alone—a one-person operation.

"Listen, Sophia," he said, "I don't want to come off pompous or arrogant, but do you know who I am?"

"Yes, I do," she replied.

"I have to thank you for being respectful and not asking for pictures and autographs."

"I'll have your autograph on that check you're about to write," she joked.

"Not when you cash it. But what I would say is allow me to be your benefactor? I love what you do. Let me be a part of it, even if only financial."

"I'm trying not to cry, but that would be amazing. Can I hug you? Or would that be inappropriate?" Sophia asked.

TJ pulled Sophia into a bear hug. "Okay, this is a check for the adoptions. I'll call my accountant, and he will be in touch. I'll also tell Susan about your work, and I bet you won't be a one-person operation long. Sophia, I'm very thankful you pushed this through. Susan is broken-hearted."

"She's a lucky girl," Sophia remarked.

He left the check on the table, gathered up the tiny terror, and handed her to Sophia. Sophia kissed her and told her to be a good girl. She slid her into the carrier for safety. She walked Candi to the car and showed TJ how to buckle both the carrier and Candi inside the vehicle. Candi sat in the front seat with her new dad.

After he arrived at the house, TJ called Cora and asked her to open the front door because he had his arms full. He unbuckled Candi first and let her out with the leash attached to his wrist. He reached into the carrier and retrieved the baby terror.

He stepped inside and went toward the kitchen with Candi on a leash and the baby in his arms. Cora squealed, and he motioned her to be quiet.

"Where's Susan?" he whispered. Cora motioned on the lanai.

He handed Cora Candi's leash and whispered, "She's mine."

He strolled outside. Susan sat on the lounge chair, her knees up and her head in her folded arms across her knees. He went over and sat at the foot of her chair, hiding the teething terror out of sight. The puppy used his fingers as teething toys.

"How are you today, honey?" he asked.

"I'm terrible. I miss Buddy, and I'm so scared for him," Susan replied, weeping, lifting her head slightly and peering at him through red puffy eyes. "Are you aware that Coyotes steal family pets around here? It is so populated, yet animals disappear. I don't want to think that a predator took him.

"Would this little girl help you ease the pain until we find Buddy?"

"TJ, what are you talking about?"

TJ turned around to show her the baby girl. "Her name was Lily at the rescue, but you can name her what you want."

Susan took her and buried her face in her fur and cried. She was mumbling into the puppy's neck, thanking him, promising to keep her safe forever. As she hugged Lily, the puppy teethed on her hair. She lifted her head toward TJ. Her face blotchy, and her eyes were red and swollen from crying, but she never looked more beautiful to him. It was at that moment TJ realized he was still in love with his childhood sweetheart.

"TJ, I'm speechless."

"Do you like her?" he asked, his eyes wide and his eyebrows raised.

"Like her? I'm in love, and when we find Buddy, they will be best friends." She smiled. It was her first smile in a week, and it relieved him. Her smile took his breath away.

Susan stood with the little one in her arms and said, "We should bring her in. It's too hot out here for a little puppy."

"Wait. Before you go in, there is something else. What you see inside is mine. Don't get attached."

Susan gazed at him, and tilted her head tilted to the left. She hurried inside, where she heard Cora cooing. Curious, she followed Cora's voice and saw an older chubby pug. She turned to TJ. "And who is this?"

"This is Candi. She's a rescue too. She's going home with me."

Susan jumped into TJ's arms and hugged him tightly. She reached up and gently kissed him, "You're amazing. Thank you so much. Can you tell me how you found these babies?"

He told her all about Sophia and her rescue and how he was a benefactor. Just as he predicted, Susan said, "I want to help Sophia too."

"Well, you enjoy that little chewing machine. There are toys that the pup can nibble on in that bag. Sophia sent them.' TJ pointed to the canvas pouch. "I want to take my new roommate home.

He didn't realize he left his cell phone in the car. When he peered at it, there was a message from Sophia. She was crying. *"Oh my God, TJ, the adoption donation totaled seven hundred dollars, five for the baby and two for Candi. You left a check here for ten thousand dollars. Please call me."*

TJ went home and introduced Candi to his housekeeper. He took her for a walk, and when she became tired, he lifted her and carried her home. At the obnoxious click of the camera, TJs head snapped up. "Oh well, girl, I hope you like your picture taken. Will happen a lot." He called Sophia and told her to take the check and cash it. His accountant would be in touch, and he and Susan may stop by tomorrow to return the carrier. He mentioned Susan wanted to meet her.

"Tomorrow is excellent. The afternoon is better for me. Is that alright with you?"

"Yes. See you then."

Seventeen

RICHARD'S SURGERY WAS more detailed than the doctors initially suspected, but he did well despite his age. His cancer proved invasive and aggressive. The surgeon did the best he could, and now the chemotherapy would have to do the rest of the work.

Cora and Susan researched and created a diet that eliminated all processed foods and GMOs. Cora mostly cooked organic, but now she planned to be extra vigilant and prepared foods with antioxidants and foods that build the immune system to fight off cancer.

Once Richard returned to his hospital room, he found Susan passed out on the sofa. He smiled and asked them to be as quiet as possible as she needed sleep. She woke up when she sensed a presence in the room. "You're back. How are you? Do you need anything? Do you need to sleep?"

"Susan, honey, take a breath, please. I'm all right, just a little painful. I'll most likely sleep. What I want is for you to go home and eat dinner. Check on Lily and text me a picture of her. Please stay home this evening. Sleep in your bed. These are not requests, darling girl. Those are direct orders from your father."

"And if I ignore those direct orders?" she teased. "What happens? Are you going to spank me?" she joked.

"My word, 'spanked?' Your mother and I never spanked you." Richard replied, his expression pinched.

"Doc, joking. I will obey you this time." she said with a smile and a wink. She leaned over and kissed his cheek.

"My darling girl, I love how feisty and sassy you are, like that little puppy of yours. Kiss that little puppy head for me, and don't forget to text me a picture."

Susan called Jack and took the elevator downstairs to the gift shop. She chose flowers for delivery to his room, along with his favorite hard candy. The kind he always kept in his pocket and shared with her as if she were still a little girl.

Jack arrived, and Susan was home in less than an hour. Cora had her dinner warming and Lily in her arms. She greeted both Cora and her new baby. Susan grabbed her dinner from the warming oven and sat down to eat with Lily on her lap. Cora mentioned that perhaps that might not be such a wise idea as it may lead to rude habits.

"Just this one time. Lily's preoccupied, gnawing on my belt," Susan didn't think her baby teeth were strong enough to do any damage to the belt. The doorbell rang, echoing to the kitchen. Cora's brow wrinkled, surprised to hear the bell this time of day.

"It may be TJ checking in on us," Susan commented, continuing with her meal.

The voice from the other room was unrecognizable, and she couldn't hear the conversation. Cora walked in with a woman Susan hadn't met before. But the pup in the stranger's arms she recognized right away. She looked at the woman, and Buddy wiggled in excitement.

Susan grabbed the baby from her lap and handed her to Cora. She ran over to Buddy, took him from the stranger, and buried her face in his fur, crying, "Little man, where were you? I felt like it ripped my heart from my chest." She then looked up to the woman. "Thank you, thank you. Where did you find him?"

"I'm Helen, your neighbor from across the road. I just returned from vacation this morning and found this little guy in my house.

My housekeeper found him. Unfortunately, she speaks little English and hasn't left the house as she's been ill. When I unlocked the front door, I found this flyer in my bushes. I read it and never expected to see this little guy inside my house. He's well taken care of and enjoyed playing with my dogs. I'm sorry to put you through such anguish. She wanted to keep him safe until I returned."

"I can't thank you enough for this." Susan turned to Cora and said, "Please grab the reward money."

Helen smiled. Her bright blue eyes twinkled. "I don't want the reward. Donate it to an animal rescue, please."

"What a coincidence. I'm planning on volunteering with a rescue as soon as my father is on the mend. I'll do that. Again, Helen, I can't thank you enough."

"You're welcome. If it had been one of mine, I would be frantic."

Susan walked the pretty blonde to the door and thanked her again. She returned to the kitchen, and Buddy was sitting on her seat finishing Susan's dinner. The baby, Lily, bounced up and down, trying to jump onto the chair with him. "Welcome home, little man. Did you enjoy the rest of my chicken?" Susan laughed. "Now, come down and meet your baby sister."

Buddy jumped off the chair and stood still as this energetic, crazy puppy jumped all over him, nudging him with her tiny body, nipping at him. He let her do it all. He looked at Susan as if to say, "Are you crazy? What is this thing?"

Jack came in from the garage and discovered Buddy was home. "Little dude, you're back. I missed you. And look here. We have a baby too."

Jack tossed a foam ball, and the two pugs competed for it. They both lost interest and ran around the family room and kitchen until they plopped down from exhaustion. Buddy woke first, took a drink, and ran into the family room. Lily followed and did the same. Buddy climbed onto his favorite chair. Lily tried to join him, but it was too tiny to make the jump. She cried until Jack lifted her, and she snuggled in with Buddy and slept with her new friend. Susan took that picture and texted it to her father. When he didn't respond, she assumed he was asleep. Before the three of them went to bed, she called the number the hospital gave her to check in. They said her father had broth and was resting.

Richard spent a week in the hospital before being transported home to recover. Once home, Susan got him out of bed and into a chair every morning after breakfast. He refused her help in the bathroom, so Susan hired a private nurse to come every day. They had a routine, and after his shower, he would walk around with the nurse's help and then sit in the chair. Susan opened the drapes in the morning to allow sunlight to brighten the room.

Richard's first few day's home from the hospital had been rough. Being the patient was difficult for him. Susan took excellent care of him and ensured that he took his medications and ate well.

Susan spent time in the office to oversee supplies once a week for a half-day. Richard planned to be off for the unforeseeable future and to decide if he should retire. Susan opposed the retiring idea because he loved his job and asked him to return first and then choose. He agreed with his daughter's sage advice.

Maria checked in each morning before the practice opened. She brought up TJ's casual mention of marriage during a conversation, and Susan abruptly changed the subject.

"So, are you going to boff him or marry him? What's the holdup girl?" Maria asked.

"Maria. You're terrible, and nope. I'm scared. But everything you and my father said makes sense. I need to process all of it a little more."

"Don't think. You think things to death. Just do it. Tell him you accept. And when your father is well enough, make plans to go to

Malibu and spend the weekend with that hot man of yours and consummate this thing." Maria said, with laughter in her voice.

"You're bad." Susan said, laughing.

"I am, but you love me," Maria joked.

WHILE RICHARD RECOVERED, he caught up on his reading on his tablet, medical journals that he rarely had time to delve into while working. Each time Susan left the house, she'd return with the society papers for her father, his guilty pleasure. Whenever TJ appeared with her or with Candi, he would show the photo and read the clip, excitement in his voice, his eyes bright. The rumor mills ran rampant, and the headlines. The articles alluded to a committed relationship, and that made Richard happy. He wanted this for his child.

"TJ spotted with Susan Kline at Sur, having an intimate dinner."

"TJ spotted on Rodeo Drive shopping with Susan Kline, daughter of a famous plastic surgeon."

The trip to Telluride for Thanksgiving had been outstanding. Everyone went—TJ, Cora, Jack, Thomas, Nicole, Maria, and Vincent, her boyfriend. And, of course, the three pugs. Paparazzi spotted TJ around town with his Pug Candi. He and Susan both became sponsors of Sophia's rescue. TJ had professional photos taken with him and Candi. He signed them, and Sophia held a fundraiser using his autographed pictures while they were in Colorado.

He loved Susan, but she remained somewhat reserved. He wanted ed to propose at Thanksgiving because everyone that mattered would be present. She overheard him mentioning it to Maria. She approached him in private.

"TJ, I love you, but I can't proceed with any serious commitment. I'm not saying no, only that I need time to figure out what is missing in my life. Please don't give up on me yet."

"Oh honey, I won't, and when the time is right, you'll tell me. I'd be lying if I said I'm not disappointed."

Susan's heart thumped. She wanted to say yes, but her past haunted her, and she feared being intimate with him. *What was that like, would I be okay, and would he enjoy it? Would I? Should I get on birth control?* Susan kissed him and thanked him.

Eighteen

DISTRACTION WAS JONATHAN'S plan every day since Natalia disappeared. He decided that cleaning out the basement storage room would keep him out of his head. This room was ample, and Jonathan had installed shelving all around. Behind the man cave, it housed holiday decorations, the boys' sports equipment, and things from his and Natalia's past. He found her desk plate with her name and title. He keenly remembered the first time they met.

It was her first day on the job. He'd been there for two years. They worked in different office areas, but that afternoon, there was a quick training session for the new software. In the conference room, their eyes immediately found each other, and the mutual attraction was instantaneous. He couldn't take his eyes off her. The instructor asked everyone to go around the table and introduce themselves, their title, and how long they worked for the company. While sitting on the other side of the table from Natalia, Jonathan said, "I'm Jonathan Miller, a Junior Financial Analyst, and I've been with the company for two years."

When it was Natalia's turn, she said, "I'm Natalia Conte, a Loss Mitigation Specialist, and this is my first day." Most of the people wished her luck and told her what an excellent team she'd joined.

"Working with the mortgage team?". Jonathan remembered Natalia's smile like it was yesterday. It hit him like a ton of bricks. He'd met his wife that day, and he knew it.

The morning training session had proved thorough and informative. Natalia loved working on computers and enjoyed learning new software. At one time, she had thought about changing her major to Computer Science. The instructor told them to take an hour for lunch, and they would reconvene at one-thirty. He mentioned there was a buffet set up down in the oasis courtesy of the software company. Jonathan made his way over to her and asked if he could show her the way.

She smiled and said, "That would be nice. Thank you."

He asked her what college she had attended and if she lived in Philadelphia.

"No. I'm in New Jersey and was born in Philadelphia, but we moved before I started school. I attended Stockton University."

"Are you still at home?"

Natalia smiled. "Yes, I'm back home, closer to work. No siblings but wonderful parents, so no need to rent a place. I lived in a rental home outside of Atlantic City during my last year in college. My two best friends still live there, and I did until this past weekend when it became time to prepare for this job. You? What is your story?"

"Older sister, she's married and lives in New York with her husband and two little girls, Allie and Genna. They're twins. My parents live outside of Philadelphia in Quakertown. I attended Drexel University majoring in finance and currently rent a house in Northeast Philly."

Once they arrived at the oasis, Natalia remembered that she'd seen this area on the day of her interview. She said to Jonathan, "I walked through here during my interview and wondered how they used this enormous space. It was empty then." Currently, it boasted a massive buffet table with food and beverages and little café tables that sat two or four. They each made a plate, and Jonathan led her to a table for two. They chatted politely. Natalia was nervous, but Jonathan put her at ease right away.

Natalia has been working there for about a week when he asked her out on a first date. She asked if there had been a policy prohibiting dating between employees.

He replied, "If you work in the same department, then yes. We work for different departments and teams, and we're on different floors. We should be okay," he said, as his brain screamed, *say yes.*

Natalia said, "Well, in that case, yes, I would love to go to dinner with you."

Jonathan and Natalia's relationship had taken off quickly. Both had been in relationships in the past, but nothing like this. They both adored each other and got along well. They became engaged in six months and married six months later.

After the wedding, the young couple lived in Jonathan's rental house in Philadelphia. Natalia wanted to live closer to her parents, and they found a new neighborhood nearer to them. They chose the floor plan and the model they liked the most, with their future family in mind. Their home had plenty of space for children. They decided on everything together, which was easy as their design preferences were remarkably similar. In nine months, the contractors completed their home. And they look forward to beginning the next phase of their lives.

They bought contemporary furniture and put Jonathan's leather sectional in the man cave in the basement. They had requested that the builder subdivide the basement into separate rooms. The largest being what Jonathan referred to as the "man cave." For another place, they planned to buy exercise equipment. There was a small storage room, and the last one, a craft room, for Natalia. Almost two years later, they furnished the house, and they enjoyed making the home theirs.

Natalia found out she was pregnant in their second year of marriage. The news delighted them both, and they were excited to be parents. Natalia's parents couldn't contain their joy, and they were talking about buying nursery furniture. Natalia glanced at Jonathan and shook her head as if to say, "Let it go." She appreciated Jonathan preferred to pay his way. However, knowing it thrilled her generous parents, Jon wouldn't push the agenda.

Alexander and Anthony eventually followed Marc, all born via cesarean section. Their life was hectic, crazy, and joyful, and Jonathan loved it. As Natalia's return to work date approached, Jonathan eased into a discussion after returning from putting Marc to bed. "Babe, I'm aware your mom is planning to take care of Marc, but that promotion comes with a significant salary increase. Would you like to stay home and be my domestic goddess?"

She laughed at his title. "Are you sure we can swing it? This mortgage is manageable easily with both of us working, but on one income?"

"Babe, what is my job? Don't you think I've figured out everything? I'm not so sure about those wonderful vacations we've taken in the past. We can still take nice ones, just not as lavish."

"In that case, I would love to be your 'Domestic Goddess' and a full-time momma."

As Jonathan's memories flooded his mind, he found her wedding gown preserved in a box. He returned it to the shelf. "I miss you, Nat, so damn much." He finished cleaning and rearranging the storage room, tossed what he discarded into his trunk, and took it to the donation center.

Nineteen

RICHARD LEARNED TJ had planned to propose to his daughter in Telluride over Thanksgiving. He hadn't been eavesdropping, but Susan left the intercom on, and the button in the kitchen stuck when she asked him what he wanted for lunch. He understood she kept Cora in her confidence. Disappointed, he learned she had turned him down, asking for more time. Nothing would make him more content than for his child to be happy. TJ, being wealthy in his own right, made Richard unconcerned that he would marry her for her inheritance.

He worried about bringing up the conversation he had overheard to Susan. She brought up their lunch and set it up at the table in his room, which he used for reading medical journals. A deep cherry wood table that matched the bedroom set and was by the window overlooking the pool. Susan sat down across from her father.

He seemed hesitant, and Susan asked him what was wrong. She'd learned, after living with him for over a year, to read his moods and expressions.

"Forgive me, sweet girl. I understand that you're a grown woman. But you will always be my baby girl, my sweet girl. The intercom button stuck in the kitchen."

Her face paled and she licked her lips. "Yes, my love. I apologize. I overheard the conversation. I didn't intend to listen, but I couldn't turn it off from up here. TJ loves you. He has always loved you. He seems to make you smile and enjoy life more. Won't you reconsider? I understand your worries. Trust me, I researched and had private investigators searching for the possibility of you having another family. I could have grandchildren. Believe me, baby girl, we searched for you for many years. All roads led to San Francisco, and then the trail went cold. He offered her the notes from the investigators." Then he asked, "Do you love him?"

Susan nodded affirmatively, her eyes shining with unshed tears.

"Then accept the ring. Let's plan a wedding. It is time to move on with your future, my darling girl."

"Okay, Dad, I'll speak with TJ this evening. We're going out for dinner."

His heart exploded with joy. She called him, 'dad.' It was the first time since she had been home. *Dad.* For Susan, the word naturally came out of her mouth. For him, a joyful, long-awaited moment. A name he hadn't heard for over twenty years. A beam spread across his face.

Susan smiled back, but wanted to speak with Maria about her inner turmoil. Plopping down in a leather chair by the window in his room, she tapped her phone. She was now close enough to her father to hold the conversation in his presence. Susan told her everything. Her doubts and concerns and the fact that she may want to marry TJ.

Maria listened before she responded. "Susan, this is my opinion. Please hear me out," Maria began. "I'm aware the gynecologist stated, based on the cervical exam, that you possibly had a child. Perhaps you were unmarried, and maybe the child didn't make it. I would think after all this time, someone, your family, would look for you. Don't you agree? I believe you should move on with your life. You have a man, a sweet, silly man, and he compliments your personality wonderfully. You don't need to worry about him getting his grubby paws on your father's money, as he's wealthy and a popular movie star. Have you done the deed yet?"

"Oh, stop. I'm not answering that." she said, laughing. She hung up and asked her father if he felt okay and whether he needed help to get back into bed. He stated he was marvelous and thrilled she was going to say "yes" to TJ.

Susan's reply was, "You people all ganged up on me." Her father caught the smirk and realized she was joking.

TJ called Susan at his regular time after he finished work. They were wrapping things up now, and they told him they nominated him for an "Academy Award" for his last film. Excited, Susan gushed her congratulations.

TJ gave her the date and said, "I hope you will be my escort. And it would be even better if you wore my ring."

"What ring?" she asked. Unsure if he wanted to give her the engagement ring, she previously refused.

"Any ring." He laughed. "I meant the engagement ring. I would love to marry you this minute, but to deprive my mother of planning a wedding. She would behead me first."

"Alright, you propose when you're ready. Think about this, though. I don't know who or what can show up in my future."

"I understand, but I believe someone would've come forward by now, but you're mine. And I see pugs in our future."

She laughed and said, "That works." But that slight tinge of worry resurfaced. *Where was I all those years?*

TJ asked Cora if she would help him. He would like all the family present for the official proposal and inquired if she wouldn't mind orchestrating it. She wouldn't have to cook because Richard wanted it catered and hosted at their house so that Richard could be present. "This is a secret from Susan. Can you be discreet?" TJ asked.

Honored that they included her in the planning, Cora called Nicole and invited them to dinner Friday night. She mentioned

Richard wanted a family dinner. She also asked Maria and her boyfriend Vincent. Cora then spoke to the caterer and had menus emailed to her. She reached out to TJ and told him that everyone would attend and asked him if he wanted to go over food selections, telling her to choose Susan's favorites.

Hanging up the phone, TJ thought about Susan and the next step they were about to take. He had always loved her, even during the times he didn't like her. Especially during those years when she changed. This mature version of his Susan he adored. She was intelligent, kind, sweet, sexy, and every time he saw her, his heart skipped a beat. He was eager to propose.

At last, he was joining their families. He checked and rechecked the ring in his pocket. He combed his thick hair in the mirror and smiled.

WHILE SUSAN WORKED in the office, her father called a few times, with bogus questions to judge how long she would be there if there were any issues. He gathered she would be home around three. Cora planned dinner for five. He told Jack that if she were to ask for a ride home before three, to stall and pick her up no sooner. Susan made it easy when she called at three to check on her father and told him she was heading to the salon for a trim.

Richard called Cora on the intercom. "I worked everything out. Susan's having her hair done at three. Give us plenty of time to get dinner set up." Excited, Richard happily placed an order for expensive champagne after the proposal. He stood gazing out of his bedroom window for a few minutes. The sun peeked from behind the tall palm trees of Beverly Hills. He smiled, remembering Susan and the first time she saw a palm tree during their evening stroll. She had been two years old at the time and asked, "What dis?" and after he told her, she'd called it a "falm free." He padded over to his bed and climbed in for a short nap, planning his daughter's wedding in his head, until sleep took over.

Susan left the office and walked to the salon she had been using regularly. She had her hair trimmed, a manicure, and a pedicure, her routine, which was long overdue since her father's surgery. Two hours later, she called the car service for a ride. They were local, and the wait was minimal. She arrived home and strolled into the kitchen. She leaned over and watched as Cora frosted the cake. "That looks delicious. What is the occasion?"

"Your father is coming down to the dinner table tonight. He requested a family dinner," Cora responded.

Susan reached for a piece of fruit and kissed Cora's cheek, and said, "You're the best."

"Where are the crazies?" Susan asked, referring to the pugs.

"With Jack. He had a headache and is resting in the recliner, and those two can't resist a snuggle buddy. I closed the door to my suite as caterers are coming soon, and we don't want the little terrors to escape."

"I won't disturb them then. I'm glad you had dinner catered. We can be a big crowd and a lot of work. I hate when you spend the entire time in the kitchen and would rather see you at the table enjoying the food with us."

"I don't mind, but a break is nice too," Cora said.

Knowing her father was napping, Susan crept to her room to change for dinner. Family events were casual. She chose a floral sundress that she had just bought and a pair of sandals with a two-inch heels. She often wore heels around TJ because he was so much taller than her. She learned what was fashionable by watching others at various events and outings, personalizing her looks by adding her creative touches. She was often in the magazine that featured the 'Who Wore It Best' section and had been the fashion editor's selection each time she appeared.

As she came down the stairs, TJ burst through the door. He stared as Susan descended, exclaiming, "Hello," as the word dragged on, "hot momma." He waited for her to walk down the remaining few steps before planting a big kiss on her lips. He gazed into her eyes and said, "You look and smell amazing. Those lips of yours make me want to nibble them." He handed her flowers.

"You are a terrible flirt, but thank you. Where's Candi? It is a family dinner, after all." Susan stated.

TJ held up his hand and answered, "Relax. She ran right into the house as soon as I opened the door. You didn't see her run by?"

"No, you burst in with such energy I saw nothing but you." Susan replied.

"Should I be flattered or insulted?" TJ asked.

Susan laughed and stretched to kiss him again, winding her arms around his neck. They held hands as they entered the dining room. TJ realized Richard was missing from the table. He slipped out as Susan spoke with his parents and asked Cora where he was. She replied Richard was upstairs dressing. He asked Cora if he could go up. He wanted to talk with Richard in private.

"Of course, go on up," Cora replied with a bright smile.

TJ bounded up the back staircase. He knocked on Richards's door. Richard opened it and smiled at TJ, and he invited him in.

"Unk, I wanted to do this right. Can I please marry your daughter?"

"Son, you take that up with her. I'm sure by now you realize she has a mind of her own and that she's sassy and feisty. Can you handle all of that?" Richard raised his eyebrows, tucked in his chin, his smile enigmatic.

Pounding his chest, TJ laughed and said, "Me, Tarzan. Me. Strong man."

They laughed at the shared memory. As youngsters, they watched the old Tarzan movies TJ was Tarzan and Susan, his "Jane."

Once, while playing, he climbed a gigantic tree in his yard. He reached to pull Susan up and fell, breaking his arm, which ended the "swinging on the vines" for them.

"You have my blessing, but don't say I didn't warn you."

TJ escorted Richard to the elevator. They walked down the hallway together. Buddy found them first and ran toward his 'Poppa.' Buddy loved his Poppa. Lily wanted in on the action and Candi. It delighted Richard, as he loved the puppies. He teased TJ, "You need to train your 'children,' they're a wild bunch."

After Cora's cake and dessert, TJ stood up and said, "I'd like to talk to Susan for a minute."

Susan realized this dinner was a setup, and arrogantly she said, "What about?"

As TJ floundered, she smiled. He recognized the smile, one that spread across her face when she naughty. She'd surmised the real reason for the family dinner. She was standing at the table as she'd just returned from the kitchen after clearing the dinner dishes. TJ strode to her and took her into his arms, "I love you. I think I've loved you from the moment you were born, the screaming bratty baby. Will you marry me?" he asked.

"Did you just seriously call me a brat and then ask me to marry you? The nerve of you. Yes," she whispered in his ear.

Nicole panicked. She didn't hear the answer but thought TJ annoyed Susan with his smart mouth and peered around for an item to throw at her son. She found a dinner roll and plunked it on the side of his head.

"Ma, relax, she said yes." He rubbed his head. "You've got quite a throw there, Mom." he exclaimed, rubbing the breadcrumbs from his hair.

TJ chose a beautiful platinum setting with a three-carat round diamond with diamonds surrounding the band. He had the matching wedding ring in his safe.

Susan held up her hand and said, "beautiful. I love it." Everyone was talking all at once. The excitement in the room was palpable. Susan was too. However, that nagging suspicion was always there, making her pulse quicken as she thought of the unknown life she'd led. Susan glanced at her father's smile. His eyes crinkled from his broad smile, brighter than she'd seen since he confided about his illness.

Twenty

CHRISTMAS FLEW BY FOR the Millers. For the first time, Jonathan had to do all the holiday shopping himself. Natalia had always made Christmas special for their family and friends, including hosting the Feast of the Seven Fishes, a traditional Italian Christmas Eve dinner. Her absence left a massive void for her husband and sons and Christina, Alicia, and their families. Christina hosted and prepared dishes quite different from their customary seafood selections, knowing that would make Natalia's absence more painful than it already was.

Jonathan's memories of Natalia consumed him during the holidays, leaving him sad and quiet. Jonathan struggled with each day. Getting out of bed was a challenge. He looked at pictures of Natalia, praying she was alive somewhere. Vacillating between despair and anger, he spoke to the photos, yelling and crying in fear and frustration. Her absence tormented him. Several times a day, he searched social media, pug rescue chat rooms, and various other search engines using her married and maiden name, Miller, and Conte. He hoped somehow that he'd find a clue.

Early on a wintry Saturday morning in February, Jonathan climbed out of bed and padded to the bathroom, the cold bathroom floor tiles sending painful chills through his bare feet and to his ankles. At any moment, Marc would barge in, demanding a ride to an overnight camping trip with a friend and his family. Natalia would have been a nervous wreck if she had to do this. She babied her sons and hadn't readily embraced significant milestones. She'd always claimed she wanted them to be her babies forever.

As the water heated in the shower, Jonathan peered into the mirror. He saw an old and worn version of himself. He rubbed his stubble and thought, *I desperately need to shave, or maybe I should just grow a beard.* Natalia didn't like the beard he grew annually for 'No Shave November,' a fundraiser held at work for cancer awareness. The men donated the money they would have spent on shaving supplies to provide educational materials about cancer awareness. He remembered Natalia matched his donation, grateful to see his clean-shaven face on December first.

Jonathan had been in frequent touch with Mike Gorman, the private investigator he'd hired, who still didn't have any leads.

Marc stepped into the room. "Dad, are you ready? We can't be late."

"We won't be late, son. It doesn't take that long to get there?"

Marc huffed as he left the room, eager to go on his first camping trip.

Jonathan had hoped to enjoy a cup of coffee before leaving, but knowing he would not win this battle. Grabbing his car keys, he opened the garage door. Natalia's empty spot is a constant reminder of her disappearance. The insurance company paid the value of her minivan at the time of the accident, and he hadn't replaced it. He'd put the money into their joint savings account.

Marc had his new sleeping bag ready and all the gear he would need for the weekend trip. The temperatures were getting chillier, and Jonathan worried whether he'd be warm enough. His face was pink from the colder air as he tossed his gear into the trunk. He plopped in the passenger seat and grinned at his father. "Dad, I'll be careful, I promise. I'll listen to Mr. Williams. And I'll be in a cabin too. It'll be fun to sleep by the fireplace."

Jonathan thought, *oh shit, and so it begins, letting the kids fly from the nest.* He knew the cabin wasn't far away, and Jonathan could get there quickly in an emergency. Yet, he was more worried than he expected to be. Maybe because he knew Natalia would have been, and he had to be the voice of reason, and it was just one overnight.

Sunday evening, as Jonathan began preparing dinner, he thought of Natalia, as he always did. He didn't make any changes and did things just as she would.

Marc strode in from the garage just as Jonathan was placing dinner on the table. "Hi, son. Did you have fun? Were you careful?"

"Yes, Dad, careful. I had a fun time." Marc monopolized the conversation over dinner with the fun things he did and learned while camping. He turned to his father. "Thanks for trusting me, Dad."

Anthony glanced up from his dinner as he scratched the side of his head. "Dad, do we have snacks?"

"Yes, son, unless you guys polished them all off. I haven't cleaned up dinner yet, and you're worried about snacks?"

"Well, not for this minute, but my favorite action star is on TV tonight for an award. Can I stay up late and watch?"

"Yes, you can watch." He often paid little attention when Natalia turned on the award show, but Anthony enjoyed it. Jonathan checked the pantry and saw the snacks still sealed in their packages. "There are plenty of snacks in here."

They were eating dinner in the dining room, as they had a better view of the living room TV. Anthony wanted to see who his favorite star took as his date. They finished dinner just as the actors and actresses arrived. The three boys helped clear the table, but Anthony didn't want to miss his idol. His two older brothers picked up the slack and helped their father with the dishes.

Jonathan, Marc, and Alex were loading the dishwasher and putting the food away when Anthony screamed, "It's Mommy, Dad.

Mom is on TV." In his panic, his high-pitched voice flowed through the rooms. "We found you, Mom, we found you."

Twenty-one

THE AWARD CEREMONY approached, and TJ mentioned to Susan that she might want to wear a designer gown. Many designers would reach out to her, and she should choose sensibly. Someone who would style her in something Susan felt appropriate and nothing outlandish.

Once the engagement hit the entertainment newspapers, Susan had become inundated with requests from various fashion houses asking to design her gown for the Oscars and her wedding gown. She decided on an unknown designer for her Oscar gown. Joy, newly arrived from Milan, would design a dress only for her. She wanted to wait for the wedding gown until after the Oscars. It would be a fashion overload to do it all at once.

Susan expected a team to arrive at the Kline house to deliver the finished gown, do her hair, nails, and makeup. The designer herself would come to dress her. Susan, out of her element but comforted, knew that this designer would listen to her requests. The jewelry deliveries had arrived, requested by Joy to accessorize the gown.

On the day of the event, Susan woke early. She played with the pugs and went for a swim. She had just finished her shower when people arrived to get Susan ready. There were so many of them, hairstylists, makeup artists, and dress designers. They occupied her bathroom, closet, and bedroom. The pugs were very curious, but Jack thought they'd be safer inside his and Cora's suite.

The final transformation was amazing. Susan's gown, a backless navy-blue colored halter top, skimmed her body and featured a high slit and low back. Her blonde hair, worn long but pushed to the side, held a diamond clip the jeweler had sent over. She refused to wear the ring that the jeweler had sent, preferring to wear her engagement ring. She also wore a pair of long diamond earrings that the jeweler provided. The accessories were simple and elegant.

Richard, Cora, and Jack stood in the foyer, waiting for her.

"My darling girl, you look breathtaking." Richard said as she walked carefully down the intimidating staircase.

Cora exclaimed, "Oh, Miss Susan, you look like a movie star, just beautiful." She turned to Richard. "Imagine what a stunning bride she will make."

"Your royal highness, you are perfect. Those stars are going to be very jealous." Jack said.

After a few pictures, Susan kissed each one of her family and turned to her father, hugged him, and said, "Thanks, Dad, for everything. Your patience with the craziness of having so many strange people in the house and for your love. I love you."

Richard stood, hot tears stinging his eyes when the front door burst open, and TJ entered the house in all his masculine glory. Susan's first thought was, *Wow. He's boisterous when he's happy. But so handsome.*

He took one look at his future bride and said, "Holy shit, I'm the luckiest man alive. You look ... you look—there are no words that do justice in describing how stunning you look. Boy, are all the girls going to hate you. You, my gorgeous future bride. Can I kiss you?"

Cora answered for Susan, "Kiss her, but be gentle. You cannot mess her up."

He leaned over and put a peck on her lips. He whispered in her ear, "We can save the rest for later." TJ stood for photos, his chest out, shoulders focusing on the cameras while he held his fiancée. As they prepared to leave, TJ told everyone not to wait up for her as he was sure they would attend after parties and may not be home until morning. TJ assisted Susan into the limo for the trip to the theater.

It delighted Richard, knowing his daughter had come full circle and was finally safe and at home with him. Cora made a light dinner, and the three of them ate in the kitchen. They played cards until Richard yawned, and his movements were slower than usual. Cora noticed the dark circles under his eyes and his fatigue. Cora suggested Jack accompany Richard to his room, and once there, he offered to help Richard ready for bed.

He said, "No, I'm only tired. I'm going to change into my pajamas and climb right into bed."

Richard turned on the TV just in time to watch his beloved daughter on the red carpet with her future husband. She was a hit with the crowd. The TV commentators stated who she was and how stunning she looked. He was happy and proud of her. His daughter was elegant and beautiful. His heart burst with joy and love for his precious daughter.

Richard laid his head down on his pillow, prayed for forgiveness, and fell asleep for eternity. He left this earthly world loved by his child, knowing that he protected her for life.

SUSAN AND TJ SAT NEXT to each other in the limo. She asked TJ if he was nervous.

He replied, "No, I'm happy to be attending with you. This is a first for you. Are you nervous?"

"Very. The butterflies in my stomach have butterflies." A small smile appeared on Susan's lips, her eyes wide, and she gripped his hand. He peered intensely into her eyes, and she thought he would ravish her right there. Susan wanted to kiss him, but it would mess up her hair and makeup. The stylists reminded her several times throughout the day.

She leaned over and gently pecked his cheek. "I love you."

He smiled and said, "I love you too."

They arrived at the theater and waited in line when the vehicle door opened. TJ climbed out first and guided Susan from the car. Photographers, hundreds of them, were taking their pictures. Flashes exploded around them as the fans cheered for TJ, chanting his name. The spectators lined the barricades and called out to him. Smiling and waving, he held onto Susan's hand. TJ pulled her to him, planted a gentle kiss on her lips, and the crowd went wild.

Upon entering the theater, a reporter from Entertainment Now approached for an interview. The journalist asked TJ who the stunning lady was. He replied, "My love," and gave her name.

The journalist turned to Susan and asked who designed her dress. She told him it was the creation of a new designer by the name of Joy from Milan. She then asked Susan to turn around and show off her gown. The entire interview was on live TV. It delighted TJ that his fans responded so positively to Susan. The journalist thanked them, and they entered the cocktail party.

Later, an usher escorted them to their seats, and TJ asked if she needed anything.

Susan glanced around and recognized the people she had seen on TV. "No, I'm fine," she replied.

"Okay, my love, the awards should begin soon."

"Are you nervous yet? Are you prepared with a speech?" she asked.

"No speech. I'll just wing it. Who said I need a speech, anyway? I may not win. The competition is tough."

She whispered in his ear, "Forgive me, but will this be your first Oscar?"

He whispered back into her ear, "Nope. There are three at home. You smell divine, and I've already won. I have you."

She smiled at him and said, "Make it four. You'll win this one too. I sense it." She was nervous and excited to be there with him. The lights dimmed, and the Master of Ceremonies appeared. *That's my neighbor*, she thought. She whispered in TJs ear that it was the woman who brought Buddy back. He just smiled. Her naivete was refreshing.

When it came time for the best leading actor award, TJ was up against four major actors. "And the award goes to..."

Susan held her breath and squeezed his large hand.

"TJ COLLINS..."

Susan kissed him on his lips. She was incredibly proud of him. He ran up on stage with lipstick on his mouth, which the MC came over and wiped off, making a joke about what a lovely shade it was on him.

TJ thanked God, his parents, and Susan for coming back into his life. He thanked his agent, producer, and director, and others involved with the film. He then mentioned the remarkable Pug rescue where he rescued his little lady and asked people to donate to shelters and animal rescues before the music played and he had to walk off. He hurried backstage for interviews and photos but asked to have Susan brought to him.

Twenty-two

JONATHAN, MARC, AND Alex rushed into the living room. They caught the tail end of Susan and TJ's walk on the red carpet. Jonathan thought it looked just like her, and the body language was Natalia's. He hit the record button.

They sat down and continued to watch. A journalist approached TJ and his date. During the interview, they were hoping for a close view of the woman's face. When the Journalist asked her who designed her dress, they zoomed in on her face. It was Natalia.

Instinctually Jonathan yelled at the TV, "What the fuck, Nat?" He grabbed his phone and called the private investigator he had hired. "Mike, it's Jon. Are you anywhere near a TV?"

He said, "I could be, but my wife has the awards on TV."

"Can you go to the TV, please? We saw Natalia. I'm confident that we just saw my wife on TV. Her body language. Everything."

Jonathan listened as Mike thumped down the stairs. Rapidly breathing as he descended the stairs. "Jon, you're on speaker now." He turned to his wife and said, "Please tell me you recorded this."

She said she had since it was the girl's bedtime. "Next commercial break, I'll scan for the interview. I'm running into my office for that photo of her and the dog." He still had Jonathan on speaker. He placed the photo on the coffee table, and his wife said, "That's the lady TJ Collins was with on the red carpet."

Mike's heart raced, and he hoped this was a lead. "Are you sure, Carole?"

"Yes, I'm sure. Although she dressed like a movie star, that's her. The same smile, the same color hair, eyes."

At the next commercial break, Mike told Jonathan that he would call him back. He handed the remote to Carole and asked her to rewind to the red-carpet interview. It was TJ Collins with Susan Kline. He admitted she looked like the picture. He asked his wife, "Are the after-parties shown on TV?"

She replied, "You will see the winners on all the channels tonight and all day tomorrow."

"Did he win? Carole, record all that you can. You can fast forward to live TV now."

"They haven't presented the best male actor award yet," Carole said.

He stayed to watch. Once they presented the award and announced TJ the winner, Mike called Jonathan back and asked, "Well, do you still think that is Natalia?"

"Yes. That woman is Natalia. And did you hear that acceptance speech? He mentioned pugs. It must be her. It is too surreal to be a coincidence."

"Jon, do you think she ran away with him?"

"I don't know what the hell to think. I'm angry, joyful. What do we do?"

"Let me work on this. I want to find out who this Susan Kline is, who Dr. Kline is. I'll take a few days, but I'll be in touch every step of the way. Jon, you cannot involve yourself. We have to do this discreetly, as we don't want to spook her."

"I understand, and I trust you."

JONATHAN, ANXIOUS SINCE seeing Natalia last night on TV, didn't go to work and kept the boy's home. He invited Christina, Alicia, and Charlotte over to brainstorm.

They came to see the recorded version he had on his TV again. Charlotte saw it last night but missed the red-carpet interview. She watched when TJ received his award and a brief flash of the kiss. Not enough to say it was Natalia, though. Everyone agreed after viewing the recording that the woman was Natalia. But why? What made her leave?

Jonathan booted Natalia's laptop and pounded in her email password. Natalia didn't keep secrets, and he knew the passwords. He checked her email for anything that could come from TJ and found nothing, mostly spam, and the older emails were mostly PTO or related to the rescue. Jonathan logged onto her social media page, just posts from friends stating they missed her and were praying for her. He checked her favorite movies, books, and music. Nothing appeared related to TJ Collins. "There is nothing here that would link her to TJ Collins. Was he at the fundraiser, and it was love at first sight?" Jonathan asked them.

Christina pulled out her cell phone and called Kathy. "Hey, Kathy, Christina here. Can I ask you a question about the fundraiser almost two years ago, the time Natalia went missing? Did you guys have any special guests?"

Jonathan motioned, "Say nothing."

"No special guests at all. Our usual fundraiser," she answered.

"Who did Natalia hang out with?" Christina asked.

"Mostly me and my sister, like I told the police. She socialized, but we were always in the same room. I wish I could tell you more. But there wasn't anymore. We kind of hung out together the whole time."

"Thanks, Kathy. That's most helpful."

"What now, Jon?" Alicia asked.

"Well, Mike is working on it. He didn't want her spooked in the event she left us. If she didn't leave, he didn't want anyone spooked at this point."

"That makes sense, I guess." Wide-eyed, her brow creased, Charlotte ran her hand through her hair.

Twenty-three

SUSAN SAT ALONE, ENJOYING the next presentation when a young man in a tuxedo leaned into the aisle where she sat and inquired, "Miss Kline?" At her nod, he said, "Mr. Collins asked me to escort you backstage to where he's giving interviews."

Susan followed the young man backstage, where TJ waited for her. TJ held her hand and kept her close for every interview with each affiliate. Susan was proud of him and full of pride to be with him. TJ's arm snaked around her waist. The sensual, woodsy citrus scent of his cologne teased her nostrils. The warmth of his hand around her waist or on the small of her back made Susan's body tremble with TJ's nearness, keeping her in a hyper-awareness of his masculinity.

They appeared briefly at the Governor's Ball, long enough to enjoy a meal and mingle. TJ couldn't wait to be alone with Susan. He contacted his driver to tell him they would be outside in five minutes. He took his fiancée's hand and escorted her to the limo, assisting her, then following in behind her. The driver was taking them to TJ's house, with TJ grasping her hand the entire time. TJ unlocked the door and began kissing her as soon as they walked into the foyer. Susan's body trembled, her heart pounded, a sea of anxiety churning in her gut. She had scars, and she didn't remember being intimate before. She almost bolted, but TJ hung onto her even tighter.

He kissed her like he was starving. The more he kissed her, the better she tasted. He tried to slow down, not to frighten her. Even though his body encouraged him to ravish her, he couldn't. He escorted her upstairs to his bedroom, all the while kissing her. Once in his room, he kicked the door closed, not breaking the kiss.

Susan erased her mind of nagging thoughts and just went with her feelings. The intensity of his kisses brought on an unfamiliar passion stirring deep inside. Susan returned TJ's ardent kiss, exploring his mouth with her tongue. She reached up and unbuttoned his shirt, one button at a time, her moves deliberate and sensual.

A moan escaped his mouth as he unclasped Susan's dress. TJ fought to maintain self-control. No woman has ever ignited this kind of passion that he experienced with Susan. Heat turned to a blazing fire in his loins. Before he slid her dress down, she asked him to turn off the light. He didn't want to ruin the moment, and he leaned over and turned off the lamp. He turned back to face her and slid her gown down her slender body.

Susan took his shirt off and stopped. Intimidated by TJ, she hesitated until he peered into her eyes, as if he were daring her to go on. He saw her eyes in the moonlight streaming in from the windows, clouded with passion. She glanced at him and smiled. Reaching for his belt, she unbuckled it, discovering evidence of his arousal. She was apprehensive, but desired him just the same. Susan slid the strap out of his pants and dropped it. She then reached for his pants and undid the clasp and slid the zipper down. He moaned with desire. Once his pants were open, she dropped them to the floor, where he stepped out of them. They were both in their underwear. She was topless. Her full breasts pale in the moonlight, her nipples pebbled.

TJ guided Susan to the bed. He kissed her with passion while sliding her panties off. Somehow, he was out of his underwear. He climbed on top of her, touching her, exploring her body. His fingers were fanning the flames of her white-hot desire. TJ lowered himself to kiss her scar. He slid his body up again and kissed her lips deeply as he entered her, and Susan gasped, hugging him tighter. He moved deeper, a little at a time, until she begged, "All of you."

He pushed forth, filling her. As he thrust, she caught onto the rhythm and matched his moves. Susan felt the deep rumble begin, and gasped as her orgasm exploded. Her toes curled, and she grasped the bedsheets. TJ felt the quaking and released his passion.

Susan fell asleep in his arms, her head on his chest. She awoke to a trail of gentle kisses on her face and neck. When her eyes opened, TJ kissed her. They made love throughout the night. When they awoke, it was almost noon and TJ was starving. He gave her his robe, and they made their way into the kitchen. She grabbed her purse to check for a missed call. She noticed TJ's phone on the table. She brought the phone to him and said, "Your phone says you have a voice mail."

He said, "probably someone congratulating me. It can wait." He prepared an omelet, and they ate, smiled, fed each other, and kissed. They made love again on the kitchen table.

"Can I shower?"

"Of course, honey." TJ replied as he reached for his phone and walked with her to the bathroom. While she was in his bathroom, he listened to the voicemail, his mother telling him to bring Susan home straight away. He returned his mother's call and asked, "Mom, what's up? You sound terrible."

"It's Richard, son. You need to bring Susan home. He's gone, son. He passed in his sleep. Cora asked that we not tell her until she's home with them. They fear how this news might affect her. Maria is waiting there, just in case."

TJ dropped his head. His movements were hesitant. His lip quivered at the loss of a man he loved since a toddler. "Okay, Mom, the bathroom door is opening. I should go," he said, his voice quivered as he disconnected the call. TJ tried to get a grip on his emotions before facing Susan and delivering the terrible news. He used another bathroom, dressed, and waited downstairs. Susan had changed into her gown from the previous night. She walked down the stairs, holding onto her shoes and bag. Susan looked over and smiled at him.

"I hoped you'd join me," she said coyly.

"I thought perhaps you wanted privacy since it's daylight."

She raised one eyebrow and said, "It was daylight in the kitchen too."

He walked over and kissed her. "Let's go, sweetie." His heart was heavy from losing the man he called uncle and the pain it would cause his love—losing the father she had just reunited with over the last twenty-one months. They rode in silence, not even the radio played, Susan's eyes watering with each yawn. TJ was sad. He reached for her hand, his thumb caressing the top.

They had chosen the wedding date, just six months away. Richard had found and paid for the venue, flowers, and had selected the menu. It was the last gift he gave his daughter while still alive.

How am I going to help her through this? He worried as he pulled onto the driveway, knowing what waited for her behind those closed doors. He worried about how she would handle the loss. Susan was happy. Extraordinarily happy. Now her world would be shattered in less than a minute.

TJ strode around to her side of the car, opened the door for her, and helped her out. The gown had wrapped around her legs, and she fell into his arms. He hugged her, kissing the top of her head. He opened the door and escorted her into the foyer. *The dogs must be in Cora's suite*, he thought. They hadn't run out to greet them.

"Something's wrong. It's much too quiet," Susan murmured. Whispers filtered through the foyer as she moved into the kitchen. Susan drifted toward the family room. There she found Thomas, Nicole, Cora, Jack, and Maria.

"Hi." Susan looked around the room. "Where's my father?"

Cora said, "Sit down, sweetie."

"I don't need to sit. Where's my dad? Is he sleeping?" Panic built as her heart pounded in her chest, her mouth suddenly dry. "Someone, please answer me." She stared, wide-eyed, at her family.

Thomas rushed to her and grabbed her hand, and squeezed it. "He passed in his sleep last night."

"No, you're mistaken. My father was doing so well. I'm going up to him now," Susan ran from the room, flew up the stairs, taking two at a time, and flew into his room. His bed was empty, unmade. She saw needle caps and empty plastic bags strewn on the floor. The wheels of a gurney made deep impressions in the thick carpet. "Dad? Dad? Come on, Doc, where are you?"

TJ was right behind her. "Honey, he's gone."

"No, he can't be. He wouldn't leave me so soon," she said breathlessly.

TJ nodded, and she gazed into his eyes. The same face that smiled yesterday now had worry lines visible at his downcast, tear-filled eyes, and his lips set in a firm line. It was true. He was gone.

"But I didn't get to see him and say goodbye. I need to say goodbye." Susan sobbed as she slowly dropped to the floor. Gut-wrenching, painful sobs tore at TJ's heart.

"Okay, why don't we get you out of that dress and into clothing? I'll find out where they took him, and we'll say goodbye. Okay, honey? Will you change for me so we can go?" TJ asked.

Susan nodded and stood as TJ led her down the hallway to her bedroom. In shock, Susan froze in place. TJ found clothing, and he tenderly removed her gown and helped her dress. He passed her the hairbrush and a clip, seeing the mess he made of her hair. They went downstairs. TJ clenched her hand firmly and they entered the family room.

TJ asked, "Where did they take him?"

His father responded, "To the funeral home." Thomas handed TJ a business card with the address.

"Please call them. Susan needs to say goodbye now. Tell them we're on the way." TJ escorted her to the car. Cora gave him two water bottles, her hands shaking and her face, a mask of grief. TJ helped Susan into the passenger seat, and they pulled away, silent tears streaming down her face. Maria followed behind.

Richard pre-planned his funeral, using the same funeral home that he'd used for his beloved Donna. When TJ and Susan arrived, Maria followed cautiously and parked several spots away. She needed to be there for her friend, but didn't want to intrude on Susan and TJ's need for privacy.

TJ guided Susan toward the entrance. Susan's body pressed into his. He kissed the top of her head, but the clicking of the cameras interrupted them, and he yelled, "Please give us space. I never deny you pictures, but please, this is a sad and private moment."

Susan looked up at him and smiled wanly in gratitude. She squeezed his hand a little tighter. They walked to the front door and stood on the marble steps.

"Are you ready, my love?" TJ asked.

"Yes," she answered, her face moistening with tears.

"Okay, take a deep breath. Remember to breathe the entire time we're inside," TJ advised.

Susan nodded. TJ opened the door, stepped in, spied a partially opened door, and guided her toward it, assuming the funeral director was sitting behind the desk.

"Hello, this is Miss Kline. I believe Dr. Kline's attorney called to advise you she was coming?" TJ asked.

"Yes, hello, my name is Donald Deauxmare, I'm the director, and yes, I received the call. Come in and have a seat, Miss Kline. I'm sorry for your loss. Dr. Kline was well respected, and his death is a significant loss to the medical community. I have Dr. Kline's instructions. He paid and planned the funeral, eliminating that burden for you."

"Thank you," Susan said tearfully.

Mr. Deauxmare explained what Dr. Kline had planned and asked if they were ready to say goodbye. Susan's heartbeat thumped in her chest. The hammering in her ears blocked the conversation. She glanced around the room, trying to focus on something other than her breaking heart. She spied only a quiet sadness, urns, memorials, white flowers. Tears flowed, and she placed her palm on her heart. Mr. Deauxmare escorted them past the opulent foyer, down a hallway, and into a small private room. He closed the door and waited outside.

Maria waited outside until she saw them walk past the foyer. She then went in and followed in their direction and introduced herself to the funeral director. "I'm here if she needs me," Maria said.

On the other side of the closed door, Susan stood frozen in place. *How do I say goodbye to him?* Glancing at TJ, who nodded as he guided her to the casket, where she stood, silently crying, unable to speak, clutching TJs hand. She stared at the man who was her father. Still in his pajamas, his face peaceful. She reached for his stiff hand. He always had the warmest, softest hands.

"Dad, I'm so sorry I wasn't home, but knowing you, you planned this to spare me. I'm so heartbroken. You didn't spare me at all," she sobbed. "Oh, Daddy." She caressed his soft cheek and then fell to her knees, sobbing, with her hands covering her face. Susan remained on her knees while TJ said his goodbyes. Susan found it difficult to leave her father there alone. Even though she didn't remember him initially, she loved him. Susan reached in and retook his hand.

"Daddy, I promise you I'll remember everything you taught me. And I assure you I will keep the practice open and continue your mission. I love you. Be with your beloved. Sweet sleep, Daddy." Susan said as the tears streamed down her cheeks, unable to breathe through her sobs. She turned to TJ and whispered, "I need a bathroom."

TJ opened the door. The funeral director waited outside with Maria. TJ asked where the lady's room was. The man pointed to the door at the end of the hall. Susan reached for Maria's hand, and the two women walked toward it. Susan realized Maria was suffering, too. Her father was her first friend in California. They worked and ate lunch together, almost every workday, tag-teamed surgeries, and they had become good friends.

Maria waited by the vanity in the outer area, and Susan rushed into one stall. She heard her friend retching and asked, "Do you need me to hold your hair back?" She remembered the time Susan didn't realize that strawberry margaritas had alcohol in them. After they went back to Maria's place one evening, she became sick, and Maria held back her hair. It became a standing joke whenever they went out.

"No, I'm coming out." Susan then hugged her friend briefly before leaning over the sink to freshen up. "Damn, I look terrible. Imagine what the gossip rags will say when they see the shots from today."

"Don't worry about it. I threatened to 'F them up' and not repair the damage. They thought I was a crazy lady and took off."

Susan admitted, "You are a tad crazy." Her tone teasing.

"Well, I told you, I'm from Brooklyn. We don't take shit. You can take the girl out of Brooklyn, but you can't take Brooklyn out of the girl."

"Thank you for being here for me. You didn't need to hide, and you could have ridden along with us."

"I wanted to give you privacy," Maria said.

"You've seen me at my worst and held my hair when I puked up Margaritas. I don't need privacy around you. Add another milestone to the list of goofy things I've done. I just puked in a gold toilet. Talk about no class." Susan laughed and hugged her friend again. "Let's go. TJ must think I flushed myself down the toilet."

They left the ladies' room together. TJ glanced at Maria. His eyes full of concern. Maria nodded and walked to the parking lot in silence. When Susan saw where Maria parked, she turned to her friend, shook her head, and said, "Goof."

Maria laughed and said, "Tried to be discreet."

"I see, very discreet. I knew you were there the entire time. Come back to the house. I'm sure we will receive guests to offer condolences."

"Okay, I'll discreetly follow you back," Maria said, hoping levity would ease her friend's broken heart a little.

TJ listened to the banter and said, "I never figured out where the pet name 'goof' came from, but it suits you both perfectly. Let's go." The three of them returned to Susan's house.

Thomas took Susan aside and expressed his condolences again. Losing his oldest and dearest friend devastated him. He began with, "I didn't believe you were Susan when you first arrived here. But watching you care for him, going to work every day, and never being one of those women who lived to spend money. No matter who you are or where you've been, you're his daughter. And soon to be mine."

Susan cried and couldn't speak as he took her in his arms.

Thomas continued, "I have the will. Your Dad's funeral is Wednesday. Come into my office on Friday for the reading of the will and the plans for his practice."

"Alright, what time?" Susan asked.

"Can you make it for nine? It will take a while, and I must be in court for one."

"Can you tell me this before Friday? Is Dr. Ross's job safe? I should reassure her."

"Yes. Dr. Ross's position is safe. Your father thought she was a gifted doctor and a good friend. It overjoyed him when you two bonded. We will go over everything on Friday. Don't worry about anything except getting through the funeral."

While Susan sat in the living room with Thomas, TJ called Sophia and asked if she could "babysit" Buddy and Lily until the funeral. She said that wouldn't be a problem. He asked Cora to gather their things.

"Can I ask why?"

TJ said, "I called my friend in rescue. She will babysit them until after the funeral."

Cora shook her head and asked, "Is Miss Susan aware?"

"No. I just thought if the dogs weren't underfoot, Susan wouldn't worry about them getting out with all the activity here the next few days."

"Mr. Collins, you mean well, but Miss Susan takes exceptionally diligent care of her babies, as do Jack and me. Do you see them running about now?"

"No, I don't," he admitted.

"Well then, ask her first. Remember that in your marriage, you need to include her. She's very independent. If she agrees, I'll gather their things. If not, they've been in our suite, and Jack has been caring for them."

"Thank you, Cora, for your honesty. I see Susan in the dining room now speaking with Maria. I'll ask her."

TJ met the women as they exited the dining room. He kissed the top of Susan's head. "Honey, do you think the puppies should go to Sophia's this week until after the funeral?" He didn't want to tell her about his faux pas.

"I don't think that's necessary for the entire week, but perhaps she can come here the day of the funeral? I have never left the pugs alone. It might scare them."

"I'll find out," TJ replied.

TJ went into the living room and called Sophia again, "Hey Sophia, change of plans. Is there any way you can come here on Wednesday during the funeral and watch them here?"

"Sure, TJ. What time are the services?"

"Nine o'clock for the immediate family, ten for visitation," TJ responded. Sophia agreed to be at the Kline residence at eight-thirty to care for the pugs.

Twenty-four

MIKE DUG INTO HIS RESEARCH. This case intrigued him, and his heart broke for Jonathan and his boys. They were such friendly people. According to everyone he interviewed, so was Natalia. He found out so much about them that he felt he knew them personally. He learned Natalia loved her family and had a stable marriage. They did everything together, along with their extended family, Natalia's college friends. He was confident she didn't leave her family.

Jonathan told him they took two vacations a year, one with their crew and one with his family. These people always cared for each other's kids so they could enjoy weekend getaways. All three families were middle class and financially stable. He could not find any reason Natalia would disappear with a famous actor. He called Jonathan.

"Hello?"

"Hey, Jon, Mike here. How are you?"

"Anxiously waiting for your call. It took all of my self-control not to fly to Los Angeles."

"Well, I'm glad you had that self-control. I'm heading to Los Angeles this afternoon myself as I couldn't reach anyone. The practice has been closed because of a death in the family. I could get through to the answering service."

"Who died?" Jonathan asked, fearing it was Natalia.

"I'm not sure," Mike replied. "However, it wasn't Susan Kline because the girl from the answering service mentioned if I called back to ask for Susan Kline. She's the manager of the practice and could answer questions about their services. Jon, I've been mulling over everything since Sunday evening. I cannot find any reason your wife would go voluntarily. Yet she looked quite happy to be with that actor. I didn't detect fear in her eyes or face, just happiness. A major part of me thinks this isn't your wife. But I promised you I wouldn't give up, and I won't. I have one question and a very personal question."

"I will tell you anything if you bring my wife back. That's her. Trust me when I say that. That woman who calls herself Susan Kline is my wife." Jonathan said emphatically.

"Okay, Jon, how was your intimate life? Did you get along? Didn't fight??" Mike asked.

"It was fabulous for both of us. Being married for eighteen years, it wasn't every day anymore, but two or three times a week. I think that's a sizable number considering how long we're married." Jon swallowed hard and continued, "we were best friends, and sure we disagreed a time or two, but never got to where I would say we fought.

"Okay. That eliminates that Mrs. Miller left because she was dissatisfied with the marriage or tired of the arguing. Yeah, I'm grasping at straws here. I have a plan in place, and I need you not to speak about this to anyone. I don't want anyone on the west coast spooked. I will admit this is a challenge, and I'll call you with updates."

"Thanks, Mike, safe travels."

Mike landed at LAX about eleven o'clock west coast time. He had a reservation at the airport hotel. Looking for the hotel's sign, he hopped on the moving people conveyor that ended at the hotel lobby entrance. He glanced around the well-appointed and elegant lobby. Mike noticed the fresh flowers in ornate vases on decorated pillars and tables. After checking in, he freshened up and picked up his rental car, and plugged the address to Kline Medical Building into the GPS on his phone. He was taking quite a chance by just showing up and asking to see Susan Kline.

Mike arrived at the Medical Building after sitting in heavy traffic. He peered out the window at the giant palm trees and the blazing sun. *What a life.* His nerves were on edge, and he hoped this wasn't a mistake. He parked in the lot and called Jonathan. "I'm here. This place is impressive."

"What excuse will you be using to gain access to her?" Jonathan asked.

"After what I read about her and her father, their hearts are huge. I'm going to say I'm here on behalf of a disfigured child. I'm using your first name. Hopefully, that flusters her. With any luck, I'll somehow get a DNA sample. Not sure how yet, but that's my plan."

"I hope you can pull this off. If you grab the sample, how long does it take to receive results?"

"A few weeks. Jon, it seems like a long time, but if it is her, then we found her," Mike said.

"Alright then, please call me as soon as you leave her office," Jonathan pleaded.

"Of course," he replied.

Mike stepped out of his car, praying he hadn't bitten off more than he could chew. He walked toward the building and viewed the directory. The Kline practice encompassed the entire top floor. When the elevator arrived, he pushed the button that said 'Kline' and ascended to the top.

Mike's nerves sent flutters through his body and sweat beaded his brow. The elevator doors opened, and he stepped into a well-appointed waiting area. He approached the beautiful young woman who sat behind an opulent desk and smiled. "Hello. My name is Mike Gorman."

"Hello, Mr. Gorman, my name is Lisa. How may I help you?"

"I have an appointment with Miss Kline at three-thirty," he lied.

"You do? Allow me to check her schedule. No, I'm sorry, I don't see any appointments for that time, nor do I see your name on her schedule."

"You don't? I'm sure this is a mistake. I traveled from the east coast for this appointment."

"Oh my, what is the reason for the appointment? She isn't Dr. Kline, but she's in her office. Perhaps if I told her, she might see you," Lisa said.

"I'd like to consult with her regarding a severely disfigured child who desperately needs help," Mike lied.

"If you have a seat, I'll check with Miss Kline. She usually does these types of intakes via email." Lisa put her finger on a keypad. It read her print and permitted access to whatever or whoever was beyond those doors.

She came back several minutes later and said, "Miss Kline will see you now." Lisa escorted him down the hall to Susan's office. Susan sat behind her desk. She looked up and eyed the man standing uncomfortably in her office and stood to greet him.

"Welcome to Beverly Hills, Mr. Gorman. Lisa tells me, you need help with a child. Please have a seat." Susan motioned to the seat in front of her desk.

As he approached her desk, he peered at two framed photos, a photo of her dogs and a shot of her and TJ Collins, from the night of the awards. Mike sat down and smiled at her. "Miss Kline, I've been told that your father is famous for facial reconstruction."

"Yes, he was. Sadly, my father died a few weeks ago. However, Dr. Ross has been running the practice, and she has been my father's protégé for several years and is an accomplished doctor. She is familiar with all aspects of his specialties."

"I'm sorry for your loss," Mike replied.

"Thank you. Today is my first day back at work. Tell me about the little one." Susan folded her hands on top of the desk.

He stared directly into her bright blue eyes and saw the pain of her loss. "Well, his name is Jonathan. He's three and lives in New Jersey, a small town outside of Philadelphia." He peered at her. She didn't react, not a flinch at the name or place, no recognition. Her face was passive yet interested. *If this was Natalia, she was good at pretending. Damn good*, he thought.

"That is sad. I hate the thought of children with medical issues," Susan said. "Excuse my manners. Would you like coffee, iced tea, or water? The trip must have exhausted you."

"That would be great. The water is fine. Thank you."

Susan left her office and walked into the break room. Mike overheard her speaking with someone in the hall. He grabbed her empty coffee mug with a plastic bag. He placed it into his briefcase and sat back to wait for her.

She arrived with an icy water bottle, handed it to him with a smile, and then sat back down behind her desk. "Mr. Gorman, I'm not sure if you're aware, but my father spearheaded a foundation for children such as Jonathan. We will pay for everything should the patient qualify. The qualification process isn't much. They need to be medically stable for the surgery and cleared by their physician and then ours." She handed him a folder with the foundation's name and children's before and after photos. "Here is everything you need. Just complete the forms and ask Jonathan's doctor to complete the physical exam sheet and questionnaire. Once we receive it, we'll schedule his physical here.

"And then, provided his health is stable, we will set up the appointment. Mr. Gorman, please assure the family that the foundation will pay for everything, including their flight and hotel stay. We provide a driver who will take them back and forth to the hospital and a prepaid Visa card for food and necessities while they're here.

Should Jonathan need additional procedures, we'll cover those. Do you have any further questions?"

"No, thank you. You have been most helpful and thorough," Mike said. "May I ask you a question off-topic, please?"

"Sure," she replied.

"Is that a photo of you and TJ Collins, the actor?" he asked, pretending to be ignorant of the relationship.

"Yes, it is," she said, smiling.

"Wow, it must be great to live here and see and date actors." he exclaimed.

"We're engaged and will get married in a few months."

"Well, congratulations." He stood up and shook her hand. Susan escorted him to the exit door herself.

"Have a safe flight, Mr. Gorman. I'll await the return of that package."

"Thanks again." He pressed the button on the elevator. *Damn, now I doubt this could be Natalia. There was not one hint of recognition at Jonathan's name or the area where they lived or met. I hope this wasn't a waste of time.*

He returned to his hotel, deep in thought. *This news is going to be a setback for Jonathan and the boys. But I must tell him.* Once he arrived at the hotel, he bought a soda at the gift shop, went to his room, relaxed in the chair, and called Jonathan.

"Hey, Jon."

"Hey, how did it go? Were you able to make an appointment?" Jonathan asked, his body pulsed with anxiety.

"Yes. I met Miss Kline and took her coffee cup for DNA testing. To be truthful, I'm not sure about this. There wasn't the slightest hint of recognition using your name, the state you live in, or the city you met. I'm grateful to grab her coffee cup to use for the DNA matching process. That's all we can do now. I'll send it to the lab I use in New York."

"Thank you, Mike. I wish I could say I'm excited about the news. I'm trying not to be hopeful as it sounds as though it isn't Natalia," Jonathan replied regretfully.

"Hang tight. We'll find out in a few weeks. I'll try to get a rush on it," he said.

Mike disconnected the call and gathered his things. His flight left early in the morning. He planned to send the mug to his acquaintance Paul at the DNA lab. He'd used this lab before and had built a stable working relationship with Paul. Mike hoped he could rush the sample. Thankfully, his child sob story got him into her office.

Susan's heart broke for the little boy in New Jersey. Just three and had so many surgeries in his young life. Once she received the package from Mr. Gorman, she would ensure this baby received the help he needed. Maybe even a trip to Disneyland. She reached for her coffee cup and missed it. She looked up and said out loud, "I must've left it in the break room. Funny, I don't remember taking it back there." She hurried into the break room, heels clicking on the tile floor, grabbed another mug, and prepared a cup of herbal tea. As she walked back to her office, she turned at TJ's bellow.

"Hey sexy, I came to take you to dinner."

"You did, did you?" she asked as she walked into his arms and kissed him.

"You kiss me like that again, and we won't make it to dinner." he said gruffly.

"Come with me," she said. Susan reached for his hand and led him into her office and locked the door. She picked up the remote to lower the blinds. Pulling TJ over to her desk and sat on the edge. "Kiss me," she demanded. TJ pressed his lips to her, opening her mouth with his tongue. Reaching for his belt, she worked on the button. His eyes widened. She smiled and dropped his jeans to his ankles. "Step out of those please," she demanded, and he immediately obeyed. She reached down to caress him. Sliding out of her panties, she wrapped her legs around his waist. She pulled him to her and kissed him hard, sticking her tongue deep into his mouth, caressing his tongue with hers. When Susan nibbled on his lips, it put him over the edge. She reached down and gripped him in her hand.

TJ moaned and whispered, "Hurry," as she guided him inside her. Shocked and hyper-excited by her need for him. Susan was usually timid, and TJ initiated intimacy. This afternoon she was full of desire. Hot and needy for him. He pushed into her, unable to control himself. Her walls tightened around him as he thrust inside. He thumbed her pleasure center and felt her orgasm pulse through her body, pulling his from deep inside him. Afterward, he kissed her again and said, "You amaze me. That was fantastic."

She smiled at him coyly. "Yes, it was. Are you going to take me to dinner now?"

"I am."

"That," she said, pointing to her desk, "was an appetizer."

They left the practice holding hands and went to a romantic spot for dinner. Over dinner, they discussed honeymoon plans. Susan mentioned she wanted a tropical and relaxing honeymoon. Maybe a place where he could relax and wasn't popular. TJ suggested Bora Bora. He described the private cabins over the water. "We can add that to our list to research. I want to be with you. I don't need to sightsee or do any tourist attractions unless that's what you want," she said.

"You're what I want, and I'll go anywhere with you," TJ said.

She smiled and replied, "You are charming, the man of my heart."

Twenty-five

JONATHAN HAD A TERRIBLE day. Anything that could go wrong with work did. He took a shortened lunch and went back to his office, aggravated. He had a significant account, and the investor was rude, demanding, and obnoxious. Because this client is a high-profile investor, Jonathan maintained a professional attitude when dealing with him. He thought about leaving early to go home and take a nap before the boys came home, but still struggled to sleep in their bed without Natalia.

Anthony arrived home from school first. He didn't usually. However, both brothers had received detention. His father told him to go to his Aunt Charlene's until he or his brothers came home. Stepping into the house through the garage, he punched the security keypad to gain entry. Never having been home alone before, he tossed his book bag down and headed straight to his room. He over-heard his dad say his mom's new name, Susan Kline. Her father was a doctor in Beverly Hills. But he knew his Pop-Pop, her father, was Antonio Conte. Pulling the tablet out of his desk drawer, Anthony used a search engine and searched for the phone number. He found the number for Dr. Kline, but not Susan Kline. He dialed it from the landline, and after three rings, a woman answered.

"May I please speak to Susan Kline?" Anthony asked.

"Who may I say is calling?" the woman asked.

"Anthony."

"Miss Anthony, are you from the medical supply department?"

He lied, "Yes." He had almost said, "I am not a girl," but he thought maybe she would put him through if he played along.

"Hold on the line, please. I'll patch you through to Miss Kline," she said professionally.

Anthony waited as the phone clicked. And then she was there. "Hi, this is Susan Kline. How may I help you?"

He recognized his mom's voice at once. Tears streamed down his face, and he said, "Mom, mommy, it's me. It's Anthony. When are you coming home, Mommy? I miss you," he sobbed.

Susan was speechless. She took a deep breath and said, "Honey, I don't have any children. Could you possibly have the wrong Susan Kline?" Her heart broke for the child. She listened to him sob through the phone, the catch of his breath. She couldn't do anything for him. "Sweetheart, can you take a deep breath for me?"

He inhaled and sobbed.

"Is there an adult there with you?" she asked.

"No," he whined. "The boys received detention, and Dad isn't home yet. I'm supposed to be at Aunt Char's." He cried harder.

"Okay, sweetheart, why don't you go to your Aunt Char's, then? You shouldn't be alone. I'm sorry that I'm not your mom. You sound like an awesome boy."

Anthony choked, sobbed, and disconnected the call. Anthony threw himself on his bed and cried.

Susan hung up on her end and felt terrible for the little boy. She remained frozen at her desk, her eyes burning with unshed tears. *What if?* She strode into Maria's office, plopped into the chair, and told her about the phone call.

Maria asked, "How did you feel when you received the call?"

"My heart broke for the little boy. Is that what you were looking for?"

"No, I was just thinking about what you said when the gynecologist's exam revealed you had a pregnancy and could have delivered a child."

"When I answered the phone, he said, 'Mom? Mommy, it's me, Anthony.' I thought, could it be they found me? My primary concern was to calm him down. He hung up after I asked him to breathe and not to be alone." Shaking her head, she left and returned to her office.

TJ had a few early days on the set and had been picking Susan up from work. When she climbed into his car, still unsettled from the call, he noticed her face lacked color, and her hands trembled. Tears glistened in her eyes. "Sweetheart, what's the matter?" TJ asked. His eyebrows raised, and a small V appeared on his forehead.

Sighing as a lone tear slipped down her cheek, she quickly wiped it with her palm. "I received a phone call from a little boy. He thought I was his mom. It nearly broke my heart. What if he is, TJ? Mine, I mean."

"Your father searched extensively to track down any family you might've had and came up empty. I doubt it, honey. And to be truthful, I'm grateful. I don't want to be a parent at my age. I like it this way, just us two."

Annoyed, Susan turned her head away from him. She knew they might not have children, but if she had a child and they found him or her, wouldn't he welcome the chance? She was pensive on their way to his place. Once they arrived at his house, he stepped into the kitchen and pulled steaks out of the refrigerator. Susan called home to check on her fur babies, and she cuddled with Candi. After the phone call, she padded barefoot onto the deck, with the dog at her heels.

"I love steak cooked on the grill. Is there time for a swim, or do you need me to make a salad?" Susan asked.

"I can do it. Go for a swim, love."

After changing, she stepped onto the stone patio, headed to the pool, and then dove in without saying a word. She swam back and forth the entire length of the pool several times to rid her brain of the turmoil. She hoped the warm water would calm her internal demons. That phone call and TJ's remarks upset her in separate ways. Her heart was sad for the little boy missing his mom. She understood that sadness as she missed her father. She tried to lift her funk by doing laps.

Calmer, Susan swam over to the edge of the pool where TJ was grilling and said, "Hey, hot stuff, come over here and kiss me."

He dropped the grilling fork and bent down to kiss her. She grabbed him by his shirt and pulled him in. He came up, sputtering, "How the hell did you get the strength to do that?" His eyes widened, and his brows lifted.

"That's just a warning. Don't mess with me, dude," she said, laughing. "How private is this yard? Paparazzi?" she asked.

"I doubt they can get here unless by helicopter, but you'd hear them. Why?" TJ asked.

Susan stepped into his arms and kissed him. "Because I've had a terrible day, and I need this to forget." She caressed him through his shorts. Susan reached for his board shorts and exposed him. She moved her bathing suit aside and guided him inside of her.

"Whoa there, let me help you so this isn't over before it begins." He guided them over to the stairs and made love to her in the pool as the sunset. Flames shot from the grill as the steaks ignited, as did their passion.

Laughing, TJ tossed the charred meat into the garbage can. They enjoyed salads and fruit outside in the moonlight before going inside. They cuddled on the sofa with Candi, and the three of them were in bed by ten. TJ had an early call in the morning.

Susan's sleep was restless. When she fell asleep, she dreamed of a tow-headed little boy running into her arms, a baby boy on a blanket, and a kindergarten-age boy with dark hair playing with his dad. She couldn't see his face. In the dream, she smiled and looked upon her family with love, happiness, and pride.

When morning hit, TJ left Susan asleep with Candi, took a quick shower, and then kissed his girls before rushing to the set. Susan slipped from the cozy bed and readied for work, unsettled about that dream. She called home again to check on the pugs and then checked in with Maria to ask if she left for work yet. She had but was just a mile away from TJ's house. His house was directly on the route that Maria took when going to practice. "Can you swing by TJ's and pick me up?"

"Yup, be there in a flash."

"Great, thanks." She kissed Candi goodbye and informed the housekeeper she was leaving.

Maria arrived a few minutes later, dressed in a black sleeveless dress with a beige bolero jacket trimmed in black, the slim-fitting dress that hugged her curves. Her shoes were black heels. Maria never dressed down for work.

"Good morning, friend," Susan said with a smile.

"Right back at you." Maria smiled back.

"Maria, I want to learn to drive. Can you help me with that? I don't want to tell TJ yet. He is as over-protective as was my father and Jack. I don't see any reason I can't drive. Do you?"

"No, I don't. How is Saturday? I know the perfect spot where you can't kill anyone," Maria said, laughing.

"Thanks for the vote of confidence." Susan exclaimed, laughing.

SATURDAY MORNING, SUSAN woke excited to see if she could drive. Dressed in shorts and a tank, she bounced on the heels of her sneakers, waiting for Maria. She zipped into the circular driveway, and Susan hopped in the passenger seat. Maria pulled into a parking lot of the local high school and parked in the vacant lot. "Switch seats," Maria stated as she climbed out of her car.

Susan walked in front of the vehicle and slid into the driver's seat. She didn't have to adjust the seat or the mirrors and maneuvered the car in and out of cones.

Maria asked, "Any idea where your birth certificate is? We can get you tested for your driver's license."

"Probably the safe. Doc kept paperwork inside. My parent's marriage license, my mom's death certificate. Will you take me to the Department of Motor Vehicles?"

"Of course." Maria exclaimed. "Drive some more, this time out on the road."

"Ugh. Do you trust me with your car? And on the road?"

"Of course, you didn't knock over any of those cones. You'll be fine, have faith in yourself. I'll direct you. Hey, I taught my kid brother to drive. I've got experience." Maria teased.

Susan eased the car onto the road. She was terrified of driving outside of the school parking lot. She reached into the pocket of her shorts, searching for something, yet coming up empty.

Maria provided directions in enough time for Susan to react. Thirty minutes later, they arrived at their favorite cafe. Susan pulled over as a valet rushed to the car. After a carb-laden lunch, Susan took the returned vehicle from the valet, sliding a tip into his hand. "Where to, Princess?" she teased her friend.

Maria gave her directions, and twenty minutes later, Susan pulled into her driveway. "Thanks, Maria, this was fun. And the lunch, oh my gosh, I feel so full. I love that pasta." Susan leaned over a placed a kiss on her friend's cheek.

After the lesson, Susan strode into the kitchen and found Cora with the puppies. They went crazy when they realized she'd arrived.

"Hello, Miss Susan. How'd your driving lesson go?" Cora asked.

"I did great, and Maria thinks that I'd driven before."

A FEW WEEKS LATER, after a long day at the office, Susan stepped into the kitchen and greeted Cora. She raised her head to Susan. "The contractors left. They're finished." Richard left instructions he didn't want his room to be a tomb or a memorial to him. He wanted his daughter to occupy the main bedroom as the new head of the household. Modernized and brightened with contemporary furniture, the area boasted a new bathroom and a dressing room. Cora moved Susan's stuff inside earlier. Susan loved the result. It was elegant and would suit both her and TJ's styles. Except TJ wasn't sure if he wanted to move there after their marriage. As Susan predicted, it had been a cause of disagreement.

As the wedding date approached, they still hadn't resolved where they would live. Susan felt a strong need to live in her father's house. She called TJ on location in England, where he was filming his new movie. His role was of a double agent. "Hey honey, how did shooting go today?" she asked sweetly.

"Hiya, Babe, it sucked. The stunts are killing me, and I'm exhausted. How was your day?"

"It was good. The bedroom's finished, and I'm moved in and will spend my first night there tonight. I wish you were there with me," she said wistfully.

"Me too. It's going to be a long few months. Is there any chance you can fly here soon?" he asked.

"Sure. I planned on it. Not sure when, though. Perhaps within the next few weeks. I planned on heading over to your place and get Candi for a few days. Are you okay with that?"

"Honey, I'd rather you didn't. She seems to get stressed when the two youngsters get all crazy around her. She's doing well with Carlotta."

"Okay," she replied, disappointed and annoyed. Candi loved playing with the puppies, visiting her home, and never appeared stressed by the younger pugs.

TJ sensed her annoyance. But he was too tired to care.

"If the stunts are too much, why not use a stunt double? TJ, these stunts are going to hurt you." Susan was cranky because her cycle started.

"Susan, are you implying I'm too old to do my stunts?" he grunted.

"No, honey, but when you do dangerous things that tax your body, it wears you out. Don't be so touchy." Susan exclaimed, frustrated. "You're annoyed and tired. I'll let you go. Call me when you're free and can chat."

"Okay, babe, love you." He hung up before she could reply.

She thought, *Maybe I don't want to go to England if you're going to be in a miserable mood.* In the suite, Susan approached the safe, unlocked it, and looked through all the envelopes. She found her birth certificate, her parent's marriage license, and an old wallet that contained her driver's license, long since expired.

She grabbed her phone and tapped on Maria's contact information. "I found my old license and birth certificate. What more do I need?"

"I think that's it. But bring something else official with your name on it, just in case. Maybe a credit card statement or something. I can take you tomorrow morning," she said, flipping through her appointment book. "There aren't any appointments scheduled because of the installation of the new equipment. Did you plan to go to work?"

"No. Let's do it tomorrow. Today, I want to buy a car. My very own car."

"That's great, but let's get you licensed first." Maria said, laughing. "With all those cars Doc left you, you want to buy another?"

"Yep, a girly car."

Everything went as planned. Susan renewed her license and they went to a car dealer. Susan had her heart set on a Jaguar SVR convertible. She chose the F-Type Model in cream, with cream quilted seats. She loved it and was excited to own such a beautiful vehicle.

As she pulled away from the dealership, she was aware of the paparazzi taking photos. She was a little annoyed but waved. They had no privacy. Mostly, photos were usually of her and TJ. She could imagine what the caption would be on this one. Susan relished being independent.

Twenty-six

THREE WEEKS PRIOR, Jonathan shuffled into the kitchen, and his gaze found Anthony sitting at the kitchen table with his head in his arms. The sun cast a warm glow over his son's head, and Jonathan peered at his profile. He looked just like Natalia. he shared the same natural blonde hair that became lighter in the summer. A lump formed in Jonathan's throat when he realized his son was crying and rushed over to him. "What's the matter, son? Why all the tears?"

"I miss Mommy. I talked to her today," he said between sobs. "I miss her even more now."

"Ant, what do you mean you talked to her?"

"I found the number for that doctor on my tablet, and I called it and asked for Mommy," Anthony sobbed. "She answered the phone, Dad. It was her voice, and it was Mommy. And she didn't remember me. She said she didn't have any children."

"Oh God, Ant. Don't you remember what the investigator said? Not to make contact, to let him handle this?" Jonathan stopped to his level.

"Yes, but I missed her, and I wanted to hear my mom's voice. I was going to hang up, but it was her, and I needed her. I want my mom," he sobbed.

"Oh, buddy," he said, pulling into son into his arms. "I know this is so hard on you and your brothers. We're just waiting on the test results." He hugged him tighter. *Well, if this isn't the icing on a shit-*

224

ty day. He's brokenhearted yet again. Jonathan asked where his brothers were. Anthony shrugged his shoulders, unwilling to get them in trouble.

Before he could respond, the two boys sauntered in. "What the hell, guys? Why are you two so late?"

"Detention. We had to take the late bus, and it goes all over town, dropping kids off," Marc answered.

"Why did you both get detention?" Jonathan asked.

Marc said, "I tripped a guy who made a rude remark about Mom running away."

"Great, just great, Marc." Jonathan replied, his voice dripping in sarcasm, his face red, "And you, Alex?"

"I didn't turn in my project," Alex said.

"Let me say this just once. You two will do your work and ignore people who say stuff about your mom. No more tripping people and focus on your damn homework." Jonathan banged his fist on the kitchen table. Anthony stared wide-eyed at his father. Jonathan stared at his two older boys, waiting for a response. He looked away when they nodded.

"What's for dinner, Dad? We're starving." Marc asked.

"We were going to go out, but I just don't have it in me. Order a pizza, Marc. Here is my card." He tossed the card onto the kitchen table and left the room.

As soon as the pizza arrived, the landline rang. The caller ID showed Mike, the private investigator, calling in, "Jon, that woman is Natalia. The DNA was a positive match using the toothbrush and hairbrush you provided. Jon, we found your wife."

Jonathan couldn't even speak, his mouth suddenly dry, and his heart raced. He was thankful she was alive. Yet, he was angry that she left them and how much they had all been suffering from her absence.

"Jon, are you there?" Mike asked.

"Yes, I am. Sorry. I'm stunned. So many emotions all at once. Mike, how do I thank you for this?"

"Can you meet me later? I want to give you the results and what we used to gather them."

"Sure. Are you free at seven? I'll meet you at the coffee shop on Main Street. Halfway for both of us? I'll buy." Jonathan grinned.

"Sure can."

Two hours later, Jonathan zipped into the parking lot of Kurley's Kafe. He hurried inside and found Mike waiting at a table in the back. Mike stood as Jonathan approached. Jonathan shook his hand and asked, "What are you having?"

"A Kurley Kroller, chocolate glazed, You?"

"Same, they're my favorite, Natalia's too." Jonathan placed the orders when the server appeared.

Thirty minutes later, Jonathan was on his way home with a dozen assorted pastries and the DNA report, along with the coffee mug and toothbrush. During the ride home, Jonathan thought, *thank goodness this was the last day of school for spring break*. He needed to reserve plane tickets to Los Angeles. Mike was going to email him the location of the medical building where she worked.

Jonathan returned to the kitchen to tell the boys. "Guys, the phone call was from Mike. He received the lab results, and they proved that the woman we saw on TV is your mother. And yes, Anthony, that was the woman you spoke with today. For whatever reason, she doesn't remember us. Mike met her and said she was a kind woman, but when he mentioned my name, where we live, and where we met, she had no response to the information. None of it seemed familiar to her. Something happened to mom, and we need to get her."

"Yes, Mom liked the movie star and dumped us. That's what happened," Marc said crossly.

"Marc, I don't believe that, and you don't either."

"I do, don't buy me a ticket. I'm not going out there," Marc said.

Alex stood frozen, noticeably quiet.

Anthony said, "I told you, dad. That was my mom."

Jonathan called the girls and told them the latest news. He told them they would leave tomorrow and that he was online trying to get a flight.

The girls cried and said, "Tell her we love her and miss her."

Marc came over and said, "Dad, get me a ticket. I decided I'm going."

Jonathan mumbled quietly, "As if you had a choice." He booked a flight, leaving Philadelphia at eight-twenty in the morning eastern time and arriving in Los Angeles at eleven-twenty Pacific time.

They packed light as they planned to bring her home right away. Each just had a carry-on bag. They were quiet most of the trip, each lost in their worries. The flight arrived in Los Angeles without delays.

The Miller family left the Los Angeles airport and hailed a taxi to the Medical Center. Jonathan was nervous and anxiety ridden. He hadn't set eyes on his wife in person in over twenty-one months. In his rush to travel to LA, he hadn't made a reservation at a hotel. They arrived at the impressive medical building forty-five minutes later because the driver was a maniac on the road. The boys were quiet. It was as if it scared them to speak about why they were there, as if it might somehow reach her before they could.

As the taxi pulled into the lot, they watched a beige Jaguar zip into the lot, right to the front door. A valet waited, rushed over to the car, opened the door, and a woman exited. It was Natalia. Her hair was blonder and longer, but it was her. They watched as she thanked the valet and dashed into the building. Jonathan thought, *wow, it has been a long time since she dressed like a professional.* Her entire style was different, and she walked with an air of confidence.

Alex almost yelled, "Mom," through the open taxi window. Jonathan sensed it and laid his hand on Alex's shoulder and admonished, "Quiet, son, we can't scare her. We don't want the police involved." Jonathan thought it might not have been a bad idea to invite Mike to come with them. *Too late for that now.*

The taxi pulled up and let them out, and the foursome made their way into the building and approached the elevators. In his bag, Jonathan had a portfolio with their marriage license, the DNA test results, the mug in the plastic bag used to gather the DNA, and Natalia's toothbrush from home they used for comparison. He also brought the missing person's flyer with a picture of her and their dog Buddy.

Jonathan and the two older boys approached the elevators with trepidation. Anthony ran up to it, nervously bouncing on his toes, and turned to watch his family walk toward him. He pushed the button, and the elevator arrived in seconds. Sweat beaded along Jonathan's scalp and forehead as they ascended. He wiped it with the back of his hand while watching the numbers on the elevator panel light up.

At last, they arrived, the elevator stopped, and the doors opened. They stepped into an elaborate waiting area. Jonathan approached an opulent receptionist's desk to speak with the woman who sat behind it.

She smiled and said, "Welcome to Kline. How can I help you?"

"We're here to meet with Nat ... Susan Kline," Jonathan countered.

"Do you have an appointment?" she asked.

"No, we don't," Jonathan said.

She looked down at the phone system and said, "Miss Kline is on the phone. Please take a seat. Once her line clears, I'll reach out to her. Who shall I say is calling?"

"Her family." he said with frustration and worry.

"Oh."

Dr. Kline told the staff he found Susan many years after being missing, but nothing more. They made their way over to the chairs and sat down. Alexander couldn't sit still, nervous and scared his mother would reject them. He stood by the window and looked out at the expansive view of Beverly Hills.

They waited about five minutes, which felt like an eternity when Lisa walked over and said, "Would you like anything? Water, coffee, herbal tea, juice for the children?"

"No, thank you," they said at the same time.

Twenty-seven

SUSAN DISCONNECTED the call and sat at her desk, glaring at the computer screen, unable to focus, feeling unsettled. She reached into her pocket again and found nothing. *Why do I keep on doing this?* Rubbing her forehead, she leaned back into her chair, wondering if TJ was okay. Were her instincts telling her he was injured? She jumped when her intercom buzzed and pushed the button for her office and heard Lisa whisper, "Miss Kline, you have visitors. A gentleman is here with three young boys who say they're your family. Should I call security?"

Susan tapped a few keys and glanced at the security cameras, showing her the waiting room. They appeared non-threatening. The view was grainy, and she didn't recognize any of them. "No. Bring them back and have someone from security wait unobtrusively in the reception area. Ask for Craig. He's the department supervisor and doesn't wear a uniform. He'll blend in better."

Lisa rang for security and asked for Craig. She explained the situation, and he assured her he would be up right away. Lisa buzzed Maria, as well, to inform her of the problem. Lisa made her way over to the family. Jonathan was restless, wiping his palms against the pocket of his tan slacks. The children fidgeted, paced, and were anxious.

"Miss Kline will see you now."

They followed her to the door, and when Lisa placed her finger on the keypad, the door clicked and opened.

Anthony exclaimed, "cool."

Lisa turned and smiled. "It is very cool. Good for me too, as I've lost keys a few times, but ssh, that's our little secret," she said, winking.

She knocked on Susan's office door. Natalia's voice came through the heavy door, "Come in." *Her voice. The voice he hadn't heard in twenty-one months.* His brain screamed at him.

Lisa opened the door, and Jonathan stepped inside first, followed by the three boys. She rose, and no recognition dawned in her eyes. He knew Natalia like the back of his hand. Her facial expressions showed all emotions. Now all her face expressed was fear.

Oh God, Dear God, my knees feel like they're going to give out. I'm lightheaded. Susan thought as she reached for the small button on the intercom to Maria's office so that Maria could listen in and interrupt if things became ugly. Susan spoke first, "How can I help you?" Her voice cracked.

Anthony exclaimed, "Mom, we're here to take you home." Susan was spiked with fear, these people who claimed to be hers, of the unknown.

Jonathan gently said, "Son," and Anthony went quiet, his face flushed, his smile wide.

Susan moved her eyes to the youngest of the three and said, "Are you the little boy that called me?"

He smiled proudly and said, "Yes."

Susan looked at each boy carefully for an iota of recognition. The youngest, known as Anthony, looked a lot like she did. "Please sit." They scared her, and her heart raced. She turned to Jonathan and asked, "What makes you think I'm your wife and their mother?" She pulled back, narrowing her eyes. Hints of memories left her blinded by a gripping migraine. Susan was just a woman trying to piece her life together.

"This." Jonathan pulled out the bag with her coffee mug, the lipstick mark still present, and a toothbrush. She stared at the plastic bag, not sure what to make of it. Jonathan placed the DNA report on her desk, sliding it toward her.

Susan reached for it and read the typed report, unsure if he fabricated it. She buzzed Lisa and asked her to take the information to Dr. Ross and wait for her to read it. She also asked Lisa to prepare a beverage cart. Susan turned to Jonathan. "You haven't introduced yourself. I'm at a disadvantage here."

Jonathan said, "I'm Jonathan Miller, your husband. This young man is our oldest son, Marc. Here is our middle guy, Alexander, and this is whom you always referred to as 'the baby,' Anthony."

Susan took a deep breath and let the name 'Miller' roll off her tongue. She licked her dry lips and said, "I'm sorry, I don't remember any of you. Please sit, and let's talk."

They sat down and stared at her. She began with, "One day about two years ago, I woke up in my house with my father and his housekeeper tending to me. A little dog too."

The boys simultaneously yelled with joy, "Buddy?"

She smiled. "Yes, Buddy." She continued, "What I learned of my past was that I was a terrible teenager, did drugs, and ended up missing after my high school graduation. My father found me unconscious and brought me home. I don't have any memories of a time before the day I woke up. None, nothing. It is a total blank slate."

Jonathan muttered, "Hard to believe."

"Frankly, I don't care what you believe. That is my truth, and just as you have DNA, I have medical records from several physicians," she stated, her voice rising. "The neurologist's diagnosis was a severe concussion that caused retrograde amnesia. I couldn't remember people or events, yet I remembered skills. The doctor told me that came from muscle memory." She spoke sincerely, and she sounded truthful. Natalia never lied, but his patience was thin.

He was tired and emotional. Jonathan took a deep breath and spoke, "Allow me to tell you *'Your'* truth," he said with a touch of sarcasm. "You are Natalia Conte Miller."

Her mouth fell open, and her brows raised.

"We married eighteen years ago. Your parents are Antonio and Catarina Conte. We met after college at work. We married, built a house, and had these fabulous boys, who were the light of your life. Twenty-one months ago, you took a trip to Myrtle Beach, South Carolina, for a pug fundraiser. You left the evening before you originally planned to leave and were rerouted by detour signs. You had a car accident, and you and Buddy vanished. Until the Academy Awards, where you walked the red carpet with your *fiancée*." Jonathan said the word fiancée through gritted teeth.

She was overwhelmed, and tears streamed down her face. Everyone remained quiet. There was a gentle knock on the door, and Lisa appeared with the cart containing coffee, tea, water, juice, pastries, fresh fruit, and cookies.

Lisa mouthed to Susan when she saw the tears streaming down her face, "Do you need Dr. Ross?"

Susan nodded and reached for tissues, dabbing at her eyes. She motioned towards the cart and said, "Can you please give me a minute? Help yourselves to the snacks. I'll be right back." Susan opened the door inside her office and stepped into her bathroom.

He was very genuine, she thought. *Could this be? Those boys are precious. Are they mine? That little one. He's feisty and looks just like me.* The door opened to the bathroom, and Maria stepped in. Susan turned on the exhaust fan to drown out their conversation.

Maria took a deep breath and began. "I think he's authentic. They could be your family. The shocking part is him saying who you are and NOT Susan. Did you change your name when you ran away? Who are you, my sweet friend?"

"I don't know." Susan replied tearfully.

"Okay, we can't stay here much longer. Why not do this? TJ is away. Invite them to stay and spend time with you. Perhaps your memories will return. I'll call Dr. Saker to see what he has to say. Go home and take care of this."

"Okay. Thank you."

Maria pulled her into an embrace, wiped her face, and they stepped back into Susan's office. Maria knew that her closest friend was on the verge of a full-blown ugly cry, so she took over. "I'm Maria Ross. I was Susan's doctor when she arrived. Dr. Kline found her in South Carolina. He brought her here after the accident. That's all the information that I have. When she arrived, she had nothing, just Buddy. Susan arrived unconscious, and that's how she remained for twenty-four hours. When she awoke, she was in her room at her father's house, without her memories. She didn't even remember being Susan, nor did she recognize her father. Everything she's telling you is true. What I suggested to Susan is to get to spend time with you and see if memories emerge." Maria turned to Jonathan. "Can you stay, or do the kids need to return to school?"

Anthony chimed in, "Woohoo, we're on spring break. Dad, can we stay? Can we go to Disneyland?"

For the first time since they arrived, Susan smiled and said, "Of course we can go to Disneyland. I haven't been there. At least not that I remember, anyway."

"Dad, can we, can we please?" Anthony begged.

"Ant, I didn't even make reservations yet. We must find a hotel because we only brought a change of clothes. Remember, we thought we were bringing your mom home."

Susan intervened. "No need to worry. The house is enormous. You can stay with me. We'll go out later for necessities if your father agrees to stay."

Jonathan looked into her eyes, and they reflected only pain and sadness. He didn't want to stay and planned to take her home. But that wasn't happening, and he had to wait to give his family this chance. "Okay, just until spring break is over. I don't want you guys missing school."

Anthony cheered, Alex, smiled, while Marc looked relieved.

"Thank you. Gather your things, and I'll call for my car." Susan reached for the phone and said, "Jose, can you kindly bring my car around? I'll be down in a few minutes." She was silent, overwhelmed, and tearful. She stopped by Lisa's desk. "Lisa, I'm taking the week off to tend to a family matter. Please put my private line on voicemail. If anything comes up with the Foundation, please reach me on my cell. I'm waiting for the packet for a little boy named Jonathan from New Jersey. I assured them I would push it through right away." Her voice quivered as she spoke.

Jonathan interrupted with, "That packet isn't coming. That was my private investigator's fabricated story about meeting with you for the DNA. He used my name, where we live, and the city we met to see if you showed any recognition."

"Oh, tricky. I see I need to step up security." She smiled feebly. "Okay, let's head down."

Lisa spoke out loud, "Enjoy, and best of luck to all of you."

"Thanks, Lisa."

The children bounded into the elevator first, followed by their parents. Jonathan stood next to Natalia. Her perfume tickled his nostrils. From the corner of his eye, he glanced at her. She was tanned, and her body thinner but fit. He was so worried she wouldn't choose their family. She looked fantastic in a cream pencil skirt and a light blue short-sleeved summer sweater. Her beige heels were higher than she'd worn at home. His mind was a cacophony of thoughts, and heartbroken that she had forgotten him and their kids.

The car she had arrived and was idling outside, with the valet beside it. He opened the door for Susan and assisted her in the car. She peered in the rear-view mirror. "Everyone buckled up?" She snapped her seatbelt in place and carefully headed to the residential area of Beverly Hills.

The giant palm trees impressed the boys, and she listened to parts of their conversations. With the top-down, conversation was a challenge.

Jonathan remained quiet as his thoughts barraged his brain. *How can we compete with all of this? I want to kiss her. Will she choose us? What will I do if my marriage ends? I love her. What if she's so different that I don't like her anymore?* His thoughts came in waves of worries.

They arrived at the house, and she opened the garage door using a button housed next to the rearview mirror. The boys hadn't ever been in a garage this huge, and they were awestruck. As they exited the car, excited barking came from inside the house. Susan closed the garage door and then turned to unlock the house's door and deactivate the alarm. Of *all the times to send Cora and Jack to the Maui house for vacation.* The door opened, and Buddy waited his tail wagging.

Anthony squealed, "Buddy. Dad, look, Buddy." Buddy caught Anthony's familiar scent and leaped with joy, and he jumped from one boy to the other and bounded into Jonathan's arms, licking his face.

Susan remarked, "He hasn't done that before."

"Yes, he has. Every night when I got home from work, this was the greeting he reserved for me, and he has done this since he was a puppy."

Susan realized Lily wasn't there, and panic set in. "Lily?" she yelled, and a faint bark came from the kitchen. "Damn it. You've locked yourself in the pantry again." Susan rushed farther into the kitchen with Anthony at her heels. She opened the pantry, and a little black pug jumped and carried on.

"Okay, little girl, no need to be so dramatic. No one murdered you," She peeked in, and the area was clean, with no messes, and Lily hadn't dumped the dog food. She was not inside long enough to do much damage. "If the pantry door isn't closed properly, this little one often pries it open to help herself to snacks," she informed the boys. "This is Lily, Buddy's best friend."

The boys stooped to pet her. Alex said, "She's so cute and little. How old is she?"

"Not yet a year old. Lily weighs only twelve pounds. And she's a troublemaker. Twelve pounds of terror. But she's so loved, and she makes me laugh. She keeps Buddy on his toes too. He enjoys her," Susan rambled, as she did when nervous. "My housekeeper is on vacation. We're going to have to fend for ourselves this week. Is anyone hungry? We can go to lunch, raid the refrigerator, or I can have a delivery. Do you guys like Pizza?"

"Yes, we do," Jonathan responded, his mouth dry and his nerves on edge.

"Okay, pizza it is." She called her favorite place and ordered enough food to feed an army, then she asked her visitors, "Would you like to tour the house and your rooms?"

Marc said, "Holy cow, look at that pool. That is sick."

Alex and Anthony ran to the glass door in the kitchen to see the pool.

"Mom, can we swim?" Susan didn't realize he was talking to her until Anthony came over to her. "Mom, can we swim?"

Susan was speechless, and a lump formed in her throat. *These kids are fantastic. Why couldn't she remember them?* "Sure." She walked them through the kitchen, past the closed door of her father's study.

She hadn't been inside since his death, and tears burned her eyes as she thought of the kind man who had been her father.

"What's in that room, Mom?" Anthony asked.

She took a deep breath and said, "The doctor's study." She walked them past the closed door, into the living room, and through to the foyer so she could show them their rooms.

Jonathan, eyes popped open at the marble staircase and foyer, exclaimed, "Holy Moly, I've only seen houses like this in magazines."

Susan smiled. "I didn't decorate it, but it is a beauty, and I had the same shocked reaction the first time, too." She escorted them upstairs and showed Jonathan to her old room, redone as a guest room. He dropped his bag on the bed and followed her. "There are four rooms here, guys. Each has a bathroom. You can choose among yourselves which room you want. They all have TVs," she said. The boys scattered, and each chose a room.

Anthony said, "Mom, where is your room?"

She walked them to the end of the hallway and opened her double doors. "This is my room now. I used to stay in the room your father is using."

Anthony went in and checked each side room. "Wow, Mom, a sauna. Can I use it sometime?"

"Just with your dad, never by yourself." she replied.

"What is that control outside your shower?" Anthony asked.

"This luxury is embarrassing, and I don't use it much. See this control panel? It controls the experience." She laughed.

"What experience? You just jump in, lather up, rinse, and get out. That's what you always preached to us when we use all the hot water, Mom," explained Alex.

"That's true, and that's just what I do. However, there are times I'm super stressed or sad, so I use this setting." When she pushed it, a gentle spray of water came from the showerhead, a light scent enveloped the bathroom, and soft spa music played.

"Is there one in my bathroom?" Anthony asked.

"No, use this. Each button tells you what the setting is," she replied.

The three boys went over and tested all the buttons. They determined they all wanted to use the rainforest mode.

The doorbell rang, and Susan jumped. "That must be lunch."

She ran downstairs and opened the door. She escorted the delivery into the kitchen and tipped the delivery guy with a handful of cash. She closed the doors behind him and called on the intercom, "Lunch is here."

She set the table as the boys ran down the stairs, with Jonathan telling them to slow down and be respectful. The kids did all the talking. They were excited to go into the pool. After everyone cleaned up, she asked if the boys had swimsuits, which they didn't.

"Can you swim in your shorts for now?" she asked. "You have a change of clothes for later, and then we'll go to the store, or we can order stuff online and get it delivered. I can bring my laptop out here, and you can choose stuff online should you not want to go out shopping."

The boys looked at each other and their dad. Their father's face reflected exhaustion and sadness.

"Online is good. This way, Anthony can exhaust himself in the pool," Jonathan responded to his father.

"What is that?" Alex asked, pointing to the grotto.

"That's the amazing grotto, and it looks like a cave. Here, let me show you." She walked the boys in, with Jonathan following.

"This is a relaxation area for when you want to escape the sun."

The boy's mouths gaped open when they looked at the big screen TV on the wall and the pleasant furniture.

"That's a bathroom with a changing room inside." Susan moved to the right. "And this is a kitchen, and over there is a swim-up bar. This refrigerator here has soft drinks, juices, and iced tea. This one has bottled water and this one, alcoholic beverages. You guys can take whatever you want out of these two. The other is for adults. These cabinets contain glasses and plates, and we pack this pantry here with junk food. Help yourself. Just don't make yourself sick."

The boys each grabbed a bag of chips. They were shoving chips in their mouth, leaving a path of crumbs on the patio. Each boy with a different flavor, tasting a sample from each other's bag. Afterward, they canon balled into the pool.

She turned her head toward Jonathan. "Would you like a beer, wine cooler, anything? Help yourself. I'm going upstairs to change into my swimsuit. Being poolside or in the pool is my favorite place."

"It always was at home too," he said woefully.

"Can you tell me more when I come down?" she asked.

Jonathan nodded. He thought, *how can we compete with all of this?*

"I forgot, guys. There's a sliding board built into the side of the rock formations that encompass the cavern area, and back here is the diving board. She showed them how to access each. Please don't go in without your dad being out here." She turned to Jonathan. "Will you be swimming?"

"I think so."

She nodded and hurried inside. She returned a few minutes later in her swimsuit and cover-up with the pugs in swim vests. Lily ran to the pool and jumped in. Susan threw her favorite toy in, and Lily swam after it. Buddy went and jumped in his dad's lap and licked his face.

The silence was uncomfortable between Susan and Jonathan. Jonathan tended to the kids in the pool, particularly the youngest, because he was fearless. Susan peered at him, and then the boys, back at him again and said, "I'm sorry that I don't remember any of this, of the life we built together. Those boys seem amazing. You did an excellent job with them."

"No, Nat, you did all of that." He pointed to the boys. "You quit your full-time job and became a full-time wife and mom. You raised those boys to be the amazing young men they are."

"Tell me about our life," she asked, feeling at a disadvantage of only knowing the life she lived now. Susan loved TJ but wasn't sure what affect her past life would have on their relationship. She was thankful they hadn't yet married. She was also grateful he was in England, so she could sort this out before he came back.

Jonathan told her everything about how they met, what a wonderful marriage they had, and the birth of each boy. He explained their extended family with her friends from college and the pug she found in the snowstorm that started her love for the breed. Jonathan showed her pictures in his wallet. A photo of her he took when they were first dating, then their wedding pictures and pictures of the boys.

She cried and became noticeably upset. Her hands shook, and she grasped them together to quell the shaking. Jonathan went to her and kissed her forehead, and wrapped his arms around her. She accepted it despite feeling uncomfortable. The tingling that coursed through her body felt like a betrayal to TJ.

She pulled away and said, "I'm going inside for a sec to get the laptop and compose myself. Help yourself to anything, and there's plenty in both pantries. Cora worried I wouldn't eat in her absence."

Susan returned several minutes later with the laptop and a bowl of fruit salad and placed it on the table. She stepped inside for bowls and silverware and stacked them next to the fruit. Sitting at the outdoor table, she booted up the computer. She took the fruit, went onto the Neiman Marcus site first, logged in and navigated to the casual men's apparel shop, and slid the computer to Jon. "This is the Neiman Marcus site, casual men's wear department. Order what you need. Please don't add a credit card. I've already logged into my account. They'll deliver the clothing. Please call the boys over when you finish."

Confusing thoughts barraged her mind. *If I am Jonathan's wife and NOT Susan, was Doc aware? Will the media think I'm an imposter and a thief after inheriting Doc's fortune? Should I call Thomas? No, he'd alert TJ, and I don't want his short fuse to make him walk off the set.* Lost in thought, she didn't notice that Jonathan tried to get her attention until he touched her arm, leaving it tingling.

"This stuff is way too expensive. I can't order using someone else's money," Jonathan said, sliding the computer back.

"Yes, you can. Please, just do it. Once we get over the clothing hurdle for you and the boys, we'll address activities. I want to spend as much time as possible with you all, hoping that my memories return. Please, can you just order the stuff you need while here and not look at the prices? Please?" Susan rubbed her head and pinched the bridge of her nose. She was getting a migraine from the stress.

Jonathan sensed her distress, and he didn't want to cause her to cry yet again. He slid the computer back and chose a few items.

She smiled at him and said, "Don't forget a few swimsuits. I think this pool will get regular use."

He finished placing his items in the cart and passed the computer to her. He never bought such expensive casual items. There wasn't an item close to what he paid back east. He ordered the minimum, knowing he could launder them. He kept an eye on the boys, and for the first time in their marriage, he was speechless. Relieved, worried, and without a way to converse with his wife.

She called the boys and asked, "Who wants to place their order for clothes first?"

Anthony yelled back, "You do mine, Mom, please, you know what I like." He went back to playing with Lily.

"If only," she said exasperated as she turned to Jonathan. "What size does he wear?"

"Size ten."

"Okay. You may need to approve of my choices, though. That is if we can get those two out of the pool," she referred to Anthony and Lily. She added several things to the cart. But before she finished, she went over and looked inside his shoes for his size, then added sneakers to the list of items to get. She checked the cart to ensure she had everything Anthony needed before calling one of the older boys over. "Who's next?"

Alex walked over shyly. She slid the computer over to him. She had it set up for the boys' clothing department. He added a few things and passed the laptop.

"Thanks," Alex said.

Susan smiled at him, "You're welcome." She called over to the oldest, "You're up."

Before she hit send, she checked the cart to be sure they ordered everything they would need. *Of course.* Both the boys had forgotten underwear and shoes. Looking inside their footwear, she retrieved their sizes. She added sandals for the pool area along with new sneakers. She wondered aloud if she should ask what their favorite brand was or just buy what she had seen the boys wearing now. They all said "anything," so she ordered what she thought they would like.

While Jonathan swam with the kids, she looked at his shoes and ordered him shoes. She added a few more things to his items. She completed her shopping and requested delivery by the end of the business day. Confirmation of delivery pinged her phone. She glanced at the boys, who were getting red from the sun. *What an idiot. I didn't remind them to put sunblock on.* She hurried into the dressing room and came out with several towels and several bottles of sunblock.

"Hey, you're all getting sunburned. Please dry off and use this. A little late now, but I should've thought of this before."

They begrudgingly climbed from the pool and toweled off. Anthony took a bottle of sunblock and went to his mother. As if nothing had changed their relationship. He handed it to her and waited. She applied the sunblock, as any mom would do. He looked up at her adoringly. Susan pulled him to her and buried her face in his hair. He smelled like pool water and a little boy. She inhaled him. No memory. But she enjoyed the moment as much as he did. He was a precious child, full of life and joy. The two older boys seemed much more reserved, but sweet. She offered the boys fruit and asked if they were hungry.

"Yes." they all exclaimed in unison.

Susan laughed and asked their father, "Do they always do that?"

"Yup, three peas in a pod."

"Alright, what would you like? We still have all that food from lunch in the kitchen refrigerator, or you can raid either fridge or help yourself. There are also pantries in both the grotto and kitchen, you remember the one, and Lily's famous hiding spot." She laughed.

The boys raided the kitchen first. Lily and Buddy were cuddling on the sofa inside, both snoring softly. Susan placed a towel over them and turned on the ceiling fans to increase cooler airflow inside the cave-like area.

The boys mesmerized Susan as they ate at the outdoor table. She smiled and turned to Jonathan and said, "They're awesome, and they make me happy."

"Yes, they are. The boys kept me sane while you were missing."

Susan removed her engagement ring when she changed into her swimsuit, out of respect for Jonathan. She loved TJ and wanted to marry him. But Jonathan's anguish broke her heart.

When Susan returned, Jonathan realized she wasn't wearing TJ's engagement ring and didn't comment, but she wasn't wearing his ring either. He assumed she would share when she was ready. His concern, the constant worry, was if she would return to their family or stay in the warm climate with her fiancé. How could he agree to a divorce? She was the love of his life. His knee bounced as his thoughts buzzed in his head. He gazed at the children, knowing their hearts would be crushed if she didn't choose them.

They had a lovely afternoon, and Susan realized it was getting close to dinnertime. She asked the boys to get ready for dinner. Picking up after these little guys exhausted her. She went upstairs to change into a sundress with a pair of sandals. She found the boys in the family room watching TV and Jonathan with the pugs by the pantry. He said, "I found their food but not bowls."

She took the bowls out of a cabinet and handed them to him, "Just one scoop, their cooked food is here. Cora cooks for them."

"That scoop is super small. Is that dog food?"

"No, just a supplement they get twice a day. We add home-cooked food." Susan split the warmed-up food between both bowls and placed it on the floor. Like typical pugs, they scarfed it down.

"What do the kids like to eat?" she asked. "We'll go somewhere casual."

Jonathan laughed. "Ask them but wait for it. You're in for a treat."

"No, you ask them. I'll watch and learn." She grinned.

"Guys, we're going out for dinner. What do you want to eat?"

The three boys responded differently at the same time and began arguing over whose turn it was to choose. She laughed and said, "Oh, wow, I think you opened up a can of worms."

"Happens every damn time."

She said to him, "You choose, and I'll say I did."

"Mexican," he said.

"Hey guys, we're going to the nice Mexican place I love, a fun and casual place." She pulled up the address on her phone. "Good? And next door is an arcade if you like that kind of thing." She checked her email for updates to their clothing order. "It appears everything will arrive by ten p.m. I'd like to be home to receive it." She looked up as she tossed her phone into her purse. "Alright, let's head to the garage." Anthony padded next to her, barefoot. "Anthony, did you forget something?" she asked, laughing.

"Oh, yes, my phone. Dad bought me a phone." he exclaimed.

"That's nice, sweetie, but I was referring to your shoes. The restaurant is casual but not relaxed enough for just toes."

"Duh." He slipped into his shoes and ran after his brothers. Susan checked to make sure the pantry door was closed and engaged. She set the alarm and locked up the house. She found the boys running around the garage investigating her father's cars. "Are you guys ready? We can take my car. Was it uncomfortable for you in the back?"

"No, the convertible is cool," Marc said.

"Alex, are you okay? Do you like the convertible? I can put the top up if you prefer."

"No, don't," Alex replied.

Susan took a hair tie out of her glove box and pulled her hair back so it wouldn't blow too much. "Off we go. Buckle up."

The relaxed restaurant was inviting and done in traditional Mexican style artwork. The boys commented on the colorful chairs, each different. Susan glanced around at the unique style. "It is beautiful," she responded to the boy's comments. Dinner arrived, each family member ordering something different.

"Wow, I'll come back here. Those were the best street tacos I've ever had." Susan mentioned, wiping her mouth. She watched as the boys perused the dessert menu.

After the restaurant, Susan took the boys to the arcade and bought a family package of coins. She split them three ways and told them to have fun and not to leave the building. The parents sat in the café in the back. Grateful that she had looked at the area online while the boys ran around the garage and saw the café on the arcade's website. They found a table near the window that gave a complete view of the arcade and ordered coffee.

The server returned with two steaming cups, and Susan started the conversation. "I'm sorry for all the pain you and the boys are going through. I don't have any recollection of our life together. Are you one hundred percent sure I am who you say I am? Could I look just like your wife?" After getting used to her life, now the slammed her with another identity—the forgotten one.

"Nat, I have the DNA proof." He leaned in closer and lowered his voice. "Natalia, I can describe your body. There's a scar on your lower abdomen near your pelvic bone—a Cesarean section scar from giving birth to the boys. Also, a birthmark on your right butt cheek. It looks like an upside-down heart." He looked into her eyes, and he knew it was true, but he asked her anyway. "Right?"

Tears formed again, and she replied, "Yes."

He took the tissue out of her hand and wiped her tears. "I didn't mean to make you cry. It destroys me when you cry. It always has. I never want to cause your tears. Somehow, we will get through this and decide in the best interest of every one of us, I hope."

She nodded.

Just then, the boys ran in. "That was awesome."

She checked her phone for the first time. One missed call from TJ. And it was time to head back and wait for the delivery. There were pajamas for the boys in the delivery.

"Are you guys out of tokens?" she asked.

"Yes, mom. We're all out," Anthony answered. He seemed to be the only child willing to speak to her.

"Let's go. We should be home for the delivery. We can do this again another time since you enjoyed it so much."

As they walked to the car, Susan listened to the whisper of the breeze through the trees. Glancing at the sunset, the pinks and deep orange that lit the sky below the moon, she knew it predicted another sweltering day. Shivering from the cool evening air, she raised the top of the convertible and got them home.

They weren't in the house but a few minutes when the front doorbell rang. She opened the door to the delivery service with their packages. She tipped the delivery man and locked up behind him. The boys stood behind her, Anthony rubbing the sleep from his eyes.

"Can one of you grab me a pen off the desk in the family room? We'll sort this stuff into piles so I can make sure everything is here. Also, grab four sheets from the printer."

Jonathan returned to the foyer from the family room, where he'd played with the pugs.

She printed each name on a piece of paper and went through the boxes, thankful that everything they ordered had arrived. The boy's excited chatter filled the room as they compared their stuff. Susan scored massive points with the new sneakers. They were the latest release, which thrilled the boys.

"Guys, please grab a box and put your stuff inside. We'll take it all up in the elevator." Once the boys filled the boxes, she escorted them to the elevator, and the five of them rode up in silence.

"Just put all the wrappings in the boxes. Put your stuff into the dressers. Good night, guys." She left them to their own devices and hurried downstairs to retrieve the dogs. Susan reached for her phone and realized it was six A.M. in London. She returned to TJ's call. His assistant answered and stated he was in makeup but would give him the message the next time he took a break.

The following morning, she woke with a start and climbed wearily from her bed. *Was it another dream? Was the family that claimed her here?* Stepping into a lightweight robe, she opened the bedroom door. The pugs flew down the stairs in their typical fashion. Standing on the small patio, as the dogs ran around their little play area, Susan turned toward the pool. The pool water glistened. She stared at the calming water as the robotic vacuum moved about, creating the peaceful flow of the water. She stepped into the kitchen to brew a cup of coffee when Jonathan appeared.

He leaned over and kissed her on the lips as he said, "Good morning."

The kiss left her flustered and unnerved. Her lips quivered from the gentle kiss. She showed Jonathan the brewer and told him to help himself with anything. "I'm going upstairs to get dressed," she said to Jonathan, and she ran up the steps.

After she dressed, she listened to a voicemail from TJ. He seemed angry, and she suspected he had read the papers. The industry newspaper's morning delivery had several photos of them at various locations, the practice, last night's dinner, and the arcade. Of course, they caught the damaging shots. Jonathan wiping her tears, opening the car door for her, a picture of Anthony with his arms around her.

TJ sounded furious. His message simply said, "What the fuck, Susan. Call me."

She decided not to call him back, giving him time to calm down. Susan couldn't worry about TJ right now, not with this decision looming over her head. She was in love with TJ, but she had also had a family and a husband, even if she couldn't remember them. Didn't that mean she had some responsibility toward them? She wanted to spend all the time she could with her family. They still had time before the children were due back at school in New Jersey.

The day they went to Disney, the weather was perfect, not too hot. Even with Marc and Alex being older, they had a fun time. Susan had no memories of being there before. She enjoyed it as much as they did. They were all exhausted, but happy. Industry papers and gossip magazines had a plethora of photos and bits of conversations overheard. The paparazzi, once amusing, were now very intrusive. It relieved her when they got home, secure behind closed doors.

Twenty-eight

JONATHAN SAT ALONE in the kitchen with a coffee mug. Reaching for the newspaper, and thought it was the morning news. Flipping through it, he found photos of them and headlines. He grimaced and said, "Uh oh."

Susan stepped into the kitchen wearing a swimsuit and cover-up. She watched as he read the paper and shook her head, knowing full well what he read. The TV volume was higher than usual as an action movie captivated the boys. TJ's call riddled Susan with anxiety and sorrow. She asked Jonathan, "Will you come with me to my father's study? I haven't been inside since his death."

"Sure. Let me tell the boys to stay put."

He followed her into a study. Richard had decorated in darker masculine tones with a huge ornate desk in the room's center. Leather seats with the gentle reminders of male cologne lingered. She stepped over to her father's desk and began opening drawers, looking for anything about her past. She pressed on and found a safe in the deepest lower drawer. He told her the combination to the upstairs one was her mother's birthday. She punched the numbers into the electronic keypad, the safe hummed and popped open. Inside, laying on the top, was an envelope addressed to her, in her father's chicken scratch. She opened it.

Dear Natalia,

It seems strange to print that name as during the last twenty-one months, you were my Susan. If you are reading this, I've gone to be with my beloved Donna.

I must beg your forgiveness. I didn't learn of your identity until recently, and when I knew the end was near. My heart broke. I didn't have more time with you to express my sorrow in person.

When I found you, I placed your purse and cell phone in my safe. Not sure why I did it. Perhaps in the furthest recesses of my mind, I wanted you to forget your past. I genuinely believed you were my Susan. The resemblance is uncanny, and I should have known why.

Before I became sick, I was in heart failure and knew I was on my journey. I removed your purse from the safe and opened it. I almost died on the spot when I read the name "Natalia T. Conte-Miller" on your driver's license. I didn't panic as I thought that could be the identity you took on after your disappearance.

I looked at your photos and realized you had a husband and children that I deprived you of and denied them. I was heartsick at what I had done. I located your social media page and read all the tributes to a missing friend. After contacting a Private Investigator, I asked him to find out about you, sweetheart.

The information he supplied left me sicker than cancer ravaging my body. Your parents were Antonia and Catarina Conte, who died several years before our paths crossed. You married Jonathan Miller, a loving man, eighteen years ago, and you are the mother of three sons.

I am sorry. I know it seems inadequate and meaningless. But I am sorry, profoundly so.

As Susan Kline, you inherited my fortune. As Natalia Miller, that fortune is still yours. Once I found out who you were, I had everything transferred to you in your actual name. There are three fully funded college grants for your sons. Any college they want. From the first year through to comprehensive education to their doctorates. They will dis-

perse any remaining funds to them on their 30th birthday. I wish I could've met them, knowing you raised them.

You were my angel, both before I became ill, but even more so after. I am very thankful you followed my care and took total control of my health as any daughter would. Know that I left this world a fortunate man, having spent my last twenty-one months with you.

Do all you can, find your way back to where you belong, choose wisely, and lead with your heart. Please convey my most profound regret that I inadvertently kept you from them.

Remember our promise about Cora and Jack. Your management team is the best and remember that YOU sign every check to keep your inheritance safe.

Be a happy, sweet girl. You can't understand how your presence brightened my life.

My sweet, funny girl, my precious daughter, I'm grateful we had this time together, and I hope you can forgive me—our Royal Highness.

I love you,

Dad

xoxo

Tears streamed down her face as she read the letter. Her hands shook, and her body trembled as she folded the letter back into the envelope. She needed to talk to Maria, who always supported her and explained things reasonably.

Jonathan sat next to her on the floor and wrapped his arms around her. "I'm sorry, honey. This situation is pretty messed up, and I don't know what to do for you."

"There is nothing you can do. I just need to remember. I try so hard that my brain hurts," she replied, her lower lip quivering.

"We should go tend to the kids. I hear a commotion out there," Jonathan said. He helped her up from the floor and kissed her lips tenderly. She was flustered, but didn't complain.

They enjoyed a lovely day together as a family, and Maria arrived after work with dinner. She spent time with Jonathan and the boys, and after dinner, the two ladies went upstairs to Susan's bedroom. She looked at Maria and burst into tears. "What am I going to do?"

Maria began, "Susan, you are my best friend, and I would be remiss if I didn't help you find your bliss. You're supposed to marry TJ, and I think you love him, but are you in love with him? From what Jonathan has told me, you were a match made in heaven from day one. Could he be lying? Perhaps. However, look at the letter from your father ... um ... doc. He investigated him. All satisfactory results, he is a good guy. This choice is tough but think. Think about the qualities each man has."

"I agree, but it has just been days with Jon to observe his qualities."

"And think of TJs. You've told me he babies you, and you think it's an insult to your intelligence and independence. Sometimes that's the beginning of a controlling person. I'm not accusing him, but just subtle trivial things I pick up. Spend time with Jon, both with the boys and without the boys. TJ is on location now. Try to avoid him for the time being so you can concentrate on your family. When you decide, you must clear-headed."

"You're right. Thank you. No matter what happens, we will always be best friends. You're like a sister to me," Natalia assured her.

"You too," Maria responded. "One other thing, as your doctor, I think you should begin thinking of yourself as Natalia. Start using the name. Perhaps memories will return, or you will feel more comfortable using your real name. I conferred with Dr. Paulson, and he recommended it as well."

"Okay," she let the name roll off her tongue. "Natalia Miller. I am Natalia Miller."

She was in love with TJ, and the thought of ending it with him hurt her heart. But she also had a family and a husband, even if she couldn't remember them. She wanted to spend as much time as she could with her family. They still had time before the children had to be back at school in New Jersey. Inhaling, she called TJ. She loved him and couldn't just ignore him.

"Hi," her voice quivered.

"Babe. What the hell is going on there? Who is this guy? And those kids?" TJ asked.

"My family," she replied in a faint voice.

"And how do you know for sure they are your family? Susan, you're not stupid. Why are you falling for this scam?" he admonished.

"They presented the DNA proof that I'm his wife and their mother."

She went into detail about how the PI captured her DNA. She mentioned they had the mug they used and the tests verifying accuracy. He was angry, disappointed, and shocked. He said he was coming back to the states to find out what's going on.

She begged him not to. "TJ, please don't. You'll violate your contract and possibly ruin your career. Also, I need time to decide."

"Susan, how can I compete with them?" TJ asked pitifully.

"He said the same," she replied wearily.

"He has an edge, him, the kids, and history."

"You also have my love. It doesn't mean I love you less. I need to decide between you and a family I don't remember," she responded as she disconnected.

JONATHAN LAID IN BED, alone and lonely. He wanted her but couldn't add sex into the mix right now. *How can I compete with all of this? A movie star fiancée, mansions, money, cars?* He knew finding the letter upset her and knew how to help Natalia in the past, but this new Natalia was different. She still had the same kindness, but she also had more substantial confidence in herself, somewhat of a detached vibe. Jonathan knew he loved her, still in love with her. The old Natalia and the new. She was his wife, and he wanted her back.

After a fitful night's sleep, he woke up earlier than usual, slipped into a pair of shorts, headed out the bedroom door, and heard the pugs crying in her bedroom. Opening the door slowly, he listened to his wife's gentle, familiar breathing pattern for a few seconds as the dogs darted from the room, then Jonathan followed behind at a slower pace to the kitchen.

After turning on the brewer, he reached into the pantry for their food. Sitting at the breakfast bar, sipping coffee, he perused a magazine she had laid there yesterday. His gaze left the glossy pages of the fashion magazine and met her shining eyes as she entered the room. Her lips curled into a sleepy smile.

"Good morning, beautiful. Would you like coffee?"

"Yes, I need it. Thank you. Were the puppies out yet?"

"No, the alarm's on, and I didn't know the code. But I fed them."

Natalia padded into the laundry room and disengaged the alarm. Jonathan stepped outside with the pugs and his coffee. He threw the ball, and they brought it back to him. Natalia poured a cup of coffee and joined him. She stood by his side as he tossed the ball to the pugs. She was calm. He asked her if she was hungry.

"A little." She smiled at him. The bright early morning sunlight cast a ray across his light brown hair. The pugs ran to the back door when they had enough of the yard. Jonathan opened the door, and he knew there were dog treats on the shelf. He reached for the jar, opened it, and passed a treat to each pug. Following them into the kitchen, Jonathan pulled open the refrigerator. He looked at Natalia, watching him sleepily. "There aren't any eggs. Is there a store nearby?"

"We usually order groceries online. But what if we go to my favorite breakfast stop? I think the boys would like it, and there are often sightings of movie stars," she asked.

Jonathan replied, "I think they would love it. Let's wake them."

They strolled into the foyer together as they climbed the stairs. Jonathan snaked his arm around Natalia, and she didn't step away. When they reached the top of the steps, he walked into Anthony's room.

Natalia was closer to Alex's room, and she tapped on the door, no response. She glanced toward Anthony's room as Jonathan closed the door behind him. He nodded for her to go in. She walked into Alex's room. He was asleep on his back, his arms crossed behind his head. She caressed his cheek until his bright blue eyes popped open. "Wake up, sweetheart."

He offered her a sleepy smile and sat up in bed, rubbing his eyes. "Morning, Mom." That was the first time he'd called her mom.

"Good morning, handsome. Your dad and I thought about taking you to my favorite breakfast spot. How does that sound?" she asked him.

"Sounds good."

"And then maybe I could take you guys shopping. You can pick out some fun things."

Alex gaped, his eyes glistening, "oh, consolation prizes?"

"No, honey, I just want to get you fun things, that's all. This situation has been rough for you guys and your dad. I'll be honest with you. I'm bewildered, and my memories are not coming back yet. But I'm thankful you're all here and that you found me."

Alex had tears floating in his eyes. She pulled him into her arms. Tears streamed down her face, as she knew she had hurt him. "I promise you I will be honest with you always, no matter what happens. I want to get to know you and your brothers more. You guys are amazing."

"Dad too?" he asked.

"Yes, Dad too." She kissed the top of his head and didn't want to let him go. "You get ready, and I'll do the same. Meet you downstairs. We'll have fun today."

It took Natalia thirty minutes to get ready. She wore a slim-fitting dress, which showed how hard she worked to be fit and healthy after her accident. When she arrived downstairs, everyone was waiting in the family room.

"Are you guys ready?" she asked.

Anthony ran to her and hugged her. "Yes, Mom, we're ready. Is the place nearby? I'm starving."

She laughed. "Yes, little man, it is close by."

She looked up, and her family stared at her. "What? Why are you looking at me that way?"

Marc said, "You always called us 'your little men.' Maybe memories are coming back to you."

Not wanting to disappoint them, as she had no clue why she said it, she smiled at Marc and said, "I hope so."

She took them to the Cabana Café in the Beverly Hills Hotel, and the hostess showed them to an outside table. Unfortunately, the boys didn't see anyone they recognized. A few of Dr. Kline's acquaintances stopped by to say hello. As usual, the paparazzi were outside and took a few shots as they entered the hotel. Natalia enjoyed breakfast and friendly conversation. She was happy to be part of this family.

After breakfast, Natalia brought them to the Apple store. She mentioned to Jonathan earlier that her phone broke that morning after dropping it on the bathroom floor. As soon as they entered, the boys scattered. She looked at Jonathan, smiled, and said, "I guess they like this store."

An associate approached her with a tablet. "Good morning. How may I assist?"

"Hi and good morning, I need to replace my phone. It's in terrible shape." She laughed and handed him her shattered phone.

He smiled and said, "That is bad. What's your name? I'll assign a technician."

"Susan Kline." It was instinctual to give that name. She wasn't used to being Natalia and worried that Jonathan overheard her slip. It appeared he hadn't heard because Marc preoccupied him.

He typed into the iPad, smiling. "The wait isn't long."

A young man approached her. "Ms. Kline, my name is Jerome. How can I help you?"

She gave him her shattered phone. "I dropped this. I don't think we can salvage it."

"Is it insured?" he asked.

"I'm not sure, but I doubt it. I had the phone for a while now. Can I just buy another? This one." She pointed to a phone on display.

"Of course, I'll be right back with it," Jerome said.

Natalia glanced at her family as they tested out a display tablet. She experienced a rush of tenderness toward them. When Jerome returned, she asked him about the electronics that intrigued her family. He explained the two younger boys were playing with iPads, and the older one and her husband were trying out the newest MacBook.

"Are any of those devices good for school?" she asked him.

"Well, the Mac book is an asset for homework and research. And the iPad will be useful."

"Okay, can you get me four more phones, five iPads, and two MacBook's?"

"Yes, ma'am, I'll send someone over from sales," Jerome said, waving to a young woman, who hurried over. "Mrs. Kline, this is Stacy. She can help you with your needs."

"Hello. Stacy, do you have my order?"

"Yes, Mrs. Kline, I have it. I just have a few questions. Do you want the iPad Pro?" Stacey showed her the larger tablet.

She pointed to the boys. "No, I like the size my sons are looking at now."

"Okay, and what about memory?" Stacy asked. After discussing memory sizes, the sales associate hurried into a room in the store's rear.

Natalia walked over to her sons. "Having fun, guys?"

"Yes," Marc answered for his brothers. "I think I'd like to work in a store like this someday."

"Maybe during college. You'll go to college, right?" she asked, her eyebrow raised.

Marc nodded in reply.

"My phone should be ready soon, and then we can head out and do other fun things. Stacy and Jerome hustled over to them, carrying three shopping bags. Natalia handed them her American Express card for payment.

Jonathan stepped over and took the bags. He asked Natalia, "These all yours?"

"Yep," she replied.

Jonathan inhaled and sighed. *This is over the top.* They almost didn't fit into the trunk of the sports car. Next was the La Brea tar pits. She kept a watchful eye on the boys. After they walked through the entire museum, she took them to lunch at a different arcade than before.

While the boys played, she looked at Jonathan. "Are you okay? You seem a bit off-kilter?"

"I'm okay, just thinking about the boys. They need to be back to school on Monday."

"So soon? Can you stay for another week? Are their grades good?" she asked him.

"Unfortunately, their grades slipped since you went missing. And I don't want to pull them out."

"Can you email their teachers and ask for their work? I can hire a tutor for them." Her voice quivered as the tears sprung to her eyes, "I need more time with them, with you."

"Okay, honey, please don't cry. That's all I make you do is cry. I was hoping you would come back with us. Maybe being in our home, you will remember?" he suggested.

"Maybe, I could do that," she replied, chewing on her lower lip.

When they arrived back at the house, Jonathan unloaded the bags and placed them on the breakfast bar.

She dropped her purse right next to them. "Cora and Jack are coming home later today. I'm grateful you'll get to meet them." She emptied the bags and asked Jonathan to get the boys.

She handed each of them a phone. It excited them to receive the latest phone and an iPad. They were at the kitchen table, opening them, and Marc came over and said, "Mom, I think this one is yours. It's pink." He had called her mom and smiled.

Her heart burst. "Marc, honey, I think you're correct. This one must be yours."

"Guys, there are two MacBooks here. One is for you three to share, and the other is for your dad." She handed Jonathan a stack of Apple products. The phone, the iPad, and the Mac.

"Honey, this is too much. We can't take this," he exclaimed.

"I bought this with the money which I earned. Not the inheritance. And look at those smiling faces. I wanted to do something special for them. I promise not to make it a habit." She smiled at him. "Besides, I missed Christmases, right?"

He looked into her eyes and smiled back. "Okay, I'll back off this time," he said, winking at her.

"How about a dip? I just love the pool." she said.

"Sure, but I wouldn't count on them," he replied.

She peeked in on the boys, who were unpacking everything. The room was a mess. But it made her happy.

Twenty-nine

NATALIA SAT IN HER room, her legs crossed on the plush cream brocade comforter, and tapped TJ's contact information. She smiled, remembering the day he typed it into her phone. Her timing was impeccable, as he was on break.

"ello, my love, how are you?" he asked, using an exaggerated British accent.

Natalia giggled, "I'm okay. How are you?"

"Busy but missing you."

"I miss you too."

"How are things going with the family?" he asked, his tone changing to sarcastic.

She sighed. "TJ, the boys need to go back to New Jersey for school on Monday. I'm going with them."

"You decided without coming here and giving me a chance?" his tone reflected annoyance.

Exasperated, Natalia responded, trying to keep her voice even, "No, I didn't decide, I just want to go, and perhaps something will jog my memory."

"Do you plan to come here at all?" he asked.

"Yes, I planned to ask you if the third week in May was alright with you. Will you have time for me?" she asked.

"Yes, we're breaking for a few days. Will you fly commercial?"

"Yes, it's wasteful to fly private for one person," she admitted.

"Okay, love, I'll call you tomorrow." Placated that she was coming. "I love you."

"Love you too."

He didn't hear her return the love, as he'd already disconnected. Natalia undressed and slipped into her swimsuit and cover-up. She walked past Jonathan's room and heard him on the phone as she made her way downstairs.

Jonathan had called his parents to update them, and then the girls. They were happy that Natalia was okay. He told them he would come home on Sunday, and he had asked her to join him. He hoped Natalia would agree. After his call, he dressed his swim trunks, went downstairs, and peeked in at the boys. They wore earbuds and had movies playing on their iPads.

Jonathan stepped out onto the patio and glanced to the pool area. And he couldn't find Natalia. He peeked into the cavernous space and found her behind the bar, making drinks. He joined her, grabbed her, and kissed her greedily. She didn't pull away and kissed him back. He wanted her, but refrained from taking the kiss further.

Natalia hugged him and laid her head on his shoulder briefly, backing up. She smiled and handed him a drink, took hers, and walked out to the pool. She had set up the lounge chairs with thick towels and terry cloth pillows. There was a table between them, with a bowl of pretzels and sunblock.

Jonathan took full advantage of the sunblock. He asked if she needed lotion on her back. She said yes and turned to him as she lifted her hair. Jonathan applied the sunblock, caressing her back. He handed her the bottle and asked her to do his back. She was gentle, and her hands were familiar on his back. He thought this was not such a great idea as she was stirring feelings in him. He worried he couldn't control them.

After they sat down, he began, "I hope you agree to come home with us. I think it may help with your memory." He worried that should she decide not to, the divide between them would grow larger.

"When do you plan to leave?" she asked.

"Sunday? Does that give you enough time with Cora and Jack?"

"Yes, I know the boys need to go back to school. I'll come with you," she replied.

"Okay, I guess I should set up that iPad so I can make reservations for us," Jonathan announced.

"No, please let me call our pilot so he can file a flight plan. This way, we can take the pugs too. I don't want to leave them behind."

"Okay, as you wish," he said, leaning back into the chair.

They made plans for the trip home when Anthony came outside. "Dad, can you buy me this game?"

"Which game is it, Ant?"

Anthony handed his father his iPad and showed him. "It's the same game that is on the computer at home."

"Okay, grab me my wallet. I left it on the dresser upstairs," Jonathan said.

Natalia listened to the banter, smiling. "Sweetheart, my wallet is right there." She pointed to the bar. "I'll buy the game for you. What do you think of this? I'll buy gift cards for you to load into iTunes. Every month I'll replenish it as part of your allowance if you keep your grades up and do your chores. Deal?"

"Deal, thanks, Mom." Anthony ran to the bar and returned with her wallet. He sat next to her on the lounge chair, and she plugged in the info and completed the sale. He kissed her and ran back inside and told his brothers about the new deal. Jonathan stared at her.

"What now? Shouldn't I have done that? They do chores, right?"

"That's fine. Yes, the boys have chores. Just don't spoil them too much." Jonathan worried about how the money might affect them.

"I will try to behave," she said with an eye roll and mocking him.

He shook his head. "Some things are vastly different, and some things are very much the same. I'm taking a dip. Are you coming?" he asked.

"Yes, I just want to put a call into the pilot first. We should get the flight plan started."

Natalia made her call and returned outside. Jonathan was asleep on the float. She stealthily entered the pool. He wasn't sleeping but watching her the entire time, his eyes shielded by his dark sunglasses. Inching over to him, she was just about to tip him over when he grabbed her arm.

She shrieked in surprise. "I thought you were asleep."

"Oh no, I knew what you were up to the minute you walked toward the pool. Like I said before, some things are different yet so familiar." He slid from his float and into the water.

"Tell me about our life?" she requested. "Sugarcoat nothing. If I was a bitch, tell me. I'm struggling and very fearful of going to New Jersey. Will I fit in?"

"Honey, life differs from the one you have here, that's for sure. We own a pleasant house that you and I designed together. We chose everything and raised our boys there. A pleasant town, good people, and wonderful friends who are delighted you're coming home. Mrs. Hannigan next door worshiped you, and she's over the moon that you were found alive. I can't tell you the number of rosaries that woman said for you."

"What about us, what were we like? Did we get along, were we friends?"

"Babe, we were best friends. Soul mates. I don't want to fill your head to confuse you, but that is the truth. You will learn more when we arrive home. I can show you our wedding videos, videos of the kids when they were babies. Our friends will tell you. Your girls won't hold anything back."

"My girls? We have daughters too?" she asked, her eyebrows raised.

Jonathan laughed. "No, your best friends from college. You did everything together. You referred to them as your girls. They may be at the airport waiting for you," Jon joked.

She smiled. "What things do I pack?"

"Jeans, maybe Capri's. It's spring there, and the temperatures could go from freezing to warm. It is a crazy season back home, but there's a closet full of your clothing. Don't worry."

"Okay, I won't worry."

She placed an order for everyone, as she knew Cora and Jack would be home in time for dinner. She wanted to be home when they came and wanted them to meet her family. Natalia spoke to Cora every day and was excited for them to get home. She also placed an order for flowers, expected at five o'clock. Natalia scheduled dinner to arrive at six. Their flight was arriving at three. She sent a car for them and was eager to see them.

Natalia returned outside and found Jonathan in the hot tub. She stepped inside and sat beside him. "I placed the dinner order. Friday nights are our family nights. We order in, play games, or watch a new movie. Sometimes we bowl in our pajamas, and the loser has the clean-up patrol."

"You bowl in your pajamas? How does the paparazzi not grab shots of it?" he asked, surprised.

"I forgot to show you and the kids. There are two lanes in the basement."

"Wow, Nat. The boys would love that."

"Okay, then we bowl tonight after dinner."

He put his arm around her and looked into her eyes. "Nat, I missed you a lot. It was tough without you, and I lost part of myself."

"How did you find me?" she asked.

"Anthony saw you on TV, on the red carpet."

Natalia remembered that night. It was the night she'd slept with TJ for the first time. He had told her he took Susan's virginity years ago, but she did not know that because she wasn't Susan. Doc had Susan declared deceased many years before, even though his heart remained ever hopeful to be reunited. Torn, Natalia loved TJ, but she had feelings for Jonathan. *How did I get myself into this mess?*

She glanced at her phone, checking the time. "It's three-thirty. I'm going to get ready for dinner. Are you staying out here?" she asked Jonathan.

"No, I'm coming in."

Natalia peeked into the family room, and a movie had engrossed the boys. Jonathan walked upstairs, holding Natalia's hand. Stopping outside of her room, he pulled her to him, her body slamming into his, and kissed her. Natalia slid her arms around his neck, deepening the kiss.

He pulled away and said, "Unless you want to take this to a different place, we should stop," he said as he looked over to her bed.

"Okay, I'll see you downstairs in a little." After a quick shower, she pulled her hair up into a clip and changed into a pair of Bermuda shorts and a tank top. She touched up her makeup and hurried downstairs to be with her sons. They were just finishing watching their movies as she sat down on the sofa. The pugs jumped off the recliner and right into her lap.

Jonathan called home and told the girls he was taking Natalia home with him. They were squealing and acting like teenagers. He laughed and said, "Take it easy. She has no memory of our lives. She's different and yet the same. I hope she chooses us. I've always loved her and always will. I fell in love with her all over again."

Christina said, "Oh, we will make her remember, trust me. Don't forget, Jon. She was ours first, and we have many sordid stories to bring her memories back. We can't wait. As soon as you know the flight arrangements, we will pick you up."

"No, don't, she's overwhelmed easily. That's one different thing. She cries a lot. But justifiably so, a lot has happened to her. She arranged a car to take us home. Let me show her the house first, and then I'll call you over for dessert? Can you grab things to bring with you?"

"Okay, Jon, I'll bake her favorite things. We'll wait for your call," Alicia said. Out of all the girls, Alicia loved to bake, and everything she made was excellent. Natalia often told her she should open a bakery.

"Thanks, girls, I need to win her back."

When Christina heard that, she started teasing him, "Jon, you just need to ..." She mimicked sounds from a porno movie. "And she'll fall all over you."

He chuckled. "You are terrible, but I love you both. Talk to you later."

Jonathan hung up the phone and bounced downstairs, smiling as he walked into the kitchen. He didn't see Natalia, but heard her voice floating from the family room. She sat on the sofa with the two pugs half on her lap and half off. She looked healthy, glowing, and gorgeous. Jonathan wished she would have invited him into her bed.

Jonathan told her about his phone call to their friends. She smiled and seemed apprehensive. He didn't want to mention the dessert invitation and increase her worry. He learned it was best to give her a little information at a time. As he approached the kitchen, the front door opened, and he noticed a woman who could only be Cora come through the front door.

Natalia heard the alarm and ran into the foyer. "Cora." She ran into her embrace.

The two women held each other when Jack walked in, shook his head at the two women, and said, "Your highness, no love for your court, jester Jack?"

She walked into his embrace and hugged him. "I missed you both very much. Where is your luggage?"

Jack said, "The driver brought it around the side door to our suite. He said you asked him to do it that way."

"Yes, I did. I just forgot in my excitement."

"Come meet my family."

Cora never saw her so happy. Her face lit up when she called them her family.

Natalia reached for Jonathan. "This is Jonathan. Jon, this is Cora and Jack, my lifesavers."

Jonathan stepped forward and he shook Jack's hand. He leaned over to Cora and kissed her cheek. "Thank you for caring for my wife and keeping her safe."

Natalia walked with them into the kitchen. "I tried not to be messy, Cora. I didn't want you to come back from vacation and clean up our messes. I'll call for the boys." The pugs already found out Jack and Cora were home and jumped all over them gleefully, Lily squealing.

Natalia appeared in the family room and said, "Boys, I would like you to meet two incredibly special people."

The boys stepped into the kitchen timidly.

"This little man is Anthony. He's the youngest. Here is Marc, and he's the oldest, and this guy is Alex," Natalia said with pride.

"Oh, Miss Susan, they're very handsome. Come over, boys. May I please get a hug?" Awkwardly, but once in her embrace, they sensed the love and kindness emanating from her.

Jonathan heard her refer to Natalia as "Miss Susan." He said nothing, as it wasn't his place. He assumed it would take time.

Jack gave each boy a fist pump. They smiled, and everyone chatted at once.

"Cora, it is family night. Are you too tired for fun and games?" Natalia asked.

"I'm fine. What have you planned?" Cora asked as she sorted the mail. Cora planned the evening with Jack and Natalia's help.

"Well, dinner will arrive at six. Then I thought we would bowl. I forgot to show my family downstairs, and I thought tonight we could hang out down there. Are you up for it?'

"I know Jack is. He slept the entire flight. Thank you very much for that amazing vacation. And flying first class was unbelievably special."

"Are we bowling in pajamas?" Jack asked.

"Yes. We'll change after dinner. I think I hear the catering truck now," Natalia declared.

The dinner was delicious. Natalia gazed around the dining room with pride. She loved Cora and Jack and these boys of hers, and her feelings for Jonathan grew stronger each day. After dinner, the four adults put away the leftovers. Cora and Jack went into their rooms to change, and Natalia asked the boys if they wanted to change into their nightclothes. The boys wore basketball shorts but slept in their underwear. The nightclothes she bought remained new, with tags still on them.

She walked upstairs to her bedroom, and as she passed her old room, Jonathan stepped out of the guest room in basketball shorts and a T-shirt. He smiled and asked her if she would like him to escort her to her room. "You can come in. My stuff is in the dressing room. I'll get changed inside."

He sat on her bed and joked, "It's not like I haven't seen you in the buff before. We made babies together."

"You remember that, but I don't." she yelled from the dressing room.

She stepped out in her pajamas. A pink T-shirt with tiny flowers and pink matching pajama bottoms. Innocent, yet so provocative to him. She slid into her favorite slippers and took his hand.

"Let's go. I've got ass-kicking to do."

"You? Kick ass? Bowling? You're terrible at bowling, with any sport." Jonathan exclaimed.

"Hmm, we shall see. Would you like a wager?"

"Well, how is this? The winner gets a make-out session." Jonathan announced.

"Um, no. What if Jack wins? I cannot." she laughed.

"No, silly girl, I meant we play opposite each other, and if I win, I get a make-out session with you."

"And if I win? What do I get?" she inquired.

"A make-out session with me." he joked as his eyes shined bright.

"Tricky, aren't you?" she said, laughing with him.

Natalia and Jonathan walked downstairs and realized the rooms were empty. She turned to Jonathan. "I guess they're downstairs already." She walked him past the laundry room and opened a door. They heard the boy's laughter floating upstairs.

Jonathan's mouth gaped open at the room's size, and he salivated at the freshly made popcorn. Natalia showed him the party room, the kitchen, the gym, and the bowling alley. Marc and Alex helped Jack prepare for their games. Setting bowls of popcorn around the room, Anthony was with Cora in the kitchen, shoving beverages into an ice bucket. Anthony and Cora carried it together into the bowling area.

They played several games, and Jack won them all. Natalia was disappointed because she looked forward to the "session." But she also wanted to be loyal to TJ. She was in constant turmoil, torn between the two men.

SATURDAY MORNING, SHE woke up later than expected. She knew Maria liked to sleep in on the weekends and assumed calling now wouldn't be rude. Natalia sat up in bed. "Hello, are you awake?" Natalia asked.

"Yup, awake, worked out and dressed. What's up?"

"I'm going to New Jersey for a week or two. Then heading to London. The boys need to be back at school on Monday, and Jonathan feels if I returned, it might jog my memory," Natalia explained.

"What do you think?" Maria asked.

"I think it's a promising idea, although I would rather stay here. I fell in love with those kids, and the thought of not being near them breaks my heart," she said.

"What about Jonathan? Anything there yet? I can tell you that he loves you."

"Well, there are feelings. I like it when Jon kisses me or touches me, you know, those butterfly feelings. I'm very attracted to him."

"What is holding you back?" Maria asked.

"Guilt, loyalty to TJ. Like I'm cheating on him," Natalia explained.

"Nat, this entire situation is messed up. You're all suffering, trying to muddle through it, you, TJ, Jonathan, the boys. Let the guilt go. If you're feeling romantic feelings for Jon, go for it. He's your husband."

"I need to speak with TJ first. I love him and have a life planned with him. I should take my time because I'm an emotional and confused mess. Do I want to be intimate with Jonathan? Yes. Do I tell him I was intimate with TJ? That, I cheated on him?" Natalia responded.

"You didn't cheat, damn it. How could you even think that when you had no idea who or what happened in the past? You thought you were Susan. And to be honest, if I were in your shoes, I would try it with Jonathan to be sure there is something there. He might just be amazing in the sack." Maria exclaimed.

"Re, you are so silly, but I love you regardless," she replied, laughing. "I think we're hanging out by the pool today. Jack is going to have a BBQ for the boys. They hit it off. Those four are inseparable already. Last night we bowled, and they argued over who was going to be on Jack's team. We had such a fun time. Re, these kids are amazing. We can talk tomorrow about the practice unless you join us."

Thirty

JONATHAN WOKE UP EARLY because he wanted to take care of their laundry today, and it was easier to pack clean clothes than balled-up dirty clothes. He threw on his basketball shorts and a T-shirt, left the room, and banged into Natalia, who had her arms full of dirty laundry.

"Sorry, honey, did I make you spill all that laundry?" he asked.

"Good morning, and yes, but it isn't like you intended to." She smiled warmly.

They both bent down simultaneously, banged heads, and she giggled.

"Shh, you're going to wake the monsters," Jonathan said, laughing with her. "I was hoping to do the laundry to pack clean clothes."

"I planned to do it as well, but leave it here unless there was something the boys were fond of and wanted to take home?"

"Here? Why?" he inquired.

"Well, I thought maybe summers they would spend here," she said.

Jonathan's nostrils flared, and a deep red began at his neck, rising to his scalp. His pulse sped, and his body tensed. He stood, his body rigid and backed up, his mouth in a grim line, his temple twitched, and he spewed, "Oh, I see, you decided they will spend summers here with you? That's it, you made your decision?" he remarked angrily.

"No, no, no. I haven't decided, Jon. I thought if we stayed together, we would all come here."

"I work, Nat, I can't," he sighed, peering at her, his eyes in slits.

"Look, Jon, please don't be angry. It was a random thought that popped into my head, don't put any stock into it. Can we finish gathering the boy's things, and we can talk over coffee? Just you and me? Or better yet, let's go out to breakfast, just us, we can talk without the boys or anyone else around."

"Okay, I know we need to talk, but every time I try, you cry. I'm not blaming you, but when you cry, it breaks my heart. It always has," Jon replied.

"I understand, and you're right. I will promise to try not to cry. Let's get this stuff started. We can finish when we get back," Natalia said.

They gathered the boy's laundry, sorted it together on the floor, and started the first load. While Natalia's comment upset Jonathan, thinking the worst, she decided and wasn't strong enough to say it aloud, leaving him devastated and defeated. Once in the bedroom, he changed and called Matt, Alicia's husband, and one of his closest male friends. Matt is a tell-it like it is guy, and Jonathan values his opinions.

"Dude, is everything okay there?" Matt said when he connected the call.

"Damn, Matt. I just need to vent. I have no clue where I stand with Natalia. I see she's enamored with the boys. Me, not so sure. How can I compete with all of this, Matt? This house is tremendous. And she inherited several more. We're ordinary people with bills, a mortgage, and car payments."

"Calm down, Jon. Let me ask a few questions. Does she act repulsed or fearful of you?"

"No, she's sweet. Like my wife, but there are differences. She's more confident about some things, not that she wasn't before. She's different. I can't describe it," Jon said.

"I don't want to intrude on your privacy, but did you make any moves on her?" Matt asked.

"Kinda. We kissed a few times. One time it was intense, and she responded. I think if the location were more private. It might have gone further. Last night, I tried to make a bet that she would owe me a make-out session if I had won in bowling. She seemed to agree." He told Matt about all their interactions as they're etched in his memory. "Matt, I'm still in love with her, and it destroys me that lost her memories of us. I cannot lose my wife again. This morning she mentioned the boys coming for the summer. What the fuck am I supposed to think about that?"

"Okay, Jon, I think you need to talk to her. Soon, here, or there. You're coming home tomorrow. With any luck, the troublemakers will trigger her memories. I know Alicia went shopping last night for the ingredients for all her favorites. Today, she told me to make plans with the kids as she planned to bake her ass off because her girl was coming home. Char, Chris, and I are taking the kids to the shore for the day," Matt informed him.

"We're going to breakfast, alone, for that very reason. Thanks, Matt. I appreciate you letting me bounce thoughts off you. I'll see you tomorrow," Jonathan replied.

Jonathan ended the call and readied himself for his date with his wife. As he left his room, her bedroom door opened. They locked eyes, and he couldn't help himself. She looked gorgeous. She wore a white sundress that showed off her tan and curves, high-heeled white sandals, and her blonde hair worn down and flowing freely. Her makeup was always impeccable. At home, she was a mom, wore jeans, sweats, and shorts. Casual and comfortable. She always looked beautiful to him then, but this fresh style made her seem like a different person.

He kissed her, pressed his lips firmly onto hers, and took her hand. It was a challenge not to open his bedroom door and make love to her.

She laughed. "Jon, turn around to face me," she asked.

He did, and she ran her fingers over his lips and laughed.

"This is not your shade. I can't have you wearing lipstick that doesn't match your complexion. Not to mention the paparazzi will have a field day with it," she said, laughing.

Natalia took him to an upscale restaurant. She had called ahead to reserve a table for two in a secluded location. The staff chose the perfect spot as the table was near a beautiful picture window to look over the city. Next to the table, a beautiful indoor plant sat that provided ample privacy. Jonathan was as upset and nervous as she was.

Natalia thought she was closer to deciding, but the unknown in New Jersey frightened her. She knew she couldn't be away from those boys, her boys. Her heart couldn't take separation from them. Jonathan was fun, and she enjoyed spending time with him. He was easygoing primarily. She sensed his impatience in wanting things to go back to whatever they had before. They were getting closer, and she had feelings, but didn't understand what they were. Natalia was attracted to him yet still unsure and nervous. She loved TJ, but the lifestyles were not the same. She loved her life now, her job, Cora, Jack, and Maria. But her kids, those boys who stole her heart in a week. She needed those kids.

Their server appeared with crystal glasses and a coordinating pitcher of water. He poured them each a glass. "Welcome back, Miss Kline." He turned toward Jonathan. "Good morning, sir. My name is Jacob. I'll be your server today."

"Good morning, Jacob. Thank you for the water. I'll order the fresh fruit plate along with a hard-boiled egg. Please, can we have two cups of that delicious coffee blend you introduced to me last time?" she asked.

"Of course, I remember the blend you enjoyed, and I just brewed a fresh pot." He smiled at her. "Sir, can I take your order?"

I'm sick to my stomach. How can I eat anything? "Yes, the same, please," Jonathan responded, not opening the menu.

Natalia was thankful she didn't see any familiar faces, especially the paparazzi. They were too high up to get a shot from outside. They would need to be in the restaurant to grab one. She began the conversation. "Jon, I'm still very unsure of what to make of all of this. I'd like to tell you what I'm feeling, what I know, and what I don't. Okay?" she asked.

"Yes, go on, but Nat, you always told me everything. We had that kind of relationship. Hold nothing back. Don't worry that whatever you say will anger me."

"Thank you. I will not start from the beginning. I assume you know all of that by now. After I healed, I created a new life for myself, one that I enjoyed. My career is amazing, and I love working with Doc's foundation. I made good friends, and I fell in love with TJ. I rarely left the house because of my insecurities, but he helped me become confident and enjoy life. I can imagine that hearing that I love TJ hurts you." She reached across the table and squeezed his hand. "I didn't say it to do that. You asked me not to hold back, and I need to be truthful, one hundred percent because I can't live a lie."

Jonathan was quiet, and he nodded as she spoke. His mouth was dry, so he gulped water. Their food arrived, and Natalia remained silent until the server left.

Then she continued, "Being that I had a relationship with TJ, you need to know, it was an intimate one. That's exceedingly difficult for me to tell you because I cheated on you, although I didn't know 'you' existed. In my heart, I was disloyal to our marriage and our vows. Getting to know you, it upsets me further."

"Honey, don't you think I didn't know that? You are gorgeous and sexy. You thought you were single, and as much as I hate to say it, he's not bad looking either. When I saw you together on the TV, I knew I couldn't compete with him. I would torment myself and search the web for photos of you. It tore me up, but I had to see you. I wouldn't look at him, only you."

"Thank you for understanding. This morning when I mentioned the boys coming here for the summer, I wasn't thinking. It wasn't a hint as to my decision. I need to make that on my own with no reservations. I know this much. I can't be without the boys. There are a lot of things that come into play here. Things that I can't discuss that affect me and the decision I need to make. I have feelings for you, Jon. They're confusing to me as I'm in love with TJ. But you make me feel safe, loved, and happy to be near you. You must be the most patient person I know besides Doc, and you remind me of him in so many ways."

"Nat, I love you. From the minute I saw you in that conference room, I said to myself, 'your future wife just sat down across from you.' How I knew it, I don't know. I was grateful you took your break with me. From then on, we were inseparable. Trust me when I tell you, we had a fantastic marriage. I would be upfront and honest if it were less than that. But it was terrific, we seldom argued, and if we did, it didn't last." He smiled at a memory. "If I were at fault, you would steam for a little while, call me an 'asshole,' and it was over. If you were at fault, you would either apologize or ask, 'was I being a brat?' or I would call you a brat, and we'd laugh, and it was over. It was near perfect, honey. I promise you it can be again. I'm aware you're different. Sometimes those differences scare me, but other times I'm proud of how you handled this. This a lot for anyone to manage, unusual, unbelievable, and scary." Jonathan leaned back in his chair and sighed. "But we found you. Whatever your decision is, I know you will arrive at it using all the knowledge you now have.

One other thing, as I know, you're too polite to ask. Our sex life was outstanding."

Natalia's face pinked, and she giggled. "Well, alright then. No holding back there, Jon." I can tell you this. I love being near you, in the same room as you. You're handsome, kind, and loving. When you hold me, I inhale your scent. Somehow, it's familiar and comforting. And to be honest, I want to make love to you. However, I can't. It wouldn't be right. I know you want to, but I think it will confuse me more. I don't want to confuse sex with love. If I commit to you, it needs to be with no doubts and forever."

"I understand, and I think you coming home with me will help. You can sleep in our bed, and I'll sleep on the pullout in the office. I promise not to hit on you any longer, but I cannot promise not to kiss you." Jonathan smiled, a little less nervous, and said a silent prayer she chose him.

Natalia and Jonathan didn't touch their food during their conversation. She smirked and said, "It's a good thing we ordered cold food."

They stopped speaking and picked at their meals. The restaurant wasn't full of customers, no one nearby overhear their conversation, just two men across the room at a table. Jacob brought the check over in a leather portfolio.

She signed it and smiled. "Thank you, Jacob, for the great service. See you again soon."

"Thank you, Miss Kline." He nodded toward Jonathan and left.

Jonathan stood and pulled her chair out. He took her hand, and they walked to the front doors, holding her hand. *I said I wouldn't hit on her. Never mentioned I wouldn't romance her or treat her like I did before.*

Jonathan reached for her hand as they walked into the bright sunlight, and the valet ran to her car. Unbeknownst to them, the hidden paparazzi took great shots. The papers and gossip columnists went wild with the scandal. Natalia lowered the top for the drive home. She did it for two reasons. The weather was glorious, and it was challenging to converse. Her brain was frazzled, and her thoughts were all over the place. She was eager to return to the house.

Cora peeked up from the sink when Natalia and Jonathan walked in. "Good morning, love. You look stunning this morning," Cora said.

"Good morning. Thank you for taking care of the boys," She pointed to her boys shoving chocolate chip pancakes into their mouths. "Did you see the note I left you, Cora?"

"Yes, I did. Your boys are precious. I trust you enjoyed your breakfast date?"

"We did." Natalia turned and smiled at Jonathan, but she stayed at the kitchen table with her sons. She studied them. Her heart swelled with love. She created these kids even if she didn't remember. As she peered at their sons, Jonathan scrutinized Natalia. Her face softened, and she beamed. He hoped it was enough to keep their marriage intact. To remember how in love they were when she disappeared.

Cora noticed the pain in his eyes, and it broke her heart. After Natalia left the room, Cora reached for him and pulled him into her embrace. "It will be okay, Mr. Jonathan." She patted his back. "Enjoy your time with her, she's wonderful, but I can see you know that already."

"Thank you, Cora, and please, just Jon or Jonathan will suffice. I know you do that out of respect, but we are friends now."

"Jon, if you ever need to bend an ear, both Jack and I will listen. I know you feel like an outsider here and so alone in this, but please don't. Jack and I spoke last night. We could sense that Susan—sorry, Natalia was here, that a vital part of her life was missing. She's changed in the week you've arrived. Both Jack and I sensed a peace about her that hadn't existed before."

"Cora, thank you. That means a lot. It has been almost two years since I have laid eyes on her or held her. It is killing me, but I will be patient. I must be. I cannot rush her. Natalia should choose me because I'm me, not because of a sense of responsibility to her family."

The boys played games on their iPads, wearing earbuds as they enjoyed the excellent breakfast Cora prepared for them. Jonathan mentioned it was rude, but Cora assured him it was okay, that they had asked first. They heard Natalia's footsteps and stopped the conversation.

Natalia had been in Doc's study, signing checks the courier had sent over from her financial team. She learned a great deal from Doc and would protect his finances, as she knew how hard he had worked for them. Natalia retrieved Thomas's voice mail, saying that he made the name changes on the accounts. His voice brisk.

She opened the safe to look in her old purse. After reading the letter from Doc, she looked in her wallet, but never in the entire bag. She found a tube of lipstick. The shade was like what she wears now. She also found ATM receipts from Myrtle Beach, a dead mobile phone, a shopping list, a tissue package, and a sealed envelope with Doc's return address. Inside, she found an engagement ring and matching wedding band. She assumed these were from Jonathan, her life before her memory loss. She placed them in another envelope and sealed it. *I wonder why Doc hid this from me. What was going on with him that he thought this was okay?*

She walked down the hall and rode the elevator upstairs to her suite. She put the envelope in her bureau drawer next to the box containing her engagement ring from TJ. Her mobile phone rang.

"Hi, Fred," she answered.

"Miss Kline, they approved the flight plan. We will leave LAX at seven in the morning. Can you all be here by six-thirty?"

"Yes, Fred, we can, and thank you," she replied.

"I've also planned for a limo to be waiting in Philadelphia to take you to your destination. Will there be anything else? I'll make sure there are child-friendly snacks, and beverages are onboard, and your favorite wine."

"Thank you so much, Fred. You're very thorough. I appreciate it," she responded.

Natalia changed out of her dress and into yoga pants and a tank top. She ran downstairs and found her boys playing a game together on an iPad.

Marc came over to her and said, "Mom, I set up your iPad for you."

"Thank you, sweetheart. Does it work just like my phone?" she asked him.

"Yep, just like it."

She hugged him, and he let her, snaking his arms around her waist. She kissed the top of his head and hugged him tighter. He squeezed her back. She was happy to have reached him.

Natalia turned to Jonathan. "The flight plan is in place. The flight leaves at seven tomorrow morning. Do you think we can all be ready for six? The pilot would like us to arrive by six-thirty at the latest."

"That's fine," he replied.

She turned to her boys and asked what they would like to do on their last day. "Would you like to go to the beach? I'll show you the Malibu house."

She turned toward Jonathan. "That sounds like fun. Guys, what do you think?" Jonathan answered for them.

The boys were excited to experience Malibu beach after watching reruns of a TV show filmed on a nearby beach.

"Alright, you guys, grab your bathing suits. You can take your tablets in the car. Should we take my car with the top down or the town car?" she asked.

Jack overheard the conversation and said, "Your highness, I can drive you. I just need to repair the lock on the outside shower. Is that okay?"

Natalia asked Cora, "Would you like to join us?"

"No, but thank you, I will stay here with the puppies. I'll make a nice dinner for your last night here," Cora replied, her voice quivering.

"That sounds wonderful. Jack, thank you for offering to drive. I appreciate it. Okay, kiddos, let's get ready."

Natalia rushed upstairs to grab a beach bag for all the kids' swimming gear. She met everyone in the kitchen.

"Everyone ready?" she asked.

"Jack is waiting in the garage. He gathered the tools he needed and is ready to go when you are," Cora said. "I called the caretakers to open the windows and to make sure there are ample beverages in the refrigerator."

"Thanks, Cora. The last time we were there, it was full. And we haven't been back since."

The boys piled into the limo and were excited as Jack put snacks and juice in the cooler.

"Seat belts, guys, buckle up," Natalia told them.

Jonathan laughed and said, "You remembered a lot of your mom things."

"Well, not sure, I remember. But a responsible adult should remind them to put the seat belts on."

The boys plugged into their iPads the entire trip. Jonathan sat next to Natalia and held her hand. His thumb is caressing the top as he glazed out of the window.

After they arrived in Malibu, Jack set out to work on the outside shower door. The kids ran through the house investigating. Anthony appeared in the living room with a ball cap embroidered with TJ's

Oscar-nominated movie title. The film that TJ won the award for Best Male Actor.

"Mom is this TJ's ball cap?" he asked, his face beamed, and his eyes were wide. "I found it in that bedroom." He pointed. "Is that your bedroom? It's all girly."

Heat flooded her face, and she glanced at Jon, and he tried to remain nonplussed. "Yes, and yes, Anthony," she replied.

"Can I, have it?" She knew TJ had no idea he'd left it there, as he had several.

"Sure." She looked at Jon again. She was embarrassed and uncomfortable, knowing what she had disclosed earlier. His face was emotionless. "Okay, kids, get into your swim trunks. I'll do the same, and we can head out back."

The boys ran toward the back of the house, and she said to Jonathan, "Are you going to change into your trunks?"

Jonathan nodded, his teeth clenched, his movements abrupt. He wasn't speaking, as he knew he couldn't hold his annoyance and jealousy back. His stress level was at an all-time high, envisioning his wife with another man. It was an image he was struggling to clear from his mind.

Natalia sensed something was amiss, grossly amiss, but wasn't sure what to do. She went to him, pressed her lips to his in a gentle kiss, and walked away. She strode into her room, stepped into her bathroom, and changed into a swimsuit.

When Natalia stepped into the bedroom, Jonathan waited in the middle of the room, his face red and his body stiff. He stared at Natalia, unblinking. "Did it happen here?" he asked, glowering. His ribs felt tight, as though a tourniquet squeezed him. Sweat beaded on his forehead despite the chilly air flowing through the vents.

Wincing, she responded, "Jon, please. Do you want to go there? Does it matter where? It happened. I told you it did. Please don't torture yourself." She crossed her arms as though they were armor. She looked down, unable to meet his eyes.

"Nat, it has been over twenty-two months since the last time I made love to you. You're going to decide between your two lives, and you don't remember us together intimately, or our relationship, our family, but you know him that way. I don't think the playing field is fair."

Natalia's eyes sought for the boys and found them outside with Jack. "Are you friggin' kidding me, Jon? Are you going to guilt me into having sex with you to make the playing ground fair? Don't you think the timing should be right?" She was furious and continued, "None of this is fair to you, those kids, TJ, or me."

Her face flushed, her chin jutting out, her jaw tight. Natalia pointed her finger. "I thought you graciously accepted what I told you this morning. I didn't have to reveal anything. I don't talk about TJ or our relationship with you or in front of you. I'm trying to keep him out of the equation when I'm with you. I know Anthony finding that hat and being excited about it threw you for a loop. But this"—she waved her index finger back and forth between them—"is unnecessary. Don't ruin our last day in California like this."

Jonathan didn't respond. He knew he shouldn't have said it, but he was human. She was his wife, and the thoughts of her with another man made him crazy. Added to his frustration, he hadn't been with her in a long time. He walked out to the back porch and plopped down on a deck chair. He stared at the beach and the ocean. *How do I do this?*

Natalia sat next to him. She had no clue how to ease his mind. She wanted to make love to him. But being in a relationship with TJ stopped her. Should it? Maybe not, but she had to follow her instincts, do what she thought was right. "Jon, what can I say to you to calm you down? I'm at a loss here."

He looked into her eyes and smiled. "Call me an asshole."

She laughed. "Okay, asshole, can we get the kids on the beach?"

She leaned over and kissed him. He held the kiss, reached for her hand, and walked with her to their boys. Her sons entertained their mother as they roughhoused in the sand. Natalia and Jonathan barely spoke, not because of anger, but because she didn't want another conversation about TJ. A shadow appeared over Natalia. She glanced toward the sun to see Jack.

"Is it time to head back, Jack?" she asked.

"Yes, if you want to be home in time for Cora's dinner," he replied.

She yelled for the boys to head to the outside shower to rinse the sand off. They followed Jack. She and Jonathan went into the house, and she walked toward the bathroom. As she passed Jonathan in the living room, she said, "You can change in my room or the main bathroom there."

"Can I shower with you?" he asked.

She smiled and said, "You know the answer to that."

Jonathan chose the other bathroom. After he finished, he walked into her room. Knowing it was rude, but she was his wife. He found her in her bra and panties. She was wearing lace panties, a matching bra, a demi-cup, almost transparent. She raised her head and peered at him and found his face flushed. "Forget something in here?" she asked, her tone sarcastic.

"No, I didn't. You did, though. Your identity, me. That we always made love after a day at the beach. You're killing me, Nat."

"Jon, please, not this again. Let this occur organically, and don't guilt me into it." She continued to dress. She wanted to make love with him, but it wasn't just a release. It was confirming commitment and devotion.

The cool air brushed across her body as he closed the door when he left. She applied light makeup, gathered her things, walked to the car. Her movements were stiff and her mouth in a grim line, with daggers shooting from her eyes. She climbed in, and the boys were fighting over seats, and she waited for Jon to say something, but he seemed unbothered by them.

"Hey guys, knock it off, find a seat, and buckle up," she said, annoyed.

They stopped what they were doing and listened to her. Anthony looked at her wide-eyed.

She looked back at him. "Is there a problem, little man?" she inquired.

"No, you used your mom voice," he answered. Anthony hoped her memories were coming back.

"Well, I didn't realize I had another voice," she answered.

Natalia hoped at least one boy wouldn't use air buds, so she and Jon didn't have to converse. She didn't reach for his hand, nor did he grab hers. She glanced in his direction a few times, but he just stared ahead, his lips in a firm frown, his temple twitching. *Did it always twitch when annoyed? Did I know that before?*

When they arrived at the house, the boys jumped out of the car first. Jonathan climbed from the car and offered his hand to assist her. She reached for it, and as she climbed out, she whispered "asshole" just so he alone could hear it.

He replied, "Understand. A horny asshole."

She shook her head *as if I couldn't tell.* The house smelled like a little of heaven, and Natalia's mouth watered. Cora had the dining room table set and the food ready to serve. Thanks to more traffic than expected, they arrived later than planned.

"Dinner smells heavenly, Cora," Natalia said. "The beach always makes me hungry."

As Jonathan pushed her chair in, he whispered, "That's not all it does, my love."

She rolled her eyes and ignored him. They had a nice dinner, and Jonathan seemed to relax more than he had all day. The boys were hungry but behaved like gentlemen at the table, telling Cora about their time at the beach and complained about going back home to school.

"Boys, okay. This place is ours," she said. "We can come back anytime. Why don't you guys do something, like bowling? The adults will clean up here. I need to speak with Cora and Jack about my time in New Jersey."

The boys left the adults and raced downstairs. Jack had explained to the boys how to turn everything on during the game night.

"Cora, I'm not sure how long I'll be away. I replenished the household accounts. Call me if you need anything. Then during the third week of May, I'll be in London."

"What the hell, Nat. You're going to London?" he asked in disbelief, his voice raised and his face heated.

She ignored his outburst and continued her discussion with Cora. After, she left the room and stomped upstairs to gather things together for the trip. Jonathan looked at Cora pleadingly.

"Go talk to her, Jon," Cora said. Cora didn't know their conversations earlier. Otherwise, she may not have offered that advice.

Natalia was angry. She didn't recall feeling this intense before. She pounded up the stairs and hurried into her suite and slammed the door with such ferocity the wall shook.

A few seconds later, Jon barged in and stood gaping at Natalia. Her face was red, and her mouth was curled downward into a frown. She glared at him and said, "I didn't hear you knock." Her heart was thumping, and her hands dropped to her sides.

"I didn't," he replied sarcastically. "Why didn't you tell me you were going to London? What is the purpose of the trip? Business? Or your *fiancée*?"

"If you don't change your tone and stop acting like a jealous asshole, I won't discuss it with you any further. Jon, we've been over this several times today, and honestly, it's exhausting."

"Yes, we have, and I'm still not satisfied that *he* doesn't have an advantage," he yelled.

"Lower your voice. I don't want the kids upset. And I will not be intimate with you for any other reason than the timing is right, and I want to. Can you please let it go already?"

Jonathan stormed from the room and didn't join the family downstairs for the rest of the evening. He called Matt and vented about his day. Matt tried to help him, but Jonathan's mind couldn't understand that he wasn't at a disadvantage.

"Dude, listen. You're not at any disadvantage. You have kids, a family. That guy doesn't," Matt told him. "She'll realize that."

"He's a movie star. You should see the life she has out here, Matt. Why would she leave all of this for a boring life in New Jersey?" he stressed.

"Jon, your life isn't boring, and she was happy. I know this is hard, especially from what she told you, but let it go. Don't nag her about it. It may cause her to shut down. Just be you, not this pissed off you, just you," Matt advised.

SUNDAY MORNING'S WEATHER was dreary, *just like my mood, dismal.* The rain pelted against the windows, stopping after twenty minutes. She passed Jonathan's room on her way downstairs. She heard the water running in his bathroom and walked toward the stairs. *At least I can grab a coffee before the bull shit starts again.*

Natalia knew he was angry, frustrated, and upset, but understood his position, but it wasn't pleasant. She regretted telling him the details of her relationship with TJ. Standing alone in the empty kitchen, waiting for the coffee brewer to finish. Reaching for the industry papers, she stepped into the family room to enjoy her first cup.

The pugs cuddled together on the chair and were snoring peacefully. Natalia sat on the sofa and opened the first newspaper. There in print was Jonathan holding her hand, another photo kissing her. There were photos of them on the beach with the kids, a photo of her kissing him. Just as she thought, *oh shit,* her cell rang. It was TJ. She thought about letting it go to voicemail, but she took the call.

As soon as she said, "Hello," his tirade began. "What the fuck are you doing out there, Susan? Every fucking time I open a newspaper, there you are with *him.* You're on the Entertainment TV shows, every damn one of them. I'm sick of this shit. You better get your ass over here this week." he demanded.

"Are you through with your tantrum? I'm not coming this week. Get that through your head right now. I will not now or ever take orders from you or anyone. I explained all my plans to you, so nothing should come as a surprise. And my name is *Natalia.*"

"Okay, *Natalia*, why are you kissing him? Did you fuck him too?" he screamed at her.

"That was crude and unacceptable. If you knew me, you would know the answer."

"I know nothing about you anymore, Susan. Excuse me, *Natalia.* You're now a stranger to me, a stranger with a boatload of kids."

"Okay, TJ, if that's how you feel, I think we need to end this now. I cannot have a relationship with you if I'm a stranger. I don't like the way you're speaking to me. I understand it's a messy situation, and we are all suffering. I'm trying my best to muddle through things as painlessly as possible."

"You're choosing him over me?" TJ yelled into the phone.

"No, I'm choosing *me*. I haven't decided yet, but I know this, it cannot be with you. You made it known you don't want children. I have three. Three exceptional boys. You didn't even ask to meet them. No matter what I decide, these kids will be part of my life. Goodbye, TJ."

She pressed the end call button, shaking, her eyes stinging with tears. She stepped into Cora's opened door. Cora rose from her sofa and pulled Natalia into her arms. Jack left and closed the door behind him and passed by Jonathan, sitting at the breakfast bar with coffee. Jack nodded and mumbled, "Good morning," and walked out back with the pugs.

Jonathan peered into the family room to the strewed newspapers on the sofa. He was wondering if Natalia left the house. He peeked on the lanai and found it empty. Reaching for one newspaper, he took it into the kitchen to read with his morning coffee. He took the wrong one, an entertainment paper. He didn't know many of these people, but he looked through it. Recognizing their pictures and he read the small article. He smiled at first but imagined how he would feel if he were in TJs shoes. He returned it to the sofa. Then he gazed through the French doors when Natalia came breezing from the hallway.

"Good morning," he said, turning to her.

"What is so good about it?" Natalia replied, annoyed, storming by him to hurry upstairs.

Jonathan debated if he should follow, aware that Natalia was still mad at him. He was a jealous idiot yesterday but took the chance. Although he knew his wife, he didn't understand this version. Natalia's bedroom door was closed. He tapped on it gently, not to wake the boys.

The door ripped open forcefully. "What, Jon, I'm not in the mood for any more bullshit."

"I want to apologize for yesterday. You're right. I am an asshole and ruined a perfect day with our family. I'm sorry. Forgive me?" he asked.

Natalia sighed. "Jon, I understand how frustrating this is for you. But please, can we let it drop and move forward at a more natural pace? I'm conflicted and would like to get to your home in New Jersey and try to make a new normal."

"Honey, *our* home, not mine. And yes, things will be better, I promise."

"Thank you, and just so you don't stew over England. I'm going to interview a family whose child needs facial surgery. My Dad, I mean Doc, established the foundation that will cover the expenses, and Maria will perform the surgery if he qualifies."

"Thanks for telling me." He thought about hugging her, but knew she wouldn't welcome it. "Did you eat breakfast? I can make you my famous French toast. I would offer to take you on a date, but I know nothing about this area."

"No, I didn't, but I'm not hungry, and there's no time. I had breakfast sent to the plane. But thank you. I'm just going to gather a few things before we leave. We should get the kids up."

No sooner had she said that than Anthony ran into the room and jumped on her rumpled bed. "Morning, Mom, morning, Dad," he said as he jumped. "Can someone help with my suitcase? I can't close it."

"Okay, little man, come down before you get hurt. Hug me, and I'll fix your suitcase," Natalia ordered.

Jonathan knew something was very off with her, but couldn't put his finger on it. He apologized, but worried that he had pushed her too far. He silently hoped that things would improve as the day went on.

Anthony hugged her for a long time, and she hugged him back. The way she hugged their son and buried her nose in his hair reminded Jonathan of how Natalia used to embrace the boys before. She had told him she was inhaling them before they grew, and she wouldn't be able to reach their heads any longer. It made his heart happy that he found her "inhaling" their son. Perhaps memories were coming back bit by bit.

After his conversation with Matt, he let go of the "sex thing." He would wait for her.

Natalia helped the boys pack. She asked Jack to get the luggage stored inside the basement closet. Her family had only arrived with backpacks and one change of clothing. She thought about leaving what she bought them here for their next visit but realized they would most likely outgrow them. The boys packed, and their backpacks now held their iPads and cookies that Cora had baked for them. They hurried because of the early flight time, and it was time to leave for the airport.

Natalia was on the brink of losing it when Cora grabbed her into a hug. "Everything is okay, love, calm down, take deep breaths. I know you're scared, but what you're doing is the right thing. He's a lovely man and those boys. Those boys brought joy and life back into this house. I can see Doc smiling down on us. You'll be back.

"I'm just a phone call away. Follow your heart and allow yourself time to grieve and time to decide. No matter what, kids are resilient. Travel safely, my love, and call me when you land. Deep breaths, honey." Cora kissed her and hugged her one more time. She hugged the boys and Jonathan, too. "Safe travels," she called to them as they walked out. Tearfully, Cora wiped her face with a nearby napkin. She knew Natalia would be back and prayed she would choose without pressure, hoping it was with her family.

Natalia was the last to climb into the town car. She felt breathless. Jack waited good-naturedly. She looked up at the house that had been her home for the past twenty-two months and thought of Doc, Cora, and Jack. Her sole memories were of this place, those people whom she loved, her safety nets, and her home. She heard the pugs barking in the car and getting the boys all riled up. She climbed in. Jack closed the door. The gentle click was reminiscent of the end of Susan and the new beginning of Natalia.

"Boys, calm down, please. I have a headache," she told them.

Marc responded without delay, "Sorry, Mom, I know this is hard for you. It'll be okay."

A sob escaped, and she turned her head. She didn't want to cry in front of her children. Alex heard the sob and looked up and said, "Now look what you did, Marc, you made Mom cry."

Natalia didn't want them to think that she didn't want to go with them and remembered Cora's advice to breathe. After inhaling a deep, cleansing breath, she expressed her gratitude to Marc. "The simple part is being with you guys. The hard part is the unknown. Alex, he didn't make me cry, honey. I'm just going to miss Cora and Jack. They were like parents to me." Jack looked in the rearview mirror and smiled. She would get through this. She had to.

Jonathan reached for her hand. He couldn't wait to get home and hoped she would remember once she was home. They arrived at the airport, and Natalia hesitated to leave the car. The boys jumped from the vehicle first. Natalia motioned for Jonathan to go ahead of her. He panicked, thinking she changed her mind. Jonathan walked a few feet along and glanced back. He saw her in Jack's arms, clinging to him, sobbing. He had moisture in his eyes as they broke apart. Jack called to Jon, "take care of my Royal Highness for me."

Jonathan nodded, returned, and took his wife's hand, and guided her toward the plane. She sobbed as she approached the aircraft. The pilot waited by the cabin door, and the flight attendant stood on the tarmac by the stairs. Jonathan stepped aside to allow Natalia to go up first.

Nodding hello to the flight assistant, she climbed the steps toward Fred. She nodded and walked to the back of the craft, into the bedroom. She sat on the bed to compose herself. Her life had begun in this room, and now she would fly into the unknown. It scared her. *What if he was an asshole all the time? He could put on an act. If she chose not to stay and divorced, would he let her go amicably and raise the children in Beverly Hills?* Her mind was a jumble of conflicting and confusing thoughts.

Fred gazed into the room, "Miss Kline, we need to take off. Will you take your seat, please?" He left, assuming she followed him. Jonathan overheard and realized she hadn't come out.

Jonathan said to the pilot, "Give me a minute, I'll get her."

Jonathan knocked on the wall outside the room. He couldn't see Natalia from where he stood. When she didn't respond, he stepped inside and found her sitting on a bed. He sat next to her and began, "Honey, if this is too much for you, we can leave now, and you can come when you're stronger. I cannot imagine how you're feeling right now, but you're worth the wait, and we'll be there for you. Would you like to do that? Call Jack to come back for you?"

Natalia's eyes widened, and she realized she behaved like an inconsiderate ass. She wiped her face and reached for him and pulled him into her embrace. "No, I'm okay. Let's get started." She followed Jonathan and ensured her sons had buckled themselves onto the sofa. They belted the pugs into their car seats on the love seat. The remaining seats were the chairs with the table between them or two bucket seats. Jonathan chose the bucket seats and guided her next to him.

The flight attendant prepared the cabin for takeoff, and the announcement came over the intercom, "Miss Kline and guests, we will arrive at Philadelphia International at approximately four PM eastern standard time."

She smiled and knew perhaps that was the last time anyone would refer to her as Miss Kline, her identity for the last twenty-two months. Digging into her purse for her headache medicine, she reached for the bottle of water Jonathan held. She fell asleep on Jonathan's shoulder with his arm wrapped around her and slept most of the flight until she heard someone coughing. She bolted awake. "Who is choking?" she asked abruptly.

"Mom, it was me. I'm okay. I just choked on the huge gulp of soda I took. Marc and I are having a contest. I bet him I could down this bottle of root beer quicker than he could," Alex replied.

Raising her eyebrow, she turned to Jonathan and asked, "Do they compete with stuff like this all the time?"

"Pretty much."

"How long was I asleep?"

"A few hours, you needed it." He handed her a bottle of water. "Here, drink this. Is your headache gone?"

"Yes, thank you, I feel a little better." She unbuckled her seatbelt, grabbed her purse, and moved to the bathroom.

Jonathan yelled back, "Hey, mile high club?"

"Smartass," she replied, laughing.

"Dad, what's the mile-high club? Can I join it too?" Anthony inquired.

"No, just a silly term for getting a little drunk on a flight," Jonathan lied, unsure if Anthony even knew what drunk meant.

Natalia returned to her seat. She had washed her tear-stained face, touched up her makeup, and appeared calmer than before. She slipped in next to Jonathan and said, "Your big mouth landed you in a bit of a jam there, didn't it?"

"Yes, it did, my love, yes it did. I said it because they're listening to music." He pointed to his ears. "I didn't realize Anthony had pulled his earbuds out. But the result was worth it. You smiled."

Thirty minutes later, the pilot's voice came through the speaker, reminding them to fasten seatbelts and for the flight attendant to prepare for landing. Jonathan sensed his wife's body tense. He regretted giving the okay for the girls to come this evening. Jonathan reached for her hand, unsure if it was the landing that scared her or the unknown. What was familiar to them was a source of great apprehension for Natalia.

Jonathan squeezed her hand. She knew he couldn't be an "asshole." He seemed to sense when she needed his support the most. She squeezed his hand and somehow knew he was apprehensive, too. The plane landed with ease. A few minutes later, Fred stepped into the cabin.

Natalia thanked him for the safe flight and all the treats for the kids. "Fred, can you put me on your schedule for the third week in May, for England? I'll email you the details in a few days. It will be for the foundation business. I would rather have you there in the event we need to fly back with a patient. I'll keep Dr. Ross in the loop. She may meet me over there. She'll decide once she receives the medical records."

Jonathan listened to his wife and the pilot's conversation. She didn't mention TJ, but that was because he was in earshot. The door opened, and the boys exited the plane. Marc carried Buddy, and Alex took Lily. The flight attendant hustled to the limo with the seat belt attachments and the dog's car seats. The boys secured the dogs in their seats. They entered the limousine and were excited about being right on the tarmac with a ride waiting.

As Natalia entered, she heard Alex comment, "so fancy."

She smiled and said, "Well, guys, we're off to a new normal for me, and you guys, your old routine, school tomorrow." She lifted her head to Jonathan. "And work tomorrow for you?"

"No, I took the week off. We have things at home to get settled. I need to buy you another minivan since the accident destroyed the old one."

Marc started laughing and looked at his father. "Dad, I don't think that Mom is the minivan type anymore. Did you see that sick car she drives?"

Jonathan's face pinked, and he glanced down, unsure of how to respond.

Natalia retorted, "If a minivan provided my family with safe transportation, then a minivan it is." She smiled at Jon and asked, "All good?"

He leaned over and kissed her. "All good, as I didn't even know what kind of car it was, but knew it was out of my budget."

Budget? She didn't spend obnoxiously. She didn't want to throw the money around or stand out as differently in her new home.

Thirty-one

THE LIMO ARRIVED AT their small New Jersey town forty-five minutes later. She knew they must be close, as John reached into his pocket for his keys. She breathed deeply to calm down and clear her mind. Anxiety pulsed through her, worried about neighbors and best friends she didn't remember. A life she didn't understand, and how to adjust to it. The limo pulled up to a lovely house with a well-maintained lawn. There was a floral wreath on the front door, with a ribbon with the word 'Welcome.'

Jonathan sensed Natalia's angst and handed Marc his keys. He reached for his wife, guiding her from the vehicle. As soon as she stepped out, Mrs. Hannigan, their neighbor, rushed over from her front porch. "Oh, Natalia, I'm so happy that you're safe and home. I opened windows to freshen up the house. Dinner is warming in the oven."

Jonathan whispered, "Mrs. Hannigan, Abigail, you called her Abby. You love her. She's great."

"Hello, Abby, thanks for the warm welcome," Natalia replied politely.

Mrs. Hannigan knew she didn't remember her. Jonathan kept in touch while in Beverly Hills. "You look wonderful, my dear, but you go on inside. The neighbors are noisy, and the children saw the limo pull up. We can catch up once you're acclimated."

"Thank you," Natalia replied, relieved that Abby didn't expect her to hold a conversation. Jonathan escorted her inside, and she glanced around the unfamiliar rooms. "It's lovely, looks like a cheerful place," she said.

The boys were running around, showing her things. She laughed and said, "Can someone take the dogs out? I'm sure they need to go to the bathroom."

Anthony took the dogs into the backyard while the limo driver brought their luggage in, and Natalia tipped the driver liberally. She walked him to the front door, and someone across the road waved to her. She waved back, clueless who they were.

After, she followed Jonathan into the kitchen and asked him where the bathroom was. He showed her to the powder room. She needed a minute to compose herself. She was disappointed because nothing was familiar.

As Natalia exited the bathroom, the house was a bustle of activity. The older two boys took the luggage upstairs. Anthony tended to the dogs, and Jonathan went through the mail. She found her way over to a wall of photos, the boys when they were babies. Natalia recognized each boy. She approached another and knew it was her parents. Staring at the picture, she felt their love surround her.

She turned to Jon, who followed her movements. She had tears in her eyes and said, "My parents." Relieved she recognized her parents. That was a significant breakthrough.

He nodded and reached for her and showed her the cabinet with the cremains in the ornate wooden box. "Whenever you were upset, you would talk to them. You told me they always helped you, even from heaven. I wasn't sure I believed it, but you did. One day I struggled with your disappearance. I asked them to guide me to you. That night Anthony saw you on TV. I believe now." He hesitated to tell her about the girls coming over. He hoped it was just the girls not to overwhelm her.

She stepped into his arms and kissed him. "I'm glad you found me."

They had a casual dinner that Mrs. Hannigan prepared. Roasted chicken, mixed vegetables, and Jon found a salad in the refrigerator she'd left. Natalia was hungrier than expected, and she enjoyed the meal in the kitchen with her family. She helped Jonathan clean up and load the dishwasher. She fed the pugs and followed Jon into the office.

He took the new MacBook out of its packaging and set it up. He still needed to transfer the files from the old. But he knew Matt could help with it. He opened the sofa bed and pulled the sheets from the closet. Natalia helped him make the bed. As soon as they finished, John heard the front door open, and he heard Marc exclaim, "Oh, Aunt Alicia, did you bake my favorites?"

Natalia froze, her body upright and rigid. She raised her eyes to his.

"Honey, I'm sorry I couldn't hold them back. It is Alicia and Christina. They know you as much as I do, perhaps more. Wouldn't you rather do this with me here? They love you and understand. They just needed to see you. I couldn't decline."

They overheard Alicia respond to Marc. "Of course, I made chocolate chip cookies for my favorite nephews. I made some with macadamia nuts too, Alex. I know you love them. Just be careful around Buddy."

Jonathan stepped from the office, grasping Natalia's hand. Christina gasped her name and ran to her first, and just wrapped her in her embrace. Alicia enveloped them both in her embrace, and they remained in that position for a few minutes. He'd seen them do this before, many times. When Natalia's parents died, and when their pug, Dolly, who they raised together, died. Any time of sadness, they embraced each other.

Matt stepped into the dining room with more pastries and said, "Okay, break it up, let me look at her and grab a hug."

Natalia was overwhelmed and speechless. She felt like a spectator as Christina and Alicia took over, setting the baked goods on the table. Cakes, cookies, and pies. Alicia spread them out on plates as though they were pieces of fine art, and they were. Glancing at the cakes, she wondered if she knew her friend was talented with confections. Although quiet, Natalia enjoyed the back-and-forth banter. Her headache returned as she tried to remember them. She rubbed the side of her head as her bright eyes watered.

Alicia handed Natalia a plate. She smiled and said, "Your favorites."

Jonathan made coffee for everyone. He was relaxed, different, his face was calmer, and he laughed a lot. The children ran into the family room, and they decided what to watch on the TV while the adults caught up.

She watched Johnathan as he moved with ease and talked with their friends. Christina's wife, Charlotte, kneeled by Natalia and whispered in her ear, "Everything will be okay, Nat, it will come back. I've missed you a lot, don't be nervous. I'll help you in any way that I can." Charlotte leaned over and kissed her cheek.

Natalia's eyes stung with tears. She took a deep breath, nodded, and picked at the delicious dessert. Their friends didn't stay long. Alicia and Christina cleaned up while Natalia chatted with Charlotte. Charlotte told her she was a stay-at-home mom, and Natalia hung out with her during the day. They were both members of their children's PTA. Once everyone left, she looked at the time and said to Jonathan, "Think the boys need to get to bed for school? Is it bedtime?"

"Anthony is in the shower now. He takes one the night before school, and Marc and Alex prefer to do it in the morning," Jonathan responded, surprised by how things that were once overwhelming were now routine.

"What time do I need to wake them up, and do they take a bus?" she asked him.

"Marc wakes up early. He leaves first, around six-thirty. Alex leaves at seven-fifteen, and Anthony needs to be at the bus stop by eight-ten. Don't worry, I'm off, and I'll help you with their routine."

"Thank you. You're so sweet," Natalia replied.

"Unless I'm an asshole." he joked with her.

"Can you show me where I'm supposed to sleep?" Natalia asked him. "I'm exhausted, and my head is pounding."

"Sure, sorry. Everything happened so fast I forgot to show you upstairs. Follow me, my love." He showed her the boy's rooms first. The joining bathroom between the two older boy's rooms. The main bathroom that Anthony used. And then their room. He lifted her suitcase onto the bed for her and raised his own and unpacked. Confusion spread across her features.

"Honey, to be honest, I don't know where all of your stuff goes, but that's your dresser. That door is the walk-in closet, and that's our bathroom over there. Just find spots for your stuff." Jonathan unpacked, hung his stuff, and couldn't wait to get out of there. He knew if he stayed, he couldn't trust himself to be good. They had a lot of fun in that bed, and he hoped they would again. He didn't even kiss her, just said, "Night, sweetie," and hurried downstairs.

"Okay, thanks." Her head throbbed as she unpacked. She took her medication and climbed into bed, too emotionally drained to decompress. Natalia didn't even know what side of the bed hers was. She tossed and turned and then remembered to call Cora. She told Cora she was okay and would talk more in the morning. Natalia had a rough night and turned on the TV, eventually falling asleep in the morning. The grinding of the garbage trucks and the cans slamming against the macadam woke her, and she glanced at the brightly lit alarm clock. The red numbers showed it was seven in the morning. She groaned, because it felt like she had just fallen asleep. Realizing she missed Marc but wanted to go to the bus stop with Alex, she flew out of bed. She stepped into her clothes from the previous night and ran downstairs, banging into Jonathan on his way up.

"Woo there, are you running away?" he asked, laughing.

Natalia's brow furrowed and she shrugged, followed by a yawn. "I overslept. I need to walk Alex to the bus."

"Alex goes to the bus himself, babe. Go back to sleep. I can take Anthony. You can learn the ropes tomorrow."

"No, I want to. I'll change and go with you." She ran back upstairs and took a quick shower. When she stepped out, a cup of coffee waited on the vanity. She smiled. *When he's not an asshole, he's damn near perfect.*

She dressed in jeans and a T-shirt, her long blonde hair flowing. She bounced down the stairs and into the kitchen. She greeted the pugs and kissed the top of her youngest child's head as he ate his breakfast. "Morning, little man," she said.

"Morning, Mommy," he answered with his mouthful of pancakes.

She smiled at him and made her way into the kitchen. "Good morning, and thanks for the coffee. It was thoughtful," she said as she rinsed the cup and stuck it into the dishwasher.

"Good morning, love. After Anthony is off to school, can we get groceries in and then get you a vehicle? Are you okay with that?" he asked.

Natalia stepped onto the front porch as the sun peeked out from behind the trees. Smiling, she glanced behind her as Anthony struggled with his backpack. Jonathan lifted it on his back and untangled the straps. They walked Anthony to the bus stop since he was the youngest child on the block and the only child at this pickup. She was thankful that it was just the three of them, and she didn't meet another person she'd known before. Anthony chatted about his friends until the bus arrived. He kissed them both and hopped onto the bus. She waited until she couldn't see the bus any longer.

Jonathan grabbed her hand and walked her home. He took his car keys off the hook in the kitchen and walked with her to the garage. They had a fun morning at the grocery store. They joked, teased, and Jonathan made fun of the healthy choices she threw into the cart. Natalia seemed more comfortable being out of her element. After they stored the groceries, he showed her a list of minivans he had pulled off the internet and asked her what kind she preferred.

"What kind did I drive before?" she asked.

"They don't make them any longer. This one is in our price range. And it has the highest safety features."

Natalia ignored the price range comment, as she was clueless about his budget. She knew she could afford it but didn't want to embarrass him.

"Who pays the bills, Jon?" she inquired.

"Well, you did. My company deposited my pay into our joint account, and you took care of that stuff. Of course, I had to muddle my way through when you disappeared," he responded.

"I can do it again if you catch me up," she said. Natalia had ulterior motives. She wanted to be in charge and hoped he wouldn't know when she paid for something from her account. Jonathan had already alluded to the ability to care for his family. She'd work on him about allowing her to assist monetarily.

"That would be great. I hate it. Working with financing all day long, that is the last thing I want to think about."

They arrived at the dealership before lunch, and a middle-aged sales associate greeted them. Jonathan showed him the vehicle he had in mind, and he took the car on a test drive. It had a lot of features and a smooth ride.

Jonathan asked her, "Do you want this one? Would you like another color? Is there anything you would prefer in a minivan?"

As Jonathan dealt with the salesperson, she listened in as he explained their needs, and she realized that everyone who encountered him was polite and kind. She thought back to their week in Beverly Hills, how he respected and responded to Cora and Jack. How patient and loving he was with the boys. Her heart pounded at his nearness, his scent. Emotions she didn't expect coursed through her, her body tingling as tiny bumps appeared on her skin. At that moment, she realized she loved him, without a doubt, even if there were no children involved. *It's him.* She had never experienced such intense joy like this that she could ever remember.

"Honey? Honey, you're a million miles away. The salesperson asked if you like this gray one?" Jonathan asked her.

"It is nice, not a huge fan of the drab color. Does it come in another color, maybe red or blue?" she asked the salesperson.

"There is red in stock. It just came in on Friday. It has a tan interior, heated leather seats, and a heated steering wheel. Back up camera, fully loaded. Every bell and whistle. Would you like to see it?"

Jonathan said, "Sure, sounds nice. Let's look at that one." He had the minivan brought around. The cost was considerably more than Jonathan planned, but he didn't mention it. He wanted her to buy the vehicle she wanted. "Honey, what do you think? Do you like this one?" he asked her.

"Yes, I love the color, and the interior is nice too." She turned to the sales associate. "All the same safety features? My children will be in this vehicle."

"Yes, Ma'am, five-star safety features, rated highest of all minivans."

Jonathan said, "Okay, let's talk numbers."

There's enough in my checking to pay for this now. What do I do? When the sales agent walked away, she turned to Jon and kissed him.

"What was that for?" he asked, and smiled.

"I don't know, for being you, was just compelled to do it," she replied.

Teasing, he asked, "Feel compelled to do anything else?" He raised his eyebrows suggestively.

She laughed out loud and pressed her hand over her mouth. "Maybe." His eyes widened. *Did Natalia say, maybe?* This car deal could take forever.

The salesperson returned with payment calculations based on the sticker prices. She knew Jon was suddenly eager to leave the dealership. Jonathan was nervously looking at the paperwork. Now was her chance. She turned to the sales associate. "If you can give it to us for this price." She wrote the number down. "I'll write you a check now."

"Wow, okay. Let me ask my manager," he said as he walked away.

Jonathan turned to her. "What are you doing?"

"Trying to get us home quicker. There are only a few hours before our boys are home," she replied, glancing at the clock on the wall.

Jonathan was gob smacked, and his mind was spinning. *Is she ready? What does this mean? Has she chosen me?* "Are you serious, Nat? Are you implying what I think you're implying?" he asked incredulously.

"I don't think there is an implication at all in what I said. Let's get out of here as fast as we can," Natalie answered, raising one of her eyebrows.

The sales agent returned and said, "We've got a deal."

Natalia said, "Great, total us up, and can you make it quick? We have an appointment that we cannot miss."

"The invoice is ready." He showed her the total.

She wrote the check, passed it to him. "Can you detail it, and we'll pick it up this evening around six-thirty, please?"

"Yes, Mrs. Miller, see you then."

Jonathan paced as she stood up from her chair and reached for him.

"What's next on your agenda?" she asked, giggling.

At first, Jonathan didn't realize she was joking. "You. Let's get out of here."

He peeled out of the parking lot like a crazy man. Fortunately, the dealership wasn't far from the house. He ran into the house, grasping her hand and pulling her along. *I don't need a neighbor to stop me now.* As soon as he locked the door, she stepped into his arms and kissed him.

The kiss reaffirmed what Natalia already knew. *It's him. I know it's him I want. This feels so right.* He kissed her hungrily, and they both ran up the steps to their room.

Jonathan yanked Natalia's shirt over her head and pulled her to him. They fell onto the bed together. He was afraid to speak, as he didn't want to break the spell. He kissed all his favorite spots on her body. Her neck, behind her ear, down her cleavage to her stomach. As he followed the trail of kisses left up toward her neck, he eased himself inside of her, unable to hold back any longer. Natalia clung to him as he whispered words of love into her ear. They fell asleep, holding each other.

Jonathan heard a school bus nearby, and he jumped up and laughed. "Wake up, honey. Marc will be home any minute. I don't think we want to get caught."

"I'm up. I can't find my bra. Where did you toss it?"

They were giggling like teenagers, trying to find their clothing. At last, they found each piece, and they walked down the stairs as Marc walked in.

"Hi sweetheart, how was your day?" she asked innocently.

He looked at his parents, his eyebrows raised. Something was strange. He shook his head, thinking, *all parents are weird.* "Mom, your lips are puffy and red. Did you have an allergic reaction?"

She touched her lips and realized how swollen they were from all the heavy kissing. Jon stifled laughter. He left it up to her to respond. "I might be. I just had a new-fangled latte from the coffee shop. I won't get that flavor again."

"I think there's Benadryl somewhere," Marc replied, buying her story. "Going upstairs to start my homework. What's for dinner?"

Jonathan answered, "We're ordering pizza, we didn't plan a meal, and Mom and I need to pick up the new minivan at six-thirty."

Marc looked at his mom and snorted. "A minivan, Mom, for real? I thought you'd convince dad to get you a cool car, like the one in Beverly Hills."

Jonathan laughed. "It is cool, Marc."

His mother was still laughing.

He looked at them like they were crazy and mumbled, "Dorks," as he continued to his room.

"Marc, this isn't Beverly Hills, and that convertible isn't practical for our family. However, when we visit Beverly Hills, Dad and I will use it.

"I still think you should have gotten a cool car. Can I go for a ride in it too?" Marc asked.

"The minivan, sure. But then you will be a dork too." Natalia retorted as Marc went to his room, shaking his head. He didn't understand what was so funny.

They both looked at each other and continued to laugh, as they had envisioned their afternoon at the dealership. Natalia had to wipe her eyes because she was laughing so hard.

Jonathan turned to her. "I'm delighted that tears of happiness come from your eyes."

She kissed him. "Let's wait on the porch for Alex as I can't trust myself near you right now."

Alex ran down the street toward the house. He offered them a big smile when he saw his parents waiting for him.

"How was your day, sweetheart?" Natalia asked him.

"It was okay. Did you guys buy a car?" He looked over at the empty driveway. He knew his mom hated driving into the garage and always left it in the driveway for his dad to pull it in for her.

"We found something, and we'll pick it up later," she answered.

"Cool, can I have a snack? I'm starving."

"Of course, Dad and I went to the grocery store. There is plenty in the pantry. Pizza for dinner," she yelled after him. She turned to Jon. "Will we take the boys tonight?"

"Nah, Marc is here. We shouldn't be too long. We just need to sign the registration papers. I bet Anthony will want to come. He loves cars."

An hour later, they walked to the bus stop. Jonathan reached for her hand. They waited a few minutes before it arrived, and Anthony jumped off.

Natalia laughed and asked, "Anthony, do you jump onto everything? You have a lot of energy. Can you spare a little for your mom?"

"Yup, I'm your jumping bean." Anthony exclaimed as he ran home.

Jonathan was laughing. "He's halfway down the block now. And yes, he's a jumper. You used to say he used your bladder as a trampoline when you were pregnant with him."

Natalia wished she could remember being pregnant, how it felt to have a life growing inside. She helped Anthony with homework as Jonathan ordered the pizza and set the table. After the pizza arrived, she helped Jonathan serve the boys.

As predicted, Anthony went with them to pick up the new car. The van was ready, and the paperwork. Jonathan signed it, and he asked her, "Do you want to drive the new car or my car home?"

"I can drive the new one. But you need to go slow so I can follow you. Don't fly out of here like you did this afternoon."

"Hey now, I was on a mission, a serious mission." He kissed her.

"Yes, you were. Let's grab our son before he tries to get me to buy that sports car he's hanging around," Natalia joked.

Jonathan called him, "Let's go, son, we're ready to go home. Are you riding with Mom or me?"

"Mom, in case she gets lost," Anthony said, looking at his mom.

"Thanks, kid, for the vote of confidence. I'll be following Dad."

Once they arrived home, she glanced at the clock on the stove, "Jon, do you mind if I borrow your office? I need to make a few business calls."

"Honey, this is our house. Use whatever room you want."

She strode into the office and called Maria.

"Hey, you, how's the east coast treating you," Maria asked.

"It's nice. The weather is mild. Now don't laugh. We bought a minivan today." Natalia said, giggling.

"Why can't I laugh? You are. You're now a typical suburban Mom, laughing at minivans."

"The van is nice and practical. I like it." Natalia exclaimed.

"Okay, enough chitchat. I have a patient in a few minutes. I received a call from the doctor in London. He wants to push up the date for us to review his patient's case. I received the medical records this morning. The patient is a baby, and he has a severe cleft palate and a cheekbone deformity. He's tube-fed," Maria said. "It breaks my heart, and I hate to ask you, but can you push up your trip?"

"Oh God, Maria, that poor baby. I guess I can, but I feel bad. I haven't been here long. I don't want Jon or the boys to feel abandoned already. Do you think you can go? You know the criteria. I'm confident, without seeing him, that he meets it. Maybe you can just arrange the flight for them if you can't go. I know you're running the practice yourself." She rubbed her forehead.

"Alright, I'll call the physician and ask specific questions about the family. We'll need accurate answers to satisfy the foundation. I'll ask you to send the plane," Maria replied.

"If you're unsure, we can always ask Nicole Collins to fly over. She's a board member and loves getting her hands wet."

"Sounds like a plan. Before I go, how are things with Jonathan? Are they improving?"

"They're marvelous, Maria. It's him, Jonathan's the one. I had this light bulb moment go off this afternoon, and I just knew."

"My sweet friend, I'm happy for you. I must run. My patient is in the exam room. What time do you go to bed? Can I call you later this evening?"

"No, I'll call you at your lunchtime tomorrow. I'm hoping we go to bed early."

"We? We? Nat, I hope it's amazing."

"It was wonderful the entire afternoon. I'll call you tomorrow." She giggled.

She finished her calls and sat next to Jon on the family room sofa. Marc and Alex were studying for a test, and Anthony watched a movie. His favorite action movie. It was one of TJ's. She was about to panic, but took a deep breath. When he came into view, she felt nothing but gratitude. If she hadn't met him and asked her to the awards show, her family wouldn't have found her.

Jonathan glanced at Natalia with a smile and knew whose movie was on the TV. He didn't care. Natalia was home, and she chose him. He was a fortunate man, and he whispered in her ear, "Do I have your permission to sleep in the bedroom with you this evening, my beautiful wife?"

"Of course. Where else would you be, husband? I have plans for you. Good thing you're on vacation. Otherwise, you would be mighty tired at work."

Jonathan glanced at his watch and groaned. At least another hour before bedtime. Marc said his goodnights first. He wanted to finish his studies upstairs. Alex joined him as Anthony was very distracting as he interacted with the actors in the movie.

Jonathan watched as Natalia read through her emails on her iPad. There was one from TJ. She opened it, and he asked for his ring back. She had left it in California and responded that she would have it delivered to his home. Nothing more. He wasn't aware that she called him to end things yet. He assumed she did since she became intimate with him. But he didn't know when it happened.

After the kids went to bed, she reached for Jonathan's hands and pulled him up from the sofa. They made love most of the night. He was ecstatic that she was back. No memories, but it was okay. She was here, in his bed, in his arms, and his life.

Thirty-two

JONATHAN RETURNED TO work, and she was alone for the first time in their home. Natalia knew the routine now, and Charlotte came by on the first day after putting her girls on the bus and asking Natalia if she wanted to go to the mall and have lunch.

Natalia enjoyed herself hanging out with her new friends. New to her, but many years for them. She adapted to her new life and her friends. To them, it was almost like she never left. To Natalia, it was new and exciting. The first month on the east coast, she had the checks sent overnight delivery for her signature. She promised Doc she would sign everything, and she intended to keep her promise. She just wasn't ready to leave her husband or kids, even for a few days.

The second month, she did the same. She was very much in love with Jonathan. She couldn't stand the days apart when he went into the office. Maria had everything under control at the practice. Natalia promised to fly out in June to interview a new physician to ease the load off her. Doc's medical practice was a busy one, and Maria needed help.

In early June, the week Natalia planned to fly to the west coast, Anthony came home sick with a stomach bug that lasted for two days. Jon came home feeling unwell, too, exhibiting the same symptoms. Natalia planned to leave in the morning for LAX, as Maria had set up the following day's interviews. Natalia would be away for three days. One to travel, an entire day of meetings, and one to fly home. It would exhaust her, but her need to be with her family was great. She hated leaving while they were unwell. Since Jon was not feeling well, Christina offered to take her to the airport.

"I could've ordered car service, Christina. I hate to inconvenience you this way," Natalia said as she stepped into the car.

"No inconvenience. I have a meeting at an office complex right past the airport. Are you okay? You look pale."

"I feel like shit. I think I caught what Jon and Anthony have. Very queasy."

"I can take you home and dial into the meeting. Can you cancel your appointments?" Christina asked.

"No, I'm okay. I brought saltines from home, and the crackers helped Jon and Anthony. So, I'll be fine."

"Eat them now. Why suffer?" Christina said.

Natalia ate a few crackers, took a sip of water, and felt a little better. Christina dropped her off at the curbside and said, "I have your flight info. I'll be here on Wednesday to pick you up. Text me when you land. No luggage?"

"Nope, no need. Everything I need is in my closet there. Easier this way, just me and my iPad. Marc taught me how to video chat. I feel terrible leaving Jon and Anthony sick. But Jon insisted, he said, 'You're hovering, and I don't need you sick too." Natalia mimicked her husband. "But I think it's too late. That bug may be here. See you on Wednesday, and thanks for the ride."

Natalia hurried to the gate, and she breezed through security. Grabbing a large black coffee, she sat down to read on her iPad. As soon as she put the coffee cup to her lips and smelled it, she wrinkled her nose and became queasy. She ran to the ladies' room and retched. *Great, I caught the bug.* After tossing the coffee in the trash, she bought a cold apple juice, drank it, and her stomach settled. She found ginger chews in a convenience store and grabbed a bag for the trip.

The flight boarded on time, grateful that she ordered a first-class seat. She felt frivolous but was glad she did, because she knew she would rest better. She fell asleep and slept for the entire trip. Once she landed in LAX, she woke refreshed and much better. Natalia couldn't wait to arrive at the house and be with Cora and Jack.

She followed the exit signs and found Jack, holding up a sign that read "Her Royal Highness." She ran into his embrace. "How I've missed you, my favorite jester."

He had tears in his eyes. "I missed you too, your highness. Cora is beside herself, and she prepared your favorites. You look great. Are you happy?" Jack asked as they walked to the car.

"Jack, I'm incredibly happy. The sad part is not being with you and Cora every day," she replied.

"Aww, the house is empty without you and my favorite furry friends. I miss those two little clowns very much. They were such a great company for me. Especially after Doc passed."

Natalia made a mental note to reach out to Sophia. Perhaps she had a rescued baby that needed a home. She would do that for Jack. They caught up and arrived home in no time, as traffic wasn't too bad. Natalia jumped from the car and ran into the house. Cora was just coming from the laundry room when she saw Natalia come through the foyer.

Natalia rushed to her. "I missed you, Cora."

"And I missed you, my sweet girl, let me look at you. You look the best I've ever seen you. You're so happy you're glowing. Are you hungry? I made your favorite bowl for lunch."

"Yes and thank you. You'll both eat with me?" she asked. "Right?"

"Of course." They ate and caught up.

Cora said, "Why not relax by the pool? I know you missed it."

"I think I will."

Natalia went to her room. It was just as she had left it. She slipped into a bathing suit, dismayed that it was a little snug. *I guess I gained a few pounds, not swimming or working out every day.* She turned to grab the sunblock and peered at the calendar she kept hanging on the back of the bathroom door. She realized her last period finished the week before Jonathan arrived. In all the commotion, she hadn't kept track. She opened her vanity drawer, and her birth control pills were right on the top. She should have taken them the week her family arrived and never did.

"Oh shit, I can't be. I'm too old. I was thirty-eight on my last birthday. I must have just caught what Jon and Anthony are suffering from," she said.

When Cora served dinner, she was very nauseous and couldn't eat. She apologized and excused herself to lie down. "I'm exhausted." She fell into such a deep sleep that she missed her FaceTime call with Jonathan and the boys.

Jonathan called the landline at the house, and Cora answered.

"Hi, Cora, it's Jonathan."

"Hello, Jon. Are you feeling better?"

"Yes, I am, thanks for asking. Is Natalia available for a chat? Unfortunately, she missed our video call," he said.

"She went to bed right after supper. She wasn't feeling herself. The smell of dinner upset her stomach. I think she caught that bug. She slept by the pool this afternoon and went to bed without eating. Shall I go wake her?" Cora asked.

"No, please let her sleep. It is only a twenty-four-hour thing. Both Anthony and I are feeling better. Please let her know I called, and I'll talk to her tomorrow."

"I sure will. I know she has an early day. She misses you and the boys," Cora announced.

"Well, we miss her a lot. It was hard having her leave," Jon replied. "Thanks, Cora, for taking care of our girl. I would love for you and Jack to visit sometime. Anytime you are family.

"Oh, Jon, that's lovely. We would love that," Cora responded. "We have missed her so."

Jonathan checked on the boys. They were doing homework, and he ate the soup Natalia had made and left for them, enjoying it. *She's getting her cooking skills back.*

Jonathan worked from home while Natalia was in California. He missed her and thought about how funny she was trying to learn things about their life. She cried and gripped his hand when he showed her their wedding video, the videos of the children's birth, and the holiday footage he saved.

And after Natalia was home for a few weeks, she went on a massive cleaning spree. When Jon arrived home from work, she was a mess. Her hair was in total disarray, and she was sweating. Yet, she never looked sexier to him. When she observed the way he leered at her, she recognized the look in his eyes and said, "Dude, are you kidding me? Not right now. And where the hell is the maid? She hasn't been here since I came home."

He remembered laughing so hard at her. Annoyed with him, she tossed a dust cloth in his direction. He loved her. Their marriage was different but perfect—just another kind of perfect. She always was sassy. She was just a funny-type sassy now. Two more days, and his love will be home.

NATALIA WOKE UP ON Tuesday morning, thinking she slept for an hour. Then, realizing the sun was up, and it was the next day, she climbed out of bed, begrudgingly, and went to the bathroom. She ran the water and ran back to the toilet and threw up. *Gosh, I feel shitty.* She showered but threw up again before she went downstairs.

"Good morning, Cora," she said as though it was an effort and yawned several times.

Noticing the dark circles and Natalia's pale face, Cora said, "Oh, dear, you look ill, honey. Can you cancel the interviews?" Cora asked.

"No, I'll be fine. I just need to get through the day. It'll pass."

"Can I make you breakfast? Maybe toast?" Cora asked.

"Yes, toast, please, no butter. I'll be right back. These pants are too tight. I need to change into another pair."

Natalia hurried up the stairs and into her room. She tried on three pairs of pants before choosing a black sleeveless dress as it hid her bloated stomach. She felt puffy and unwell. Natalia swallowed the toast. Natalia fell asleep on the drive to the practice. It was very unusual, and as soon as Natalia arrived and stepped into the building, Jack called Cora and told her it worried him. Cora assured him that her family was not feeling well, and she most likely caught the bug.

Natalia arrived early purposefully. She was the first one there, strode into her office, grabbed the supply cabinet keys, and walked down the hall. She found what she was looking for and took it with her into her private bathroom. Natalia took the test and placed it on the toilet tank. In seconds, it was positive. Excitement and panic ripped through her. *I'm thirty-eight. How did this happen?*

Natalia heard Maria's shoes tapping on the marble floor. She yelled, "I see your office light. You're here. I'm coming, girlfriend."

Natalia stood in her bathroom in total shock as Maria walked into her office. After a moment, Natalia yelled, "I'm here. Please come in."

Maria opened the door to the bathroom, and Natalia handed her the test. Maria's mouth fell open, and she stared at her friend. "Do you feel okay?"

"Am I safe, Maria? I'm thirty-eight. Is it safe?" Natalia was a mess. She was pale, looked unwell, and had dark rings under her eyes.

"Nat, when you left, you were in perfect health. Has anything changed?" Maria asked.

"No, I just started feeling sick. I thought I caught the stomach bug from Jonathan and Anthony. When I went back to my room in Beverly Hills, I checked my calendar and realized that my last period ended right before Jonathan and the boys arrived."

"We did the deed at the optimal time, and I never realized that I missed my period—a couple of them. I came in early to take this test."

"This is exciting news. I'm happy for you. Jon loves you, and he will be happy too," she assured her friend. "Did you have time to review the resumes? We can go quicker if there is someone that stands out to you," Maria said.

"There are three, but my first choice is Dr. Marissa Stanton. Do you think you can work with a woman?"

"She was my first choice, too," Maria smiled. They compared notes and agreed on the second and third choices. Then Natalia reached into her briefcase and pulled out a folder. She slid it over to Maria. Maria raised her eyebrows, but opened it. In it, she found documents making her a full partner in the practice.

Maria's mouth gaped open. "Are you serious about this, you're sure?"

"I'm one hundred percent sure. Just sign the damn papers. And I'll courier them over to the attorney's office." The day flew by, and they decided on Dr. Stanton. She was a personable, skilled, and warm person. She was their age, and the three women had a comfortable interview.

Dr. Stanton left after they assured her she would hear something in the next few days. Natalia went into her office, set up the courier service, and then took her and TJ's photo off the desk, shoving it in her desk drawer. She logged onto her social media page, pulled up a picture she liked before the accident, and printed it. She now related to her life as "pre-accident" and "post-accident." Natalia placed the photo of her family in the frame that formerly held her and TJ. She closed her office and knocked on Maria's door.

"Hey, I'm going to call Jack for a ride," Natalia said.

"No, don't, I'll take you home," Maria said. "Just give me a few minutes. I need to return a call."

Natalia reached out to Sophia while she waited. Her financial managers were sending monthly checks to Sophia's rescue. Natalia also paid for the nonprofit status for Sophia's rescue.

"Hi, Sophia, it's Nat... Susan Kline. How are you?"

"Hi, Susan. How are you? I heard you went back east. Are you home now?" she asked.

"Just for a few days. I'm heading east tomorrow. So, you're receiving regular checks from my financial gurus?"

"Yes, thank you, I am."

"Well, the reason I'm calling is to ask if you have a pug that needs a home. I'd like to rescue one that can stay with my dear friends here. An older one is okay."

"I might. Candi's here. TJ is staying longer in London, and his housekeeper quit without notice. She had to go home, as her mother was ill. He asked me to care for her. He hasn't officially surrendered her, but I think he might. His new girlfriend has allergies, and rumor has it he may stay in London indefinitely."

"Oh no, poor Candi. That's so sad. I don't want TJ to know that it is me who's interested. He might not want to give her to me. It wasn't good, the ending."

"I'll just call him and tell him I have a pre-approved adopter. Let's see how that goes. I'll call you later."

"Thanks, Sophia. I appreciate it. If it doesn't work out with Candi, please keep me in mind."

Maria took her back to Beverly Hills, and again Natalia fell asleep. "Nat, when you get home, go to your doctor. You need prenatal vitamins."

"I will. I need to show Jonathan this first." She reached for the stick in her purse and pulled it out. "Am I crazy to be this excited?"

"No, not at all. I would be just as excited," she replied as she pulled into the circular driveway in front of Natalia's house.

Maria leaned over and placed a kiss on Natalia's cheek. "I need to rush to an awards dinner, but I'm coming east next month. I'll come by, or perhaps you guys can come to New York? We can do touristy stuff. I bet the boys would love it. Love you."

"Love you too, and New York sounds like fun." She waved as Maria zipped out of the driveway.

Natalia rushed into the house and wandered into the kitchen, where Cora was making dinner.

"How are you feeling?" Cora asked.

She debated telling Cora she was just exhausted, but couldn't hold it in. "Cora, I'm fine, better than fine." She took the test out of her purse and showed Cora the stick.

"Is this what I think it is? Oh, honey. A baby. Is Jon excited?"

"He doesn't know yet. I just found out today. I'll tell him when I get back tomorrow."

Thirty-three

JONATHAN PICKED NATALIA up from the airport. The kids were in school, and her flight arrived early. He missed her and hoped she was feeling better. Jonathan arranged for Mrs. Hannigan to get Anthony off the bus. He wanted to surprise her. Jonathan couldn't wait for his wife to return. He received her text and ran to the doors, where he stayed with a bouquet for his bride.

Natalia exited and searched for her ride. When she saw him, she ran into his arms, "I missed you so much." she said as she kissed him.

"I missed you even more. Are you feeling better, honey? Did Cora fix you up?" he inquired.

"I'm fine. Where are you parked?" Natalia glanced along the curb.

"Right over there, in the short-term parking lot," he said as he handed her the flowers.

"They're beautiful. You are so sweet."

He grabbed her hand. She loved when he did this, held her hand all the time. They walked to the car together. Natalia planned to tell him later that night when they were alone. She hoped he was excited, too.

They hit traffic but made it home in time for dinner. Jonathan called the kids and mentioned they were going to go to their favorite restaurant for dinner. The guys enjoyed their dinner and ate with gusto. Natalia ate morsels. The quesadilla, her favorite meal, turned her stomach. She munched on the tortilla chips instead. After they left the restaurant, the boys finished their homework, and the long-awaited bedtime came.

Jonathan knew something distracted Natalia. He had to call her a few times before she responded, and he couldn't help but worry. *Did she miss Beverly Hills? She had eaten so little.*

Soon after, their boys had gone to bed. Jonathan let the pugs out back for their last break of the evening. They followed him upstairs. Natalia was in the shower. Jonathan opened Anthony's door since the dogs preferred to sleep with him. Sometimes they slept with him and Natalia, but tonight Jonathan had other ideas that didn't involve two snoring pugs.

He stripped down and joined her. It was a little uncomfortable attempting to make love in the shower, so Jonathan said, "Let's take this to the bedroom." He stepped out first, dried himself, stood ready with her towel so that when she stepped out, he dried her.

"Honey, I need to talk to you." She watched his brow wrinkle, and his smile was strained.

"What?" he asked, snappier than he intended as he wrapped a towel around his waist tighter. Natalia opened the vanity drawer and showed him the test. He looked at it, at her, then back at it. His mouth opened, he swallowed hard. Then the enormous smile spread across his face, lighting his eyes, the smile she adored. She watched as the emotions spread across his face. He pulled her to him and asked, "Oh, honey, are you okay?"

"I'm fine. I'm happy, excited. Are you okay with this surprise?" Natalia asked with trepidation.

"Yes. Yes." He pulled her to him and wrapped her in his comforting embrace.

"Who is my doctor here, Jon? I need prenatal vitamins," she explained.

"I'm working from home tomorrow. I'll find his information in the morning. Now come to papa, my love. I've missed you."

They made love, and she fell asleep in his arms afterward. She made an appointment with the doctor for the following week. He advised her to take another at-home test to be sure. She did, and it was another positive result.

They waited to tell the boys until after Natalia saw the doctor. Other than morning sickness and exhaustion, she felt great. It delighted her she was expecting another child. Natalia and Jonathan had discussions about moving to a larger house or adding on to their current home. Natalia was confident it would be another boy and thought that Alex and Anthony would share a room, and the baby could take Anthony's smaller space. She hoped Jonathan could get the day off to go with her.

Jonathan took off to attend her appointment. Over breakfast, he felt tendrils of apprehension because of her age, his age too. Would they have the patience? The energy to manage a newborn. He also had something else on his mind. "Honey, can I ask you a question and promise you won't get upset?" he asked her with trepidation.

"Of course, you goof, you made me pregnant. Why do you feel as though you can't ask a question? You can ask me anything."

"Did you ever end it with TJ? Is he still filming and knows nothing of this?" he asked, pointing back and forth to them.

"Yes, I ended it before we left Beverly Hills," she answered.

"You left me confused and in turmoil until we came home? Why?" He needed to know.

"I wasn't there yet. Cora told me to follow my heart, and at some point, the light bulb would go off, and I would know either way. I knew in Beverly Hills that I was falling in love with you. But the lifestyle was different, and I felt somewhat pressured." She raised her eyebrow at him. "I wanted to be in our home, to see if my feelings were the same and if you were that amazing guy here. And that light bulb moment happened at that dealership. I looked up at you, and my heart jumped, and I felt chills all over. I knew then it was you, just you, and could only be you. I fell in love with you all those years ago with a different brain but the same heart. I love you, honey. You were made for me. And now we're being blessed with another little treasure."

Jonathan was speechless. He leaned over and kissed her maple-flavored lips. "Honey, you know how I feel. You are my entire world. I loved our old life, and I love watching you learn your new life. I don't care if you ever get your memory back. If you remember, you are my wife. My knocked-up wife, who cannot get those pancakes in her fast enough," he teased.

She smiled. "I know I'm starving. I seldom eat these, but I think our new little one is insisting. Did I get huge with the boys?"

"No, honey, you gained the weight the doctor thought you should, and because you nursed, you were back into your old clothes in no time."

The doctor took another test, and after the exam, he told Natalia that everything was fine with the baby. They listened to the baby's heartbeat and received the sonogram printout. At eight weeks pregnant, the due date was January first.

On the way home, she said, "I guess we can't go to Beverly Hills for the Christmas holidays. Not even Thanksgiving. Would you be okay with having Cora and Jack here?"

"Darling, of course. We can make up Marc's room as a guest room, and he can sleep in the office or Alex's room."

"I'm going to call them now. They should be awake," Natalia peered at her watch.

In her voice, Jonathan heard the love she had for Cora and Jack. Jonathan stepped into the kitchen for a cold drink.

Cora had placed their call on speaker. Cora and Jack would visit for both holiday periods, and they would stay at Christmas until the baby was born. Natalia's face beamed, and her cheeks glowed during the conversation. He loved seeing her happy.

"Thank you, Cora. I'm extremely excited about your arrival. The boy's first day of school is September fifth. I would love to fly out with the family before I can't fly any longer. I just need to check with Jon and his schedule." She listened for a minute. "No, I haven't discussed that with him yet, but I will. Cora, I'm ordering an iPad for you, so we can see each other when we chat. Go with Jack to pick it up, and the associate will show you how to use it." Natalia hung up the phone and saw Jonathan standing in front of her with a cold glass of juice.

Handing her the glass, he asked, "What's up, Nat? What do you need to discuss with me?"

She took a deep breath. "You can say no, but before I take the next step, I wanted to ask you. I just learned that one of my lead financial people on the wealth management team is retiring. I wanted to know if you wanted the position," she asked nervously.

He didn't answer right away. He seemed dazed and shook his head. Then, before speaking, he inhaled and replied, "Is this a ploy to get us to move to Beverly Hills?" His tone was brisk.

"No, asshole," she joked. "I didn't even think of that, nor did I think of you to fill the position. Wes did. He's the team leader. He knows the firm you work for and started his career there, years ago in the New York branch."

Jonathan's face relaxed, relieved she didn't ask to move. "Honey, I don't know. Let me think about it. Can I speak with Wes before I decide? It's risky, leaving my job after all these years."

"What's the risk, Jon? You don't have to work. I... I mean, we can live off the interest of Doc's estate comfortably. I just doubted you wanted to be a 'kept man.' Although I do like the idea of it though, I can keep you naked in our room. That sounds like great fun to me."

"Okay, I'll talk to Wes later. But for now, meet me in the bed-room," he replied, reaching for her.

Thirty-four

THE MONTHS FLEW BY without incident, and Natalia's scheduled date for surgery approached. Swollen and uncomfortable, she was eager to meet their next child. Natalia loved her house and didn't want to move. In September, they added a guest room to the back of their house and a bathroom for Cora and Jack.

Catarina Cora Miller was born on December twenty-ninth at eleven sixteen in the morning via cesarean section after a healthy pregnancy. She weighed six pounds, eight ounces, and came out of the womb screaming. However, after placing her on her mother's chest, she quieted and looked at her mother. Natalia was in awe. *A daughter.*

It came as a shock as Natalia and Jonathan had never wanted to know the sex of their unborn baby. In their hearts, they had convinced themselves it was another boy, and they were happy with it.

When her doctor yelled, "We have a little princess," everyone in the operating room applauded, knowing they were parents to three boys already. Natalia and Jonathan cried happy tears.

Jonathan was present for the birth. But because it was a surgical procedure, Cora couldn't be with her during the delivery but waited at the hospital with Christina, Alicia, and Charlotte. Jack took care of the boys and dogs back at the house.

After the delivery and recovery, Natalia dozed off in her room, her husband snoring softly in a chair and Cora rocking their daughter. Pure joy radiated on Cora's sweet face.

After dinner, Jack brought the boys over to meet their sister. Natalia gazed around the room at her beloved family. She thanked God and her parents for finding her and sending her precious daughter from heaven to join their family. "Well, guys, what do you think of the peanut?" she asked.

Everyone answered at once. Marc claimed he wouldn't change poopy diapers, but he might change them if she went pee. Alex refused to change any diapers, and Anthony was happy that he wasn't the baby anymore. The boys took turns holding their new baby sister, and her tiny features entranced them.

The joy she felt being with her family was immeasurable. Natalia scanned the room again. She chose well. All those years ago and again last April. She looked at her husband, and they locked eyes. She said to him, "I'll love you forever."

He smiled and said, "Ditto, my love."

Epilogue

A WOMAN SAT MEDITATING serenely in an open field, lush with colorful wildflowers in a small community in rural Tennessee. She had lived here most of her adult life, and this place was her passion. Songbird loved the tranquility of her home, her community, her husband. She had been living there for over twenty years. Although Songbird had no professional training in childbirth, she was the community's midwife. She just assisted as nature took its course. She had a very calming way, and the expectant mothers often requested her presence at their births.

She observed many children as they learned about nature, ran about, and played all over the land. Most of which Songbird had assisted into the world. Sometimes, parents honored her by allowing her to name their newborn.

Songbird had married River under the moon years ago. He was the current elected leader of their community. However, he didn't need to lead much, as their community was a peaceful, respectful, and loving group.

Often, either Songbird or Meadow, the youngest keeper of the pantry, would go into the nearest town to ask for contributions or sell homemade and home-grown items. With the small donations and sales, they bought necessities they couldn't grow or make themselves. They lived ninety percent off the land. But the residents sometimes needed things they had to buy from the stores in town, fabric for clothing and diapers, cooking utensils, and tools.

Meadow returned to their community and watched Songbird as she walked back from the field. Meadow waited for her friend and mentor with a smile.

"Peace, Sweet Meadow. How was your trip to town for supplies? Were you blessed?" Her smile was pleasant, and her face relaxed as she peered at Meadow.

"Yes, Songbird. People were very generous today. I got pieces of fabric from the fabric store for diapers and several yards for clothing. Also, some thread along with needles. They were quite kind at the store today and appreciated the exchange of fresh vegetables." Meadows smoothed down her shirt and broke eye contact several times.

"That's wonderful, Meadow. Walk with me. You seem troubled. What's wrong?"

Meadow hesitated as she knew of news from the outside world, and gossip wasn't welcome in their peaceful community. Her gaze lowered as they walked. "I am troubled." She looked into Songbird's kind eyes. "I read an article in a magazine at the fabric store. It was an obituary. The employees were discussing it."

"Why would that trouble you?"

"Because I think it may have been your father's." She licked her dry lips.

"My father? How would you know him?" Songbird's heart raced, and she felt a lump form in her throat.

"Well, I don't, Songbird, but a long time ago, when I planned to leave our community, you spoke to me about your past life and all that you gave up being a better person. You told me about your father, Dr. Richard Kline, a famous doctor, and how in your previous life, you were Susan Kline."

"Yes, I was Susan Kline."

TO BE CONTINUED....

Made in the USA
Middletown, DE
11 July 2021